MW00776999

#56259

RADIUM

RADIUM

by John Enger

NDSU | NORTH DAKOTA STATE UNIVERSITY PRESS

Fargo, North Dakota

NDSU NORTH DAKOTA STATE
UNIVERSITY PRESS

Dept. 2360, P.O. Box 6050, Fargo, ND, 58108-6050
www.ndsupress.org

Radium
By John Enger

Copyright © 2022 Text by John Enger
First Edition
First Printing

LCCN: 978-1-946163-33-2
ISBN: 2021939682

Cover design by Jamie Trosen
Interior design by Deb Tanner

The publication of *Radium* is made possible by the generous support of the Muriel and
Joseph Richardson Fund and donors to the NDSU Press Fund, the NDSU Press Endowed
Fund, and other contributors to NDSU Press.

David Bertolini, Director
Suzzanne Kelley, Publisher
Sarah W. Beck, Executive Administrative Assistant
Kyle Vanderburg, Assistant Acquisitions Editor
Oliver M. Sime, Graduate Assistant in Publishing
Megan G. Brown, Editorial Intern

Book Team for *Radium*: Meghan Arbegast, Grace Boysen, Megan G. Brown

Printed in the United States of America

Publisher's Cataloging-In-Publication Data
(Prepared by The Donohue Group, Inc.)

Names: Enger, John, 1991- author.
Title: Radium / by John Enger.
Description: First edition. | Fargo, North Dakota : North Dakota State
    University Press, [2022]
Identifiers: ISBN 9781946163332
Subjects: LCSH: Brothers--Minnesota--Fiction. | Runaway teenagers--United
    States--Fiction. | Fugitives from justice--United States--Fiction. |
    Poor youth--Minnesota--Fiction. | Red River Valley (Minn. and N.D.-
    Man.)--Fiction. | LCGFT: Domestic fiction.
Classification: LCC PS3605.N454 R34 2022 | DDC 813/.6--dc23

To Robin for teaching me to read.
To Leif for teaching me to write.
To Emily, my lovely wife, for teaching me to edit.
To Reed for teaching me everything else.

CONTENTS

1.

Billy held the bottle up to the sun and looked through it. The glass was green and thick and smeared with mud. He squinted.

"Hey, kid," he said. "I think there's something in here."

He was up to his knees in a section-road ditch a couple miles north of Radium, not far from our trailer house. It was spring, and the prairie was more water than dirt. The sun gets all its muscle back at once, you see. Melts three feet of snow in three days, and suddenly the drainage ditches turn to rivers, and the lowland fields fill up like big square lakes. It happened nearly every year we lived in Marshall County, and every year Billy and I went out scavenging. It's amazing what kind of stuff drifts loose on the floodwaters. Tires and tarps, and cases of beer, and on that day, an old Jägermeister bottle with something inside it.

"Is it a frog?" I said. "It would be cool if it was a frog."

Billy dipped the bottle back down in the water and wiped it on his pants. He had to use his pants because pants were all he was wearing. It had been a long winter, and his skin was already pink in the spring sun—everything except the scar on the left side of his chest, which was white.

He polished a little window in the scummy glass and looked again.

"It's paper," he said. "Rolled-up paper, tied with a string."

All my arm hairs rose up at once. I'm not the smartest dude on the planet, but I know what it means when there's paper rolled up inside an old bottle. That's a secret message right there! I ran into the ditch so fast I tripped. Went face first into the dirty water. You'd think it'd be warm—with everything melting so fast—but it wasn't. It was so cold I almost gasped in a lungful. So cold I thought my skin was peeling off.

Billy dragged me out onto the gravel road, and then he had to sit down he was laughing so hard. I jumped around to warm myself up.

When he calmed himself, he had another look at the bottle. There was a big gob of electrical tape around the neck and lid. He bit a corner with his teeth and peeled it away, one wrap at a time.

"I'm not sure about this," he said.

"I am. Open that bad boy."

"It seems pretty old, kid. Thirty years at least."

"Cool."

"What if it's a clue, or a treasure map?"

"Then we're rich."

"Then maybe you kill me and keep the treasure for yourself."

"I won't. I promise."

"Maybe I kill you instead. Money corrupts, little brother. There's no telling what I might do."

"Jeez, Billy."

"I should probably just throw it back. Yeah. It's for the best." He wound up and fired it out across the floodplain. Only he didn't. It was still in his hand. He grinned and shook the note out of the bottle.

"You wanna read it?" he said.

"You read better."

He slid off the string and unrolled the little scroll. "Under the leaning tree," he said.

"That's it?"

"I think there's something on the other side," he said. He turned over the paper and smoothed it with his palms. His hands moved so slow. It made me crazy! He held up the paper and squinted. Right in the middle was a perfect square, drawn in pen, with a red X along one edge.

"X marks the spot," he whispered.

"Holy shit!" I yelled. "It *is* a treasure map!" I jumped up and down, but not because I was cold. I just couldn't contain myself.

"I bet the square represents a field," Billy said.

"Treasure!"

Billy took a deep breath and looked around. He ran his fingers through his hair. "There sure are a lot of fields," he said. "They're all square."

I snatched the paper from his hands and squinted hard, scoured it for clues. Anything we may have missed. Billy got up off the road and slowly brushed the gravel from his jeans. He walked over and put his arm across my shoulders.

"We'll need shovels," I said.

"There are too many fields, kid. It would take years to search them all."

"We'll get metal detectors," I said. "We can sell the truck. Dig full-time."

Billy chuckled. His arm tightened around me. "People go nuts looking for treasure," he said. "I won't let you go out like that."

We walked home and didn't talk much on the way. I didn't even look for any other cool trash in the ditches. I was too disappointed. I just watched my own feet sink into the soft, wet gravel, one at a time. The hell kind of secret message is, "under the leaning tree"? And who draws a map that's just one dumb square and an X. You expect a level of mystery. Possibly some riddle-type material, with a good payoff at the end. But this was just cruel.

Then Billy stopped in his tracks.

"Hot damn," he said. I followed his pointed finger with my eyes. We were coming up on the beet field where our trailer house was parked, one of the drier ones, lucky for us. In the nearest windrow lay a great huge oak tree, uprooted long before we moved in.

"Thirty years ago," Billy said, "I bet that old girl was just starting to lean over."

He looked at me and I looked at him, and then we ran. Flat out across the sticky field, so fast I fell down again. Billy didn't stop to laugh. He dragged me along. We came up panting on the fallen tree. The root mound had come out of the ground in one piece, those years before. It spread out in the air like a fan of woven snakes, washed and bleached white in the sun. Billy dropped to his knees in the hollow they left and dug with his hands. He seemed to know just what he was doing. And sure enough, in a minute his fingernails scraped something solid. He pushed the dirt away and pulled out a coffee can. Folgers. Rusted shut.

I thought I was gonna fall down for the third time in one day. All my blood rushed into my head. The world spun around me. Dirt and water and sky. Round and round. Billy caught me by the shoulders.

"You okay, little brother?"

"Treasure!" I said.

I sank down on my butt in the dirt. He let me get my breath. Let the world stop spinning, then he pried the lid almost off, and put the coffee can in my lap.

"You should do the honors," he said. So I did. Oh man. That thing was so full of cool stuff! There were agates and spent bullet casings and old padlocks that didn't have any keys, but were pleasing nonetheless. And right on the bottom was a pocketknife. One of those tactical folders, with a heavy blade and black aluminum grips. I fished it out and felt the weight of it in my palm. It was solid and smooth in the corners, chilled from the earth around it. There was a feel to the thing. You know, power. Like low-grade electricity.

"That's a nice knife," Billy said. I passed it over, and Billy opened it with a flick of his wrist. He felt the edge with his thumb and grinned. "Very nice," he said. Then he closed it with one hand and gave it back.

"Give that a shot," he said.

It opened easy enough, but the knife had all kinds of safety locks on it. One to stop the blade from folding shut on your finger, and another to stop the first lock from letting go on accident. You gotta press the levers in the right order to close the thing.

"Try and do it with one hand," Billy said. "I bet that would be good for your fingers. For dexterity. Like a workout."

I fiddled with it for a while, but the levers were too stiff and far apart for my dumb fingers. I went to give it back, but Billy didn't take it.

"That's yours," he said. "Everything in there is yours."

I held the knife in my open hands. It seemed too nice to be buried in the ground. Too nice for me to have. The world wanted to spin again, but I kept it steady.

"Why?" I said. "You found it."

"We found it. And kid, it's *your* birthday."

I blinked and looked at him, to see if he was kidding. It was hard to tell with Billy. Plus, it didn't feel like my birthday. Not that I could call back any particular dates, but I sort of thought my last birthday had been in the wintertime.

"You're fifteen today," Billy said. "You remember, don't you?"

I looked down at the ground. Fifteen is a lot of years. More than I remembered living. I thought hard. Added things up. Twelve seemed more accurate.

There's something you should probably know about me, right out of the gate. I have some, well, let's just call them defects. There was an accident when I was a kid. Car wreck. I went through the windshield of Dad's Buick LeSabre at sixty miles an hour. Hit the road so hard my head changed shape. There's a flat spot on one side, like a melon. My hands got all mangled up in the same accident. Some of the tendons were sliced clean through. Some of the nerves. They didn't heal right. My fingers were numb for a long time. Then tingly. They still cramp up in bad situations. But the worst is my stupid memory. Maybe memory is the wrong word. I don't forget things as such. It's more like bits of time go missing. I get this screaming pressure in my ears, like I'm way down underwater. And reality gets slick and my dumb hands can't hang on. Then I blink and I'm somewhere else, in the middle of something. Once I walked into a gas station for a bag of peanuts and came 'round three days later in a knee-high cornfield,

with a frog impaled on a sharp stick. Another time I found myself
in the woods with my dick in my hand and a JCPenney underwear
catalog in the other. That's why fifteen seemed like too many years. I
wasn't strictly around for all of them.

I tell myself it's like autopilot. My brain just edits out the boring
stuff. It doesn't feel so bad that way. But I shouldn't drone on. Nobody
likes a complainer.

"Yeah," I said. "Fifteen. I remember."

• • •

We cut across the field to our trailer house. Billy carried the treasure
can and I fiddled with the knife. It still wouldn't close.

"Who do you think buried this thing?" I said.

"Some kid."

"Somebody who was a kid thirty years ago, before the tree fell over."

Billy reached out a cigarette and lit up. "Yeah, I guess."

"Oh man! Do you think it was Dad?"

"I don't know, buddy."

"He grew up around here, and the timing's right."

"A lot of kids grew up out here."

"Maybe he left a clue so his sons could find it one day."

Billy nodded kind of slow and looked away. "I guess it's possible," he said. "Yeah. Real possible."

The knife snapped closed. I had to use both my crippled hands,
but it was still a victory. I held it in my fist. It felt good to touch a thing
that Dad might have touched back when he was young and alive. Billy
threw his arm across my shoulders. He passed me the cigarette, and I
smoked it.

√2.

Billy gave me a choice that night. We could go hang out with Carl or sneak over and visit Maggie-Grace. It was still my birthday, he said, so it was up to me.

Carl was Billy's best buddy. He drank the same liquor and smoked the same cigarettes and liked to fistfight sometimes. Bare knuckle, just like my brother. He was cool enough, and he was good to me. But Maggie, man, she was just excellent. Billy'd been seeing her on the down low for a couple months. When she came over, she always brought food. Tater Tot hotdish for everyone to share, and a Snickers bar for me to eat outside while she and Billy had some privacy. She used to put the candy bars in her deep freezer overnight. The caramel was hard as rocks. Took me forever to eat, but it was worth it. Nothing's as good as a Snickers.

It was a no-brainer. I wanted to see Maggie.

We waited till it was dark and piled into Billy's old Silverado. He called her on the way. They spoke in whispers even on the phone. It was risky going to her place, because her place was actually her parents' place. Maggie's dad was this sanctimonious prick named Randy. Sanctimonious—that's the word Billy used. It's the only time I ever heard it in regular conversation. Anyway, Randy didn't want his little girl hanging out with my brother, what with the cigarettes and alcohol and occasional redneck fistfights. He'd gotten wind of their budding romance maybe a week before and hadn't taken it well. He forbade Maggie from seeing Billy anymore. Then he came by our place and explained how it was. He said that we were garbage people living in a garbage trailer house. He didn't say "garbage." He used a nicer sounding word, which I've forgotten. It meant garbage. He said it wasn't our fault. Our parents had been garbage before us, and that's why they were dead or shooting-up in an alley in Minneapolis or whatever.

Their garbageness was in our DNA, like early-onset Alzheimer's, or
Down syndrome. We deserved government help, he said, but not his
daughter. He couldn't let us wreck her life. It was nothing personal,
but if he had to, he'd take, "preventative measures." Man, the way he
said it, with nothing behind his eyes, like God was speaking through
him, turned my stomach all cold and quivery.

Billy just laughed it off, of course. Strong young men always
underestimate threats, and I guess I see why. What the hell was Randy gonna do to my brother? Randy was rich, sure. Well-connected
and vengeful in an Old Testament sort of way, but Billy could drop a
well-fed farm boy with one single left hook. I'd seen him do it a gang
of times. And so we ignored Randy's little speech. We did more than
ignore it. A little danger makes everything more exciting.

Billy took us south, into town. It was just a couple miles, but big
chunks of road were submerged. We had to go real slow, and even
then the tires launched gallons over the windshield. We drifted in on
Main Street, pushing up a bow wave. Homes and businesses rose up
from the water. Not one sandbag in sight. Flood season was just that in
Radium. A season, like winter or spring. No point in fighting it.

A lot of other little towns in the area built massive flood diversion
projects. Their streets were dry all the time. Not Radium. The Army
Corps of Engineers came to town one time, with big plans. They wanted to build a four-mile levee, all the way around Radium, to hold back
the water. They said the floods would only get worse, on account of
climate change. They said the federal government would pay for the
levee. But there's a lot of paperwork involved with federal funding.
Radium's tiny city council didn't understand the process. They didn't
like talking about climate change. Plus, nobody in town wanted to
take handouts from The Man. The Man always wants something in
return. So they sent the engineers packing and handled things their
own way. The people of Radium just ripped the soggy Sheetrock and
insulation from their houses, up to the high-water mark, and left it

that way. It looked pretty trashy and was cold as shit in the winter, but at least they didn't have to worry about black mold. And who really cares about resale value? Nobody left Radium anyway.

We parked in a dark corner of town and walked a block and a half or so through ankle-deep water, then scrambled up a hill toward Randy's backyard. Randy had the only dry lawn in all of Radium. The town may have turned down a ring levee, but Randy didn't. He had one built all the way around his house, a five-foot-high berm of compacted earth, covered in perfectly manicured grass. And he put a chain-link fence on top just in case the townsfolk got crazy and made for high ground. We scaled the fence and dropped down into nice green grass. Billy paused to dig his heels into the levee. He kicked at the grass. Tried to make a hole. He grinned. "How about that Randy?" he hissed. I had to bite my lip to keep from laughing.

Maggie's room was on the second story, but a tree grew up past her window. Billy helped me into the lower branches. We climbed by feel till her bedroom light clicked on, and everything became too bright to see. The window scraped open and by the time my eyes adjusted, Maggie was leaning out, already locked on to Billy's lips.

She pulled away after a good long time, blinked, and started back. "Oh," she said. "Hello, Jim."

"Hi, Maggie," I said. I was a few branches down and I guess she hadn't seen me right away. That's okay. She didn't look too disappointed.

"You brought your little brother," she said to Billy. "That's so great."

"It's his birthday."

Maggie looked down at me and smiled. She had a great smile. It always looked real.

"Happy birthday," she said.

We kicked off our muddy boots and sat around on Maggie's girly furniture. She and Billy on her twin bed, and me on this puffy red footstool set up by her mirror. Everything was super girly in there. Not frilly. Just, you know, girly. It smelled nice. Her clothes were draped over things. Girls' clothes. They gave me a tingly, carbonated feeling in my guts.

She reached under her bed and came out with a box of Little Debbie Swiss Rolls. "I keep these for emergencies," she said. "I think there's still one left."

She said "one," but Little Debbies come in packs of two, and that's what she tossed over. Two rolls! I couldn't believe my luck. Maggie was fantastic!

"So, what did you turn?" she said.

"I'm," I said. I was tearing at the packaging with my teeth. I was distracted, and I started without knowing the end. "I'm," I said again. This time I tried to concentrate, but the number was already out of reach. Shit! What a moron! Then Billy caught my eye and flashed all five fingers three times, down by his leg, so Maggie couldn't see. "Fifteen," I said.

"That's a great age," she said. "I bet you grow six inches this year."

"I hope so," I said through half a Little Debbie.

"You know, girls are going to start noticing you pretty soon."

She leaned back against Billy, laced her fingers in his. It made my heart beat fast. Even with most of a Swiss Roll down the hatch, my guts tingled like crazy. You have to understand, Maggie was real pretty. She had that smile of course, and so many freckles you couldn't tell the actual color of her skin. She was half freckle, pretty much. Billy liked that about her, and I did too. Not in a creepy sort of way, but I may have carried a small torch.

"Girls won't notice me," I said. "Not in a good way."

"Why is that?"

"They'll just call me names. They do already."

"What names?"

Damn it. I never should have talked about school. Maggie was one of those caring people who can't seem to let things go. The type who will root around in your personal embarrassments for hours, just trying to help. I knew this. But she was so pretty. I've never been able to keep secrets from pretty women. Any women, really. They have power over me.

"You know," I said. "Names."

"Are they . . . bad names?"

Of course they were bad names. I had a melon head and bad hands. I never knew what was going on, because of my glitchy memory. At that time, I was maybe the second- or third-easiest kid to pick on in the whole world.

"They think I'm slow," I said.

"Is that what they say? Slow?"

I jammed the whole second roll into my mouth at once, had to ram it in with my hand. "They use a different word," I choked out.

"Do they call you . . . " Maggie's voice dropped way down low, "the 'R' word?"

"Not anymore. We're not allowed to say retard this year."

"Well, that's good, isn't it?"

"They call me SPED now."

"SPED?"

Billy ran his fingers through his hair. He took a deep breath. "Special Educated," he said. "It means retard. I'd like to do something about it, but he won't let me."

"Nobody likes a complainer," I said.

Maggie didn't say anything for a little while. She blinked and wrapped her arms around herself. She looked like she was gonna cry. Her breath hitched on the way down. Oh man! I didn't know what to do. Nobody likes to see a girl cry. I met Billy's eyes, and he seemed just as confused as me.

"Hey, kid," he said, "show Maggie the thing you found."

"What did you find, Jim?" her voice cracked in the middle.

I pulled out the knife and went to snap it open, the way Billy had done. Just a quick flick of the wrist. I figured that would maybe impress her a little, maybe head the tears off at the pass. And the knife did open, sure enough, but then my dumb hand let go and BAM! The blade stuck right in the floor.

"Oh my," Maggie said. She even giggled. It was working.

"We think it might have been my dad's," I said. "He buried it in a coffee can and left us a treasure map. It turned up on my birthday, too! How lucky is that?"

And for some reason, that just opened the floodgates. Tears streamed down her face. She rolled over and buried her head in Billy's chest. The things that set people off. You never know.

• • •

Maggie eventually pulled things together enough to tell me about some leftover cake her parents had down in the kitchen. She said it was from a church event, and thus not an actual birthday cake. It *was* chocolate however, and pretty good, and angry old Randy was asleep. She said she had some important stuff to discuss with my brother. I could stay if I wanted, but I could also go have some church cake if I felt like it.

Of course I felt like cake. I also felt like getting the hell away from that room, and the tears, and the important stuff she had for Billy.

I slid downstairs and found the pan on the kitchen table. About half a cake under cellophane. I took a seat and dug right in. Man it was good! Rich and spongy and loaded with blow-your-head-off sweet frosting. It was even better than the Little Debbies, which is saying something.

I was maybe half a slice deep when the lights came on. Heavy footsteps echoed down the hall. It was Randy, rousted in the middle of the night and no doubt reaching a whole new level of pissed off. I looked for exits, but they were all too far away. No time to run or even snag the cake on my way to the pantry closet. I wedged myself in and eased the door shut behind me. It came almost to my nose, barely enough room to take a full breath.

In a moment the footsteps were prowling the kitchen. "Hello?" Randy said. I closed my eyes.

"Anybody there?" His voice was right outside the pantry door. Any second, he'd throw it open and drag me out by my ratty hair. Probably call the cops. I wanted to throw up.

But Randy just shuffled around and took my seat at the table. I could hear chair legs scrape the floor, the crinkle of cellophane and clicking fork tines.

"Yes sir," he muttered through a mouthful of frosting. "Already dry." He took three more bites and worked to get it all down. "I tell her. I say, 'Cover the food when you're done.' Is that too much to ask? I don't think so."

He was really going to town on the apparently dry-as-dirt church cake. "But no," he said. "Nobody listens to Randy." He thumped his fist on the table and wolfed another few bites.

Randy, on paper, was a pretty ordinary dude. He owned the Nelson Company Grain Elevator, a family business and the only reliable moneymaker in Radium. He was a deacon in the local Baptist congregation and a member of the Lion's Club. But there was this other thing, too. A rumor. The kids at school said a few years back Randy had caught an employee embezzling thousands of dollars from the elevator. The guy was named Derek, I think. Anyway, Randy gave Derek a choice. He could either call the cops and turn himself in, or he could let Randy chop the thumb and forefinger from his right hand with a hatchet, the fingers he'd used to nab all that embezzled cash, metaphorically speaking. According to the kids at school, Derek was terrified of getting defiled in prison and took the hatchet option.

That's some Old Testament shit right there. I never really believed it before, but honestly, how well did I know Randy? Was he one of those undercover psychopaths, white-knuckling it through a regular American life, just looking for another Derek to hatchet? Maybe. A guy who can stay angry through half a pan of chocolate cake is capable of anything.

I gritted my teeth and tried to keep from hyperventilating. There wasn't much air in the closet, and it was warm already and thick. Sweat trickled down my low back. My legs went weak and jittery, and the tendons in my wrists rose up like bridge cables. The fingers bent back, doubled over at the last knuckle like animal claws. I couldn't stop them. Couldn't even close my hands.

Then a knocking came at the pantry door. One, two, three knocks. Randy knew I was there. He was toying with me, the prick. "Here we go," I thought. The whole thing flashed through my mind in a moment. Randy would drag me out of the closet and strap me to a kitchen chair. Then he'd pull out most of my teeth with pliers. He'd tell me it was a fair punishment for eating his church cake. He'd leave the molars, probably, and count himself merciful. I could already taste blood in my mouth.

But a fourth knock came, and a fifth. It wasn't Randy at all. It was my own damn forehead on the door. I was spinning my head around! Shit!

That's a thing I do, by the way. Because ruined hands and a faulty memory aren't enough for one kid to deal with, sometimes my neck decides to spin my head around for no reason. Not all the way, like owls do. Just in a big circle like I'm watching a Hot Wheels car do a loop-de-loop. For sure you've seen a challenged kid spinning his head around at the Walmart. I'm that kid, and I'm not even challenged, not all-the-way challenged, anyway.

I reached up with my cramped claw hands and pinned my head steady. Silence spread out in the dark closet. Forever it seemed. Maybe he hadn't heard my dumb head bumping around. I let myself hope. Then chair legs scraped back from the table. Footsteps padded over.

The doorknob turned real slow. "Here's the end," I thought. "I hope he leaves the molars."

But as that door latch clicked open, a whole new worst-case scenario came to mind. If Randy hurt me, or even just roughed me up a little, Billy would come downstairs and kill him with his hands. It would be easy for him, but he'd have to go to prison after. Probably forever. I'd be lost without him.

A thing rose up in my chest. Fear or adrenaline, I don't know, but I couldn't be still another second. I threw my weight at the door, shoulder down, everything I had all at once. It flew open right into Randy's face. He fell back in a pile, holding his nose, and I went out the front door at a dead sprint.

• • •

"You broke his nose?" Billy said.

We were back in the truck, making time out of Radium. Billy had one hand on the wheel and the other was wiping tears from his eyes. He could barely make words he was laughing so hard. "That's the best thing I ever heard," he gasped.

"Do you think he saw me?"

"Kid, have you ever been punched in the nose? I mean, right there. Direct hit."

"One time. Baby Arm Jeff hit me with his regular-sized fist. The left one."

"And could you see anything after?"

"No. I guess not."

"Because?"

"Because I was crying like a total wuss."

"Boom!" Billy said. He slammed his palm down on the dashboard. "Randy didn't see shit, because you made him cry. You made him cry, kid! Tell me, did it feel as great as I imagine?"

"Mostly I was just really scared."

"Unacceptable," Billy said. "This has been an amazing night." He slammed the dashboard again. "A record night! For both of us, kid, and I'll be damned if you let fear take that away."

"What was good about your night? Maggie was sad. That's no fun."

"Never mind about me."

"What was that important thing she told you?"

"Some really good news, kid. But right now we're talking about you and your brazen escape! Think back, little brother. Relive it."

Billy lit a cigarette, rolled down the window so the smoke could escape and so he could float his arm out into the wind like a bird in flight. "Close your eyes," he said. "Remember the sound of his face hitting the door. Feel the rush of blood in your veins. Yes?"

"Yes."

"Is it good?"

"It's good."

"Goddamn right!" he shouted. Then he leaned his head and shoulders out the window and let out a scream. A long animal thing that rattled in his throat and between his ribs. He thumped his chest, and then he thumped my arm with his fist.

"A record night!" he said.

He was right about that. Buried treasure and chocolate cake. My father's pocketknife. My brother's joy. Even with a crying girl thrown in, I was having a pretty great birthday. Maybe the best one ever.

Then a loping form came into my peripheral vision. A white-tailed deer bounded up from the flooded ditch. She was sleek and strong and wet to the belly. Poor thing, she'd have made it except for the headlights. She skidded to a stop in the middle of the road, turned her smooth head and hollow eyes toward the Silverado. It must have looked like the rising sun. Billy found the brake pedal and dropped his cigarette getting at the horn. None of it helped. I felt the impact in my lungs. The thump of it, thick with the sound of cracking bones.

Billy stopped the truck and flicked the burning cigarette off his leg. Didn't say a word. He pulled a three-point turn and found the doe a hundred yards back, laid out on the tar. He parked and got out. I followed him into the high beams.

Her blood glowed like neon. It was thick and stinking, and so bright I see it still, when I let myself. She thrashed in a pool of the stuff, looked up with panicked eyes at my brother and me.

"Give me the knife," Billy said. Some distance of time must have passed, because he touched my shoulder. "The knife," he said again, and I gave it to him. He flicked open the blade and circled around behind the deer. She tried to rise up, but her legs didn't work. The bones moved in a way they shouldn't.

Suddenly, I found it hard to think straight. The world moved slow, and pressure built in my head. A sound like water rushed in my ears. I reached out to steady myself, but there was nothing to hold onto. Just a bloody road, and Billy with my knife in his hand.

He patted the doe's straining neck with the palm of his left hand, then slid his fingers under her jaw.

"Be still, my friend," he said. Spasming limbs went loose as he raised the doe's head off the road. She blinked and breathed in little puffs. Her eyes calmed as he placed the sharp blade to her throat, relaxing into nothing. I felt very far away now, and yet I watched.

Billy's grip tightened on the knife. His knuckles turned white.

"Look away, kid," he said. I couldn't hear a damn thing over the roar in my ears, but his lips moved clear and calm, and I read the words. He was right. It was time for me to go. I knew it. I closed my eyes and was lost in that sound, the sound of water, rushing louder and louder, till the world slipped from me.

3.

The roar drained from my ears in a hallway packed with kids. They had backpacks and thermal sweatshirts and boots still dirty from the morning chores. I blinked in the bright light of day, tried to line things up. Was I in the right school? The right year? A bunch of the kids looked strange to me. I can only hold so many faces in my mind at once. Then somebody socked me in the arm, and I whirled like a boxer, fists up to protect my face.

"Jesus, dude." It was Clive Pissarky, a kid from my grade. Clive and I hung out a lot. If he was there, I was in the right place.

"Sorry," I said.

Clive leaned against the wall and cracked his knuckles. "No biggie," he said. Man, Clive was one weird, disagreeable little guy. He always looked like he had scurvy, and every single one of his joints could bend the opposite way. It was disconcerting.

"You can't have that in here," he said. "Against the rules."

"What?"

Clive pointed to the bulge in my pocket. I'd forgotten to leave my new knife at home. That's the danger of autopilot.

"No knives in school," he said. "They gotta keep you from going all Sandy Hook on our asses."

"Don't talk about that." This was Jeff, another friend of mine. His full name was Jeff Clopp, but no one called him that. They called him Baby Arm, or, if he was real lucky, Baby Arm Jeff. Jeff's dad accidentally slammed his arm in the sliding door of a minivan when he was about six years old. It shattered something Jeff called the "growth plate," which sounds made up to me. Either way, Jeff was stuck with one regular arm and one six-year-old-sized arm. He was real sensitive about it. He was sensitive about other things, too, like all the mass killings happening at public schools.

"I don't know why you have to bring that up all the time," Jeff said. "I get nightmares still."

Clive just grinned his chalky teeth. "Let me see it, Jimmy," he said. "I won't tell."

We huddled with our backs to the river of students. I slid the knife from my pocket and saw—with some relief—that it didn't still look like a murder weapon. Billy must have scrubbed away the deer blood. What a stand-up guy. Clive snatched it from my hand, quick as can be. He snapped it open and then closed. It was easy for him. His weird knuckly fingers were still way better than mine.

"I bet you can't do that," he said to me. "You either, Baby Arm. This town is full of cripples."

"My left arm is regular sized."

"The fact that you have to clarify is depressing as shit. Where did you get this thing, Jim?"

"It was in a time capsule."

"What?"

"We found a coffee can buried under a tree," I said. "It had agates and padlocks, too. We followed a treasure map and everything."

"Aw man!" Jeff said. "I never find cool stuff."

"That's because your big brother doesn't bury cool stuff."

"Billy didn't bury the time capsule," I said. "It was too old. We think it was probably our dad's, when he was a kid."

"That's real cool," Jeff said, but he couldn't look at me. He fiddled with the loose sleeve that hid his little arm.

"It sure is," I said.

Clive grinned wide. He snapped the knife open again, and closed it. Then he put it in his pocket. "I'm gonna keep this," he said.

"Like hell you are."

"SPEDs can't have knives, Jimmy," he said. "It's the law."

I thought hard. No such law existed in my memory, but we've already established that my memory doesn't work for shit.

"You just want to keep my knife," I said. "And I'm not a SPED anyway."

"You must be. This is a new knife. You know that, right?"

"I guess so, but."

"So, your old man couldn't have buried it in a time capsule and left clues or whatever."

Jeff put his full-sized hand on Clive's shoulder. "Come on, man," he said, but Clive didn't listen. He couldn't help himself.

"Because he was dead as rocks five years before this thing was made."

We all had defects—Clive and Jeff and I. That's what held us together. You already heard about my contributions and Jeff's little arm, but Clive's issue was the most recent. The freshest disappointment. Up until the seventh grade, he was almost a normal kid. Double-jointed and malnourished, but basically okay. Then one day, he got a bad expression on his face in the middle of English class. When it passed, he stood and moved his pant leg around, and a little pebble of shit rolled out onto the ground. Hard and round like a deer turd. He just kicked it aside like no one would notice, but people did. After that, Jeff and I were the only kids weird enough to hang out with him. He was still bitter about it. Still mean, and he took it out on us.

Clive laughed hard. He had this nasty high-pitched chuckle. "Your brother really pulled one over on you," he said. "I can't believe he told you it was your dad's knife! What a dick."

I didn't know what to say. I looked down at the ground.

"Oh, shit," Clive said. "He didn't tell you that at all, did he? You came up with it yourself. That might be the saddest thing I've ever heard."

For about half a second, I felt paralyzed. My vision slanted red. Heat climbed into my throat till I couldn't take a breath. Then I noticed my fist was moving. Back at first, like a pitcher, then forward at great speed. It landed in Clive's guts. He bent double, sank to his knees. I watched it happen. And wouldn't you know? It felt even better than breaking Randy's nose.

"How about that, Clive?" I shouted. "Do you think I'm a SPED now?"

"Hnnng," he wheezed.

Then I blinked, and Clive wasn't bent over at all. He stood in front of me with a funny look on his face.

"What's wrong with you?" he said. "Your lips were moving, but no sound came out. Jesus, Jimmy, are you crying?"

I was. Heat poured down my face. I mopped it up with my shirt sleeve.

"I bet you spin your head around next."

"Shut up, Clive."

"Take your damn knife," he said. "Pathetic."

• • •

After that, I couldn't keep things straight. I wandered down the hall. Washed my face in the bathroom sink. Then suddenly I was out on the flooded streets of Radium, alone. I didn't even know if I'd gone to the rest of my classes. I didn't care. Billy's job wasn't too far away. He worked at the sugar beet mounds on the edge of town. Spent his days pushing the stinking things around with a Bobcat. I figured I could go there and maybe have some of the chili Mr. Hasskamp kept in a Crock-Pot in his office. It was good stuff. I'd have some of that, and then maybe steal a few of Billy's smokes and just relax for a while.

I headed that way, but the next thing I knew, I was many miles down a road I did not recognize. Everything looked different half covered in water. I blinked, and thought, and finally just sat down on the soggy ditch bank. That's what Billy always told me to do if I got myself turned around and lost. "Just sit and wait, and don't get *more* lost," he said. "I'll find you."

I fished the knife out of my pocket and snapped it open. Then I couldn't get it closed again. My hands were too stiff. I set the blade beside me in the grass and rubbed my palms. The scar tissue goes real deep. All the way to the bone. It feels like ropes buried under the skin. I dug in there with my thumbs till the hardness softened. Till my fingers moved right. Then I picked up the knife and tried again. This time it closed easily. I opened it and closed it. I practiced and practiced with those sharp steel mechanisms and wondered if my father had done the same thing, many years ago.

I don't have a lot of super clear memories of the old man. That accident, you know. It took a lot of the early stuff, and he wasn't around after. Billy remembered him though, and sometimes he told me things. Here's what I know then, secondhand.

Karson Quinn was a fighter. Not one of those trained mixed martial arts killers you see today, tearing each other apart with arm bars on pay-per-view. No. He was just a rangy farm boy with an empty place two kids and a pretty wife could not fill. This is what Billy told me, mind you.

Our father was something of a big deal on the Indian casino boxing circuit. He had bouts at Red Lake and White Earth, and even a few out west. It's not that he was all that good. People just liked his style. Dad never backed up, Billy said, not once in his whole life. He didn't raise his hands. Didn't bob or weave or any of that shit. He just smoked a little bit of methamphetamine in the locker room, then stormed out into the ring and slugged the living crap out of people.

But how many drug-fueled wars can one man fight? How many punches can he walk through? I suspect it's different for everyone, but our dad used himself up when I was about ten. Took one too many punches to the frontal lobe, Billy said. The morning after his last fight a blood vessel gave out. He was behind the wheel at the time. His brainpan filled with blood, and he drove head-on into oncoming traffic.

Dead before impact, Billy told me, though I suspect he padded the truth a bit for my sake.

Billy kept an old fight poster pinned to the inside of his closet door. Karson Quinn squaring off against a big fat guy named Buck the Butcher. I used to spend hours looking at that thing. Dad flexed shirtless and made a face like he was yelling. He wasn't really yelling though. It was posed. You could tell, just looking at it.

I closed my eyes and tried to imagine that man, with his arm across my shoulders. I clutched the knife like the end of a rope and tried to pull him back from wherever he was. The guy in the poster had my brother's high cheekbones, the same hard jaw, and hard knuckles. I started there. Built Dad up in my mind, with Billy as scaffolding. I added squint lines around the eyes and some gray hairs. His bony arm slung over my shoulders—that would be like Billy's too. I took the smell of Billy's cigarettes and added that slight chemical whiff left behind by amphetamines. I could almost feel Dad there with me, by the side of the road. Hear him breathing heavy in the spring sun. I wondered if maybe this wasn't my imagination at all, but a memory. Something I'd lost and found again. But my father wasn't yet fully rendered. I wanted to see his whole face. Make him as real as I could. I forced my eyes closed even tighter and filled him in . . . his busted nose, then down to his mouth. That's when the whole thing went to hell. I saw his lips, thin and peeled back, like in the fight poster, baring teeth in a silent scream.

A shiver ran through my body. I opened my eyes. He had to be fake screaming in the damn poster. He couldn't have been smiling, or even gritting his teeth. I could have worked with some gritted teeth . . . imagined him like Clint Eastwood in the first *Dirty Harry*. Wouldn't have been too far off. But that's not my luck, is it?

I opened my hand and looked at the knife. Really looked at it this time. It *was* brand new. Clean and factory sharp. There was no way Dad could have hidden it away in a time capsule. He couldn't even have bought such a thing back then, with all its complex mechanisms. The timeline didn't make any sense. It became clear. Billy did it. He buried all the things he knew I'd like and helped me find them. It was a kindhearted trick. That's not the part that bothered me. What bothered me was Clive. That double-jointed little bastard was right. I'd told myself lies to feel close to my dead father. Shit! What a pathetic, naïve, SPED thing to do. I put the knife in my pocket. Put my head in my hands. How the hell did Billy let me walk around with that idea in my head? Telling people. Telling Maggie! I wanted to throw up. I wanted to step in front of a bus. I'm telling you, if there'd been a bus going by right then, I'd have stepped in front of it.

• • •

Billy's Silverado coasted up with the setting sun. He was in a wild, happy mood. Everybody was. The whole truck was packed with guys. Billy and Carl in the cab, and a handful of others in the bed. He rolled down the driver's window and levered his whole upper body out past the windshield.

"Hop in," he said. "Ralph's back, and he's got the goods."

Just then a stream of sparks flew up into the sky and exploded. My ears rang. Everybody cheered. Ralph leapt up and danced on the bed liner. The whole truck rolled and swayed like a boat on the ocean. "All hail Ralph," somebody shouted. "Bringer of fireworks!"

They hauled me up over the sidewall and slapped me on the back. They gave me a cigarette and a sip of their whiskey, and Ralph touched off bottle rockets as we rode along.

Ralph had the size and strength of a small grizzly bear. In the summer, he worked the beet fields outside of Radium. Every winter, he drove home to Mexico to see his parents and all his little sisters. When he returned, he always brought these super powerful Mexican fireworks. He had a whole box of them in the bed of the truck. He launched them from his bare hands. All the hair was burned off his knuckles and most of the way up his arms, but he didn't seem to mind.

"They're supposed to corkscrew," he said. "The guy said they'd corkscrew."

"I don't think it matters." This was Josiah, or maybe Travis. Those two guys were such baseline, ballcap-and-Copenhagen rednecks, I had a hard time telling them apart. Anna was along too. She was one of those cowboy-boots-wearing type of girls. Tank top in the summer. Carhartt in the winter. Big, crooked smile all the time. I liked her. She was Josiah's sweetheart, I think. Or maybe Travis's. Shit. Maybe she couldn't tell them apart either. Doesn't really matter. She was just as crazy as the rest.

Ralph lit another rocket and tried to throw it like a football, tried to force the promised corkscrew. Instead, it blew up about three feet in the air. The blast slammed Ralph flat on his back. The truck swerved below us. When the smoke cleared, Anna was straddling Ralph and slapping at the small fires that had sprung up on his shirt. "Stay with me, big guy," she said. Dang. Maybe she was with Ralph. It was so hard to tell.

Ralph blinked many times and screwed his fingertips way into his ears. Then he pulled them out like two waxy corks.

"Boom!" he said. Everyone whooped and yelled. I did too. I might have been a pathetic SPED, but you can't stay sad around some Mexican fireworks.

4.

The night went about like you'd expect from a bunch of bored farm boys with access to alcohol and low-grade explosives. They built a massive bonfire and threw in bottle rockets, danced away from the explosions. They roasted bits of road-kill deer on sticks. They broke out more whiskey and drank. And when everyone was suitably revved up, Carl got to his feet and peeled off his shirt. He threw that into the fire, too. He flexed his muscles and roared. Carl was always the first to take these little gatherings to the next level. He was the shortest after me, and for that reason he felt the need to prove himself.

He made fists and boxed the air, then he pointed to Ralph. "You," he said.

Billy shook his head. "Relax, Carl," he said. "Finish your drink first."

But the others were too wild to let it go. The fire lit their eyes and their teeth, and they cheered Ralph on. I watched it all from this spot I liked, under the trailer house. There was a shallow dip in the earth, down between the cinder-block piers. Just my size. It was cool and dark and small under there. Life felt manageable, understand?

I squinted through the rotting latticework, watched Ralph heave his great weight upright. He laughed aloud. Popped his knuckles. Swung his huge arms back and forth.

"Alright, little man," he said.

Carl came at Ralph with everything he had. Slammed his fists into Ralph's big hard gut, and Ralph just pushed him away. The others laughed, reached for their wallets. Anna took Josiah's hat and ran around collecting bets. Five dollars said Ralph would crush Carl with his grizzly strength. Ten said he would tire and Carl's speed would win out in the end. They filled that ballcap to bursting.

This is what my brother and his friends did at night, when their energy became too much to bear. Who cares if somebody loses a tooth or some synapses? To hell with it. Good things had a way of slipping through our fingers. Bad things had a way of happening to careful people. No point in trying. The young men of Radium saw no good future for themselves, so they raised their fists and felt the rush and fear and desperation. Everything at once.

Carl leaped up on Ralph's back and wrapped his arms around his throat. He cranked down till Ralph's eyes bulged from his head. The great man wobbled. Forward at first, then back. Carl realized his mistake but couldn't move in time. It was like watching a tree fall on a lumberjack.

I could hear Carl's lungs empty. They wheezed down to nothing. "Mother," he hissed. He heaved at Ralph's bulk, but it was no good. Ralph came to himself some moments later. By then Carl was feeling pretty narrow. Ralph rolled over and pinned both of Carl's wrists in one massive hand. Poor Carl. He looked like a small child in Ralph's grip.

"It's not over," Carl wheezed.

Ralph looked up for approval. Billy nodded and money changed hands. Ralph tried to help him up, but Carl slapped his hand away. He staggered to his feet and worked at recovering his wind.

"What the hell?" he said. "That wasn't over." He looked like he was gonna cry.

"Yeah," Billy said. "It was, Carl."

"I was about to do some jujitsu stuff. You don't know."

"Don't be a sore loser," Josiah said.

Carl lunged, but Billy stopped him. "Okay," he said. "You got me, buddy. I called it early."

"The hell for?"

"I got bored. Jesus. Is there nothing to do in this town but brain damage each other?"

Carl stormed around, throwing more shit into the fire. Beer bottles and whiskey cups, which rose in plumes of fire. Everyone but Billy edged away. "Of course you're bored," Carl shouted. "You're a goddamn killer. There's no challenge in it anymore."

This was true. Billy never seemed to lose his fights. He never seemed to try all that hard either, while thrashing his buddies. It was the way he moved. Everything was loose and easy. Josiah or Travis would come after him in a blunt rush, and he'd just ghost to one side or the other. Then, all of a sudden, his tendons would snap tight as bowstrings. Instant acceleration. He had the touch of death in his hands. That's what his friends said. They hated him for it, and they loved him too. They called him Bare Knuckle Billy.

"Maybe you're right," Billy said. "I need a challenge."

"Give me a baseball bat," Carl said. "There's a challenge."

Billy grinned and scratched his stubble. He looked tempted, but then he shook his head.

"I've got something else in mind," he said.

"What is it?"

Billy tapped out a cigarette. He reached a stick from the fire and lit up. He took his time. "I don't know, Carl. It might be too crazy for you."

"Try me. And screw you by the way."

Billy took a drag. "How do you feel about a swim?" he said. The words came out in a cloud of smoke. His buddies chuckled.

"Like in a pool?" Carl said.

"Across the Red River. To the Dakota shore and back again, at flood stage. Now there's a challenge."

Carl grinned, and that's all it took. Everybody cheered and knocked back their drinks and followed my brother to the Silverado. They would have followed him anywhere. Even I crawled out from under the trailer house and piled in. Billy's late-night ideas weren't something to miss.

We flew down gravel roads. South a few miles, then west. I was in the cab this time, wedged in between Billy and Carl. Anna sat on Carl's lap, one hand on his chest and the other on the dashboard to keep herself steady. It was cramped, but I felt lucky all the same. Half the roads were flooded. Every time we hit the water, the Silverado threw huge waves on the guys in back. They sputtered and shouted curse words and Carl gave them the finger through the back window. He laughed. Talked a mile a minute, all about how he was gonna crush my brother and how he'd had real swimming lessons. "My teacher said I moved like a fish," he said.

"How old were you then?" Anna said.

Carl hung his head. "Six," he said. She laughed and socked him in the shoulder. Was she with Carl? She was very comfortable in his personal space. No way. He was too short and angry. Ralph was a way better dude, and besides, he'd dominated Carl in the fight. I suspect that might mean something to women.

Billy was silent. I watched him in the dashboard glow, in the tobacco smoke that eddied around his face. His eyes never left the road for thirty miles. Then he pulled onto the shoulder and parked. We splashed across a field of ankle-deep mud and into a line of trees. Their branches stopped the moonlight, and we had to feel the way forward with our hands. Carl turned on his cell phone flashlight, just in time to walk into an oak tree and drop the damn thing. It made a sound like a pebble hitting the mud.

"Mother!" Carl said.

Some distance in, the ground sank away below sluggish water. The Red River, swollen right up to the top of its banks and beyond. All the snowmelt for a hundred miles goes into the Red. And the Red flows north. That's the real problem. The ground's still frozen, deep down. Nothing soaks in. Billy stopped when he was up to his knees. The water was icy cold, but he didn't seem to mind. He stood there with his friends, looking out toward the main body of the river. The place where the trees ended, and the water went rough and black with current.

As we watched, a refrigerator floated past. It was fish-belly white in the moonlight and drifting fast. Probably came all the way from Grand Forks. A soggy mattress followed close behind.

"Jesus," Travis said.

Billy shrugged. He pulled off his boots and tipped them so the water ran out. Then he stepped out of his pants and peeled off his shirt, wrapped it all up in a bundle. He put the bundle in my arms. He took the cigarette from his mouth and wedged it between my lips.

"If you get cold," he said, "go start the truck. Don't feel bad if you have to."

I nodded, and he turned to Carl.

"How about it my friend?" he said.

Carl was already stripped to the waist from his fistfight with Ralph. His skin looked as white as that drifting refrigerator.

"Hell yeah," he said, "I'm gonna crush you." He tried to strip off his jeans, but the pant legs got all tangled up around his ankles, and he fell into the water. Ralph had to help him up and hold him by the shoulders while another guy wrenched the wet denim past his feet.

"Are you sure about this, Carl?" Ralph said.

"Yes, I'm sure," Carl replied. "And why didn't you ask Billy that? He's swimming, too."

"Billy's not shivering already."

"Screw you, Ralph."

Carl threw his pants over a tree branch and went down to meet my brother. They stood in their boxers in thigh-high water, squinting across the river. The far shore was just a black silhouette, low and distant. They waded out toward it. In five steps the water was up to Carl's nuts. He groaned, gripped his crotch with his hands, and kept going. In five more, it was waist deep. Their bodies pushed up mounds of black water on one side and cut roaring canyons into the other.

"Be careful," Ralph said. "Don't make me fish your bloated bodies from this goddamn river."

They were clear of the woods now, and the moon lit them up, bright as a cold sort of day. Billy was ahead, leaning hard now, skidding downstream on his heels. He put his hands down in the water. I could hear the current ripping between his fingers. Then he dove and was gone, Carl close behind him.

Ralph and the other dudes stood in the flooded forest looking out at the empty river. It was cold, and the whiskey was wearing off. Ralph blinked and rubbed his face.

"This might have been stupid," he said.

"Carl's gonna drown for sure," Josiah said. Anna backhanded him in the sternum.

"You suck," she said.

They breathed in and out. Lit cigarettes and smoked them down.

"Twenty bucks says Carl dies," Josiah said. She backhanded him again.

"I'll take that bet," Travis said. "Against my better fucking judgement." Anna went after him, too. Everyone laughed.

We all waded back to where the woods were only mostly flooded. We sat on stumps and logs and didn't talk for a long time. My feet went numb, but I didn't mind so much. It's the warming up that hurts, when the nerves awaken. Your toenails feel like they're peeling off. But all that pain was way off in the future. Right then, my brother was racing Carl across the flooded Red. Probably kicking his ass. He'd be back any minute. Victorious. Joyful. His buddies would tell about it for years. They'd tell their kids and grandkids about my brother. Big, strong Billy Quinn, who could do things other people couldn't.

But Billy did not return. The night got darker in the small hours. No moon left at all. I hugged Billy's empty clothes and tried to keep my guts warm. That's the important bit. The guts. Finally, we heard splashing coming through the trees.

Here comes Billy, I thought. I jumped up to welcome him, but it was Carl who staggered into the light of Ralph's cell phone. Carl's lips were blue, and his fingers were blue, and he reached out to block the glare.

"Holy shit," Travis said, and slugged Josiah in the shoulder. "You owe me twenty dollars."

Ralph wrapped the little guy in a bear hug, and Carl didn't complain. He soaked up the warmth. "Where's Billy?" he said, into Ralph's meaty shoulder.

"He's not here. You won."

Carl broke from Ralph's arms. "Shit!" he said.

"Yes. We're all very surprised."

Carl shook his head, tried to gather himself. His hands quivered.

"I lost him," he said. "On the way back. It was so cold. We decided to stick together. But I lost him. I thought he was trying to beat me, right at the end."

"Well, he's not here," Josiah said. "And I'm out twenty dollars."

"Shut up," Carl said. "Shit, man. We have to look for him. And somebody give me my pants."

They fanned out through the trees. I could see their tiny cell phone lights bobbing along. Anna stayed back with me. She looked into my face.

"Let's go back to the truck, kiddo," she said. She tried to sound calm, but there was something wrong with her voice. It was thin as paper. Her face was wrong, too, all drawn and white. It looked like fear to me. The real kind. "You shouldn't be around for this," she said.

I nodded. "Okay," I said. "But you can stay here. I know the way back."

"Well, give me a shout if you need anything."

She stared down into the water that swirled around her boots. She put one hand over her mouth, like she was gonna be sick. I hate seeing people like that. Girls especially. Girls are so nice; they shouldn't ever have to be sad. It tears up my insides to see it.

"Hey, Anna," I said. "Can I ask you a question?"

"Sure thing, little guy."

"Are you with Carl, or Ralph, or Travis, or Josiah?" I said. "I can't tell."

She looked back up at me. That big, crooked smile spread out across her face again. "Guess," she said.

"My money's on Ralph," I replied, "because he can beat up Carl and probably the other guys, too. Everyone but Billy, and Billy's taken."

She laughed and slapped me on the back. "I'm not with any of these losers," she said. "I've got a full ride to Concordia College. Theoretical physics, bitches! I'm blowing this shithole in about three months. Now go wait in the truck, little dude."

"Okay," I said, and I walked away through the trees. But I didn't go to the truck. I circled back and snuck down to the shore on my numb feet. I could hear those guys around me. I could hear Anna. They shouted my brother's name. They debated calling 911 and decided against it. Too much liquor involved. Too many priors and green-card issues.

I waded out to where the current tugged at my pant legs, and that's where I stayed. I squinted over the black water and held the stub of Billy's last cigarette between my lips. And here's the thing. I wasn't worried. Not really. Billy would make it out of the river. He'd live. Deep down, I knew it.

See, Billy had this idea about himself. It started when he was young. We were in that car accident, Dad and Billy and me. Like I said, I went out the window, but Billy was strapped in. The frame of our car crushed right down on top of him. A piece of the roof support broke loose and staked him in the chest, all the way through and out the back of his seat. The whole car was mangled and horrible. Glass and blood and bent steel, and everything on fire. Dad died quick. Which is good, since he burned to charcoal. Billy should have gone the same way, but he did not. There's no clean explanation on how it happened—none you would believe—but my brother woke in the hospital three hours later with a pair of white bandages on his front and back and a bunch of doctors squinting at his X-rays. They were puzzled. They called it a miracle. They thanked God. It's a small town, you know. Even the men of science are devout. Billy nodded along, but he had his own suspicions. He didn't think he was immortal or anything. What kind of asshole just walks around thinking he's full-on immortal? No. Billy just figured he was different from other men. That his mind was different. That he could will his body to do things.

He tried out this theory a handful of times in the years that followed, to make sure it was still true. When our lives became complicated, when we were in bad trouble and the way out was not clear, Billy went looking for challenges. Wild, dangerous, potentially lethal things. He drove his truck across barely frozen lakes, climbed a cell phone tower, hand over hand. Once he crossed the Fargo rail bridge with a train coming. Took the last dozen yards at a sprint and missed the engine by a foot. He called them tests. And when he finished one, whatever problem was headed our way, Billy knew he was equal to it. This was his ritual, the closest thing he had to religion.

Whatever you think about all that stuff, I'll say one thing. Billy might have looked like the man in that fight poster on our closet door—dear old Dad, fake yelling at Buck the Butcher—but my brother had something Dad did not. The light in his eye. The things he could do. Different rules applied. Understand?

So, I did not fear for Billy. He wouldn't die like our old man. He was stronger than death. I'd say I had faith, but that's not it. I had proof.

• • •

When the eastern sky turned colors like a bruise, a form walked up out of the river. It looked like a sea monster, or maybe a troll, all lumpy and hulking and growing taller all the time. As it came near, the form clarified. It was Billy with a railroad tie thrown across his shoulders. He grinned when he saw me.

"Hello, little brother," he said. There was a spark in each of his eyes. Probably just a reflection of the early dawn, but it looked like more. It looked like the whole inside of his body was on fire, and somebody had drilled two little holes. He came up beside me and threw the timber down in the shallows. That's when I noticed the barbed wire. There was a mangled nest of the stuff trailing off the wood, and up around Billy's leg. The points sunk into his thigh.

"That doesn't look so good," I said.

"Yeah." He sat down in the water and uncoiled his leg. The barbs were so deep, they pulled up little tents of skin before letting go. He laughed under his breath.

"I thought a squid got me," he said. "A giant squid, like in the movies."

"In the Red River?"

"It pulled me right under," he said. "I couldn't get loose. I had to reel this beast in, hand over hand. I had to carry it in my arms."

"A *giant* squid?"

"I had to run along the river bottom, holding my breath. It got pretty narrow. Forget it. Just reach me a damn cigarette."

I lit it for him and passed it over. I could hear Ralph's voice booming through the trees. Not the words, but the pleading tone.

"Your buddies think you're dead."

"Did you think that?"

"No."

"Why not?"

"You know why."

Billy sat in his underpants in the freezing water, yet his hands were steady. His eyes were bright, and his body seemed to be throwing heat like a woodstove. I could feel it on my face. He pulled a stray chunk of barbed wire from his thigh and splashed water up over the punctures. Tiny threads of blood wicked from them and slithered in the current.

"So, what was it this time?" I said.

"What's what?"

"This was one of your tests, wasn't it? What are you preparing for?"

He grinned and blew a smoke ring right up into the sky. The tree branches sliced it to pieces.

"Maggie's knocked up," he said.

It took a minute to land. Billy was gonna be a father. Oh man! Babies are such good news. Television pretends they're not. Dads are super uncool. Men fear responsibility worse than death. But come on now. Who doesn't want to carry a son or daughter on his shoulders? To look into a child's eyes and see his own. I wanted to laugh aloud! I wanted to scream and shout and jump around. But if I did that, the others would hear. They'd come running, and then Billy and I wouldn't be alone anymore. So I kept my words hushed.

"Holy shit!" I hissed, and socked him in the arm.

"Things will be different," he said. "No getting around it."

"They'll be better. Way better. Hey—that's what she told you on my birthday, wasn't it? That important thing."

"Yes, sir."

"Oh man! No wonder you had to ape-roar out the window."

Billy nodded. "It's good news," he said. "Real good news." But he was too quiet. Too still. I squinted at him.

"Why was she crying then? Before she told you. Why did you have to do one of your tests?"

He finished his cigarette and flicked it out into the water. He ran his fingers through his wet hair. "She thinks her dad might do something terrible," he said. "You know, when he finds out."

"Did she offer specifics?"

"She said we don't know him. We haven't seen how he gets."

"Maybe he'll come after you with the hatchet," I said.

"They never proved that. Derek says it was a farming accident."

"Of course he'd say that. He wants to keep the rest of his fingers."

"Nobody's hatcheting fingers, kid. Don't believe everything you hear."

I sat down beside him in the water. We listened to it run through the trees, listened to Ralph's big voice, far off. Listened to our own breath in our lungs.

"You're probably right," I said. "Lucky for you, since he wouldn't go after your hands."

"What would he go after?"

I nodded down at his submerged crotch. "You know," I said.

He laughed aloud. Loud enough for his friends to hear. Then he tipped his head up at the purple sky. "Come on!" he shouted. "What the hell could Randy do to me?"

5.

I couldn't bring myself to go to school that day. No sleep the night before, and then there was the whole deal with Clive and me being a SPED, and probably having to go to the principal's office to answer a bunch of questions about why I blew off half my classes. Or maybe I hadn't blown them off. No way of knowing for sure. It was a real sucker of a situation. The thought of putting on clean underpants and facing all that caused me real pain.

I told Billy I had stomach problems, like Clive, and I might shit myself for no reason. I told him I couldn't afford another defect, and I better stay home. I let my head spin around in circles just to drive home the point. Not that he took much convincing. Billy always let me skip school when I really needed to.

So, he went to work, and I crawled under the trailer house for a whole day of relaxation. Oh man. That was a great spot. The whole trailer was up on cinder block piers, about two feet off the ground. At some point, before we moved in, somebody had nailed up sheets of wood latticework all the way around the outside. They left one sheet loose, so you could get in and work on the plumbing. Well, I didn't know a thing about plumbing, but I went under there all the time. The great thing was, I could see out, but it was hard to see in. It was like being in a cave. All cool and dim and close.

I pulled back a little flap of fiberglass insulation and got my Pop-Tarts down from their hiding spot, between the joists. Then I reached down an L.L.Bean catalog I kept in the same spot. The summer issue from last year. The lady swimsuit models lived on page twenty-six. I had a JCPenney underwear catalog as well, but that was some high-grade stuff. I had to work up to it.

I got my things and crawled to my favorite spot of all. I had this hollow down there in the dirt. It was scraped out between two piers, about six inches deep. I think a dog lived there before me. There were claw marks and hair and stuff, but I didn't mind. That dog did me a big favor. Ever since the accident my structure has been kind of warped. Regular chairs don't fit my back. My bones land in all the wrong places. But that dirt was carved out just right. The best easy chair in the world! I just curled up in that baby and breathed easy. I ate the Pop-Tarts while my eyes adjusted to the darkness. Then on to the catalog, taking my time on the way to page twenty-six.

I found my dirt easy chair the very day we moved to the trailer. It was summer then, too. Three years back. We had to leave our old place in Radium in kind of a rush. There was this whole thing with bankers and social workers and, anyway, we had to get the heck out. Billy was just sixteen then, and already working at the beet mounds. Old Mr. Hasskamp ran the place. He always liked my brother, and he had this trailer he wasn't using a few miles from town. He said we could buy it for cheap. Even cheap wasn't cheap enough, but he and Billy worked out a deal—Dad's old .30-30 deer rifle for the structure itself, and twenty-five dollars a paycheck for the patch of field underneath it. Hasskamp was a generous man. He even helped us move in. Well, he helped Billy. I found my way under the trailer in about thirty seconds. It felt so safe under there. I didn't leave for a week.

• • •

After Bean, I considered stepping things up to the JCPenney level, but I wasn't in the mood. Billy was gonna be a dad! The thought kept popping into my head. A surprise every time. Things would change. He'd been right about that. Maggie would move into Billy's room, of course. The baby could have mine, and I could sleep in my dirt hollow under the trailer. I already did that sometimes. It was no big thing at all, except in the winter. I lay back in the dirt. At the time, I did not believe a child would ever call me father. A guy like me—nobody's lining up to make genetic copies. But my brother had a shot. I could be something to his children. I closed my eyes and saw how things would be. Billy and Maggie on a quilt in the field grass with the baby between them. Me hanging around the corners, watching them all grow up. It was gonna be so good. I smiled and slept.

I woke to Billy pulling back the loose bit of latticework. He got down on his hands and knees and crawled under.

"Hey," he said. He had a bag of cheeseburgers from a place in town. We ate them in silence, on our backs. Then Billy put his hands on the steel I beams that held up the trailer.

"How much you bet I can lift this mother?"

"I don't have any money."

"If you had money?"

"Twelve bucks."

"Twelve bucks I can, or twelve I can't?"

"Can't."

He set his shoulders against the dirt and adjusted his grip on the beams.

"Are you sure?" he said. "I ate a deer's heart yesterday. Everybody knows if you eat a creature's heart, you get its power."

"Deer aren't that strong."

"Buzzkill."

"If it was an ox heart. Or maybe a gorilla heart. Different story."

Billy gritted his teeth and pushed. And for a moment, I doubted myself. In the days after one of his tests, Billy had command over a great strength. He could do almost anything. Maybe he *could* lift our home with his own two hands. It was hard to rule out. He pushed till the veins in his neck and arms rose up like snakes under the skin. Once I thought I saw it shift, but that was just in my head. The trailer didn't move. Of course it didn't. It weighed a few tons at least. After a while he let his arms fall back down at his sides.

"You win," he said. "You should have bet more."

• • •

The weather turned with the setting sun. A day of blue sky, then sunset and storm clouds rolling in like a stampede. Such a shift, I could feel it in my joints. The rain hit our trailer all at once. No lead-up at all. One minute we were debating which kind of animal heart would make a man the strongest and for how long, and the next we could barely hear over the roar. Billy reached his hand out through the lattice.

"It's like marbles!" he shouted. He laughed and lit a cigarette, blew the smoke out into the storm. Up until then, our field had been one of the drier ones. It was a bit higher than the rest. Just a few inches, but it had been enough to avoid the floods. That storm was too much. In ten minutes, water was trickling in. In ten more, we were crawling through inches of the stuff. We laughed and splashed each other. We reveled in it.

We were having so much fun, we didn't notice the trucks till they were right in our yard. Headlights shown through the lattice work, then clicked off. Car doors slammed. Boots approached the trailer, sucking and popping in the thick field mud. Five, maybe six men.

I waited for them to knock on our door. Instead, there came a blow so heavy it sent a shiver right down into the cinder block piers. A sledgehammer probably, to break open a door that was unlocked already. Billy dropped to his stomach. We made ourselves flat. So flat we had to reach up sometimes for a breath of air. Another blow came and then boots slammed up into our trailer. They stomped around no more than two feet above our heads. Shouts came. Glass shattered, and they piled back out into the rain.

We crawled up to the lattice and squinted out into the night. High-powered flashlights scanned the field. I couldn't see their faces, but I knew these men. Randy and his buddies. Had to be. No one else hated my brother enough to come to our trailer in the darkness and bash down the door.

Billy doused his cigarette in the streaming mud. "Well," he said. "Time to pay the piper."

"What?"

"Never mind." He watched the flashlights and flexed his hands into fists. His jaw muscles worked back and forth like chewing steak. He took long slow breaths, gathering himself.

"Are you gonna go thrash those guys?" I said.

"I'm thinking."

"I bet you could do it!"

"There are five of them," he said. "Only one of me."

We both knew that didn't matter. I could see the strength building in his muscles. The energy, shimmering around him. My hands wanted to reach out and touch him, to feel that crackle. Randy and his asshole friends didn't know what they were in for. How could they? They didn't know about the car wreck or the tests Billy made for himself. They didn't watch Billy stride up from the Red River with a railroad tie across his shoulders. But I did. I saw it all, and I knew the truth. My brother wasn't just some garbage redneck. He was a wild, dangerous, joyful beast, wearing the skin and bones of a man. He could do anything, and Randy didn't have a prayer.

This line of thinking got me real wound up. "Break Randy's face," I hissed. "I broke his nose. You break the rest of it." Billy's eyes glowed in the darkness. Two bright sparks and a grin of fangs. I guess he was pretty wound up too. "Randy thinks we're trash," I said. "I hate him. Even Maggie hates him. Tear his head off. You can do it. I know you can."

Then Billy's smile fell away. The light went out of his eyes.

"Maybe so," he said. "But I'm not going to."

"Why?"

"Every woman loves her father," he said. "Deep down. They can't help it. Maggie won't admit it, but there it is. One day she'll choose him over me. If I can't bring Randy to terms, I'll lose her."

"Well don't tear his head all the way off." I don't think he even heard me.

"Maybe if I let him box me up a little," he said. "Black my eyes. Crack my jaw. Let him feel like a big man. Get his pride back, you know?" He turned to me with a weary smile. "Maybe he'll forgive me. Worth a shot, right?"

"Jesus Christ, Billy."

I grabbed at him, but he brushed my hands away. He crawled to the loose panel and pushed aside the rotting lath. The rain splashed up on his muddy skin. Flashlights swept the earth just beyond him. He paused there, and looked back at me.

"There are only five of them," he said. "I won't let them hurt me too bad." He winked, and then he was gone.

• • •

I watched the field from my safe dirt hollow, down in the water. The flashlights moved with impatient glances. I could see little in them. Just water and dirt and blackness. For just a moment I caught a glimpse of Billy, standing before a heavy short man who carried a baseball bat. But then the flashlight beam swung away and there was nothing for a long time. Nothing but grunts, and the slap of knuckles meeting bone. I ground my teeth. I clenched up fistfuls of mud and dirt. I may have wept. A man shouldn't let himself be beaten. It's not right. I told myself he wouldn't let it happen. His instincts would take over.

Then one single bolt of lightning sliced the sky. By its light I saw five men in a cluster, kicking at something on the ground. A slick, clay, mangled thing. I blinked in darkness with that image stamped on the backs of my eyeballs. It took some time for my brain to process it. I don't know how long. Thunder rolled in so loud the water around me shook into ripples. In the silence that followed, I could hear their boots thumping into Billy's ribs. A bad, wet sound. I didn't know what to do. I felt paralyzed. I wanted to throw up.

Then I heard one more set of boots, slogging through the rain and mud. One man, alone. He came alongside the trailer, so quiet and slow

I nearly missed him. He stepped up through the ruined trailer door and moved around above me. I lay still. I held my breath. Waited. I could hear him up there, talking like he would to a friend.

"I ask one thing," he said. "Don't fuck the redneck shithead. Don't let him knock you up with his dirty bad-luck genetics." I knew the voice. The cold tone of it. The quiver of rage. "Is that too much to ask?" he said. "I don't think so. But does she listen? No. Fuck no. Nobody listens to Randy."

He was doing something in our trailer, besides just talking to himself like a goddamn psychopath. I couldn't tell exactly what he was up to. It sounded like he was pissing on our stuff. What a prick! It trickled down through the floorboards and insulation, spattered my face. I gagged, but it wasn't piss at all. The tart stink of gasoline stuck in my nose, and a moment later the night lit up as bright as day.

I crawled through the first swirls of smoke and put my face against the lattice for a gasp of clean air. I saw him out in the field. Randy, wearing a plastic rain poncho. He carried a red gas can in one hand and a long-nosed grill lighter in the other. The firelight reflected in the wet folds of his poncho, like he himself was set ablaze. He smiled a big crazy smile. He was out of his mind! He'd chopped off Derek's fingers, and now he was gonna burn me to death and probably kill Billy, too.

I knew what I had to do. My home was burning. I had to get out. I had to kick through the lath and crawl into the storm. My brain told my body to do it, but my stupid limbs would not obey. Randy was out there, being his crazy self. I feared him more than the flames.

I crawled back to my dirt hollow and dug—with my fingers first, splashing down through the water—to the hard-packed soil below. My nails bent back, so I opened my knife. I plunged the blade down, sideways like a tiny shovel. I hated to do it. My wonderful dirt hollow. It would never be the same. I dug and coughed, and bits of trailer fell into the water around me. They hissed and spat steam. The fiberglass insulation made horrible black smoke. It stung my eyes, so I shut them. I tried to lie down in the hole. Tried to bury myself, but it wasn't deep enough. The ground was too hard, and the air was too hot. It was time to crawl out and face Randy, but I couldn't see the way anymore. I couldn't see anything at all. I reached out with my torn fingertips. Everything I touched burned my hands. Every breath burned my insides.

Then a great weight came down on me. A section of floor dropped all at once and pinned me to the ground. Plywood and burning two-by-fours. I couldn't get off my belly. Couldn't get my head all the way out of the water. I gasped mud and smoke. My hair smoldered.

I reached out again, and this time a hand wrapped tight around my wrist, dragged me loose and out through the ash slurry.

When the clean air hit my lungs, I screamed and flailed. I couldn't see, but I knew it must be Randy who pulled me from the fire, just to fuck with me, the crazy asshole. That knife was still in my hand. I swung blind. I squirmed and fought and tried to run. But the man caught me in a bear hug, and I heard his voice.

"It's okay, little brother," he said. "Breathe."

6.

The flames from our trailer rose up to meet the rain. Steam rolled out as thick as the smoke, which was as thick as any smoke I ever saw. I sat on my butt in the field and watched. Billy paced back and forth. Steam rose from him too. Blood dripped from his chin, ruby red in the firelight. It ran from his split, swollen lips and down his neck. He spat blood, and dirt. He bared his teeth at the fire, at the thought of the man who sparked it.

I can remember that first part, if I really think about it. Billy's red teeth. The hellfire look in his eye. But from there I have to admit my grasp on events became a little squirrelly. My head got all heavy and pressurized. My ears roared, and the world didn't seem right somehow. Like squinting through somebody else's glasses. It hurt my eyes. I blinked, and suddenly Radium's one and only fire engine was parked in our field. A bunch of giddy volunteers wrangled the taut hose. It got loose and slammed one of them to the mud. None of the water got close to our burning trailer, but I didn't care. The trailer was almost gone anyhow, and the firemen seemed to be having fun. There were so few fires in Radium. It was always a big treat.

I blinked again, and this time I sat alone on a hospital exam table. It was very bright and very cold, and my shirt was off. So were my pants. All I had on was one of those weird gowns made of blue paper. I shivered, but the skin on my back didn't twitch and slide like the rest. It was all glued in place, felt like layers of duct tape back there. Billy was out in the hall, talking with a woman. Arguing. I couldn't hear them clearly, but they seemed angry. I wrapped my arms around my body. I shook. I was so cold. I wanted my pants.

Then Billy was there with me. Right beside me on the table so his shoulder touched mine. He was solid and warm. "Check this out," he said. "I can do a magic trick." He lifted the bottom of his shirt.

Underneath, a big section of his ribcage had gone purple and black. It was the wrong shape too, like a ruined basket. He pressed down on the black skin with his fingertips. It flexed in about an inch and a half. Made a sound like chewing ice. "Pretty cool, right?" he said.

I blinked a third time, and the hospital vanished. Billy sat beside me still, but in the Silverado now instead of on an exam table. The cab was dark and full of that nice low engine rumble. Like a heartbeat. The rain had stopped. He had the heat on full blast and a cigarette between his lips.

I rubbed my eyes and clawed the wax from my ears. I breathed in the rich warm tobacco smell, held my hands out to the heat vents. It was night still, but almost morning. The neighborhood streets we drove looked familiar in the headlights. Wide and flat and full of water. I could have reached back into my memory and figured out where we were, but I tried not to think about it. I didn't want to remember just yet. The past is always full of nightmares. And the present seemed pretty nice. I was with my brother in a warm truck. That was good enough for me.

Billy cracked his window to let the smoke out. His fingers drummed on the steering wheel. Then he swung the truck down another wet street, and this one I couldn't help but recognize. It was the last place I wanted to be—Randy's street. But the fear didn't have time to sink in. Because there on the curb, in a pair of red rubber boots, stood Maggie-Grace. Oh man, she *was* a sight. Everything about her was bright with color. Her red boots and her red hair. Green eyes. She held a crazy zebra-stripe suitcase, which must have been heavy because she had to lean way over to keep it out of the water. Looking back, I guess she was just lit up in our headlights, but my head wasn't quite right. I thought she was glowing, like an angel.

I turned to Billy to see if she was real. If he saw her too. If we were really so lucky. He grinned and put the truck in park. Flicked away his cigarette and jumped down to the street. He made these long loping strides through the water. He threw the zebra suitcase over his shoulder and wrapped one arm around Maggie's body. And they kissed. Of course they kissed. You know that. I wouldn't even have to say it, except this kiss was special. They were spotlit in the headlights and framed by the windshield. Billy with a nice big shiner. Maggie looking all sacred and pretty and in love. It was like the best movie I ever saw. Not just one scene, either. The whole plot flashed through my head in a second. They'd run off together. Cruise out west. Eat at gas stations and have hot sex in cheap motels. Billy would win gas money boxing at the Indian casinos. Maggie'd patch him up after. And finally, when the baby came, they'd find a new trailer house, but this one would be parked under an orange tree, in a place where the sun always shines. The child would never have to be cold. It would never know hunger.

Not a complex film, I admit. More of a country music video, really. But I saw it all in that windshield movie screen. It was right there! Right within Billy's strong grasp. Tears streamed down my face. The fire had been so terrible, the fear of it. The loss. But what a payoff. So what if Randy didn't accept us? So what if he took everything away? He showed himself for the vengeful asshole he was, and now Maggie was ours. Forever! She chose Billy.

Heat filled up my whole body. My head tugged at my neck cords. It wanted to spin, and I was too happy to slow it down. I thumped my hands together. I shouted for joy.

But something was wrong. Billy was staring at me. So was Maggie. I figured Randy must be right behind me. I whirled, but we were alone. Slowly it came to me. I wasn't in the truck anymore. I don't know when, but I'd gotten out. I stood next to it in the cold water, weeping, and clapping my hands together. My head ground to a halt, mid-rotation.

"Hi Maggie," I said. Maggie's eyes shrank from me. She looked at the water, at her hands, anywhere but my stupid head. She backed away. Oh God, the look on her face! Like she'd just seen a dead puppy, or maybe fifty dead puppies. Or one of those cancer children from the TV ads. I wasn't that sad, was I? Not childhood-cancer sad? I reached out after her. I could still fix it.

"I'm not challenged," I said. "I promise. It's just my head. I don't know why I do it."

Then I caught a glimpse of myself in the side-view mirror and, man, the news was not good. A lot of my hair was missing. Burned off, I guess. My head is a real bad shape, if I haven't mentioned that before. Flat on one side and pretty scarred up. It needs the hair. But that wasn't even the worst part. I was still wearing the hospital gown. Only the hospital gown! I wasn't *just* cancer sad. I was crazy burned-kid-in-a-hospital-gown sad. That kind of sadness can suck all the joy right out of a beautiful thing. Goddamn. That kind of sadness has its own gravity.

At that point I just climbed back into the truck, and put my hands over my eyes. What else could I do? The damage was done.

"I'll get him some pants," Billy said. "We'll laugh about this later." He even mustered a chuckle, to lighten the mood. It didn't work. Maggie cried. They tried to keep their voices down, but Billy's window was cracked open, and the standing water had an amplifying effect. I heard every word.

"Our baby can't grow up like that," Maggie said.

"Like what?"

"Don't make me say it. Don't be cruel."

I didn't want to be there anymore. I wanted to hear that roar in my ears again and wake up someplace else. Maybe perched on the edge of a tall rail bridge, with a deep, fast river down below. Or standing on a clean piece of highway, watching a bus come screaming up from the middle distance. Yes, that was it. I took a deep breath and squeezed till blood sang in my head. I imagined the bus. A really big, fast one so there was just no doubt. I concentrated. Built the whole thing up in my mind. I could feel the road under my feet. The cool morning air. I could hear the bus, its big diesel engine thrashed to the red line. It came closer and closer. Faster and faster and then BAM! I imagined all the funny ragdoll things my limbs would do. I imagined the road and sky flipping, over and over. I tried to make it so, with my mind. But it didn't work. Of course it didn't. I had to stay and listen.

"He wasn't born like that," Billy said. "We had some bad luck is all."

"There's always bad luck with him," Maggie said. "It follows him around like vultures. I can't even breathe when I get too close."

The conversation went on for a while, but I'll just leave it there. It hurts too bad to think about, and besides, you know how it ends. She didn't come with us. I guess she was probably conflicted to start with, but seeing my weird head certainly didn't help.

Just to be clear, I don't want you holding any of this against Maggie. She made the right call. It's one thing to run away forever with big, strong Billy Quinn. But with Billy's damaged little brother? That's too much to ask. If only Billy had left me at the hospital. Swept up that pretty girl and run. Hell, he should have just left me under the trailer. They would have had the life I saw for them, with the baby and the orange tree. There's a reason I left myself out of that beautiful story line. I ruin everything.

They talked for a little while. Then Billy walked her suitcase to a piece of high ground, and we drove away. I watched her in the side-view mirror, weeping in her pretty red boots. That was the last I ever saw of Maggie-Grace, though I think of her often. Maggie, and her child. My brother's child, whom he never knew.

7.

Billy and I got real drunk. Didn't know what else to do, I guess. We parked by the railroad tracks and Billy fished a bottle of Everclear grain alcohol from the glove box. He kept three things in there all the time. The owner's manual, the Everclear (for emergencies), and Dad's old .45 pistol. Loaded. Also for emergencies. We lay down in the bed of the truck and passed the liquor back and forth. Waited for sunrise. Everclear's not as bad as you'd think. After the first few sips it stops tasting like gasoline.

We didn't talk till it kicked in. I started. The words came out all slurred and thick.

"Why am I in a gown?" I said.

Billy tipped the bottle up at a steep angle. It had a built-in airlock in the neck to keep people from drinking too fast and passing out. I could hear it wheeze as Billy drank. He let it down after a good long time and wiped his mouth on his sleeve. "The hospital wouldn't release you," he said. "Because we're homeless. They said you were an 'at risk youth.'"

"So they took my pants?"

"They wanted to send you to a family," he said. "Like a foster family. Just for a while. Till I got a new place."

"What does that have to do with my pants?"

"I'm not explaining this well," he said. "I had to sneak you out. We had a small window at shift change. No time to get your clothes." He took another sip. "Technically, I kidnapped you," he said. He laughed, and the booze stuck in his throat. He coughed a few times. Then he had to get up on his knees and grip the tailgate and really hack away for a while. I got up behind him and thumped on his back with the flats of my palms. He spit dark snot. When he was done, we knelt beside each other and looked around. The sky was brighter. A ribbon of blue hung where the horizon should have been but wasn't. The land was all covered in mirror-smooth water. Not a breath of wind. It was like floating in space.

And as the sky grew brighter still, a huge black shape materialized. More of an empty place, really. A void in the shape of a tower. Billy had parked less than thirty yards from the Nelson Company Grain Elevator. I don't even think he'd done it on purpose. It was invisible at night, but as the sun cracked the horizon, the elevator held our gaze. It was an impressive building, the tallest thing in fifty miles. From what I've been told, Randy's old man built it. Hired a crew of farm boys to layer up the planks and nail them down. Solid wood-cribbed walls, one hundred feet into the air and clad in tin.

Billy stood, and jumped down to the soggy gravel. He swigged Everclear. The first bits of sunlight shown through the bottle like a magnifying glass. He set it on the rear bumper and scooped a stone up off the ground. He felt the weight of the stone in his hand, and then he wound up and fired it off at the grain elevator. A great arching flight, right into the center of the black shape. Seconds went by. I began to wonder if the stone would ever land, or if the elevator really was just a void in the sky, sucking in bits of trash and songbirds and the hopes and dreams of Radium. I wondered if the stone might just sail right through the emptiness and disappear from this earth.

Then the stone rattled off the corrugated tin. A clear, metallic sound. It was very satisfying. I hopped down from the truck and threw another stone. And another. And then handfuls. Soon Billy and I were breathless, shotgunning fistfuls of gravel into the elevator walls from six feet away. We screamed curse words and nonsense. We went crazy. We busted out the windows. We couldn't stop. Billy found a chunk of four-by-four and swung it into the elevator door like a baseball bat. Over and over till the doorframe flew into splinters. We raged through the dusty inner workings of the place, opened the spill gates so wheat and corn poured out like water. Chaff rose up in clouds. We laughed and coughed, and then we found Randy's office. I tipped over a filing cabinet and ripped up the papers. Billy climbed up onto Randy's desk and pissed on his chair. It took him a long time. I couldn't stop laughing.

When we got tired, we staggered back outside. I bent over, put my hands on my knees. I gasped for air through the laughter. I'd never felt so crazy before. Giddy almost. My lips tingled.

"I can't believe you pissed on his chair!" I said. But he didn't hear me. He was walking back from the truck, stripped to the waist, trying to jam his shirt down the half-full bottle of Everclear. "This goddamn airlock," he said. "Give me the knife."

I tossed it to him, and he snapped it open. He set the bottle on the ground and stabbed the knife blade down the neck hole a bunch of times, like putting out somebody's eye. Then he rolled up his shirt and screwed it down into the bottle. He stood and watched liquor wick up through the cotton. He lit a cigarette and squinted in the morning sun.

I wasn't laughing anymore. Neither was he. With his shirt off, Billy looked like a murder victim. Dark blotches covered his body. Purple, and a sick shade of yellow that looked like vomit. One patch of ribs was stove in and all the way black. I probably looked just as bad, with the burns and the missing hair and the hospital gown. We were just a pair of dead boys, he and I, waiting for grain alcohol to saturate a cotton T-shirt.

I think of that moment often. If there was ever a time to talk my brother down, that was it. Molotov cocktails never end well, and that's just a fact. I didn't have much pull with Billy when his blood was hot, but I could have begged. I should have. Things might have turned out different. But something kept me quiet, and then Billy spoke up.

"I went to the police station," he said, "while you were in the hospital. Talked to an officer. I told him everything, kid. I showed him my ribs. I showed him pictures of your burns. Do you know what he said?"

Billy's voice turned to gravel at the end. He bent double and coughed for a long time. When he could breathe again, he stood and wiped his mouth with the back of his hand, smeared a streak of blood across his cheek.

"The officer told me I must be mistaken. Randy could not have burned our trailer, because Randy was with this very officer all evening. He told me they got a whole crew of volunteers together to clean up some garbage. He said you gotta take care of garbage right away or it gets out of hand. Starts thinking it's not garbage. Starts laying down roots."

Billy reached down and picked up the bottle. The shirt was dark and wet and reeking like gasoline. He took a good hard draw on the cigarette, till the ember glowed red. Then he looked at me one more time and grinned. His eyes burned as bright as the cigarette.

"Let's bust out of this shithole," he said.

And you know what? I didn't want to talk him down anymore. Randy came to our house with his friends and burned it to ashes. The place Billy clawed up from nothing after our father died and our mother slipped away and everything went to shit. Our own place, understand? The only place I ever felt calm. Ashes. Randy did that. So yes, I wanted to burn something of his. Hell, I wanted to burn Randy, but the elevator would do.

Billy leaned in and lit the T-shirt off the end of his cigarette. Blue fire leapt into the air. He held the bottle at arm's length for a moment, watching the flames. They floated an inch above the cloth. It seemed like a magic trick. He stepped back and lobbed the bottle through a busted window. The space inside flickered, squealed, and glowed like the sun.

• • •

We drove fast. Real fast. Billy got his foot down hard. The truck shimmied on soft gravel. The seat below me rocked and tilted, but Billy leveled things with speed. Mud flew from the back tires. We plowed through deep lengths of flooded road. I put my hands on the dashboard just to keep my ass in the seat. We didn't say a word for ten miles. Then Billy glanced up in the rearview mirror and stood on the brakes. I hit the end of my seatbelt. The Silverado slid sideways and stopped on the hard shoulder. He kicked open his door and we went out onto the road.

The world was different. Red. Our bodies cast long, black shadows on the ground, even in the daylight, and the air seemed to vibrate. A hissing, shrieking sound. We turned our heads back toward Radium. There on the horizon rose a three-hundred-foot pillar of fire. It burned so hot there wasn't even smoke.

"Holy hell," Billy said.

8.

We headed west, because we were young and because Billy had just committed felony arson, and lost his girl, and west is where you go when events line up in such a way. We drove up from the floodplain, where the ground is dry and topsoil swirls into the wind. Billy cranked up the radio, and cranked down his window, and then he snapped his cell phone in half and tossed it out. Cold air roared through the cab and counteracted the liquor in our veins. There wasn't much talk between us, and that's just fine. The road is a good place to be. There's something that happens in a truck at highway speed that words will wreck. A peace that comes.

We drove a long time. Many hours. Hills and windrows shrank with the miles until all the world was a pan of brown dirt, with blue sky above it. Finally, a town grew up from the flatland. Low, weathered buildings and tall, dying elm trees. A dog stood in the road on the outskirts of this town. Right in the middle, like a guard. A pit bull, I think. Large and black and standing very still. Billy slowed way down and edged as far over as he could. The dog's eyes followed us as we idled past. I remember them still. They were like black marbles.

"Jeez, that's creepy," Billy said.

He found the center of town and pulled over. He got out and stretched. His vertebrae, and his shoulders, and every one of his knuckle bones crackled like popcorn. He didn't have a shirt on, and I didn't have anything but the gown, but the streets were empty, so we didn't worry about it. Billy just lit another cigarette, and we drifted down the sidewalk. We were both a little drunk still, I suspect. And beat to shit. And sleep deprived. We moved pretty slow.

"My back itches," I said.

"I bet."

"Could you maybe scratch it for me? I can't reach."

"Doctor said leave it alone. It'll infect if you pop the blisters."

I blinked in the bright sun. My head hurt. My stomach sloshed around, all full of bad liquids. And my back really did itch. It was all ants back there.

"Just a little scratch?"

Billy took a deep breath and then he coughed up a big toad of jellied blood. About the size of a silver dollar. It was hard for him to do. He was doubled over by the end. He breathed through his teeth, straightened halfway up, and touched the ruined place on his ribcage. The bones made sound grinding against each other.

"Your ribs are busted," I said.

"No shit."

"Busted ribs are no good, Billy. They knife around in your guts and do all kinds of damage. Aw man. Now I feel dumb for complaining about my back."

A minivan idled past on the street. The only vehicle we'd seen in fifty miles. An old woman was driving. Her face was as hard as a bag of rocks. Billy waved to her from his gasping hunch. She didn't wave back.

"Don't worry, kiddo," Billy said. "This is temporary. My body will rebuild because I have told it to do so. I have power over it. Muscle and bone do as I say. And I say heal."

• • •

The town was only a couple of blocks long. No stoplights. All the businesses were either empty or closed. At the bitter end of Main Street was a pawnshop. The sign said "OPEN." Billy stopped under the awning to finish his cigarette. The place had bars on the windows. Plaster siding crumbled off the wall in palm-sized chunks. Billy scratched the stubble on the side of his bruised face. "Greg's guns and pawn," he read aloud. "We buy your unwanted gold!"

Just under the "unwanted gold" sign was a piece of tagboard taped to the wall. "Divorced? Sell your ring to Greg!" Billy didn't read that last line. He dropped his cigarette and ground it into the concrete with his boot heel.

A lot of people look down on pawnshops, because all the merchandise is tainted with failure. But you know, we were in no position to judge.

"Look for clothes," Billy said. "I need a word with Greg."

I cruised up and down the aisles, but there wasn't much of a clothing section. Of course there wasn't. It was a pawnshop. Nobody pawns underpants. And if they did, those are not the underpants you want.

I nearly gave up, and then I saw it—oh man, the best-looking leather jacket in the world. It was the kind where the zipper comes down at an angle. It had the chrome snaps. I took it off the rack and felt the weight of it in my hands. The leather was heavy and worn. Almost gray, except for a couple spots on the back, which were jet black. Patches had blocked the sun, but they were torn off now. I could read the letters still in the marks they left behind. "Highwaymen," right across the shoulders.

Remember the knife I found in the time capsule, on my birthday? I told you about the feeling it gave me. The electricity that came off it. The jacket carried the same kind of power, only stronger maybe. Holding it, I could almost see the previous owner. Tall and strong, with a square jaw, and probably several venereal diseases. I could see the miles he rode and the bar fights and the joy it all gave him.

I put it on. Suddenly I was that man. Six feet tall, with good muscles and a regular-shaped head. I wanted a cigarette. I wanted to run around and tear shit up.

I swaggered up to the front of the store to show Billy. He was still shirtless – leaning on his elbow over the glass counter and chatting with a greasy long-haired guy. Greg, probably. They had something on the counter between them.

"One-fifty," Greg said.

"He paid five hundred," Billy replied. "Fired it once."

"Bad investment," Greg said. "One-fifty."

That thing on the counter was my dad's old .45 pistol. My heart sank. We didn't have much from Dad. The pistol was pretty much the only thing we hadn't sold years ago. I felt small again. My shoulders shrank inside the leather jacket.

"I'm starting to think you're ripping me off, Greg," Billy said.

"Sure I am. This is a pawnshop, asshole. What did you think was gonna happen?" Then Greg's eyes drifted up from the counter and landed on me. "Oh Jesus!" He started back. "When did you get out?"

"Out from where?" I said.

"The mental hospital. You escaped like, what, five minutes ago?"

"Leave the kid alone," Billy said. Greg ignored him.

"Take off that jacket," Greg said. "You're getting retard all over it."

"You can't say that word anymore," I said, but the air got all tangled up in my throat and nobody heard me.

"Speak to my brother again and I'm coming across this counter," Billy said.

Greg turned his glare slowly back to Billy. He ran his greasy fingers over the .45. It made me sick to see him touch it. "It ain't fair," Greg said. "You know it, and I know it. But you're fresh out of options. You know how I can tell? You're beat to shit. Your brother's got no pants on, and you're pawning your dad's heirloom pistol. That's Hard Luck 101."

Billy's hands quivered down at his sides, trying not to make fists. Greg went on. "I haven't seen you before, which means you're just passing through. And nobody stops here unless they have to, so you're almost out of gas. Hungry, too. Am I right?"

Billy didn't respond. Greg smiled. "Take the one-fifty and go," he said. "Defend your idiot brother somewhere else. This is not a place of dignity."

Billy gritted his teeth. "Can you do one-seventy-five?"

I couldn't watch. I took off the jacket and hung it over the counter. The gown was cold, so I wrapped my arms around my body. Suddenly I hated everything. Greg, and the pawn shop, and myself for being there. If it wasn't for me, Billy would be flying down the highway with Maggie-Grace, not pawning Dad's gun for pants money. Most of all I hated my big spinning melon head. What a piece of garbage. The damn thing was at it again. Tugging at my neck cords. Trying to spin around. Testing the resistance.

I had to concentrate; another humiliation was more than I could bear. Billy always told me, in such situations, I should focus on a single object off in the distance. He said that would level things, like seasick people looking at the horizon. A dirty old TV was bolted up in the corner. I clung to the flickering advertisements.

A peppy housewife demonstrated the joys of a certain kind of detergent. It could clean all kinds of things. Toilets. Floors. Even fry pans. The housewife made a big thumbs-up with her yellow rubber glove. I watched her scrub and scrub, and mostly tuned out Billy's sad negotiations. This housewife was so happy! The detergent really made her day. Then she disappeared, and by some horrible magic I was watching Billy up on that dusty glass. They had an old mug shot of him up there, with the burning elevator in the background. Some shaky iPhone footage from the peak of the blaze. It looked like a crack had opened in the sky, and behind it was hell. There were houses on fire, too. Trees. Cars. Everything burned. Print ran across the bottom of the screen. "Arsonist still on the run. Officials say suspect is unstable, armed, and considered dangerous."

Things heaved wildly for me. Colors shifted red. My legs went soft. I reached out to steady myself on the display counter, but my

hand had cramped up and become useless. It bounced off the glass
and tipped over a mug of pens. Billy looked at me, then up at the TV
screen. The video was different. High quality news-crew stuff, broad-
casting live. Radium had burned to the waterline. The studs of houses
poked up from the surface like black claws. People waded through
the streets carrying blankets and photo albums. A big National Guard
truck rolled through the background. A bunch of people huddled in the
back. They were the same color as the floodwater and the sky. Gray.
Maggie was one of them. She was far away, but I recognized her.

We watched for maybe a second and a half. When we turned back
to Greg, he had Dad's .45 pistol trained on Billy's chest.

Billy rubbed his eye sockets with the heels of his palms. He let
out a deep sigh. "What now?" he said.

"Well, if you like breathing, don't fucking move."

Greg started off pretty confident, but a thing happened over the
course of that one sentence. Billy's arm snapped out across the counter
like something made of spring steel. By the time Greg finished saying
"don't" Billy'd snatched the gun from his hand and pointed it back at
him. Punched him in the nose too, real hard. "Move," came out in a
mist of blood. Greg clutched at his face. Blood poured out between
his fingers.

"Okay, Greg," Billy said. "Here's how it's gonna go."

He told Greg to empty the till into a plastic garbage bag, and
Greg did it. He told him to empty the safe hiding under the counter,
and Greg did that, too. Then Billy smiled wide. "Take off your pants,"
he said.

"What?"

Billy fired a round through the glass countertop. Shards fell like
rain. "Pants, asshole."

Greg stripped. "Give them to the kid," Billy said. "Kid, put those
on." So, I put on Greg's pants, and then his socks and shoes, and his
shirt, till Greg shivered in a pair of tighty-whities. He pinched his

nose shut with one hand and tried not to step on the busted glass. Billy tossed him my nasty hospital gown, and Greg put it on.

"When did you get out?" Billy said.

Greg blinked.

"Say, 'out from where.'"

"Out from where?"

"The mental hospital."

Billy grabbed that cool leather jacket and the sack of cash, and we left Greg bleeding where he stood.

.

9.

First thing Billy did back in the truck was reach for the cigarettes. He pushed in the ancient dashboard lighter and tapped one up from the cardboard pack. His knee guided the wheel. He got the cigarette between his lips and pulled it free. I watched him do it and said nothing.

He lifted the bright lighter coil to his mouth, but a knob in the road jolted it loose. The red-hot thing landed in his lap. It left a black ring on his pant leg. He snatched it up with his fingertips, and it burned those too.

"Fuck!" he said, and flung the coil out his open window. The cigarette in his mouth was bent in half. It hung down like a broken limb. He threw that out behind the lighter, and ran his burnt hand through his hair. The hand shook. "Maggie's okay, isn't she?" he said. "She made it out before the fire?"

"Sure she did," I said. "She was in the news video."

A smile flashed across his face. "I must have missed that," he said. "How'd she look?"

"I don't know," I said. "Pretty, I guess."

"Anything else?"

"She looked kind of gray, from all the ashes."

He nodded. Then he groaned and punched the dashboard so hard it cracked.

The Silverado coasted out of that sad little town. I glanced through the wheel. The gas needle was right on empty. Billy didn't seem to notice, or care. We burned fumes out onto the prairie.

I took the pack from the cup holder and an old Bic lighter from the glove box and lit one up. I took a couple drags to get it going. Then I passed it to Billy.

"Thank you," he said.

I watched his face through the smoke. The bruises. The sweat running down his temples. I could see him rearranging his future.

We drove till the engine began to sputter, and then we turned off the road and parked in a stand of cottonwood trees beside a creek. Billy made a campfire with dead branches, and we huddled around it as the sun went down. We split an old stick of jerky from the back seat of the Silverado and drank from the creek, and then we slept.

• • •

The morning came cold and early. We took off our clothes, and Billy brought me down into the water. He peeled off my bandages, washed my burns with palms full of cold creek water. My teeth chattered, but it felt good. The water ran smoke-dark around us. When we were all washed up, Billy looked different than before. His bruises were yellow now, instead of purple. Nearly healed just a day and a half after the beating. His rib cage looked right again. He did push-ups on his knuckles. My brother became whole with unnatural speed.

We got dressed and sat by the ashes of our fire. Billy spread the leather jacket out on the ground and picked up the .45. He fiddled with all the little pins and levers till bits of machined steel parted from the frame. He laid them out in order on the jacket. A .45 is a complicated piece of machinery. It's gotta be cleaned all the time or it jams up. The gun clicked under Billy's thumb, and the whole slide came loose. He lifted the naked barrel and squinted at me through the bore.

"Bang," he said. Then he spit on the steel and scrubbed it on his pant leg. It left black streaks. I watched him work for a while before I got up the nerve to talk.

"Hey, Billy," I said. "What are we gonna do?"

"Right now, or long term?"

"Both, I guess."

"Right now I'm gonna clean this gun because it's something I understand, and the precision makes me happy."

"And long term?"

"I've been thinking on that." He peered at each little piece of the gun, wiped them down, and wiggled them back into place.

"What did you decide?"

"The world's getting smaller, kid," he said. "With satellites and camera phones, I'm not sure there's any place we could go where the law could not find us. And make no mistake, the law will be looking. A grain elevator is one thing. But I burned the whole goddamn town to the waterline. Then there's the pawnshop and poor Greg in his underpants. I think that's what they call a pattern of antisocial behavior."

He was using every one of his fingers to force a spring back into the .45. The matter drew his concentration. "I should just go back to Radium and turn myself in," he muttered. "Hope for a forgiving judge. That's the smart move." One of his fingers slipped, and the gun flew into pieces. "Goddamn it," he said. "There goes the firing pin."

"That sounds important."

"It is. Shit. Just help me look."

We combed around in the grass till we found the little piece. When the gun was whole again, Billy levered a round into the chamber. It sounded clean. Precise. He clicked the safety on with his thumb and set it in the grass beside him.

"What kind of prison time are you looking at?" I said. "If we go back."

Billy edged closer to the gray hole of our campfire. One tendril of smoke coiled up into the air. His eyes followed it. "That depends on legal factors that I do not understand."

"Ballpark it."

"With my record, twenty years. A lot more if anyone burned to death."

The sun became very bright all of a sudden. I couldn't seem to focus my eyes. "Jesus Christ, Billy."

"We'd have to find a place for you. I bet they'd let you stay with Carl and his folks."

"You didn't mean for the fire to spread the way it did. It's flood season, for goodness' sake. No way you could have known."

"That don't matter," he said. "And it don't matter if I feel bad. Or if I don't."

I grabbed up fistfuls of dirt and grass. My guts churned, all sick and hot. I pulled in great lungfuls of air, but it just made things worse. The heat climbed up into my throat. I tasted acid in my mouth. My brother in a cage. In a cage! Twenty years in a cage—and lost to me.

"You'd like it at Carl's place," he said. "They're nice people, and well outside of Radium. I'm pretty sure their house didn't burn down."

"I don't want to live with Carl," I said.

"You could look in on Maggie for me. Make sure that kid grows up knowing he's mine."

Tears rolled down my face. "I can't be around Maggie," I whispered. "My weird head makes her sad."

Billy was quiet for a long time. He watched that little slip of smoke, his eyes tracking back and forth as it moved in the wind. Slowly he got out his pack of cigarettes and lipped one up into the corner of his mouth. Then he leaned forward and reached down into the ashes. His fingers followed the smoke, plunged knuckle-deep in the gray dust, and came out with a bright red coal. The last one. He held it softly between his fingertips like a living thing, touched it to the cigarette and breathed. When he was done, he placed the coal back among the ashes.

"There is another option," he said. "But I have to tell you. It's not a good one."

"What is it?"

He picked up the garbage bag from the pawnshop and turned it over. Stacks of bills poured out onto the ground. It was more money than I'd ever seen in one place.

"I took five grand yesterday," he said. "It was easier than I thought." There was something in his voice just then. Something like joy. I wiped my eyes. "Maybe we could scrape up a bunch more," he said. "Buy new papers. New names. Run off to Mexico before the walls close in."

My arm hairs prickled. I smiled. I couldn't help myself. He passed me his cigarette, and I smoked it.

"The world is shrinking," he said. "That's true. But maybe it's still just big enough for a couple outlaws to go on one last tear."

"I like this option, Billy. We'd make damn good outlaws."

He looked at me across the dead fire. "Think about it first," he said. "We'd never see Carl again. Or your weird buddy. What was it? Jeff? Kid with the little arm."

"Baby Arm Jeff."

"Right. You'd never see him again."

"We weren't that close."

Billy's eyes fell away from mine. "And Maggie," he said. "We'd never see her again. Never watch my baby grow. Is that something we can leave behind? Think about it, kid."

So I did think about it, all the way through. I thought about my brother and Maggie and the life I once imagined for them. The trailer house and the orange trees and the little one growing big and strong. It was a beautiful life. But then I saw another future. Billy was in a prison cell. It was gray, and there were men shouting and rattling the bars, and Billy wasn't himself anymore. He was old and small and all alone. And I wasn't around at all, because I'd stepped in front of a bus years before. I don't know how to say this right, but that ugly life was more ugly than the pretty life was pretty.

"If I leave that child behind me," Billy said, "aren't I a monster?"

"You'd have to leave anyway. Prison. Remember?"

He reached for the cigarette, and I gave it back to him. He smoked it awhile. I watched his face as he weighed things out. The squint lines around his eyes. I knew his decision before he made it. It wasn't even a decision.

"If we do this, you might see things you'd rather not," he said. "Hell, we might get shot to death."

"Well shit, what are our chances?"

"I don't know, sixty-forty."

"Forty we get killed, or forty we get away?"

"Does it matter?"

"No, it does not."

He stood up and tucked the .45 down the back of his pants. Then he lifted the leather jacket from the ground and put it on. It fit just perfect. He rolled his shoulders and flexed his hands, and looked down at himself like he'd woken up in a new skin. That jacket was never mine. Who was I kidding, trying the damn thing on in that stupid pawnshop? It was meant for Billy from the very first. The previous owner—the guy who broke it in with bar fights and highway miles and years in the sun—it wasn't his either. He was just holding onto it for my big brother.

Billy reached out his hand and helped me to my feet.

"Alright," he said. "We need a car."

DAMN GOOD OUTLAWS

√ 10.

People don't like to pick up hitchhikers these days. They worry about criminals and perverts. No one wants to end up all cut up and dead in some no-name ditch in North Dakota. Understandable, I'd say. But we got lucky. We left the Silverado in the cottonwoods and walked to the highway. It was out of gas, and besides, the cops would be looking for our plates. We hopped a barbed-wire fence and Billy stuck out his thumb. I didn't have high hopes, but wouldn't you know, a redheaded fat man pulled over right away. He waved happily from behind the wheel of a big shiny Cadillac Escalade.

Billy popped open the passenger door and stepped up on the running board.

"Thank you kindly," he said, but the fat man noticed Billy's gun peeking out from under his sweet new leather jacket. His eyes got wide, and then he stomped right down on the gas. Black exhaust belched out and the door slammed closed on Billy's hands. Billy clung on through squealing tires and smoke. In a second, they were going too fast for him to jump. I watched him go, a wild figure careening out over accelerating tar. The SUV shrunk into the distance. In a minute it was just a speck. Then it was gone, and I stood alone on a silent highway, holding a trash bag full of money. It was all so sudden. I sat down in the grass.

After a while the Escalade came back, reversing at great speed along the hard shoulder. It skidded to a stop and the window rolled down. Billy sat behind the wheel. He gave me a thumbs-up and I climbed in.

A few miles down the road we passed the fat man in the ditch. He sat on his butt with his head in his hands. When he heard us coming, he raised both chubby middle fingers. Billy saluted.

"That man really liked his car," he said.

Of course the fat man liked his Cadillac. It was excellent in every way. The seats had magic fingers inside that rubbed your back whenever you wanted. Didn't even need to feed in quarters. You just hit a button, and they went to work. Billy leaned back and let the fingers dig into his knotted muscles. Let the massive engine take us west. He felt the power of it, and he smiled. He put the pedal to the floor and laughed out loud. I laughed too, I guess. Billy's moods were so infectious. We looked out the windows and saw a new kind of world. A bright, mad, hungry place. The sky was so big, it made the law itself feel small, abrasive—a thing we were obligated to ignore.

This is how we entered Williston, riding on four tall wheels and enough adrenaline and nicotine to keep Billy in a mood to run through walls. Maybe you don't know this. Maybe Williston has changed since then, reverted to the dusty Dakota town it was in the days before oil started bubbling from the ground like an opened vein. I suspect the boom did not last, but when we arrived, Williston was prosperous and unpredictable. There was a crackle in the air.

We passed the afternoon eating gas station food and spending pawnshop cash on all the things Billy figured we'd need for outlawing. My face wasn't on TV yet, so he sent me into a Tractor Supply superstore with a roll of bills and a shopping list. More bullets for the .45. A ski mask for me and a red bandana for him. A road atlas. A big-ass hammer for breaking down doors. A few bundles of T-shirts and underpants. A roll of duct tape. A crate of canned beans, and a duffel bag to put it all in. The cashier gave me a couple weird looks but made no comment.

When it was all packed up and stowed in the Escalade, we drove around looking for places to rob. Billy took us through town in big easy loops, eyeing the old storefronts and new apartment complexes flying together in steel beams and concrete. He watched the short-skirted ladies that walked certain streets and whistled low at the sight of a half dozen oil men beating the crap out of some poor guy in a back alley.

I was thinking we should maybe move on to another town, maybe one where a .45 pistol carries more weight, but Billy had other plans.

He slowed to a crawl outside a low cinder-block building on the dumpier side of town. A big plywood cutout of a woman hung over the door. She wore cowboy boots and a cartoon hat, and a bra made out of painted handkerchiefs. It was not a tasteful sign, and the neon didn't help. The place was called Heartbreakers and advertised "Exotic Dancers." This did not look like a good time. It looked like a place where sadness lives. Sweaty, horny sadness. I imagined the sort of lowlifes who frequent such establishments and was repulsed. Problem was, the sign had nipples. You could see them through the painted handkerchiefs. At that time in my life, anything even resembling a nipple gave me a hard-on. I covered my crotch with my hands.

Billy squinted out the side window. He drummed his fingers on the steering wheel as he drove. He didn't stop. Thank goodness. The most I'd seen up to that point was a Victoria's Secret poster in the Grand Forks mall. I was hard for a week, always sneaking off to yank it under the trailer. I couldn't imagine what a real stripper would do to me. I could die.

Billy took us out to the outskirts of town and parked where tar turned to gravel. He leaned back his seat and turned on the magic fingers. I considered asking about our next move, but he was already asleep. Billy could sleep anywhere—in fields and kitchen chairs and on the corrugated liners of pickup truck beds. He could sleep through anything, too, which was convenient after I saw that underwear poster.

I sat in the ditch and snapped my pocketknife open and closed. I looked around. There wasn't much to see. Plowed fields and dry wind. The wind carried dirt and the smell of burning gasoline. Tractors moved on the horizon, pulling trails of topsoil up into the air. Far off, the great heavy arms of oil wells rose and fell like the heads of grazing horses. I put the knife away and went off to take a leak in the field.

Billy was so far under when I returned, I could see his eyes tracking back and forth under the lids. That's some REM sleep right there. I leaned through his open window and lifted a cigarette from his front pocket. He smiled as he slept, and his body twitched. I got his lighter from his pants pocket, and even that didn't wake him.

I smoked and paced, and when it was just about dark, Billy woke up. He lifted a cigarette from his front pocket and squinted down at the pack.

"You shouldn't steal my cigarettes," he said. "These things will kill you."

"You give me cigarettes."

"On special occasions only."

"Almost every day."

"Tuck in your shirt. You don't want the dancing girls thinking you're homeless."

My mouth went dry as dust. We were going back to Heartbreakers! Holy crap! Strippers! I became very conflicted. On the one hand—strippers! On the other hand, I worried I might have a heart attack, or one of those cranial hemorrhages that kill people at times of great stress. One minute you're fine, and then your face feels like it's a different shape and BAM! Dead. It happens all the time. At least Billy kept the plan to himself for as long as he did. If he'd told me right off, the afternoon would have been plagued by worry and uncomfortable erections.

I tucked Greg's big scratchy button-down into his big Wranglers, and off we went.

Heartbreakers was different at night. Wild. Trucks lined both sides of the street for a quarter mile. We parked way back and walked. Flocks of oilmen funneled down the street, and we all cruised along together on foot. Good ol' boys with dirty hands and chafingly-new collared shirts—almost running to the one place in town you could reliably see a woman take her clothes off. The men made hoots and strange shouts and slapped each other on the back.

Billy socked me in the shoulder and grinned.

"I'm feeling good about this," he said. I was feeling better myself. The Heartbreakers sign shown bright up ahead. The cowgirl's neon legs kicked up and down. It didn't seem nearly as depressing. Maybe I'd misjudged the place. It looked pretty sexy. My heart rate climbed. Real strippers. The thought alone was staggering. Maybe it was worth a small brain bleed.

The closer we got, the more excited everybody became. We could hear the music all the way out on the street. Oilmen reached into their pockets for wads of cash, just to have it ready when they got there. Man, I was wound up.

Then we got to the door, and there was this super-big, muscly dude standing guard. He took money and let everybody through, but not me. Billy gave him money and everything. He gave him twice as much money as anybody else, and the muscly guy still said no. I was too young. He'd get in trouble. So Billy set me on a park bench just across the street and put his half-smoked cigarette in the corner of my mouth. "Sorry, dude," he said. "I see no good way around this."

I sat on the bench and watched him jog across the street in his boots and leather jacket. He had the crisp new bandana around his neck, and I could see the ghost of his .45 pistol riding in the back of his pants. He nodded to the door guy and the door guy nodded back. No fuss. Man, Billy was cool. And I was so uncool. How does that happen? One brother is Steve McQueen and the other is Forrest Gump. Of course, there was the accident and everything, but there's got to be more to it. Genetic problems. I don't know. I had this theory for a long time, that on creation day God made Billy first, when his mind was crisp and fresh and full of inspiration. He used the best materials. Muscle and bone of the highest quality. Took his time. Really got the angles right. Then he thought he better not waste the scraps, so he made me. Late one night when I was feeling sad, I ran my theory past Billy. He said there is no god, go to sleep. Maybe he was right about that. Maybe not. Either way I'm still just a boy of scraps, and guys like me don't get to look at strippers. Those are the rules.

I took a long drag off the cigarette and breathed it out in a stream. "Shit," I said.

"You're not missing much."

I nearly jumped off the bench. An old man sat beside me. I hadn't even heard him come over.

"It's not so great in there," the old man said. "Just a bunch of perverts sitting around with their dicks hard for no good goddamn reason. I understand you might be too young and delicate for such language, but that's just how it is. Perverts with erections that will lead nowhere. Do you get me? Out here is better. Count yourself lucky."

I liked this old man right away. He was very tall and thin, and his face was covered in deep lines. The word "erection" sounded so weird coming from him, I had to giggle. It was nice to have someone to sit with.

"Thanks, mister. I guess I am pretty lucky."

Just then, a guy staggered out of Heartbreakers, kneeled down, and barfed on the sidewalk. His friends came out behind him and kicked him in the butt, so he fell face first into his own sick. They all laughed, even the barf-covered dude. Fresh customers stepped over the whole mess without hesitation.

"Goddamn," the old man said. "What a shithole. What are you doing out here anyway, kid? Are you waiting for your dad?"

"My brother."

"Tell me about this brother of yours."

"Well, he's probably the coolest guy ever, and I get to hang out with him. How about that for lucky?"

"He left you on a park bench all alone. That doesn't sound very cool."

"He tried to bribe the bouncer so I could go in, but it didn't work."

"I have to say, your brother is not rising in my estimation."

"He'll come out soon. You'll see."

The old man nodded and thought. He laid his arm out across the back of the bench, so his fingers nearly reached my shoulder.

"How soon?" he said. His voice shifted a bit there. It was clearer. I turned to look at him. Really look, for the first time. He wasn't as old as I'd thought. His face was old, sure enough, but his body was younger. Maybe fifty, and corded with veins and tendons.

"Not sure," I said.

"Well, when you see him coming, you let me know."

He drummed his fingers on the back of the bench, just a few inches from me. Drummed and drummed. Knuckle-bone on wood, right by my ear. I felt a twinge in my stomach and ignored it.

"What about you?" I said. "How come you're on a bench outside a strip club?"

His fingers stopped, and a grin spread across his face. The wrinkle lines cut right down through his lips, like you see on people in nursing homes. His teeth were long in his head. "Me?" he said. "I bet you can guess."

"Probably not."

"You seem like a smart kid. Give it a shot."

"Are you waiting for a bus?"

"Nope. My car's just over there." He pointed to a shiny black Dodge Charger. A beautiful car.

"Nice," I said.

"Sure is. Try again."

"Did you get too wound up in there? I was worried about that myself. You know, you can get a brain bleed from too much stimulation. Your face feels different and then you're dead. Did you feel one of those things coming on?"

"No."

"Maybe your daughter works in there. You're gonna give her a ride home."

"Ouch. That's ice cold, kiddo. I wasn't much of a father, but my kids are not on the pole."

"Well shit, just go ahead and tell me."

"Sure?"

"I'm never gonna get it."

The old man slid around on the bench and tapped a bright silver badge clipped to his belt. "US Marshal," he said. "I'm tracking a guy. Real dirtbag. You wouldn't happen to know any dirtbags, would you?" And he winked his wrinkly old eye.

Goddamn it. I missed the badge. What a colossal screw-up! I was no good at outlawing—even the waiting-around part. Billy left me alone for five minutes, and I started up a conversation with the only US Marshal I'd seen in my entire life. What a moron.

"No dirtbags here," I said.

The marshal shrugged. He drummed his hard fingers on the bench. "I don't do this sort of thing much these days," he said. "Desk duty, on account I'm old as shit now. I'm here as a favor. See, this old college buddy of mine is a police chief over in Minnesota. Little place called Radium. Do you know it?"

I could feel my body getting ready to betray me. My neck cords twitched and ached. So did my dumb crippled hands. My heart pounded up into my throat so hard I could barely make words. "Never been," I choked out.

"And you never will. The whole miserable town burned to ashes yesterday morning." He chuckled and covered his mouth with his bony hand. "I shouldn't laugh," he said, "but Jesus Christ, the place was flooded at the time. Flooded, and simultaneously burned. Let that sink in. I mean, it's objectively funny."

"Real funny," I said. I didn't laugh though. I had my head pinned between my hands to keep it from spinning around. What a cruel old dude. I knew he had me, and he knew that I knew. Pretty soon he'd slap on the cuffs. Billy'd come back for me, and the marshal would get him, too. Off to the big house for both of us, all because I was too slow and stupid to dodge one old man. But he wouldn't just put me out of my misery. He kept talking, letting me stew.

"Anyway, this dirtbag torches all of Radium and it hits the news as these things do, and my college buddy starts to panic. It turns out the dirtbag was in the goddamn police station like two hours before it all broke loose. My buddy sat across a table from him for twenty-five minutes, and apparently didn't see any of this coming. As a law enforcement professional, I can tell you that doesn't reflect well on my college buddy. So, what does he do? He calls me in to find this guy before he does any more damage, like I'm not busy as shit already."

My head wanted to spin so bad. I had the stupid thing trapped between my hands, so my neck sent all its nervous energy down into my body. I rocked back and forth. I couldn't stop.

"Friends, right?" the marshal said. "Always asking you to do shit. Do you have any more of those?"

"Friends?"

"Cigarettes," he said, and nodded to Billy's half-burned smoke, still hanging in the corner of my mouth. "I always start jonesing when I'm about to catch a dirtbag."

My head slipped free and did a quick loop-de-loop without permission. I barely caught it.

"You can have this one," I said.

The marshal watched me rock back and forth. "Never mind," he said.

He kicked his feet out and leaned back. He checked his wristwatch, drummed his fingers on the bench. He was silent just long enough that I started to wonder if he really had me after all. He was after Billy, sure enough, but maybe he didn't know about me. Maybe he was just shooting the shit with some random teenager. Maybe I could slip away and warn Billy. I eased forward on the bench, real slow. The moment my weight came onto my heels, the old man clapped his hands together. BAM! I fell back on the bench. For a second, I thought he'd shot me.

"Hey," he said. "I never answered your question."

"Which one?"

"Why I'm here."

"You're chasing a guy."

"Yeah, but why am I *here* as opposed to any other place a dirtbag might hang out?"

"Okay, why?"

"Trade secret." The marshal slapped his thigh and laughed real hard. "I'm kidding. Jesus. It's not that hard, kiddo. The dirtbag needs money. This is a cash business, and there are also titties, which is a bonus. He's gonna rob this place. It's fairly basic human psychology."

Honestly, I hadn't even considered what Billy wanted to do at Heartbreakers. I knew we were trying the outlaw lifestyle, but to be fair, outlaws go to strip clubs just for fun, too. But he *was* wearing that red bandana around his neck, and it *was* already folded in a triangle so he could pull it up over his mouth and nose. He had the .45 with him. Aw man. He was totally gonna rob Heartbreakers with a US Marshal waiting on a park bench outside. Shit!

"Goddamn it, where are they?" the marshal said. He was looking at his watch again. "I called for backup twenty minutes ago. Local meatheads, I'm telling you."

He pulled a radio from his jacket and shouted into it for a while. He berated some dispatchers on a deeply personal level, and in about two minutes the squad cars arrived. A pack of three skidded up on the street all at once. Then a few more around the side of the building. The cops got out and stood behind their cars. They pointed their guns at Heartbreakers.

I gripped my head and rocked back and forth. I went to a very dark place. What a stupid moron I was. Billy did everything for me, and I was useless to help him. He was gonna get caught because of me. I'd never be able to live with myself. I'd have to step in front of a bus, but that's not so easy to do in prison. I'd probably just hang myself with one of those prison sheets that smells like rape. I imagined doing it. My face turning red as a cherry. The thought gave me some peace.

"I know what you're thinking," the marshal said.

"I bet you don't."

"Why does this decorated lawman sit by while a bunch of other doofuses have all the fun?"

I rocked back and forth and said nothing.

"It's simple," the marshal said. "I'm not sure what the dirtbag is capable of. He might blow away six of these assholes. He might just lie down. Either way, I'll be out here with my new best friend, safe as houses."

He squeezed my knee with his wiry old hands. Shook it back and forth and chuckled. I tried to ignore his touch. Soon I'd hang myself, and all this crap would be over. I wouldn't have to be such a disappointment.

"Any moment now," the marshal said. Just as he said it, a shot rang out from inside the club. It might as well have been a starting gun. All those cops rushed in at once. I couldn't watch. They were gonna get my brother. Drag him out in the street. Put him in a cage. The marshal patted my knee. "It's almost over," he said.

I didn't respond. After a while, the cops started taking people out of the club in groups. Drunks, shouting about their ruined night. Dancing girls making phone calls. I hunched way down, my head bounced up and down on my legs. I looked at the ground below me. I didn't want to see my brother in cuffs. I didn't want him to see me. I was so useless and bad. But time passed, and Billy was never led past in

chains. The marshal never crowed like I knew he would. Trucks started up and drove away. The street emptied except for squad cars.

The marshal started drumming his fingers again. Finally, a young
police officer jogged over and stopped in front of our bench to breathe.
I knew he was husky from a quick glance when he was still across the
street. When he got close, I turned my head away so he wouldn't look
at me.

"Well?" the marshal said.

"He's not in there."

"Look harder!"

"We did. Everywhere, sir. He slipped away. This guy is real good."

"And you checked the basement?"

"There's a basement?"

"Jesus fucking Christ. Watch this kid for me. Do you think you
can do that?"

"Yessir."

"Are you sure? Are you absolutely sure you can handle one challenged teenager for five minutes?"

"Yes."

"I don't know. He might give you the slip. Hell, he might knock
you over the head with your own damn pistol."

"I got this."

"Fine." And the marshal stormed off to search the basement
himself.

The cop slouched down next to me. "That guy is so mean," he
said. He was still a cop, but I liked this one a lot better than the marshal. Mostly because he was fat. A cop ought to be a little fat. They're
more relaxed that way. Never trust a fit cop. They get all wound up
and blow people's heads off for no good reason.

He laid a jacket over my shoulders and ruffled up my burned hair.
"Let's get you out of here," he said. He walked beside me down the
street. We passed a whole row of squad cars. The lights were on, but

no sirens. The world turned red, then blue, then red again. The officer never reached for his keys. Never slowed down. Pretty soon we passed the very last one and walked into darkness.

It was only then I noticed the jacket around my shoulders was made of heavy black leather, with chrome snaps and that cool angled zipper. I looked at the jacket, and then I looked up at the chubby cop. And you know what? He wasn't a cop at all. He was my big brother in a padded uniform. I don't know how his voice got past me. I must have been pretty freaked out.

"Holy shit," I said.

"Be cool. They can see us still."

We walked real calm and casual till the street turned a corner. Then we ran. Oh man did we run, and after a few blocks we were laughing too. Laughing and running till we couldn't breathe and we had to stop. I panted like a dog.

"How'd you do it?" I gasped.

"Oh, it was no big thing," he said. "Just choked out an officer in the supply closet. All you gotta do is get their neck in the crook of your elbow." He demonstrated his technique in the air. "Squeeze till your forearm pinches off the jugular." He flexed his bicep. He laughed.

"You killed a cop?"

"Just put him to sleep so I could borrow his clothes. He's probably waking up right about now."

"That's the second guy you've left in his underwear."

"True enough."

We walked on. Neither of us remembered exactly where we'd parked the Cadillac, and we were too elevated to worry about it. I didn't worry about anything just then. Life was great.

"Hey," I said. "How'd you manage the gut?"

Billy grinned real wide. He unbuttoned the uniform halfway down. Inside, instead of a beer belly, were wads and wads of crumpled bills. Thousands of dollars. A few singles fell onto the ground, and I picked them up.

"Dang, Billy," I said. "I think you might be good at this."

He slung his arm across my shoulders and laughed. We walked like that, with me under his arm. It was warm, and I felt safe and happy. After a while he cleared his throat.

"Listen," he said. "It wasn't quite as easy as I said just now. It got pretty narrow. I could have used your help."

"I'd be no good, Billy. You saw me back there, didn't you? Spinning my head around? It was pathetic."

"I saw it."

"Then you know you're better off alone."

"Come on, kid."

"You should be with Maggie right now. You should have let me burn under the trailer."

Billy pulled his arm off me and stepped away. I thought he'd be mad. He was always mad when I talked about myself this way. When he spoke, there was an edge in his voice, but it wasn't anger. He looked me in the eye.

"You have broken places," he said. "I know it. Your weakness has made you afraid. But you have power over all of that. I've seen you be strong, Jimmy. Stronger than me. Stronger than you've got a right to be. You know the thing I'm talking about."

"That was a long time ago."

"I needed you then, and I'm telling you, I need you now. You can be strong again."

My body shivered, but not with cold. I felt a heat come into me. It poured down my spine, through my arms, and pooled up in my fingertips. I flexed my hands, and they *were* strong. I looked at Billy and he was smiling.

11.

After that, Billy and I went on a little tear. Wouldn't you? Walk unscathed through a crowd of armed police officers in a fat suit made of stolen cash. Tell me you don't go a little wild right after.

We robbed three places in three days. A payday loan office first, because it's a crappy, dishonest industry anyway and we didn't have to feel bad. Then a liquor store, because we also needed some Jim Beam. Then a gas station, because the location seemed convenient. Beyond that, the details get a little hazy. We weren't sleeping much, and the Jim Beam had a powerful effect on me. I got overexcited, I think. My grasp on time became slippery and dreamlike. What I have left at this point are snapshots. I remember ditching the Escalade and sprinting through a cornfield. I remember shop doors shattered with boot heels. Blue lights and sirens. Midnight flights down back roads. I remember my brother pretty damn clear. He was always smiling or laughing. He seemed bigger than before. His full self.

Somewhere along the line I heard that water sound in my head and I slipped away altogether. It was like falling backward into a clean, fast river. There was plenty of motion, but I wasn't in charge. I relaxed into it, let the current take me.

I came round in Nebraska. It was dark and hot, and I was running already. My eyes opened through ski mask slits. Billy moved with violent speed up ahead of me. He gripped a steel lockbox in the crook of his arm, like a football. My heart beat fast, right up in my throat. Behind us came a series of sharp pops. Out in front, the windows of a parked Dodge Intrepid collapsed in a spiderweb of cracks. A dozen holes ripped through the trunk in a second. Apparently, this was our Dodge.

Billy opened the driver's side door and brought the thing to life. I dove headfirst over the trunk and through the ruined back window, and Billy laid rubber.

I crawled through the back seats, feeling myself over for holes. My right hand wouldn't open. It was strapped closed around my knife with a big fist of duct tape.

"Son of a bitch," Billy said, his words coming muffled through the bandana. "You okay?"

I looked around the car for clues to where I was and what I'd missed. Blood ran from Billy's knuckles and glass clung to them. His hair blew around like crazy in the wind. It was night in a vehicle I did not recognize, in a town like many others.

Later I would hear from Billy about an epic spree of robberies, burned down through a handful of Plains states. He'd tell me most were easy, and that the crazy gun shop owner who chased us with his AR-15 was the exception rather than the rule. He'd tell me that I'd been good at it, that my hands worked just fine most of the time. And the duct tape helped when my fingers could not. He said my head stayed surprisingly stationary throughout. Best of all, he told me the world was not as small as people said. The law had gotten close a couple times, but they couldn't seem to nail us down. We were too slippery. Too fast. They couldn't keep up. We were on a roll.

Later I knew all these things. That night in the Intrepid all I had to go on was the blood on Billy's hands, the knife in my own, and a strange new feeling in my guts.

My body felt coiled in a spring. Like I could flip a truck if I wanted. I wasn't sure what it meant. It could have been fear, or maybe adrenaline. I turned to Billy. He pulled his bandana down and let out a whoop. He pounded his bloody fist into the ceiling and then he socked me in the shoulder and whooped again. I looked at his face. His eyes were wild and wide. His teeth so bright and sharp I could not look away.

"I'm hungry," he said. "Jesus Christ, I've never been so hungry."

As he said it, a big sign appeared to our right. The golden arches.

He slammed the brakes and squealed into the drive-thru. Glass fell from the car. Bullet holes reeked of oil and gasoline.

"We need a dozen hamburgers," he shouted into the kiosk.

"What kind of hamburgers?"

"Hamburgers! Regular." He was very wound up.

We took the burgers to a freshly plowed field some miles from town. We sat on the warm hood and ate. Billy took big bites and washed them down with swigs of Jim Beam. He balled up the paper and made a little pile at his feet. The muscles in his face worked as he chewed. Tendons rose and fell, as defined in the moonlight as the workings of his gun. I could tell by the look of him that he had not slept in at least three days. Every ounce of fat – every soft thing was burned away. He passed me the bottle and I drank.

When we were done, he took my right hand in his and unwound the duct tape from my fist. It took a long time. That's some sticky stuff. Finally, the last strap came loose and carried the knife with it. He closed the blade and gave it back to me. He balled up the tape and tossed it down among the burger papers. Then he lit up a couple cigarettes – one for me and one for him – and we lay back on the hood and looked up at the stars.

They were very bright. Usually when the moon is full, the stars get dim. Not that night. That night everything was lit up like headlights. We smoked and watched the sky, and we did not have to speak.

I wish I could tell you that in this quiet moment I felt some remorse for all the bad things we'd done. That I thought back to Maggie and the child and the newly homeless population of Radium. Everything we wrecked. Everything we gave up to stay free. I'd look better, wouldn't I? If I felt bad right away? Billy too. He's a good man. I believe it still. I saw him baptized once and maybe that counts for something. But leaned back on the hood of that shot-up Intrepid, with his knuckles still bleeding, he was joyful. So was I. A crazy, pure, sleepless kind of joy. It's hard to explain, but I'll do my best.

You see, a lot burned with Radium, and it wasn't all good. Billy's home, his life with Maggie, his shot at a family—sure, it all went up in smoke. But so did the diapers and formula, and a lifetime of skidding sugar beets for minimum wage in a shithole town. The slow decline. That inevitable moment in five or ten years when Billy's hands weren't so fast as they once were. And the day soon after that when Maggie would realize she wanted more than a trailer house. More than Billy could offer. All that horrible, depressing stuff burned to ashes, and blew away, and we were so much lighter without it.

He was just Billy. The right-now Billy. The one with magic in his fists. And I got to be his brother, and we'd never have to be anything else, because we had no future. That's what it comes down to. We talked a good game, but our run began in fire and it would end in blood and we both knew it. That might sound bad, but goodness' sake it takes the pressure off. That's what people don't understand. Having a future can paralyze.

This world is not built for men like Billy. I'm not convinced it's built for people at all. You work eight, maybe ten hours a day. Maybe skidding sugar beets. Maybe sitting at a desk. The government takes a third and another third goes to the health insurance companies that can, at best, extend a man's final sickness by a few months. What's left is enough for food, for today. Just enough to be sure you'll come back to work tomorrow, and the day after, forever. It's like quicksand. Heavy and wet. Squeezing and squeezing. So many things you can't say. Things you can't believe. It's so tight you can't move your limbs. Can't breathe! But do you bust loose? Probably not. Why is that? You fear for your future, that's why. You gotta keep everything together so tomorrow isn't worse than today. So, you sit in your house in the evening and your mind rings with anger and distraction. You are an animal in a box made of Sheetrock. You feel your blood pressure rise.

But forget about tomorrow, and the ringing stops. I promise it does. See what you want. Take it. Grip it in both your hands, because you are strong and wild and willing to bleed. Run because you're being chased. Know that you will die. The joy of it goes back further than civilization. It's older than fire.

I will not lie to you. Those outlaw days were the very best of my life. The guilt didn't arrive till later on. And it did arrive, sure as death and taxes. The things I've done torture me. There are certain faces I see when I close my eyes, understand? But I'm getting ahead of myself. In the beginning, Billy and I were as alive as men can be. To see him that way. To be there with him. I would not trade it, not for anything. Not for innocence.

12.

"You said that old dude was a marshal, right?" Billy said. "The mean old dude outside the strip club."

We were blasting along in a rusty Ford sedan. Early morning. Somewhere in Nebraska still. I think that's where we were. The air smelled like cowpies, which suggests Nebraska, but that's all I'm going on.

"Yes, sir. US Marshal."

"Those guys only chase the real hard cases."

"He said he was doing it as a favor. We don't know if he's still after us."

"That old bastard tracked me down before Radium even quit smoking. That's commitment. He's after us, alright."

"Aw man. I don't want to hear that."

"Missing my point, kid. Wyatt Earp was a marshal. Remember *Tombstone*?" Billy grinned around an unlit cigarette. "That makes me Johnny Ringo."

"Ringo was kind of an asshole. Plus, he got shot right through the head."

"There are worse ways to go, but never mind about that. You think Johnny Ringo would drive this dumpy old Ford?"

"What are you getting at?"

"We should have a cool car," Billy said. "An outlaw car."

I had no idea what he was talking about until the decrepit Ford slid to a stop on the hard shoulder. He pointed to a "For Sale" sign pinned under the windshield wiper of a 1977 Pontiac Firebird Trans Am.

"That car," Billy said, and slammed out of the Ford.

The Firebird was parked in somebody's yard. Yard is generous. It was more like a clearing. Tall grass and garbage and that beautiful car right in the middle. Leather seats. T-top roof. Big, stenciled wings on the hood. It was basically the car from *Smokey and the Bandit*. Billy had his movie references all tangled up, but I didn't call him on it. The car was too pretty. We walked around the thing, almost afraid to touch it.

"This is the one good thing to come out of the '70s," Billy said. "Look at the craftsmanship."

"Do we steal it?"

"You don't just steal a machine like this. It's disrespectful."

He slid his hand down the ridge in the middle of the hood, between the wings.

"Well, we can't buy it," I said. "We'd have to ditch it in about three days. Tops."

Billy grinned. "Let's just ask," he said. "Can't hurt to ask."

He left me with the Firebird and trotted up the steps of a nearby doublewide. It was also from the '70s and going to shit. He knocked on the tilting screen door, and after a while a man let him in. He was gone for a long time. I paced around the car, ran my fingers over the steel. It was a very pleasing object. We couldn't have it of course. We had to save all our money for our new lives in Mexico. But it *was* a very nice car. My brother and I always liked nice cars. We liked them in the way poor people like things they can't have. We'd point when they passed us on the highway. We'd call out the make and model. The year. We'd debate which one we'd own one day, knowing all along that we never would.

It couldn't hurt to just sit in the car, just for a minute. I hopped through the open T-top. The second my ass touched the seat I got a fizzy sort of feeling way down in my guts. Almost in my crotch, but not quite. Jeez, the Firebird had big energy. It got in my blood. Gave me ideas. I put one hand on the wheel and one on the gear shift and I knew that beautiful machine would be ours. To hell with the cost. For the first time in our whole lives, we had money. It seemed stupid not to spend some of it. Outlawing is a dangerous profession. Better to have some fun right now.

Finally, Billy came out of the trailer house. A hefty, freckled man wearing only jean shorts came with him. The man was bald every-where except his back and shoulders, which were thick with white hair. Billy opened our duffel bag and dug out two big stacks of bills. He laid them down on the hood of the Ford, and the man gave up his keys. They shook hands. The man wiped tears from his eyes. "Treat her right," he said.

"You know I will," Billy replied. Then he told me to scoot the hell over. He leaped in, brought that raging beast to life, and off we went. Hot damn. It did not disappoint.

We had been something approaching careful, up to that point. Traveling at night in dumpy cars. Trying not to be around people close up, just in case they'd seen us on the TV. But we climbed into that Firebird and revved her up and, I don't know, something happened. The sound of that big engine got all mixed up with the adrenaline in our blood, and the nicotine, and the sleep deprivation. Our last shred of carefulness went right out the window. We blasted the radio and tore around in broad daylight. I stood up and felt the wind in my ratty, burned hair. I yelled for the pure joy of it, but we were going so fast the air went down my throat instead of out. So much oxygen went into my lungs I felt drunk.

When I dropped back down in my seat, all laughing and dopey, Billy had his bandana up over his nose, already turning the car into a liquor store parking lot. Didn't even ask me. I pulled on my ski mask, and we ran in. Billy drew his gun, and we did the whole thing in less than a minute. I barely remember it. Just some shouting and the blood racing in my ears and Billy lobbing a grocery bag of cash to me across the counter. We were back in the Firebird in what seemed like a single breath. Billy pulled his bandana down and laughed. He took us down an empty stretch of two-lane highway. He drummed his fingers on the wheel.

"What do you think she'll do?" He shouted.

"A hundred," I shouted back.

"She's doing a hundred right now."

"Holy shit, Billy!"

"Should we find out what she's got?"

It wasn't much of a question. He was real wound up and so was I. Of course we should find out. I slammed my palms on the dashboard and let out a scream. It was higher than I wanted. Sounded like a kid. No matter. The engine and the wind and the radio were all so loud I'm pretty sure Billy didn't even hear. He put his foot down hard. The Firebird shivered like a spurred horse. Vibrations came up through my leather seat. I could feel it in my balls. The world outside became narrow. Just the road ahead, and everything else all warped and stretched out.

Billy's hands locked on the wheel. I couldn't even see them. They were blurry with vibration. His eyes focused on that narrow strip of road.

"Call out the numbers!" he shouted.

"One-ten! One-fifteen!"

In no time at all we were cruising at 120. The speedometer crept up from there. At 121, the whole car shook so hard, Billy's gun levitated off the dashboard. You could have passed a playing card underneath. At 123 it became difficult to read the dials. I had to squint to keep my eyeballs steady in my head. I leaned in close to Billy, but not too close. He was tight as a bowstring and liable to snap.

"One-twenty-four," I said.

We let the engine scream. Watched our speed inch up over a long stretch of miles. You can do that in Nebraska. The roads are straight as runways. Clean, too, luckily. At that speed a single pebble on the roadway would have sent us into the ditch, tumbling end over end.

"Come on!" Billy shouted. The wheel thrashed in his hands like a living thing. We crossed over the center line and into the oncoming lane. He tried to ease us back, but overcorrected. Suddenly the passenger side tires hit the rumble strip. My teeth chattered together. Billy kept the throttle wide open.

"Come on!" he shouted again. "What is it now?"

"One-twenty-seven!" I cried out, and Billy finally let off the gas.

The air went quiet. Not super quiet. The radio was still on, and the wind still roared through the open T-top. But it felt very calm without the accelerator pinned. My heart thumped in my chest. I put my hands on the dashboard and breathed. My lips tingled, and my fingertips tingled. All was well with the world just then. In my experience there are few things as peaceful as coasting. Letting the wind slow you down. Like landing a plane.

Billy socked me in the shoulder.

"You good?"

I just smiled. I couldn't speak.

It was only then, at the very end of our speed run, that we met a state trooper coming the opposite way. He snapped on his lights and sirens, but by the time he skidded through a U-turn, he was miles back. An angry, flashing speck in our rearview. Billy threw us down a gravel road, and then another, and we lost that state trooper in the rural empty. He wasn't even close. We laughed about it.

Billy patted the dashboard with the palm of his hand.

"Goddamn, I love this car," he said.

• • •

In the afternoon we were tired-out and hungry from all the roaring fresh air. We stopped at a diner called Jumpin Jacks. Saw it from the road and it looked just right. It was sided in shiny stainless steel like something out of the 1950s. Billy chose a red-vinyl booth with a view of the street. He slid in and glanced out at the parked Firebird. That was a lot of car. Just looking at it made him grin like a doofus.

"Those lines man," Billy said.

"Yes, sir."

"You know, he didn't want to sell. Put the sign out there months ago but kept having second thoughts."

"How'd you convince him?"

"I told him a car like that deserves adventures. I told him we were outlaws."

"Jesus Christ, Billy. Why did you do that?"

"Seemed like a good idea."

"Goddamn it. Do you think he'll call the cops?"

Billy shrugged. He reached for a cigarette, then remembered we were indoors and put it back. "Does it matter?" he said.

"I guess not, but jeez, Billy. We can't just go around telling people about . . . ."

Then our waitress arrived, and we both forgot to argue. We forgot about everything, actually. She was a young brunette in a stiff, green polyester dress. White apron over it. The pin on her chest said, "Jenny." She pushed the bangs out of her eyes and poured coffee into Billy's mug. She poured real slow and leaned in close to Billy while she did it.

"Hey there, hon," she said. She called him "hon," right out of the gate. Have you ever heard of a thing like that?

"Hey," Billy replied. I also opened my mouth, but no sound came out.

"Can I get you two some pie?" she said. "I got the best pie in a hundred miles."

"Bring us whatever you like," Billy said.

"I won't be but a minute," she replied, and turned with a little wave of her dress. She walked like she was used to cowboy boots. We both watched her go. Here's the thing—Jenny was a fairly ordinary woman. Hard-working, I'm sure. Kind. Pretty in the way most young women are. But Billy and I were very wound up. To us, she looked like a movie star. It was her job, of course, but we couldn't even believe she was talking to us.

Soon she came back with two big slices of blueberry. Whipped cream on top. She leaned down toward Billy again.

"I gotta ask," she said. "All the other girls are talking. Is that your Firebird out front?"

"Yes, ma'am."

Jenny smiled wide. Her teeth were just a little blue around the edges. "It really is just the best pie," she said.

We ate, and it was pretty dang good. Hundred miles good? I don't know. It didn't really matter, because Billy walked out of that place with Jenny's number written in Sharpie on his palm and a date for that night. The town was throwing a big old rodeo at the fairgrounds. Jenny was just so excited we could make it. She even promised to bring a friend from the diner.

"It's the car," Billy said.

"Best money we ever spent," I said.

• • •

We killed a couple hours smoking cigarettes under a shade tree in the town park. Then Billy brushed his teeth with his finger in a drinking fountain, wet his hands and pushed his hair back, and that's it. He checked his look in the rearview mirror. He was so cool—and getting cooler every minute. He had the leather jacket, and now the Firebird. He slid on a pair of aviator sunglasses, and I thought no wonder Jenny liked him. They were both like movie stars.

When he was done, I also took a look at myself in the rearview. Total disaster, but that wasn't much of a surprise. I have come to terms.

We picked up the girls from the diner at seven. They came out in their green dresses and slipped into our back seat, all laughing and excited.

"Don't you look back here, boys," Jenny said, and they pulled off their dresses right there—changed into street clothes in about a block and a half. Billy gave me a blank stare.

"This car," he said aloud.

They fixed their bras, and the introductions started over. Jenny told us her friend Candice was a past barrel-racing champion and a fellow lover of fast cars and pie. Then she put her hand on Billy's shoulder and asked if his leather jacket meant he could ride a motor-cycle. He said sure it did. He was an excellent rider of many things. They laughed.

We parked in a well-trodden field on the edge of the fairgrounds. Shouts echoed over loudspeakers, indecipherable so far away. Groups of happy Nebraskans arrived by the truckload. They carried crates of sweating beer cans. High school guys with blatant disregard for drinking laws. There were parents and teachers around. They didn't give a damn.

The girls had obviously discussed things already. Jenny slipped her cute little hand into Billy's just as soon as we were out of the car. Candice hung back to walk with me. I looked at her hands. Her finger-nails were long and painted red. They looked very pointy. I imagined them slicing into my scarred-up palms. The tendons ached just think-ing about it. So, I dodged her hand when she reached for mine.

It was a long walk to the arena. Trucks were jammed in for acres. Candice swung her arms and watched my brother laugh with her friend up ahead. I felt bad. My stupid hands weren't her fault.

"Hey," I said, to fill the silence.

I didn't have to say more, as it turned out. She started talking right along. I'm not sure what about, barrel racing, I think.

"It's hard to enjoy these things now," she said, "when you've been as good as I was."

I nodded. Jenny led us all up the grandstand. We sat down just as the arena gates opened. An outraged bull came blasting out at great speed. Dirt flew from its hooves, and the cowboy roped to its back flopped around like a doll. His hat came off, and then he came off, and then the bull ran over him as a statement to the other cowboys. A groan rippled through the crowd, but then the trodden cowboy leaped to his feet, and everyone cheered.

Rodeos are a big deal in small-town Nebraska. We had one outside Radium every year, but it was smaller. Equally violent, of course. People just didn't care as much. This rodeo packed in every kind of Nebraskan. Little kids roamed around, their little hands covered in nacho cheese. Warped old cowboys smoked cigars. Girls swam in lettermen's jackets, and everyone cheered like hell when a local boy got his turn.

After the bulls, the rodeo moved on to tamer pursuits. There was roping and racing and kids riding sheep. One toddler tipped off a lamb and landed on his butt. He cried. His mother ran out and got him.

Jenny sighed and leaned against Billy. She put her hand on his chest like they were about to go off and make a bunch of toddlers for her to comfort at future rodeos. Candice saw them and leaned against me, put her head on my shoulder. I understood how it was. Pretty girls don't snuggle with guys like me. She was just doing it to keep up with her friend. I couldn't complain. It was nice to be there for a little while . . . in someone else's life.

But it didn't last. Never does. I looked away from Candice, just for a second. Don't know why I did it. Gut feeling, I guess. My eyes swept across the crowd at the foot of the grandstands. I saw a man there. He was tall and thin, and his presence sent all the blood draining from my face. There are plenty of wiry old dudes at a Nebraska rodeo, but this one was unmistakable. He was that mean old US Marshal, the same who sat beside me outside Heartbreakers. He walked through the crowd like he knew just where he was going. My breath stopped in my lungs. He was coming toward us.

I looked across the two cuddling girls at Billy, and he looked back with wide eyes.

"Hey," he said. "You want to get out of here?"

The girls whispered to each other, giggled, then followed Billy and me down the bleachers. They were excited, you understand, by our urgency. It was a brave move less than an hour into the date. A move worthy of the Firebird. They couldn't have known what we were running from.

Jenny took Billy's hand and he dragged her through the crowd. We left by a different gate. Almost ran. I kept waiting for the marshal to grip my shoulder. Throw me to the ground. But it didn't happen. We found the car and piled in. Billy slammed her in gear and floored it. Sod rose in two streams from the back tires. We skidded out onto the road with the two girls laughing and Billy gritting his teeth behind the wheel.

I turned around in my seat and looked out the back window. We were going fast by then. It was hard to make out the details. I squinted. I steadied my head in my hands, and I saw him. Above the sea of parked cars and people stood the US Marshal. He was perched on the cab of a jacked-up truck, shielding his eyes from the setting sun. I saw him, and I knew he saw us. I could feel his eyes on me. Then we drifted around a corner, and he disappeared beyond the trees.

• • •

Candice touched my shoulder. She leaned in, but I couldn't get my head right. The marshal was still chasing us. He was so damn close. My hands cramped into painful claws. Blood rushed in my ears till I could hear nothing but the roar of it. I clamped my eyes shut, and I guess I missed some really crucial moments.

When I opened my eyes, the car was parked on a back road some-where. The sun sunk low. It turned the Firebird gold. Billy was gone with Jenny. Candice lay in front of me on the hood of the car. Her hair was all fanned out in southern curls. The stenciled wings made her look like an angel. I stood between her knees with my shins against the front bumper. It took me a second to realize her pants were off.

Her legs glowed like porcelain in the last light. She slid her fin-gers under the elastic band of her underwear. I remember they were purple with little white flowers. She smiled up in a way that confused me, like I hadn't seen.

"What should I do?" I said.

"Whatever you want, cowboy," she replied.

The thing to do, she was saying, is to "unzip your pants." I knew it. Hell, even with my useless hands I could have managed. But I just looked at her. There was something about her eyes. The sunset put a little speck of gold in each one. What did she see through those bright sparks? Not my skinny shoulders or misshapen face, or the an-gled slash of my smile. No. None of that. Maybe she saw a workable stand-in for my brother, or one of those brave riders in the arena. What she saw, I think, was a truth-or-dare kind of story in the making. A recounted memory with her friend a decade from now with kids and husbands—remember when we were wild?

This line of thinking was no good at all. My crotch became unresponsive. I closed my eyes and tried to call back certain reli-able images from the JCPenney underwear catalog. Sexy thoughts. Sexy thoughts!

"Oh, no!" Candice said.

I opened my eyes. The world swept by, round and round. Car and sky and purple underpants. I'd been spinning my head. Damn it!

Candice pushed me away and leaped off the hood. She found her pants, and almost fell down getting them on. She looked back at me. My head was still spinning. I could tell by the look of horror on her face.

"Jesus," she said. "Jesus f-ing Christ."

She paced, tried to catch her breath. I reached up with both hands and pinned my stupid head steady.

"This close," she said. "This close to banging a challenged kid."

"I'm not challenged. Not all the way."

"Sorry. No offense, kid."

"It's okay."

After a while, Candice sank back down on the hood of the car. She put her face in her hands. "I'm a floozy," she said. "My mother was right."

This whole thing was confusing and awful. I'm no good at complicated girl stuff. All those emotions. She looked so sad I couldn't stand it. My head seemed a bit more stable, so I let go with one hand and touched Candice on the shoulder. She edged away. Man, I felt bad.

"Hey," I said. "Do you like this car?"

She sniffed and looked up through her messy blonde hair. "Yeah. It's pretty much the only reason I came along. Nice cars give me terrible judgement."

"Do you want it?"

"What?"

"The car's yours if you want it."

"I'm still not going to bang you. We're past that."

"I know. It's just, you like the car, and you seem so sad and everything."

She pushed the hair out of her face and thought. Then she got in the Firebird and started the engine. That thing sure sounded good. I grabbed our duffel from the back seat and stood in the ditch watching Candice behind the wheel. She drummed the dash with her long red nails. Then she turned to me.

"Maybe you're not challenged, but you're not totally right in the head, are you?"

"Not really, but you can still have the car."

She smiled and stomped down hard on the gas. Gravel streamed out from the back tires. Blonde hair fluttered out the T-top roof. Soon she was just a speck of taillights in the darkness. I sat down in the ditch grass and waited. It wasn't so bad. I felt around in our duffel bag and found a sleeve of Fig Newtons. You can do worse than some Fig Newtons.

• • •

A half hour later, Billy returned with Jenny. He had a cigarette in one hand and the other thrown across Jenny's shoulders. He looked happy and kind of worn out. Jenny was messing with her phone. Texting or something.

"Hey," Billy said. "Where's my car?"

"It's coming," Jenny replied.

And sure enough, the Firebird came blasting back up that gravel road at something north of highway speed. It slid to a stop in a cloud of dirt and loud country music. Billy blinked many times. Jenny kissed him on the cheek and climbed into the passenger seat. "Bye, hon," she said. Candice waved at me and stomped down hard again on the gas. This time the stream of gravel pelted Billy and me like buckshot. We watched the taillights.

"You gave away my car," Billy said, "didn't you?"

"I did."

"You didn't think to ask me first?"

"You'd have said no."

"Damn right. That was the best thing I've ever owned."

"The marshal was onto us. She had to go, Billy."

"You really think he saw us?"

"I know he did. He's getting real close."

"Goddamn it." The taillights faded into blackness, and for a minute we watched the blackness where they'd been.

"Plus, Candice really likes fast cars."

"I knew it! Women have too much power over you. We need to work on that."

Billy slung the duffel over his shoulder, and we walked. I don't know that we chose any specific direction. It was a good night for a walk.

"Did it go well at least?" Billy said. "You and Candice."

"Great. We did all the positions."

"Really?"

"No. I spun my head around and it scared her. How'd it go for you?"

"Fine, I guess. She wanted to talk after."

"What about?"

"Children. She asked me if I wanted some."

"Yikes."

"I told her I got one on the way, and it's not working out so well."

"That's a bummer."

Billy shrugged. "It's not the worst date I've been on. Do we have any more of those Fig Newtons?"

He dropped the duffel bag and unzipped it, rifled around in the wadded cash and spare underpants. After a minute, his hand slowed down and stopped. "Hey," he said. "Where's my jacket?" Oh no. It was in the Firebird, crumpled up in the back seat.

"You left it in the car, didn't you?"

I didn't want to say it out loud. He took a long breath and leaned his head all the way back. "Fuck!" he shouted into the sky.

13.

We lifted a rusting Honda and went out onto the Plains. Hunkered down in an abandoned farm. These places are common all over the middle of the country. Islands of trees and disintegrating outbuildings. Farmers get old and die. Their kids rent out the land and let the homestead rot. There's a bad storm at some point, then it's just trees. Those go too, eventually, pushed over and heaped up to make way for corn, or cows, or whatever will grow.

The last tenant of this place was gone maybe twenty years. The house was broken in the middle, folded in on itself like paper. The barn still stood. We built a fire in an old woodstove that had no chimney or door. Just let the smoke filter up into the beams and rafters. We lay down on mounds of hay caked with pigeon shit, and slept. Man did I sleep hard. Goodness' sake. It was like being dead.

We stayed there some time. Billy said we needed to let the world cool off, let that US Marshal work on some other cases. Maybe lose interest in the two of us. It was good timing for me. My brain needed rest. We lazed around and picked over the farmstead's forgotten things. We found horseshoes and railroad spikes and even a brass letter opener that looked like a tiny Roman dagger. All treasures I would have squirreled away under the trailer house back home. But we had no home anymore, so Billy and I just felt the objects in our hands and then pitched them out into the field grass.

Billy found a whole mound of china plates under the collapsed farmhouse. He set them up against the wall of the barn and taught me how to fire the pistol. Squeeze on the exhale. Let the shot surprise your hand. My ears rang, and Billy smiled. At night we heated beans on the cast-iron stove. Ate from the can.

It was at this rotting farm that my burns became well enough to shed the blister skin. Billy took it off for me since I couldn't reach back there. All the burn blisters had grown together. The whole upper half of my back came off in a single sheet. The skin underneath was pink and fresh, while the sheet itself was rough to the touch. Thick and white, like something you could make gloves with. Billy wanted to tack it up to the barn wall and see what happened when it dried, but that seemed wrong to me on a moral level. Disrespectful somehow. I buried it outside, and in the night I heard animals dig it up and fight over it. Raccoons, I think. Little bastards.

• • •

One evening, just as the sun sank from the big western sky, a pair of headlights turned down the long, overgrown driveway. They were dim and the same exact color as the sunset. Looked like two round holes in the tree line, straight through to the horizon. Billy finished his can of beans.

"Get down in that hay pile," he said. He spoke through a mouthful of beans without looking up. "All the way down, so you can bury yourself if you have to."

I did as he told me, and soon I heard tires crunching gravel just outside. I peered up from the hay. It was dark, but not so dark yet that I couldn't see. Billy stood in the center of the barn's huge open doorway with his hand around his back, holding the .45. I remember the shape of him like that. The easy slant of his shoulders.

Two men came into the firelight. One was real small. Verging on "little person" small. He had a greasy pompadour that would have given him a couple extra inches, except it was all deflated and sad and hanging over his forehead. The other man was taller but looked sick and unsteady on his feet. His eye sockets were so deep, for a second, I thought maybe he didn't have any eyes at all. What a weird, run-down couple of dudes. They gave me the willies.

• • •

Billy's hand tightened on the gun. "You can stop there," he said. The muscles in his gun hand twitched. In another second he would have drawn, I think. But then a woman appeared behind them. She was pretty and plump, and pregnant. Quite far along.

"We saw your fire," she said. "May we share it?"

Billy's hand slipped from the gun. He smiled at the woman. He got her a stool to sit on and brushed the pigeon shit off it with the corner of his shirt. She was really, very pregnant. It's not right to let a woman like that arrange her own seating, and her husband wasn't much good at all. The bony one. He was her husband, near as I could tell. He slumped down on a hay bale and just about fell over backwards. He had no energy reserves. I wondered what he was sick with. Cancer maybe. I felt bad for the child.

The woman opened a tote bag she carried and got out a fry pan, a loaf of dark brown bread, and a package of hotdogs. The hotdogs were pink and slippery in their plastic bag. When she tried to pull them out, they squirmed away from her fingers like big earthworms. The sight of them turned my stomach, but the woman seemed very excited. She counted heads and counted hotdogs.

"If we all have one, there's enough for two meals," she said. "An embarrassment of riches."

"That's very kind, miss," Billy said. "I've eaten."

"Nonsense," she said.

They introduced themselves while the hotdogs cooked. The woman was named Anna and her husband—the bony one—was John.

"Yes, I know," he said, "like John the Baptist." And he forced out an awkward laugh. Billy gave him a blank stare. Anna giggled.

"You and your dad jokes," she said.

The joke would have made more sense had we known what we found out a minute later. Anna and John were a pair of evangelical Christian missionaries driving their old RV cross-country on a crusade of revival. This once-great nation had gone rotten with sin and vice, and it was John's job to snag it before it careened off the cliff to hell. Talking about sin energized John. He sat up straighter. He admitted he'd initially hoped to go from east to west, bringing the next great spiritual awakening along the path of the rising sun. He liked the imagery of it, but God got in touch and told him that wasn't the move. God, John said, had ironed out a different plan way back at the beginning of time, which was only about six thousand years ago. But still. The beginning of time! The only thing was, God hadn't shared all the details with John just yet. He doled them out one at a time, which really messed with John's travel itinerary. One day God wanted John to save some folks in Alabama, and then next it was off to Iowa, or Upstate New York.

Billy nodded along with a great big smile on his face. John took it as a sign of support and talked in grander and grander terms. But it wasn't that kind of smile. I know my brother better than anyone. I know his face. He was smiling because he thought all this missionary stuff was the funniest shit he'd heard in his life.

"How do you know what God wants from you?" Billy said.

John looked surprised. "He tells me, how else?"

"Like, out loud?"

"God speaks in a still, small voice. If you listen, you will hear him."

"So, not out loud."

"I think you're missing the point."

Billy reached out a cigarette and lit it. He took a long drag. "What's God saying now?" The words came out in smoke and grinning teeth. But before John could answer, Billy's eyes paused on Anna and her big round belly. "Damn," he coughed, and got up to blow his smoke out the barn door.

"Don't worry," Anna called after him. "It's a well-ventilated space."

Her face was flushed and sweaty from tending the hotdogs. She was attractive in the way pregnant women often are. When Billy re-

turned, the meanness had mostly gone from him. "I'm sorry," he said
to Anna. "I forget with babies."

Anna waved him off. Billy lowered his voice when he talked to
her. His eyes were kind. "Is it a boy or girl?" he said.

"We don't know yet. John says an ultrasound would ruin the
surprise."

The group fell silent. We sat a long time listening to the fire and
the wind in the barn.

"What about you?" Billy said, nodding toward the pompadour.
"Are you a missionary?"

Mr. Pompadour looked up from the fire. He hadn't said one word
and seemed confused about how to start.

"That's Lonnie Vee," John said. "Son of Bobby Vee and heir to a
long family line of pagan rock music."

Lonnie nodded but didn't say anything. "Does God speak to you,
too?" Billy said. He couldn't help himself.

"He does now," John replied. And he launched into the saga of
how he'd met Lonnie at a county fair in Mississippi two weeks before.
How he'd stormed up on stage in the middle of Lonnie's rockabilly set
and taken his microphone under the influence of the Holy Spirit and
converted everyone in the crowd.

"Halfway through, Lonnie started playing his guitar," John said.
"Accompanying my message. It was just beautiful . . . not a song exactly, but beautiful. What do you call that?"

"The altar call music?" Lonnie said.

"No, before the altar call. When you're playing that thing. You
know, the thing. Real quiet."

"I strum some stuff while he preaches," Lonnie said. "Minor
chords when he talks about hell. Nothing special."

"You sell yourself short, Lonnie. The Holy Spirit speaks through
your fingers as clear as he speaks through my own unworthy lips."

"He does," Anna said. "You shouldn't be so hard on yourself, Lonnie."

Lonnie shrugged. He looked into the fire. His pompadour sagged so low it almost wasn't even a pompadour anymore. It was pretty clear he was done talking, but John was terrible at reading body language.

"What is it you told me, Lonnie? About brainwashing. Tell them the brainwashing story."

Lonnie protested, but Anna said please tell it, and then he had to.

"Well," Lonnie said. "My band was pissed off. I mean, they weren't happy when I decided to quit the drugs and the music scene to follow John. They didn't understand about my new . . . you know, my new calling. They said John had brainwashed me."

"And what did you tell them?" John said. "Listen to this. This is great."

"It's pretty great," Anna said.

"I told them, 'My brains needed a good washing.'"

John slapped his leg and grinned. "Isn't that just the best?"

"We thought it was pretty neat," Anna said.

Billy smiled, but there was a cruel sort of light in his eye. He looked right at Lonnie. "Neat," he said.

About that time the hotdogs were cooked. They'd gone from pink to gray. Anna cut big slabs of the brown bread and dished up a single dog onto each slice. The bread crumbled when she tried to fold it. She offered one to Billy, and he said no thanks. Lonnie took one but didn't look happy about it. John said he'd start with some bread but made no guarantees about the dog.

"You know how tricky my digestion's been," he said.

"Well, shoot," Anna said. "I wish you'd told me before I cooked all these hotdogs." She was the only one who looked hungry. Her eyes turned big and wet looking at all those gray dogs.

"We'll save them for later," John said. "Nothing is wasted, my darling."

"You should have them," Billy said. "You're eating for two."

"Is everyone sure?"

"We're sure," I said. I liked the idea of Anna eating the hotdogs. I got the sense that John wasn't much of a provider, and she needed the calories. I also liked the idea of giving the earthworm hotdogs a hard pass. Everything had worked out great. There was just one problem. The whole missionary story had been so intriguing I totally forgot I was still buried in hay. Nobody but Billy knew I was there. When I spoke up, John levitated right off his hay bale. Billy had to help him up.

"Sweet Jesus," John said. It wasn't even a curse word coming from him.

• • •

Soon after that, John and Anna went back to their RV to sleep. Lonnie stayed. Billy got out his cigarettes again. He passed one to Lonnie. Didn't even ask. Lonnie took it and we all lit up.

"The hell are you doing with these people?" Billy said.

Lonnie hung his head. "It's my new calling."

"Sure," Billy said, and let out a long stream of smoke. "Really though?"

"I don't know, man. Shit. John's such a good speaker. You wouldn't expect it just looking at him. His words got me all turned around."

"If you don't mind me saying, Mr. Vee, your heritage demands something bigger than strumming minor chords when a preacher talks about hell."

"Goddamn right." Lonnie said. He was on his feet suddenly, pacing back and forth on the creaky barn floor. "I'm the son of The Great Bobby Vee," he said. "Rock and roll runs in my veins sure as I stand before you tonight."

He may have been overselling his dad a little. Bobby Vee was a rockabilly of temporary acclaim way back in the early days when there wasn't any money in it. Most people don't remember him and, honestly, I'm not even sure Lonnie was really his son. I googled Lonnie a while back and not one single thing came up. I don't know. He sure looked the part.

He paced back and forth in his wrinkled pinstripe pants and a crisp, new, white T-shirt. Tucked in. Years shed from him like water. He ran his fingers through his hair and the rock star pompadour rose triumphant to its full height. He'd produced a seafoam green Stratocaster guitar from somewhere. It was a custom job, made at three-quarter scale to fit Lonnie's little fingers. John may have been a powerful speaker, but a few words from my brother and Lonnie was a missionary no more.

"I'm squandering my heritage!" he said. "Fuck! Goddamn it feels good to say that. Fuck! Do you know these people don't swear at all? Two weeks and not one single curse word. I've been held hostage by puritans, and now I'm free. Free!"

"Get it off your chest, buddy," Billy said.

Lonnie slung his guitar up high and tore out a string of rockabilly licks. He laughed. "I need to do something," he said. "I need a clean slate. Hey, have you guys ever tried LSD?"

Billy looked at me and smiled. "Not yet," he said.

Lonnie pulled an old vinyl microphone case from his back pocket. He ripped open the big aluminum teeth and reached out three tabs of paper between his thumb and forefinger.

"My friends," he said. "I was saving these for an emergency, but now I see they were meant for this moment, in this barn. You have freed me from the yoke of religion. In return I will ferry you across the raging river of time and space."

There are some moments in life you look back on with confusion. The moment you reach out and take mystery chemicals from a tiny stranger is one of them. Billy laid the paper on his tongue, and I did the same, and Lonnie tucked one up under his lip so he could talk.

"I ate four of these things in San Antonio and rode the Gravitron for seven straight hours," he said. "Got up on my feet and surfed the wall. That's what they call a heroic dose."

Billy moved the paper around his mouth. "This tastes like a battery," he said. "Nine volt."

Lonnie ignored him. He was way on into his own line of thinking. "You should know, there is some value in what John says, and his belief is intoxicating, but his fundamental view of our creator is warped at a level that cannot be adjusted in the direction of truth. Yes. Yes, it's all coming to me now."

Lonnie strummed a few cords. Adjusted his tuning pegs. He was talking real fast about something that he called an epiphany, and which sounded to me like the craziest of all rabbit holes. He said that John's version of God was way off. He wasn't some angry, old, bearded guy in the sky. The true God was a great universal force reaching out into the galaxy with all living creatures at his fingertips. Moles and garter snakes were cosmic explorers, Lonnie said. Everything was alive, even rocks. Reincarnation was real, but only for dolphins. They were the only animals of pure enough character to be allowed back. All religion was a little right and mostly wrong. Jesus was the first-ever hippie.

I couldn't totally follow. A half hour into his weird monologue, I started to think maybe that was just a little slip of regular printer paper on my tongue. Seems like the idea of cosmic garter snakes would make sense if I were actually stoned.

Billy took the paper off his tongue and looked at it. "When is this supposed to kick in?" he said.

Lonnie walked around the woodstove. He seemed to be getting smaller. A lot smaller. Billy was sitting, and they were about the same height. Lonnie leaned in and looked directly into Billy's eyes. Billy stared right back. Both their eyes were like black voids. No pupils at all. The world shifted under me. I put my hands on the barn floor and felt it breathing. Up and down like big lungs.

Lonnie grinned. "You have arrived," he said. "Welcome."

Billy blinked and looked at his hands.

"I don't feel different," he said. Lonnie laughed and danced away.

"Oh, Billy," he said. "Bare Knuckle Billy Quinn. You've always been different."

Billy looked up. "Hey," he said. "How do you know my name?"

Lonnie gripped his guitar, which had shrunk to match. He swung his head around and loosened up his shoulders, popped all his knuckles. He was the size of a child now. He could have fit in a suitcase.

"Hey," Billy said again. Lonnie picked out a melody, the prettiest I've ever heard, though I could not hum it now if there were a gun to my head.

"How do you know me?" Billy said.

"Does it matter?"

"Yes."

"Saw you on TV. Your old buddies talking. They had a lot to say about your freight-train punches. They called you Bare Knuckle." Lonnie slapped out a rhythm on his tiny thighs. "Bare Knuckle, Bare Knuckle, Bare Knuckle Billy. I'd forgotten, but these chemicals are medicine. They've opened my eyes, and I see you now."

He went on, but I was having a hard time hearing. He was so small his voice didn't go far. And there were all these other sounds. The sounds of fire. Shearing steel—paint and shattered glass squealing in the heat. Not sounds oak makes when it burns.

It grew louder and louder, and then I closed my eyes and saw some things.

I woke on a road. Early-morning fog in the air and a burning car in front of me. In the car was Billy. He was staked through the chest with a piece of steel. Blood ran from the wound and from his face. It felt very real, and I thought again—maybe that was just regular paper. Maybe I faded out for a while and came back in the middle of a bad situation. It was time for me to roll with it. Then I looked down and noticed my hands were on fire. LSD. Yes indeed. From there the whole trip turned really religious.

A bright light cut through the fog, and the air filled with a chorus of voices singing hallelujah, and a huge white crucifix rose from the ground. Billy looked up as the flames licked around him and opened his mouth, but if he spoke, I could not hear it over the singing angels. Then a white dove flew down and landed on the car, caught on fire and flopped, screeching at the foot of the cross.

I've since talked to a few folks about LSD. Apparently, the chemical forms connections between parts of the brain that aren't usually acquainted. Ridiculous thoughts make sense. Unrelated details become linked. I don't know about that. Aside from all the scary religious stuff, the vision it brought me was no surprise. I'd seen it before in nightmares going back as long as I can remember. Billy's bloody face, and fire. I see it still when the world seems dark.

• • •

Anna was cooking breakfast when we woke. A pot of oatmeal on the woodstove and her humming over it. I sat up real slow. Billy was still laid out, but his eyes were open.

"Did you boys have a nice talk?" she said.

Billy sat up and looked around, rubbing his face with his whole palm. "Where's Lonnie?" he said. Anna didn't know. Neither did John. We walked around the farmyard and found no sign of him. He was gone and so was our dumpy Honda.

Now, I do not hold this against Lonnie. The car was stolen to begin with, and he unloaded all our crap before he took off. All he really took was about $1,000 in traveling money, which was stolen, too, come to think of it. That's a pretty fair trade for not squealing to the missionaries. But it did sting a little, so soon after the Firebird. Also, he took off before I got another look at him. I really wanted to see if he was back to his regular size again, once the drug wore off. I never got the chance, and that remains a disappointment to this day.

Anyway, in order to avoid contact with law enforcement, Billy had to tell the missionaries he'd given Lonnie the car. He said he felt called to help Lonnie embark upon his own journey.

"Did you hear the still, small voice?" Anna said.

"Yes," Billy replied, "Yes, I believe I did." And then he picked up our duffel bag of ammunition and stolen cash, and we all piled into the missionaries' RV.

It was not a high-quality RV. Brown carpet covered the floor and walls and ceiling, and it smelled like it was harboring a fairly toxic strain of black mold. The engine was badly off. It roared like crazy just getting up to highway speed. There were no back seats. Billy and I sat cross-legged on the mattress where the missionaries slept every night and had sex too, probably. Bad, uncomfortable lights-off sex. I tried not to touch anything, but every time we went over a bump, I got bounced around all over the place.

"You know," John shouted over the engine roar. "With Lonnie off on his own, we have some room to spare. You two should ride with us a while. Witness what God has in store."

"I don't know," Billy said.

"You really should come," Anna said.

"We're headed to Illinois!" John shouted. "I got the calling last night. You don't want to miss it."

"I'll think about it."

John stopped for gas in the very first town we hit. Billy said he needed coffee. I said me too. We stepped down from the RV, and we didn't even look back. Just followed Lonnie's example and slipped away.

14

Lonnie Vee knew my brother by name. Not just the regular one either. He knew him as Bare Knuckle Billy, said he heard it that way on TV. We drove a hundred miles, but we couldn't shake the thought. My brother had a special outlaw name! All the good ones do. We watched a whole lot of westerns back in Radium, and if they taught me anything it's that outlaws just got to have a good outlaw name. Take Butch Cassidy and the Sundance Kid. Cassidy was born Robert Parker. Sundance was called Harry, but nobody used their *real* names. Real names are pretty much always a huge bummer. Fate gives outlaws names that fit. Having one meant Billy was probably kind of famous. I didn't have one, of course, but that was okay. It wouldn't have been good anyway. Melon Head Jim. I was happy for Billy.

But how famous was he, really? Morning-news famous? Folk-hero famous? We had to find out, so we broke into an empty middle class split-level to use their internet.

We got beers from their fridge and made sandwiches, and Billy found a desktop computer. It was old, with the really deep keys. You gotta press those suckers down like half an inch. He opened Google and hunted out the letters with his pointer fingers. He squinted and scratched his head. He was not good with computers. He'd always been wary of technology. Social media was a waste of his time. Touch screens were too sensitive for his knobby fingers. He feared government officials might be keeping an eye on his porn searches, waiting for him to slip up and accidentally see a naked sixteen-year-old. He snapped his cell phone in half two miles outside Radium, and I expect he enjoyed it.

Anyway, Billy took a long time finding anything. He grinned and poked at the keys. He wanted to see that newscast Lonnie had talked about. The one where our old buddies called him Bare Knuckle. He wanted to hear about his great punches. It wasn't online. He watched other news reports instead, and they were a disappointment.

"Nobody likes us," he said. "Everyone's talking about gun control."

"Gun control?"

"There are all these mass shooters now. People are seriously wigged out by guns."

"So, we're not like Bonnie and Clyde?"

"Of course not," he said. "I'm just an armed criminal, and you're the furthest thing possible from a pretty girl. There's no romance. I don't know what I was thinking."

"Bonnie wasn't actually that pretty. The real one I mean. She was hot in the movie."

"Not my point."

"I know. Sorry."

"They're not even using the outlaw name."

Billy typed a little longer. He found an interview with an old man. He turned up the sound and hit play.

"I don' wanna talk about it," the old man said. "All you people expect things, but I don' wanna." There was something really wrong with this old guy. His body was all slanted to one side, and the left half of his face hung like a badly made mask. His words slurred together so bad, there was a woman next to him translating for the camera. She was tired and drawn and wore no makeup. She rubbed the old man's shoulder.

"Tell the nice reporter," she said.

"Just a few details would help," said a voice from behind the camera. "The police said he was involved with your daughter?"

"Trash!" the old man shouted. He was real agitated all of a sudden. "Trash fucker!"

He began to look familiar to me. Something about the angry set of his eyebrows. The woman patted his knee. "Please excuse my husband," she said. "The stroke took a lot of his words."

Billy leaned back from the screen and put both fists to his forehead. "Oh no," he said. The man in the video was Randy. Older looking and badly diminished, but Randy sure enough. The sight of him was a shock.

The video came with a feature-length news article and high-quality photos. We read it. We looked at the photos. Randy's house hadn't burned in the Radium fire. It was the one thing still standing. The news crew interviewed a Baptist minister who called it a miracle. God's hand protecting a righteous man, like Lot in the biblical Sodom. The fire chief said it was probably Randy's flood levee that saved his house—it acted as a fire break. Either way, Randy's luck ended there. The elevator was reduced to a steaming crater, along with fourteen thousand tons of other people's wheat and barley. The psychopath Billy Quinn saw to that, and things just got worse and worse for poor blameless Randy. Three days after the blaze, his insurance adjuster delivered some bad news. There was something wrong with Randy's paperwork. He'd accidentally let the fire part of his policy lapse five years before—somehow that was Billy's fault, too. There'd be no payout. Randy got so mad, he had a stroke right there in the State Farm office. He spent time in the hospital. The medical bills were high. Farmers were calling about their burned grain. Randy had to sell his miracle house to pay everyone back. The family was living in a Grand Forks motel, while Billy and I raged unchecked across the Great Plains.

Near the end of the article was a picture of Billy. Not the mugshot everybody else was using. The news people must have dug back through Carl's Facebook page. Billy was fresh out of a boxing match in this picture. Shirtless. He'd won easily and was grinning. He was also giving the camera both middle fingers. And right next to Billy's raised fingers and chiseled abs, the news people decided to post a portrait of sad, stroked-out Randy. It was a very effective combo.

Billy slumped in his chair. He put his face in his hands. "I'm an asshole," he said. "I'm the world's biggest asshole."

"Screw Randy," I said. "I don't feel bad at all."

"You don't get it, kid."

"That old prick was so mean, I'm glad he had a stroke."

"That mean old prick put a roof over Maggie's head."

"Oh. Shit."

"Yeah."

"Maybe the stroke wasn't so bad. People recover sometimes."

"Look at his face!"

I did. It was bad. The left eye wouldn't even open all the way, or close. It just sagged.

"World's biggest asshole," Billy said, pointing both thumbs at his own face. "This guy."

He looked back at the screen. The interview had taken a bad turn. Randy was looking off into the corner, and his wife was busy tearing me and Billy a couple of new ones. She called us thieves and devils and evil bastards. Billy watched the whole thing like penance. When it was done, he scratched the stubble on the side of his jaw. He opened Maggie's Facebook page, then closed it right away. I was glad not to see her. She'd be showing by now. It would have been too much.

Billy reached a stack of cash out of the duffel bag.

"Go find an envelope and some stamps," he said.

I rooted around through desks and kitchen drawers. Billy shouted from the other room. "Should we send a note?"

"I guess so."

"'Sorry about your dad's face,'" he said. "Dang. That doesn't sound right."

"'We didn't mean to give him a stroke,'" I shouted back. I suggested a few more lines, but Billy went quiet. I finally found some stamps and a big manila envelope and jogged back.

"'We deeply regret whatever part our actions may have played in Randy's current health condition,'" I said.

Billy didn't look away from the computer.

"We've got bigger problems," he said. He pointed at the screen. It was a news clipping from a local paper. Short. Just a few lines and a photo of a gas station we'd robbed in South Dakota. Crime scene tape crossed the broken glass door, and just off to the side stood a man with a badge, drinking a cup of coffee. He was tall and rawboned, and even far off I knew him at once. That old US Marshal.

Billy flipped to another article. Another place we robbed. The marshal was there, too, leaning against his Dodge Charger this time.

"Look at the time stamp," Billy said. I did, but the numbers didn't mean much to me.

"That photo was taken less than an hour after we left."

My stomach turned hot and sick, and the blood drained from my face. I sank down in a chair. Billy sprang to his feet and paced. He gritted his teeth. The marshal was even closer than we thought. Minutes behind us, not days. Miles, not states.

Billy addressed the envelope to Carl. He filled it all the way up with cash and wrote, "give all this shit to Maggie," on a hundred-dollar bill. We threw it in a mailbox down the street and raised the flag. Then we hit the road. We didn't say anything for a long time. Billy squeezed the wheel like he was trying to break it. He turned off the radio and made his face like a stone.

15.

We pulled into a liquor store in north Texas. Not because we wanted to rob the place. Billy was in a dark mood and needed a drink. He grabbed a bottle of Jim Beam in his right hand and a bottle of Jose Cuervo in his left.

"I should get used to this poison if we're gonna live in Mexico," he said.

The only other people in the store were a bunch of ruddy, already half-drunk cattlemen, who got to the checkout counter before us. They had a lot of stuff to buy and different credit cards they wanted to use, and it took a long time. Billy leaned against a wine rack. He massaged his forehead with the Cuervo.

Ahead of us, the cattlemen laughed and bickered about who was paying for what. They also bickered about women and about their plans for later that evening. I couldn't help but listen. They spoke in accents and terminology I did not fully grasp, but here's the gist of it. These guys were bringing all their booze to an underground poker game out in the sticks. They were excited—hoping for big wins—all except one of them. One was nervous about the legality of the plan, and the others didn't take it too well.

"Shut up, Lawrence," one guy said. "Cops don't give a goddamn about some cards."

Another man punched the worried fellow, apparently named Lawrence, in the arm. "The sheriff might take your paycheck," he said, "but he'll do it fair and square with a royal flush."

Billy lowered the bottle and looked at me.

"Are you hearing this?" he whispered.

"Yeah."

He put the bottles on the nearest shelf. "Fools," he said.

• • •

We waited in the car for the cattlemen to finish paying. Billy kicked the door open and sat with one heel out on the parking lot. I checked the air-conditioning knobs. They were cranked all the way around to the blue side, and still nothing came out the vents. I rolled my window down. It didn't help.

Clouds hung heavy and low in the starless night sky, made the air sticky and almost too hot to breathe. Sweat formed in the middle of my low back and glued the shirt to my skin. Maybe it was the LSD coming back on me. Maybe it was the heat, but I had a weird feeling about things, and I'm pretty sure Billy did, too.

He lit a cigarette and blew the smoke away in a thin stream. His eyes were lined in the yellow parking lot light. Usually, just before a robbery, he'd have to work hard to keep his whole face from grinning. Now he looked old. All the fun was gone from him.

"I don't know about this," I said.

"This is a big one, kid."

"We stick to the little scores, don't we?"

But the crew was coming out of the bar, shouting and piling into their truck. Billy didn't answer me right away. He put the car in gear and followed them out onto the road, hung back till the taillights were just red specks. Then he spoke.

"We can't do this forever," he said. "At some point we'll knock over a pawnshop or a gas station and the cops will be waiting. Or that marshal."

"I know."

"If those cowboys aren't talking shit, this place is worth a dozen gas stations. So, we have to ask ourselves. Is it worth the risk?"

"What do you think, Billy?"

"You know what I think."

"Alright."

The taillights turned from tar to gravel, and Billy turned after them. A few miles later the gravel turned to washboard, then grass, then ran out altogether in the yard of a tall, white farmhouse. The windows shone yellow, and happy country music flowed out through the hot air. Billy parked in the grass alongside a dozen other trucks and watched. The crew we followed crowded around the farmhouse door. They were all pretty riled up by the time we got there. The door slid open a crack. Words were exchanged. The cowboys began to shout and posture. One extended two middle fingers at the door, but it was no good. The door slid closed and stayed that way. The crew retreated to their truck with sunken shoulders. The middle-finger guy scooped up a clod of dirt and flung it at the house. It flew to pieces before reaching the clean siding.

We let them go, and then Billy looked at me.

"You need to know, kid. This might be rough."

"They have guns, don't they?"

"It's an illegal gambling operation in rural Texas," he said. "Yeah. They have guns."

"Aw man."

"We have guns too, kid."

"You have a gun. All I've got is the dumb knife."

I snapped the blade open to show him how small and pathetic it looked. Then my hand decided to cramp, and I dropped the knife in my lap. I tried again, and this time my fingers wouldn't even wrap around the thing. They just bounced off.

"Goddamn it," I said.

"Hand problems?"

"Yeah."

He reached around in our duffel bag and brought out the roll of duct tape. He stripped off three feet, then bit the end and ripped it down the long way.

"Hold out your hand," he said.

I raise my right hand out in front of me.

"Do you want the blade pointing up or down?"

"Whichever way looks scarier, Billy."

He pointed the blade down and pushed the grip into the meat of my hand. Then he took one strip of tape and wrapped my fingers tight around the handle. He bent my thumb over the back of it as a stopper and held it there with another loop of tape.

"You think you could do some damage with that?" he said.

"I don't know."

"You will if you have to," he said, and pulled my ski mask down over my head. He took a long drag off his cigarette, then tied the bandana across his nose and mouth. When he breathed out, smoke filtered through the cloth like he was on fire.

"Alright?" he said.

"Okay."

Sweat poured down my face halfway across the yard. The smell in that mask wasn't good after so many robberies, like rotting potatoes. I envied Billy's bandana and his reliable hands. He turned to me at the fringes of the porch light.

"Keep your head down," he said, and ran at the door. He hit it with his shoulder, hard enough to turn the doorframe to splinters. I followed close behind, felt the electric shiver of fear and adrenaline, watched Billy raise his .45 and send a bullet through the ceiling.

"Gentlemen," he said. "This is a robbery."

It was just somebody's house in there. Wood floors and plaster walls and an unlit fireplace in one corner. Tobacco smoke filled the air above a ring of men. They looked up from a regular dining room table. Their faces held something less than fear at Billy's announcement. It was like he'd fired a popgun.

In the spreading silence, I sprinted across the floor toward the poker game, vaulted a couch, and made intimidating motions at the gamblers with my knife. Kind of stabbed at the air. It's important to establish dominance right out of the gate, but my duct-taped knife didn't seem to work. They looked confused more than anything.

"You," Billy said, pointing his .45 at a man in a bright-white Stetson cowboy hat. He was the only one at the table whose clothes weren't dirty and old. "Gather those bills."

"I mean, sure," he said. "Do you got a bag or something?"

"Use your goddamn hat."

"The hat's worth more than the winnings."

We looked. Sure enough. The cash was all in ones. Not even very many ones. You know, robbing an illegal gambling operation seems like a nice idea, but it turns out the high-stake games are just a lot less common than people think. Mostly these operations are low stakes. Like, such low stakes, they're not even illegal. They're just some buddies smoking cigarettes in a dark room. Billy rubbed his face with his free hand. "We'll take the hat, too," he said.

"Looks a bit small for you."

"I'll pawn it. Shit. I'm the one with the pistol here."

Something flashed across the man's face just then. Anger, I think, instead of confusion. But he took off his hat, and a few of his buddies helped gather up the bills. They were nearly done when I heard the barking. It came from deep inside the house—angry and muscular and getting nearer all the time. Then claws rattled down a darkened hallway and a great large pit bull emerged, straining and snapping at the end of a short leash.

A woman held him at bay. She wore curlers in her hair and thick reading glasses. "What the hell is going on out here?" she said.

"We're getting robbed," the man replied.

"Keep a tight grip on that leash," Billy said.

"He's taking my hat," the man said.

"You just got that hat. It was expensive as shit." The woman looked at Billy. Then she looked at the dog. "You see 'em?" she said to the dog. The dog's two eyes shown wild and bright. Its skin stretched taut and thin over twitching muscles and veins. It snapped its jaws open and closed.

"Don't you let that animal go," Billy said. The woman said nothing but held the leash. The dog's breaths rasped from the pull of the collar.

I grabbed the hat with its tiny payload, and we backed out of that place real slow. Billy held the gun on them till the last moment. Then we turned and jogged to the car. Billy started laughing when we were almost there. It *was* kind of funny. All that build-up for what was probably about thirty-five dollars. But I didn't get a chance to laugh. Right at the car door, I got this strange feeling like something was behind me. Don't know what it was. Maybe I heard the dog's claws on the gravel. I whirled around, and there was that huge pit bull, six feet away and coming at a dead sprint. I got my hands out in front of me just before it leapt. If I hadn't, it would have got me by the throat for sure. Lights out, just like that. Instead, its jaws caught my duct-taped hand. The weight of it drove me to the ground.

I felt each tooth pop through the duct tape and sink into my hand. The dog ripped its heavy head back and forth, spattering my own blood down on my face. I swung my other fist. My knuckles crumpled on the dog's hard skull. It lunged down at the soft skin of my throat. I forced my taped hand deeper into its jaws. The dog's thin lips split on my knife blade, but the animal would not stop. Hot air and spit gurgled from its throat. Teeth dripped red. Dog blood mixed with mine. It was too heavy. Too strong for me. Its breath was hot on the skin of my neck.

Then three sharp pops rang out, and the dog fell convulsing to the ground. Three bullet holes drained red from the pit bull's flanks. It shook and spat and bared its teeth at me in the final throes. People tell me pit bulls make excellent companions. I suspect that's true if you're the one feeding them and rubbing their killer faces. But they have the devil in them. Just try and tell me different.

I left the money and the hat on the ground by the dead dog. I crawled up into the car and Billy drove.

• • •

"You've still got a hand?" Billy shouted. We were back on tar and still deaf from gunfire.

"What?"

"Your hand. How bad?"

I felt around for the edges of the bit duct tape. The whole thing was slippery and dark, and Billy flipped on the dome light so I could work. I gripped a corner of tape with my teeth and pulled off a few wraps, then a few more till the knife fell into my lap.

"How bad?" he said again.

"It's fine," I replied and held my hand up to the light. Blood ran down my arm and dripped from the elbow.

"Aw man," Billy said. "Your hands have no luck at all."

All told, I'd guess that dog was on me about ten seconds. That's how long it took for Billy to come round the front of the car and shoot it to death. But in that tiny space of time, it turned my palm into raw hamburger. I could see where the teeth had been.

"You need some antibiotics or something," Billy said.

"It doesn't even hurt. Keep driving."

This was our formula for success, after all. Theft followed by flight. It had worked so well. But Billy did not keep driving. He pulled into a small town fifteen miles away. It was a very small town. Two blocks of business and one cattle yard grouped together and called Napoleon. There were no cars and only one place with lights on. Del's Grocery. Billy parked and helped me out.

"Let's get you patched up," he said.

So the two of us walked into an empty grocery store, deaf and reeking of gun smoke. I was still wearing the ski mask, and drops of blood fell from my fingertips by twos and threes. A pimply youth looked up from the register.

"Holy shit," he said.

Billy reached for his .45 but didn't pull. "Relax, Del," he said.

"It's Logan, actually." Logan was dialing 911 on his cell phone as fast as he could.

"Logan," Billy said. "You gotta put that phone down, buddy."

Logan's thumbs were like lightning. I could barely see them.

"I'm trying super hard here, Logan," Billy said. "I recently googled myself and I realize I have a serious PR issue. People are nervous about the gun. Who knew?"

Logan looked up from his phone. I could hear it ringing.

"This isn't easy, Logan. I'm really stressed right now. A pit bull just crippled my kid brother's already-crippled hand. What I want to do is draw this pistol and tell you that if you don't hang up that phone, I'm gonna blow your nuts off."

Logan blinked.

"But I'm not going to do that, Logan, because I think you'll see reason."

I could hear the 911 dispatcher on the other end of the line. She was asking for details. Logan set the phone down. He ended the call.

"Thanks, now where are your bandages?"

"Aisle five. Gauze is on the endcap."

I left Billy with Logan and jogged back to the tiny first aid section. I shoved a whole display of Dora the Explorer Band-Aids to the floor, then ripped open packs of gauze and medical tape and lined them up on the empty shelf. I poured a bottle of water over my hand till a puddle grew pink on the floor below. It was worse than I thought. I could see tendons and bone. I looked away and crushed a whole tube of disinfectant jelly into the torn skin. I don't know if I shouted.

When I got back to the register, my right hand looking like a gauze mitten, Logan was scooping cash into a paper bag. His long, spidery fingers moved with unnatural ease. Robbery wasn't so stressful without the firearm.

"You shouldn't be robbing grocery stores," he said to Billy. "I've got like fifty bucks in here. It's not a cash business."

He rolled down the stiff corners of the paper bag and handed it to Billy like a lunch kit.

"Congratulations, Logan, you get to keep your junk," Billy said.

"Thanks. You should learn how to do credit-card fraud. I hear that's big. Yeah. That's what I'd do if I was you."

We strolled back to the car. Billy put his arm across my shoulders.

"How's the hand?" he said.

"It's not that bad."

Billy grinned. "Tough as nails, kid," he said.

16.

I mentioned that our car had no air-conditioning. That's the problem with nicking old cars. They're easy to hot-wire and hard for the law to track, but good goddamn luck getting a breath of cool air. We drove through most of the night with the windows rolled down and sweat turning the bucket seats spongy under us. Billy stuck his whole head out the window, got a mouthful of bugs and rocked back spitting.

In the small hours of the morning, he pulled off the road and parked. We tried to sleep, but it didn't work. Everything was uncomfortable. My skin and clothes were sticky and wet. My bit hand smarted real bad. The air outside was as steamy as an armpit. No relief anywhere. Finally, Billy sat up and got out the cigarettes. We smoked till we were numb. We scanned the radio dial over and over. So many goddamn Christian stations. So much pop country. Finally, we found some Johnny Cash. Some Willie Nelson. I sank down into an empty form of sleep. No rest in it, just blackness without dreams.

• • •

When the sun rose, I had to crawl out of the car and be sick. We were parked in a field of six-foot-tall sunflowers. The prettiest place by far that I've ever barfed. I ran a little distance away to do it. Didn't want Billy to hear. He'd worry. When I was done, I sat out there in the sunflowers and took in long slow breaths. I thought I'd feel better after barfing. I usually do. The cooling sweat—guts all clean and empty—you know the feeling. It's nice. But I didn't get that feeling.

"You okay, little brother?" Billy's voice came through the sunflowers.

"Just a second!"

"What are you doing in there?"

I threw up again. Tried to do it quietly. Tried to gather myself after. I was so hot. Sweat poured down my back. The sun was so strong I could feel it burning my skin. My blood moved slow and thick through my veins. It throbbed in my bit hand. It was hard to think. Hard to see straight. Then Billy was beside me. His hands on my shoulders. He got me to me feet and helped me walk. The world was too bright for my eyes. The sunflowers looked like fire.

Billy belted me into the car and leaned my seat back. His palm felt like ice on my forehead.

"Aw man," he said. "You're hot."

"I'm fine now."

"How's your hand?"

"It's okay. I actually forgot about it."

I hadn't forgotten. My hand was feeling really unnatural. Taut. Not a good sign probably, but we had to run. We had to get very far away. I didn't know where. I just knew we had to run like crazy and never stop. Never stop once.

Billy found a half-empty bottle of water in the duffel and made me drink it. I threw that up too. Then he got us on the road and drove. I didn't open my eyes for a long time, but I could tell by the sound he was going really fast. When we finally stopped, Billy had to shake my arm to bring me round.

"We need to cool you off," he said.

"Keep driving," I replied, my eyes pinned closed by the great meditative effort required to avoid the dry heaves.

"Look at this place, kid." I blinked, and followed his pointed finger to a hotel. It was tall and full of windows. Much nicer than the places we usually slept. I mean, we usually slept in fields, but before the outlawing we only ever stayed in crappy motels. This place didn't even have any chipping paint or weeds in the parking lot. "I bet a place like this has air-conditioning," Billy said.

He helped me across the parking lot and through the glass doors. I had to rest my forearms on the front desk to stop my legs from buckling. Billy rang the little bell and smiled.

"This place will fix you right up," he said, and slapped me on the back. For a little while I did feel better. The air was cold enough to prickle the skin. Each breath of it calmed my stomach. Even my legs solidified.

The desk man hurried out from the back and settled in at his computer.

"What can I get you today?" he said, without looking up from the screen. He had pointy hair, a red vest, and no apparent love for his job.

"A room with good air-conditioning," Billy said.

"All our rooms have the same air-conditioning. There's a central unit."

"Any room then."

The desk man typed away and then raised one hand, palm up. "I'll need a credit card and photo ID."

"No, you won't."

"Hotel policy."

Billy pulled a roll of cash from his pocket. He looked at the desk man as he peeled off bills. Five hundred dollars in crisp twenties. He put the stack on the counter. "Make an exception," he said.

Things turned bad on the way to our room. The cold air was nice at first, but I started shivering in the elevator. And my hand itched. I tried to scratch, but the bandages were too thick, and I was shaking too much anyway. By the time we reached our room, I could barely control my limbs. Billy had to hold my wrist down on an end table to unwind the gauze and medical tape.

"Don't look at this, kid," he said, but it was too late. I'd already seen. The skin around each tooth hole was green and slick. It smelled bad. My stomach turned, but there was nothing in there to lose. Billy got a washcloth from the bathroom and a tiny bottle of vodka from the mini bar. He wrapped the cloth around my hand and pinned my wrist back to the table. Then he opened the bottle with his teeth and spit the lid on the floor.

"Ready?" he said.

"Wait a minute now."

He poured the whole bottle into the washcloth. Slow, so every drop soaked in. It burned worse than fire. I screamed and tried to get away, but Billy was so strong. He kept my hand clamped down like a vice. When it was done, Billy stood and shouldered the duffel bag.

"I have to go get some things," he said. "Try to sleep. Don't scratch the bite."

The door slammed and he was gone.

• • •

In his absence the world spun and lurched, and I could not keep it all steady. Nothing felt right to me. My hands were the wrong size. The right one was swollen like an inflated rubber glove. It looked like a Looney Tunes hand. By comparison the other one was tiny. Like Baby Arm Jeff's little hand! Shit! I was Baby Arm Jeff now . . . and Melon Head Jim! Every time I turned around something else was wrong with my meat vehicle.

My bit hand throbbed. The skin was so tight and hot and itchy. I scratched till it bled—or seeped—I'm not sure. Whatever dripped from the swollen skin had a bad color and a worse smell. Gangrene. I might be slow, but I've seen movies. Guys in westerns are always getting themselves shot in the arm or leg. It's not bad at first. Just a flesh wound. They figure they'll make it. Then gangrene sneaks up and just rots them away. Their buddies always realize too late but insist on whacking the infected limb off all the same.

I knew what I had to do. Amputation time, before it spread. The hand itched so bad it didn't even seem like a huge loss. Too bad I didn't have a half-dozen good buddies to hold me down or a leather strap to bite. I didn't even have my knife. Billy took it with him. The sharpest thing in the hotel room was the edge of the dresser. I opened the top drawer, put my hand in and just slammed the thing shut. I really committed. Pushed with everything I had.

It didn't do a thing. Didn't even leave a mark. I don't know what I was expecting.

"Shit," I said.

I slumped back on the bed and looked at my rotting hand. The itch was real bad. It felt like there was something living in there, growing and spreading and reproducing itself. Soon it would have my whole arm. Then I'd be dead.

"Killed by one lousy dog bite," I said. "What a wimp! What a piece of shit! I should step in front of a bus."

I often considered the bus option. It was a source of entertainment for me. When I was mean to someone without realizing, or when I spun my head around at a bad time, I'd imagine just stepping right into traffic. I'd smile and wave and then BAM! The mental image always made me feel better. Now the bus option made real-world sense. When Billy got back, I knew he wouldn't be interested in performing an amputation. He'd want to take me to the hospital. They'd recognize him there and call the cops. He'd be caught up in those sterile mazes and dragged off to prison because of my dumb hand. They'd probably fill me up with antibiotics and save me, and then I'd have to go to prison too. I couldn't let it happen. There weren't any busses around just then. I decided to improvise.

I forced myself upright and went to the window. It was difficult, but I pried open an eight-inch gap and slipped through. I straddled the window sill and looked down. It was a long way. Four or five stories at least. I smiled. You want a good long drop if you plan on going out that way. Too short and you'll just break all your bones and wake up in a hospital unable to make sentences.

I closed my eyes. It wasn't so bad. I had a good run. Fifteen years with the best brother a guy could hope for. Who else would help a defective kid like me? Keep me from wandering off in confusion. He even got me that date with Candice. What a good dude. He'd be better off on his own. I relaxed. My bit hand still itched, but that was nearly over. My baby hand slipped from the window frame. I tilted out, toppled, and fell.

BAM! My head landed first. My ears rang with the impact. They rang and rang and my head hurt like hell—but I kept not slipping away into darkness. It was supposed to be quick. I opened my eyes.

"Aw man," I said.

I was still in the hotel room. I'd fallen back onto the floor, instead of out. What a shithead! I couldn't even kill myself right. I couldn't do anything right. Not ever. I cried and scratched my hand and threw up a tiny amount on the floor. I tried hard to think of one good thing I'd ever done. There was nothing. Well, maybe just one—a thing I did for Billy when I was a child. But nothing since then. I was so broken my mother had to run away and take pills. I was an anchor to my brother. Useless. All I ever did was eat and shit and jerk off in the woods. A nothing little boy of scraps who couldn't steady his head long enough to bed a woman or kill himself like a goddamn gentleman.

A knock at the door pulled me back. Billy was here again. Maybe he'd know what to do about my hand. I got up and teetered for the door, but something was off. Billy had a key and told me to sleep. He wouldn't knock.

The door burst open. Two men in black uniforms and tactical belts rushed in. They gripped me hard and threw me back on the bed. I bounced, loose-limbed. One held his gun on me while the other flipped me on my stomach and cranked the cuffs down hard around my wrists. Just as quick, I was out in the hall. My feet skid on the carpet as they dragged me along. The two cops shouted in a tag-team way.

"You have the right to remain silent."

"You have the right to an attorney."

The carpet burned through my socks before I could get my feet under me. I didn't ask what was going on. I knew. The pointy-haired desk man gave me a stern look as the two officers rushed me past. I hung my head and tried to keep step.

One of the cops opened the back of an unmarked squad car—a black Dodge Charger. The other tossed me in and slammed the door. I lay on my side and took stock. Everything hurt. My infected hand itched in its taut, swollen skin. The cuffs chaffed my wrists. My shoulders ached, and the tops of my feet stung with carpet burn.

I sat up and looked around. The back of the car was walled off from the front with steel grating. A mobile prison cell. One man sat up front with his back to me, and across the center console lay a folded leather jacket.

"Sorry about the rough handling," the man said. "Had to call the local meatheads."

I couldn't look away from the leather jacket. It was Billy's. I recognized the faded letters on the back. "Highwaymen." The fact that it was here, and not in the back seat of the Firebird was more than my brain could process.

"I've got some jerky up here," he said. "Want some?"

He turned around in his seat and looked through the grate. It was that skinny old US Marshal, but I bet you guessed that already. The lines of his face didn't look so deep in the daylight. He weaseled a shrink-wrapped jerky stick halfway through the grate.

"They really know their way around jerky down here," he said. "Oh shit. The cuffs. I left a set of keys on the seat there. No point in brutalizing a slow kid."

"I'm not slow."

"Pretty slow with those cuffs."

He was not wrong. Those keys are awfully fiddly for a pair of crippled hands, especially when one's got gangrene. I succeeded in freeing the bit hand and figured that was good enough. I held the cuffs out in front of me. One side still around my wrist and its chain looping down to the empty shackle in my palm. They were heavy and bright. So bright. Like crescent moons bolted together at the corners.

"Hey," the marshal said. "Jerky?"

He flicked the meat stick still pinched in the grating. I shook my head, and he pulled the jerky back. Peeled it. Took a big bite. He chewed loud while he talked.

"You don't look so good," he said, picking gristle from his teeth. "Your brother treating you okay?"

Of course he was. The question made no sense. Billy was good to me. I was lucky to have such a brother.

"I'm fine," I said.

"Alright then, we'll play it that way."

The smell of jerky was making me sick. I looked down and felt the weight of my skeleton under my weak muscles. Here was the end. No slipping away this time. It could be five minutes, could be two hours, but Billy would return and I'd see his freedom taken. Men like him never get loose once they're in cuffs. Never get parole. I should have leapt from the window when I had the chance. Billy would have seen the ambulance and turned away.

"You know, kid, I've got a pretty good idea what that brother of yours looks like, but I'm old. My eyes aren't so good anymore. Maybe when he gets back, you could point him out to me. Things would go better for you, if you helped me a little. Do you think you could do that for me?"

"I told you I'm not slow."

The marshal leaned back in his seat and finished the jerky stick. He balled up the wrapper and tucked it in the cup holder. For a long time, he was silent. I could barely hear him breathing. Then he cleared his throat.

"In the late '80s I tracked a white supremacist all the way to Nicaragua," he said. "We called him Duke the Arborist. Guess why."

"Don't know."

"He liked killing people with a pruning saw. It was just about his favorite thing, after talking about Hitler and getting dumb-ass tattoos."

He spoke like he was talking to a coworker, like I was in the passenger seat and not caged up in the back.

"Duke busted out of a transport van headed for Leavenworth," he said. "It wasn't planned. He just saw an opening. You know how things happen. He was in the wind for a year and half. A year and a half! That's a good run. I got him in the end though. Brought him home in a dog kennel. Ha!"

He turned around like he wanted me to laugh too. I didn't, and he went on.

"Man, that Nazi sure was elusive. And good looking, too. Weirdly good looking for a dumb-ass Nazi. People just wanted to help the guy. Strangers would give him rides. That made it hard. My superiors gave up, you know. They closed the case, but I just couldn't seem to quit. I took the files home and pinned them all over my walls like a serial killer! I had his face over my bed. I get obsessive like that. Maybe that's why my wives keep leaving."

He turned around again with a big old smile. He kept thinking I was going to laugh at his jokes, and I kept not doing it.

"Anyway," he said. "I end up hearing a rumor that old Duke is hunkered down in Nicaragua. It was pretty thin, but fuck it. I took three weeks of vacation and flew out on my own dime. Worth it. I can't tell you the joy it gave me, putting him in a box. Goddamn, it made me hard. In a nonsexual sort of way, you understand."

He laughed aloud, then let out a big sigh.

"It's not like that most of the time. Ninety percent of this job is transporting brain-dead criminals from one place to another." His voice was quiet all of a sudden. He reached out and stroked the leather jacket with his fingertips.

"But right now, I've got that feeling again. Not the hard-on. I'm not a pervert. Just—I don't know—that feeling, man. That feeling I get when I'm about to cage a monster. God, I've missed it. It's been thirty years."

A shiver went through my whole body all at once. I sat up, and the marshal was already meeting my gaze in the rearview.

"You've lived many years with Billy Quinn," he said. "You've looked into his eyes. Tell me there's no beast in him. Tell me nothing's been mangled, deep down."

I glared back. Who was this man to talk about my brother in such a way? To call him a monster. To throw him down and bind his hands. To make me watch. Blood burned through my veins up into my head and down through my arms till my bit hand throbbed and my fists closed so tight the knuckles popped. That empty handcuff was still clenched in my left hand. It had opened as I squeezed, so a hook came out each side, with the blunt steel hinge out between my fingers.

"Stop talking," I said.

"He's an outlaw," the old man replied. "Your brother. He's a thief and an arsonist and a violent man. Do whatever you have to, to get that through your head."

My vision pulsed dark around the edges, and the metal taste of blood dried my mouth. "Please stop," I said.

"You're young. You don't need to go down with him. We can work something out."

But he'd misread the quiet in my voice. As he spoke, the tendons in my arms tightened like steel cables. I felt the cuff biting into my palm skin. Blood ran from my fist, but I could not stop my limbs. I could not calm them. I wound up and punched the window glass, the cuffs like brass knuckles. They left nothing but a red smear.

"Hold on, son," the marshal said, craning around in his seat. "Calm down."

I looked him in the eyes for some moments, and all I saw was Billy in a cage. In a cage! A great strength rose in me then. The veins in my neck coiled under the skin. I thought my eyes would burst with the pressure. Every heartbeat thumped like a drum. Boom. Boom. And I sent my fist through the window. Glass exploded into shards.

The marshal rushed with his seat belt, but he was too slow. I was out and running hard. The old man shouted behind me, but I did not hear his words.

Squad-car lights flipped on and raced across the parking lot to block my path. Fully marked city police cars. The local meatheads. They met at the front entrance and crashed into each other head-on. Airbags in both cars went off. I jumped and slid across crumpled hoods and ran again. I ran so hard I thought my legs would fall apart at the joints. Pain shot through them—through my whole body—but I kept running.

I met Billy on the access road. He saw me coming a hundred yards out and skidded the car through a three-point turn. I flew through the open passenger door, and he floored it.

"Saw the cops," he said. "What happened?"

I tried to answer but couldn't.

The local meatheads dislodged themselves from each other and let the Charger through. But Billy was a good driver. He took us down side-roads and alleys and shook that old man. He got us clear, then hot-wired a new ride and drove again.

• • •

Miles down the road Billy steadied the wheel with his knees and grabbed a brown paper sack from the duffel. He raised two small pill bottles in one hand and squinted at the labels. The names were long and unpronounceable.

"Take these," he said, holding out a palm full of chalky white pills. He poured them into my good hand and cracked open a new bottle of water. When I reached for it, he saw the bloody cuff dangling.

"What did you do?" he said.

"Got loose," I replied, through a cheekful of pills.

√ 17.

The water was clear and almost blue. The pit was deep, with walls of stone and gravel. This is where we holed up. An old mine lake with no name, down a backroad somewhere in Texas. We were alone there. Except for a few beer cans and hundred-year-old drill marks from the blasting crews, we could have been in some weird and untouched wilderness.

Big rocks tilted up through the gravel like someone buried Stonehenge and time dug it up again. We laid out a quilt under the edge of one of those rocks and found some wood for a fire. Billy set cans of beans in the coals till the sweet red liquid bubbled and sparked. We ate in silence, and I slept.

• • •

Billy hadn't been angry when I told him about the marshal, that he'd caught up with us yet again. So close this time, he had me in his car. That he stroked Billy's favorite leather jacket like a pet cat.

He said nothing when I explained about the cuffs and the car window. No, Billy wasn't angry. He was thinking. He thought a long time, and he didn't speak.

• • •

When I woke, Billy was gone. I crawled out from under the rock and looked around. The fire had burned low; the water lay still and blue, and Billy was a tiny figure many feet above it. He sat on a high stone ledge far down the shore. His aviator sunglasses reflected the setting sun.

I followed the shore and then a steep path trod through dry grasses and stone. I came up from behind and sat next to him, my feet—like his—dangling out over the drop.

"You ever think about death, kid?"

That was the first thing he said. He had a cigarette between his fingers, burned right down to the filter and cold. In a mood, I guess.

"Getting killed?" I asked.

"What it'll be like. Where we'll go after."

I told him I'd thought a lot about dying, but not the actual being dead part. He nodded and lit another cigarette.

"Dad thought it was just the end," he said. "We close our eyes and that's it. Blackness. Like a dead deer. Like we were never born. I saw Dad go, and I think that was true for him."

"Well, he knows now."

"He knows nothing at all. He's dead as rocks and that's it. Not me, kid. I'm not going out that way. I will keep myself. Understand?" He took a drag and blew it out through his nose.

"I will still be me, on the other side," he said, "and I will find you."

He finished his cigarette and flicked it over the edge. It spun all the way down. Took five full seconds. I thought he was done talking, but he wasn't.

"For us, little brother, death will be like falling a long way into cold water. It's gonna hurt. But you swim for the surface, kid. When the time comes to take that dive, remember. You swim like a motherfucker, and I swear to you I'll be there. I will not let you disappear. You and me, kid. We'll swim till we find something. And if there's nothing to find, we'll make a new place. We'll drag up land from the depths—spread hills and prairies before us. Scoop out rivers with our fingertips. We'll build our home from mountains and cook our food in volcanic springs. We will make ourselves gods. You and me, brother. That is how it will be for us on the day we die."

"But not Dad."

"Dad didn't swim hard enough. Most people don't. They give up and are lost." He stood and walked back a few yards. He took off his sunglasses and squinted at the horizon.

"Care for a preview?" he said. Then he ran. He moved so fast his feet skidded back on the stone. He leaped full-on into the void, and I watched him fall. His hands floated out like he was flying . . . it seemed like minutes. Then his arms swung around and around, and just above the water, he snapped his body into a rigid plank.

Almost no splash. I could see him down there as the water calmed. Suspended. Still. Then he pushed off the bottom and swam. He was laughing when his head broke the surface.

"It's not bad at all, kid!" he said. "Trust me!"

So I jumped too. Fast and sure like Billy. I hit the surface so clean I couldn't tell you exactly when it happened, just that water rushed through my ears and for the first time the sound of it didn't take me away somewhere.

Billy met me in the shallows, up to his waist. He grinned, and gripped me by the shoulders, said some words I couldn't hear. My head was so full of water.

"What?" I said.

"I'm calling this thing. Time to go to Mexico."

I tipped my head and smacked the water from my ear canals. "I thought you wanted to get more money first."

"To hell with the money. It's time we hang it up, kid. Your hand's all bit to hell, and I'm so tired I'm going out of my mind. Watching sunsets and talking a load of nonsense about death—like a damn poet." He laughed aloud and slapped me on the back. "Shit," he said. "You and I both know I'm never gonna die."

• • •

We stayed in the pit for a little while. We swam and ate and slept, and when the bite marks healed in raised pink scars, we hit the road.

18.

We stopped for Mexican about a hundred miles north of the border. It was late at night and we were hungry, and there was this food truck in the middle of nowhere with all its lights on. We couldn't help ourselves.

I can't even describe the smells. The words aren't in my midwestern vocabulary. And the food-truck lady . . . she was just right, too. She had white hair and white teeth and skin that looked like it had been in the desert sun for eighty years, which I guess it had been.

She was working over some unconventional pieces of meat with a cleaver when Billy and I approached, scraping chunks into a wide, flat pot of bubbling stew.

"Tacos?" Billy said.

The lady nodded. Billy scratched his head, trying to access high-school Spanish. Finally, he raised both hands with the fingers spread.

"This many," he said.

The woman nodded again. She laid out a bunch of little tortillas, about the size of saucers, and scooped out the meat. It was hypnotic. My stomach turned around in my body.

Around this time, if I really think back, I remember the sound of an engine shutting off. A slammed car door. Footsteps. But I was too distracted to look. All that good meat portioned out in front of me.

The taco lady straightened up and smiled. "Buenos días, *oficial*," she said.

Billy and I turned around a bit too fast. Her next customer was a Texas State Trooper, checking his watch.

"I guess it is morning," the trooper said. "Time flies."

He looked up from his wrist with a big old smile, the kind of smile you get when you're about to eat some tacos. Then his eyes landed on Billy. I saw recognition come into them. The smile fell from his face.

He reached for his pistol, but he wasn't quite fast enough. Billy hit him, shoulder down, right in the sternum. They went down together. A big pile of limbs. In a moment Billy was up again and running.

We climbed into the F-150 pickup truck we were borrowing at the time, and Billy floored it. Hard down on every gear. Redlined. Ninety on two-lane blacktop. There just wasn't any place to turn. If you've never been in a car chase before, you just gotta have some place to turn. It's about losing the cops, not out-running them.

The F-150 rattled and shook. Billy's hands twitched on the wheel.

"I bet you miss the Firebird right now," he said.

I did. I really did. The F-150 climbed past a hundred. It was close to lifting off. Bounding and rocking over every little knob in the road.

"The Firebird was built for exactly this thing," Billy said. "She was perfect. And you just gave her away."

"Is this really the time?"

"One pretty girl bats her eyes. One! And you hand over the keys."

"Billy?"

There were flashers behind us. Far back, but not as far as you'd like. Billy glanced up in the rearview, then grinned at me.

"You and pretty girls, kid. It's like you're hypnotized. We have to work on that."

"Okay, Billy," I said. "We'll get that ironed out."

He pushed the gas pedal further into the floor. Watched the speedometer edge toward 112. Then he looked up.

"Aw, shit," he said. Up ahead were more flashers. Barricades. Probably spike strips. They had us trapped. It was surprising how quick it all happened. We'd run so far from Radium. Robbed all these places . . . slipped all these tight situations. Then we stopped for tacos and BAM. That's it. We were cornered and about to be shot to death. It seemed real anticlimactic. I was pretty goddamn disappointed, I have to admit.

But we weren't quite as cornered as I thought. The cops screwed up their barricade operation. There was a little gravel crossroad between us and them. The first road I'd seen in miles.

Billy stomped down on the brakes. Everything they could give. He sent us at that gravel road in a great screeching arch. One wheel hit the ditch, bounced off a culvert, and nearly threw the whole thing end over end. Billy held on. He floored it. Leveled us out.

Squad cars poured onto the road behind us. Five or six of them. They were well back, but the Ford was sluggish with heat. Billy forced the thing on, shook her to pieces on washboard gravel. The lights closed in. Nowhere to go, and the road getting worse. Billy did what he could with the boiling engine, but it was no good. He knew it and I knew it. I suspect the cops behind us knew it, too.

We reached a big corner with the engine and tires and clutch all smelling angry.

"Hold on," Billy said, and killed the lights. He didn't slow down or even turn the wheel. Our tires parted from the roaring washboard. For a moment, all was calm and silent. We floated in blackness. Astronauts. One. Two. Three heartbeats.

My face snapped down on an exploding white pillow, then hard right, out the passenger window. Blood screamed in my ears, and the earth whirled around me. Faster and faster till my vision squeezed into nothing.

I was gone awhile. Not long. Less than a minute probably. My eyes opened in bloodshot slits—upside down, hanging by the seat belt. My hands lay on the crushed ceiling below me. Blood and dirt and pooling gasoline. Spider-webbed windshield everywhere I looked.

Billy was gone. His seat hung empty. Then my seat belt parted, and he was dragging me from the wreckage. He pulled me to my knees and gripped my shoulders.

"Are you with me?" he said. His face was wild. All teeth and bright eyes in the moonlight. I blinked. "Are you with me, kid?"

"I am."

BORDERLANDS

19.

We fled over rough ground, ran on turned ankles and shaky legs till our gasps came louder than the fading sirens. When they were gone, Billy dropped to his knees and panted.

"Jesus Christ," he said. "I gotta quit the cigarettes."

He found a bottle of water in our duffel bag and drank some. He passed it to me and told me to finish it. It was warm, but I drank. We picked our way through dry brush and stones and knotted trees. Bugs arrived, but we were both so burnt-out it didn't matter. Just the lack of sirens was calming, even if they were replaced with humming mosquitoes of a shocking size. We didn't even slap at them.

"Hey, kid."

"Yeah."

"Remember when Carl passed out trying to take a dump in our yard?"

"Yeah."

"Remember all the mosquito bites on his rear end?"

"It was like pizza."

"My face, right now."

We laughed, and he threw his arm across my shoulders as we walked.

• • •

The sun found us a couple hours later, on the banks of a small river. Voices drifted to us over the water. Singing. "Amazing Grace," I think, or something like that. For a moment I thought we'd been killed in the police chase and were now approaching heaven. Then I remembered a few choice robberies and knew for sure we were alive. When I'm dead there will be no hymns.

The source of the singing turned out to be a crowd of excited Christians on the opposite bank. A preacher stood in the shallows, dunking the men and women who waded out to him. A little revival— quite an odd thing to see with no warning at all.

Billy squinted through bloodshot eyes. He shaded his face with his hand.

"Church people," he said. "You know what that means?"

I didn't know.

"Food," he said, and went in boots and all.

It wasn't a deep river or a swift one. Wide and lazy and brown as a toad. The water felt good on my jittery body. My neck ached from the crash. I dipped my hand in the water, then held it to the base of my skull.

We came ashore just upstream of the baptisms. A grassy clearing by an old, white church. Picnic tables stood abandoned and mounded with food. We rushed in like animals. Oh man. They had a huge assortment of pastries. Peach pie. Sausage links. Billy grabbed a fistful of bacon. He took a big bite and then another and then he had to thump his chest with his fist to get it all down.

I found a cinnamon roll the size of my head and a cup of warm orange juice. Man, it was a good roll. They didn't skimp on the cinnamon. I finished it and set to work on a serving bowl of scrambled eggs. I had to scrape the crusty dried stuff to one side but that was no problem. The rest of it was fine.

As my guts filled, I started thinking like myself again instead of a half-crazed, probably whiplashed outlaw. My surroundings began to sink in. The more I ate, the stranger it all seemed. I pushed the eggs away and looked around. The picnic tables were cluttered with warping paper plates and half-eaten food. Goopy red sugar ran from jelly doughnuts. Flies buzzed around the peach pie. I peeked over the rim of my warm orange juice. It was full of dead wasps. I leaped back and chucked it into the grass.

"Holy shit," I said.

Billy grinned through a mouthful of bacon and sausage. "You're pretty wound up, aren't you kid?"

"I guess so."

He poured himself a Styrofoam cup of coffee and headed down the shore. "Let's check out the revival," he said. "I bet somebody starts speaking in tongues."

"We should get going."

"You afraid of a little religion?" Billy chuckled.

"I am not."

But I was. I totally was. Billy used to tell this story about a religious cult in South America. Everybody in this cult killed themselves at once. They did it by drinking poisoned Kool-Aid. Days later some poor townsperson stumbled on the compound, all covered in hundreds and hundreds of bloating dead people. Can you imagine the Kool-Aid officials when that hit the news? Billy said this was the inevitable conclusion to spiritual certainty . . . plunging stock prices for the pow-dered-beverage industry. So yeah, I *was* afraid of a little religion.

I gritted my teeth and followed Billy.

The preacher was up to his waist in the brown river. Churchgoers crowded the shore. They sang and clapped, and a big rancher-looking guy took off his cowboy hat and headed in. Must have weighed 250 pounds, this guy. His wide shins plowed up little bow waves in the river, but the preacher man just threw him down under the water like it was no big thing at all.

The rancher came up sputtering. Applause. "Amazing Grace."

It was only then that I recognized the preacher. It was John, the missionary. He didn't look much like the weak bony fellow who shared our fire not so many days before. He was thin, sure, but he seemed to have grown in size and power. Anna stood down on the shore. Her face lit up when she looked at him.

Billy shook his head and chuckled. "Hot damn," he said. We stayed some little ways back from the action. Billy nudged a guy at the back of the crowd. A white-haired black man with long legs and long, knobby fingers. "Do you know this guy?" Billy said.

"Hell, no," the man replied. "He just showed up."

"Just showed up?"

"Right in the middle of the meal."

Billy knocked back the last of his coffee. He took out a cigarette and lit it, then bumped out another for the old man.

"I know him," Billy said. "He's a crackpot. Calls himself John the Baptist. You should keep your distance."

"This from a man who just dragged his ass out the river and poached a bunch of church food."

Billy nodded and smoked. The rancher came in and hugged his wife, and somebody else waded out for a dunking. Billy grinned like a guy at the zoo watching monkeys. I tugged at his arm.

"Come on," I said. "Let's go. Nobody's even talking funny."

Billy shrugged. "True enough," he said, and turned to leave. But it's never that easy to duck a church service. If you've been, you know I'm right.

"You," the preacher called out. "Why do you turn your back on God?"

It took me a minute to realize he was talking to us—Billy in particular.

"What now?" Billy said.

"You. I see God has brought you across my path once again. He knows your sin, and he wants to free you of it . . . can you not feel the weight? Is your sin not heavy on your shoulders?"

Billy's face froze in a half smile. John could not have known the sheer volume of sin we'd perpetrated in the last month alone—or if he did, he'd kept it to himself. But there he stood in a sluggish brown river, with his hand reaching out to probably the only real sinner in his crowd.

"I'm okay," Billy said, and turned again, to leave.

"Okay? You think you're okay? Let me tell you son, no one is just okay without God."

Billy stopped and looked back. The preacher's face had become like a skull. No one clapped or spoke. No one said "amen." The happy gathering went real cold all of a sudden.

"The path leads to heaven or it leads to hell. That's it. You say you're okay. I know which path you're on."

Everyone was watching now, the earnest Christian smiles gone from their faces. They looked afraid, naked. My stomach revolted against the cinnamon roll. I wanted to throw up and then run away. Or maybe the other way around.

"I tell you the truth," John said. "The word of the Lord."

Billy was the only one without fear in his eyes. He met the preacher's stare straight on. He let the silence ring.

"Come to me," the preacher said. "Jesus Christ and the muddy current will lighten your load."

The congregation held its collective breath . . . urged Billy in all the ways that require no words. My brother looked down at the duffel bag in his hand, bulging with stacked bills and firearms. He caught my eye and winked.

"Why not?" he said, and let the duffel fall. "It's just a dunking."

The crowd went wild. They clapped and shouted as Billy waded out into the river.

The preacher didn't bother with ceremony. He just grabbed my brother by the shoulders and threw him down under the water—held him there a long time. Longer than you'd think it would take to save a soul. From what I understand, the dunking is symbolic. A quick splash should reasonably do the job. But the preacher just kept him down there, watching Billy's face under the current like he expected some visible change.

Just when I was starting to worry, he dragged Billy upright. Billy gasped, and the crowd cheered like crazy. The women sparked up another chorus of "Amazing Grace." It was a full-on revival again. People laughed aloud. Their faces glowed.

Billy soaked it in. He peeled off his wet shirt for no reason. He looked up and mouthed "thank you" to the sky. Then he looked down at his own body. He raised his brows at the ladies like he was surprised at how ripped he was. Like, "can you believe this?" Anna stood down by the river's edge. She had her shoes off and her dress hiked up a bit. She looked so honest and freckled. Billy made eye contact and twitched his wet muscles. She giggled. Couldn't help herself.

John wasn't quite done. He took Billy by the shoulder, leaned in and whispered in his ear. A few urgent words, then Billy broke away.

The crowd parted as he came ashore. Men slapped him on the back. Women reached out and touched his skin. Billy tried to make his face look earnest, but he was having a rough time of it. I could tell by his eyes. This whole thing was the funniest joke in the world to Billy. Religion. Belief. Fear of anything, now or in the afterlife. For him to be baptized. To say the words, take his dunking, and rise unchanged . . . it was a punch line. Nothing more.

But I couldn't seem to laugh. See, it was never the rare cults or group suicide that made me fear religion. It was the ring of truth. Someone calls me a sinner, and I know they're right. They say I'll be judged, and I believe it. I'm not that smart you see. The words of a preacher dig into my brain like fishhooks, and I don't have the strength to pull them out. I keep my distance, because once I hear a thing, I can't unhear it.

So I'll admit it. There on the shore, I wanted a dunking too. I wanted it in the worst way. Every line the preacher spoke. God and sin and the path to hell . . . the barbs sank deep. I knew it was probably horseshit—that's what Billy said, and he was always right. Without him I was lost. But maybe he was lost, too. Maybe this preacher knew what was up. Probably not, but what's the harm in a quick swim, anyway? My clothes were already wet.

Then Billy put his bare arm across my shoulders.

"Time to go, kid," he said.

"Right now?"

Billy nodded out across the river. On the opposite shore, a wolfish hound was sniffing our boot prints. Officers followed close behind. One was tall and thin and wore a beautiful black leather jacket.

"Right now," Billy said.

√ 20.

We stole a car and drove south. It was the shittiest car we could find. There was so much rust it was windy inside. Billy didn't care. All it had to do was carry us to Laredo, a border town on the Rio Grande. We'd cross into Mexico, Billy said, and take a new car with local plates. He worked the mostly broken radio dial and found a station playing some of those fast Mexican songs. He grooved with the music. He sang nonsense words over the Spanish.

See, Billy figured we were just about in the clear. He thought the border was only hard to cross if you were headed north. Mexico doesn't give a damn who comes in. Somebody once told him that you don't even need a passport. They said a lot of American tourists get in trouble for this reason. They forget their papers at home, and the US border agents won't let them back in. It's a whole big thing. Billy couldn't remember who exactly told him this, but he was sure they were right. We weren't planning on heading north any time soon, so there was nothing to worry about.

Billy followed signs to the border crossing and drummed his hands on the wheel. He was really getting into the music, trying to roll his r's.

"This is a great language," he said. "I'm gonna find a pretty señorita to teach me."

Up ahead was a big old gate. It looked like one of those tollway booths, with an office on one side and lift arms for each lane. It said "Mexico" on it in big red letters. Billy punched me in the arm.

"We'll find a señorita for you, too," he said. "I hear Americans are very popular down here."

"That's great, Billy."

"Damn right."

Traffic slowed to a crawl, then stopped dead. Billy quit singing. He squinted ahead at the border station, then rolled down the window and stuck his head out. Every car was getting stopped. Border agents chatted with drivers and waved them through.

"I don't know about this," I said.

"I'm sure it's just protocol."

"They're looking at papers, Billy. Everybody else has a passport."

He turned off the radio and tucked his gun down in the door pocket. He kept one hand on it and drove with the other. We inched forward. Up ahead a big pickup truck was taking forever getting through. The border agents looked concerned. They talked into their radios. Then an old white guy came out of the office. The sun was bright and hot, but he wore a black leather jacket all the same. Billy's jacket. Goddamn it.

"Who the hell is this guy?" Billy said.

"He's a US Marshal. I've told you like three times."

Billy glared at me. "I remember. It was a rhetorical question."

The marshal took one look at the truck and shook his head. The border guys waved it through.

"What's the plan, Billy?"

"Stay cool."

Then the marshal turned and started walking down the line of cars. He nodded at the drivers, looked in back windows. He took his time.

"Aw, shit," Billy said. He looked in the rearview mirror. Cars were lined up about a mile behind us. Bumper to bumper. He looked ahead. The marshal was close enough we could see the shape of his holstered pistol below the leather jacket.

"Time to go, kid," Billy said.

Billy tucked his own gun down the back of his pants, grabbed the duffel and eased his door open real slow.

"Keep your head down," he said. We left the car in the middle of the road and ran. Got some weird looks from the other motorists, but the marshal didn't see us. If he did, he didn't make a move.

• • •

We walked down the streets and back alleys of Laredo. We didn't know what else to do. Billy was at a loss. We smoked cigarettes. We walked some more.

When our legs got tired, we bought some tamales from a street vendor and ate them sitting on trash cans behind an empty brick storefront. It had been a fancy boot shop. Now it was nothing. Want ads and posters covered the alley walls. Mowers for sale. Missing people. Everything weathered and bleached by the sun. Billy ran his hand over his face. Escape plans take a lot of energy to think up, and Billy was tired. More tired than I'd ever seen him. We sat in silence for a long time. The air smelled like garbage.

It was a hot day, and tamales were salty. The water cups we got from the vender were small. Billy tipped his all the way back and slurped at the last clinging drops.

"Shit," he said.

A little boy cruised past in the middle of the potholed alley and up a flight of iron steps to an apartment above the empty store. He carried a key on a length of string. He was no more than six years old.

"Amigo," Billy said. The little boy stopped halfway up the stairs.

"*Agua?*" Billy said, and reached out with a couple folded bills in his hand. The kid started back down to us, but Billy shook his head. "Agua first," he said, "then dollars."

The little dude nodded and went away. In a minute he came out of the apartment with an old milk jug full of water. The plastic was yellow from long use. He moved to fill Billy's little cup, but Billy just caught the jug and tipped it back into his mouth. He drank his fill and passed it to me. I did the same.

"Thanks," Billy said.

"*De nada*," the kid replied.

Billy held out the cash, but a woman was coming down the alley. The kid heard her footsteps and looked for approval before taking the money. She nodded, and he snatched it from Billy's hand quick as can be. It was in his pocket before Billy's fingers closed on the emptiness. Billy laughed, and the woman laughed, but then she must have changed her mind because she started yelling at the kid in Spanish. He ran to her, and she dragged him away by the hand. We watched them rush off, all the way down the alley and out onto the street.

"Weird," Billy said, and took another drink of water. Then he lowered the jug real slow and focused his eyes on a patch of wall just across from us. It was plastered with posters and tear sheets. One was still crisp from the printer. A black-and-white photo of my brother's face, with the words, "Do not approach. This man is armed," across it in big letters. I don't know how we missed it till then.

Billy hoisted himself to his feet and cracked his neck. "Man, I'm tired of this," he said, and threw the duffel bag over his shoulder. We walked again. More alleys. Worse parts of town. We stayed away from people. Billy helped me over a chain-link fence, and we drifted through rows of parked tractor trailers. We lost ourselves in the tilting maintenance shacks and the Quonset huts. Right, then left, in no particular order. We crossed the railroad tracks. Finally, Billy put his gun through the window of a potato warehouse. It was empty, this place. Cool and dark. Abandoned maybe ten, fifteen years. We went down into the basement and sat for a long time on a pile of damp burlap sacks. They smelled of death and mold and rat piss, but we were too tired to care.

Shafts of sunlight swept the floor. They must have been moving slow. Exactly as slow as the rotation of the earth, which is pretty slow. But my sense of time was all screwed up. They seemed fast to me. I thought they were searchlights. I was real scared for a while; felt pretty stupid when I realized.

Soon the windows dimmed. Billy stood up and laid out our new plan.

"We need to find a coyote," he said. I blinked at him.

"Like a wild dog?"

"No. Shit. Different coyote."

Billy explained. A coyote is a guy who smuggles hopeful young Mexicans across the border in semitrucks, or on foot at night, or any of a hundred ways. Billy figured we could pay one of those guys to bring us along on his return trip. He figured there had to be a ton of coyotes to choose from. It's a good living if you don't mind routinely ripping off the poor and desperate. But where to find all these coyotes? They don't really advertise.

We crept out onto the street and found a dive bar. A falling-down building lit with neon, loud with Spanish music. It seemed like a good place to start. Billy went in. Told me to stay put. Two minutes later a couple big guys threw him out onto the pavement and kicked him in the guts a few times and shouted words at him that I didn't understand.

When they were gone, Billy got up. He held his side. I tried to help him, but he waved me off. He led me down the street to another bar. They threw him out there, too. They beat him first. You could hear chairs and glasses breaking in there for a good long while before he flew out the front door and landed in the street. He stayed down. He touched his ribs with his fingertips. He wiped the blood from his mouth. He held onto the bumper of a parked car and tried to stand. It didn't work. He sat down with his back against the car.

"Are you okay?" I said.

"Resting."

"If you keep walking into bars asking about coyotes, people are just gonna keep beating you up."

"Well, shit, kid. Do you have a better idea?"

Just as he said it, a gray-haired Mexican strolled out of the bar and approached. He stopped a few feet away and looked down at Billy.

"You are a crazy person," he said. "But I respect crazy."

The old Mexican helped Billy to his feet. He told us to go to a machine shed on the outskirts of town. He told us to ask for Jocko. "Tell him Francisco says hello."

• • •

The shed was 1950s untreated steel. Dents and tears in the metal were worn smooth and shiny by windblown sand and constant sun. Rows of trashed, probably stolen, cars surrounded the place. The inside flickered blue with welding flash, orange with sparks. Men looked up when Billy and I came through the door. Hard, sweaty faces.

"I'm here for Jocko," Billy said.

One of the men set down his tools. "No Jocko here," he said.

"Francisco sent me."

The man squinted at Billy a long time. "Check the office," he said.

The office was just a box of raw sheetrock and studs built in the middle of a spare engine bay. The man inside was short and thick and quick to smile. He wore a khaki vest over his bare shoulders. Jocko, I guess, though we never discussed names.

"Welcome to my sanctuary," he said. "Close the door."

It was another world in there. Brightly lit and messy as hell. Papers all over the place. Jocko eased back in his desk chair and patted the top of a trundling AC unit.

"I bought this lovely little girl a few months ago," he said. "My employees hate me for it, but that's the cost of comfort." He laughed a huge, booming laugh and put his heavy arms behind his head. Right away I felt better. At ease, you know. Everything was gonna be okay.

"Sit, gringo," Jocko said. "Speak."

Billy smiled and scratched the stubble on his chin. He looked at the floor and then at Jocko.

"Francisco says you can cross the border . . . unnoticed."

"The old man talks too much."

"Is he right?"

"Let's say he is."

"You have to cross back I assume, to pick up your northbound cargo?"

"Yes."

"And you make no money on that return trip."

"Very little money. This is true."

"I'll give you $5,000 to let the two of us tag along."

Jocko rubbed his forehead creases with thick fingertips. "It's not so hard to go south," he said.

"It is for men like us."

Jocko thought.

"Five on this side," Billy said, "and five on the other."

"Alright, gringo."

They shook hands. Jocko told us to go to the end of the street, to a low stucco building his sister kept open for transients and the unlucky. He made a call on a cell phone and told her we were coming. He said a van would pick us up in the morning. He said to have the money ready. He said bottles of water would be available for purchase at five dollars apiece. He told us to have money ready for that, too.

"It's a long trip," he said.

So we went to the low stucco building. A stout woman there showed us to an outer door and unlocked it with a key that was tied to a wooden spoon. She said nothing at all because she had no English, probably, and because a couple of grimy white guys weren't worth the effort.

The room was dark and hot. It had only one window, which was too small to pass a breeze. Two beds sat on the concrete floor, and a single light bulb hung from the ceiling. Billy tapped the bulb with his finger. It swung back and forth. He kicked the duffel under his bed and pulled back the tattered blankets.

"Aw man," Billy said. The mattress had a dark red stain the size of a dinner plate. He tucked the blankets back up to the headboard. He laid down in his clothes and tossed a crumpled pack of cigarettes at the ceiling. He did this a few dozen times and then got up and peeled his sweaty shirt off over his head. He kicked off his shoes and his socks and then just stripped all the way down to his boxer shorts.

The boxers were dark with sweat. Billy pulled the band away from his body and blew a stream of air through pursed lips. Then he tucked the .45 under his lumpy pillow and lay back down.

When I came to terms with the abiding heat I also stripped to my shorts and sprawled out on my ratty bed. I took the knife from my empty pants and held it in my hand. The weight of it calmed me.

"What do you think, little brother?"

"I think someone was killed on your bed."

"Or shit themselves."

"Hard to tell."

"Which is worse?"

I thought about it. I snapped the knife open and closed and listened to the bugs humming around our room's single light bulb. There was no switch, so we let it burn.

"Don't know."

Billy laughed.

• • •

I woke for no reason in the small hours of the morning. No reason apart from the voices outside on the dimly lit street, and they were nothing out of the ordinary. There'd been voices talking in Spanish all night. Shouting angry syllables or laughing. There was something different about these new voices. They were not angry or flirtatious . . . no nuance to them at all. They were stating facts as near as I could tell.

Then one of the voices spoke louder. "*Ahorita,*" it said, and our door flew off its hinges. Men poured in—a rush of boots and shouts and sweat-stained clothing. Men with dark eyes and guns. Billy sat halfway up before their hands were on him. He fought them back and lifted his pistol, but a shotgun stock smashed his face and the .45 clattered across the floor. All this happened in a moment, and then my own world shook into streaks of light and sound. A man dragged me from the bed and threw me to the concrete floor. My head cracked hard against it. The lights dimmed, and I was gone.

• • •

I found myself in a dream. Back in Radium. Back in Billy's old Silverado. The ditches were full of water. Billy was laughing, socking me in the shoulder. "You broke Randy's nose!" he said. "How did it feel?" I wanted to say it felt fantastic. To laugh with my brother again. But then our high beams lit the flanks of a fat doe. She stopped in front of us, turned her hollow eyes toward the truck. Her bones made bad sounds when we hit her. Then Billy and I were out on the road. He had the deer's smooth neck cradled in his left hand and my knife in his right. The eyes calmed as he placed the sharp blade to its throat, relaxing into nothing.

That's a thing that happens with prey animals. They give in when death is on the way. They see it coming and meet it in silence, their brains flooded with pain-killing endorphins.

Billy's grip tightened on the knife. His knuckles turned white.

"Look away, kid," he said.

Predators aren't like that when they go. They don't give in. They meet death in fear and pain.

• • •

When I came 'round, the world was sideways. My teeth ground against concrete, and a great weight held me down. Knees pinned my arms to my body. Across the room Billy huddled against a wall, blocking kicks with his forearms. He tried to get up, but the men caught him and threw him down on his face. Two men got his arms—one on each side—struggling to keep my brother down. A third put his foot in the middle of Billy's spine and lowered the barrel of a pump shotgun against the base of his neck.

"*Quédate,*" said the man with the shotgun.

Billy looked at me across the floor . . . both our faces pressed to concrete. His eyes were wild like those of a beast. Blood dripped from his mouth, and he bared his red teeth through thickening lips.

Then another man stepped into our little room. He was short and hefty in a khaki vest. The lines in his face turned to chasms under the swinging light bulb. Jocko, sweating profusely.

"Hello again, gringo," he said. Billy raged against the grip, but the boot in his back drove the wind from his lungs. Jocko strolled around our little room and stooped to look under my bed. "This is a real shithole," he said. "I must tell my sister to look into air-conditioning units."

He reached under Billy's bed and retrieved our duffel bag. He zipped it open and reached out a fistful of cash.

"Well done, gringo," Jocko said. "You must have gone to some trouble for this."

Billy glared up. "Burn in hell," he said through the blood in his mouth.

The coyote laughed and walked from the room. At the door he turned around like he'd forgotten something.

"*Mátalos,*" he said, and was gone.

Billy caught my eye across the floor. The hate was gone . . . the fire. He was cold.

"Look away," he said.

I waited for the calm to arrive and usher me off into the next thing. Numbness and peace. An end to all this fear. I longed for it. What came was something else.

Heat and strength and the fires of adrenaline rushed through my veins and down into my fingers. And there it was—my knife, still in my hand. The very one Billy used on that doe back home. You see what's coming here, don't you?

Above Billy, the man raised his shotgun to lever in a shell. So little time now. I wrenched my pinned arm forward, free of the knees that held me down. I pulled so hard the joint nearly dislocated. Then the cords across my back heaved me around so fast the vertebrae crackled in my spine. The blade flipped open with a snap of my wrist and met a warm, fleshy place in the neck of the man above me. Blood dripped hot down my bare arm and splattered the side of my face.

Then I was on my hands and knees across the concrete to Billy's gun. I snapped it off the floor and rose. It leaped in my hands. A clean whistle split the air, and a cone of blood painted the wall. The shotgun fell to the floor without sound. The men gripping Billy's arms closed their eyes through the pink haze, and Billy threw them off like they were children.

I slouched back on my knees and looked at what I'd done. One man gurgled blood around my knife blade. Another lay crumpled against the wall with only half a head left on his shoulders.

Billy caught my wrist and lifted the gun from my hands.

Movement and the glint of heavy firearms flashed outside. Angry and surprised men, gathering for a charge. I looked up at Billy. His eyes were bright and clear. I could not hear his voice over the ringing in my ears, but his lips moved carefully so I could understand.

"Get up, little brother," he said. "We have to go now."

He took the gun and ran at the door wearing nothing but a pair of boxers. He got three shots off before crossing the threshold. I followed in his wake—out into a night lit-up with muzzle flash. The stucco wall burst into gravel and dust as we ran. We moved like there was no earth below, like we were flying. Our feet barely touched the pavement. Lead tore the air all around our naked skin, and somehow we still ran.

We ran a long time and when we could not, Billy put the .45 through the window of a Ford Taurus. He had it going before I came through the passenger door. He put his foot down hard and took us from Laredo.

• • •

Out on the road, he slammed his fist across his chest three times so hard it left marks. He gripped the wheel and let out a long cry that rattled low in his throat like something not human. I remember that. It was the first thing I heard as the ringing left my ears. I remember how the veins in his arms rose like knotted snakes under the skin. How his teeth reflected red and white in the instrument glow and how the lines around his eyes and mouth cast deep, curved shadows. When he was done, his face settled back to the face of a man. Billy was alive and strong and immortal again. And I, well, I'm not the same as I was.

21.

Carl had a theory about me. He heard this story, this thing I did when I was young. Billy needed my help, and I became strong. Stronger than a defective kid with crippled hands should reasonably be. Carl heard about it—about how I got real strong one time—and he started telling people that Billy Quinn's little brother had something he called "special strength." He called it something else when he was drunk, but I won't use that word because it is offensive to most people now.

Please don't get mad at Carl. He was a friend, and he did not know any better. Anyway, Carl figured most people never use 100 percent of their physical power. There's an override switch in the brain, he said, which shuts things down before tendons snap and muscles tear from bone. He figured my switch got damaged in the car accident. Most of the time, I was weak as cardboard, but when it was required, I had access to every fiber of muscle tissue. Every ounce of will and drive. I could break my own bones if I had to, he said. I could tear my arm off and beat someone with it.

Carl liked this idea a great deal. I guess it makes some sense. I *was* able to put my fist through the marshal's back window. I was strong enough to stab a man in Laredo and shoot another, though both were much larger than me and well-armed. Most people probably couldn't do that stuff. Maybe my override switch is busted. Maybe Carl was onto something. Seems kind of like bullshit though, doesn't it? The whole thing was based on this one story. I guess you should probably hear it, so you can make up your own mind.

I told you about the accident already. The one that took our dad. This thing I'm gonna tell you about happened right after. I woke on the tar with blood in my ears and a cry rattling from my throat. The sky was pale blue above the morning mist. This is my very first memory. It's how I came into the world. A birth of sorts. Before it, there was only blackness.

My face was hot and sticky with blood, and vision came bright and streaked with color. Around me squares of broken glass reflected sky. A boot stood upright and alone. Not mine. Then I saw the car. It was mangled up with the front of a semitruck, head-on. Red tongues licked around the crumpled hood and made paint squeal and pop. I saw a young man on the passenger side. The frame was caved-in on him. A length of steel bar had bent down from the roof and punched through his chest. Just in from the shoulder. It held him upright, while the rest of his body slumped away. An older man was behind the wheel. The police report says the older man was Karson Quinn. My father, but I didn't know him. Only Billy. I reached in through the jagged steel and touched my brother's face. He didn't move or twitch or anything, but I knew he was alive. Felt it in my guts.

I tried the door handle. Useless. Everything was mashed up together and fused. What remained of the window openings were too small and jagged to drag him free.

I took the doorframe in my hands. Broken glass sliced all the way to the finger bones and stopped. My tendons popped like busted shoelaces. Blood ran out between white knuckles and down the door, steaming and boiling as it dripped. I did not care about the pain. Flames reached for Billy. I could not let them take my brother. I looked at my hands and willed them to move. Commanded them, and a great power came into me. The steel bent under my fingers. It crumpled and tore.

I pulled the door right off its hinges and threw it down on the road. I dragged my brother out behind it. I pulled the bar from his chest and put my hands over the wound. His blood mixed with mine. He woke in the ambulance. The other man died.

I am strong sometimes. Maybe it's just another defect. A busted switch. I hope it's not that, but I guess it don't matter much either way. I am strong when Billy needs me . . . when he is weak, that's when it comes. I was ten years old the first time it happened.

22

The next day comes back blurry now. Billy in his underpants, driving that stolen Ford. Him leading me into somebody's backyard, blasting me clean with a garden hose, telling me to do the same for him. Strange-smelling clothes from a small-town thrift store, then back on the road. I was so out of it. I didn't even ask where we were going.

Then the sun rose, and the Taurus began a ten-mile decline. At first it was just a few coughs here and there, but it got worse. Billy squinted at the gas gauge. It registered a quarter tank, just as it had for many miles. He scratched his head, then reached through the wheel and tapped the glass. The needle dropped to empty.

"Don't screw with me, Taurus," Billy said.

We were way the hell out in the middle of nowhere at this point. Not the sort of nowhere you get in western Minnesota. Those are just farm fields. I'm talking about the real nowhere. I'm talking two-lane highway where people barely drive and never stop, and if your car breaks down, there's a better than even chance you'll end your life in a ditch trying to dig water from the parched earth with bleeding fingertips. That's some nowhere, and that's where Billy had his disagreement with our car.

He cocked the .45 and held it to the dashboard, execution style.

"I dare you," he said.

And so, the Ford called my brother's bluff and died right there on the desolate side of the road. I rolled the window down half an inch so the gunshot wouldn't pop our eardrums, but Billy never pulled the trigger. He just patted the dash with the palm of his hand and left the keys in the ignition.

The wind blew hard, nothing to slow it down. The air smelled like dirt. Dry dirt. Billy tucked the .45 in the back of his pants and leaned against the Ford. He reached around for a cigarette—tried and failed to light it. The wind kept swallowing the flame.

"Thoughts?" he said around the cold cigarette.

"We walk a lot."

He laughed and we set off.

For hours there was nothing to figure distance. No one coming or going. Just dry grass and sand and heat in all directions. We walked and did not speak much, and in that great emptiness, things became strange and jumbled in my brain.

Sounds seemed muffled and far away. My skin was like paper, reporting touch or pain at odd times and for unpredictable reasons. Life didn't seem quite real . . . like a very accurate forgery.

Billy told me a story once about a man who got hanged. He's tied up with a noose around his neck and dropped off a bridge, except the rope breaks and he gets away. He runs for miles, nearly to his front door. Then on his very threshold the world slips away from him and he's dead on the end of the rope. It was all in his head in the instant before death. Billy got this story from English class, one of the few assignments he actually read before dropping out.

As we walked, I thought maybe this wandering was a closing figment. Some strange purgatory out there on the Plains. Maybe I was still back in that tiny room on the border, my mind rushing after life as the bullets ripped through. Maybe I had not killed anyone. Maybe it would all be over in a minute or two. The idea was not unwelcome. I wasn't right in the head just then.

I squinted across the shimmering flats. The earth burned white for miles and miles in all directions. Very far down the road, a brown knob seemed to float above the tar. In the absence of other things, the knob took on deep significance. I watched it grow as we walked—imagined what it might be and what its presence might suggest about this empty reality.

As we got closer, the thing settled down onto the ground. The knob turned out to be a dead dog. A big black pit bull lying on the edge of the road. It wasn't bloated or smelly or even eaten out by anything. There was no obvious cause of death. It was just dry as a bone. We stood there and looked at it for a long time.

I thought back to that story about the hanged man who didn't know he was dead. Wasn't there a dog in that story? A dog who followed the poor dead man, all the way to his doorstep? Yes, there was. Not in the original, I don't think, but Billy usually saw fit to improve the stories he told me. In his version, a huge black dog followed the man for many miles. The man feared the dog but didn't understand its meaning till the end. It was a death dog, Billy told me. He said sometimes before you die you see such an animal. They've been spotted all throughout history, he said, during times of war and sickness.

We stood over the corpse dog, on the side of the road. It was rangy even for a dead thing. Its lips shrank away from long white teeth. The sight of them made my hands tingle. Billy nudged it with the toe of his boot. The skin crinkled like a pop bottle.

"Hey, Billy."

"Yeah?"

"Are we dead?"

"I don't think so. Why do you ask?"

I told him I thought maybe this dog wasn't a regular animal, that it might be a death dog like the one he told me about, come to take our souls away. Billy laughed. "That was just a story," he said. "Besides, I already told you how death would be."

But I think he could tell I was a little crazy right then and not easily convinced. "Even if this is a death dog," he said, "you gotta realize it is, itself, dead. How is it gonna take our souls if it can't follow us around for a while first?"

I nodded. Billy made good sense. My thoughts cleared a bit. I blinked and looked around. If we were alive, I had other questions.

"Hey, Billy."

"Yeah?"

"Where are we going, anyway?"

"Away from this dog. It's giving me the creeps."

"Which direction?"

"North."

"Mexico is south."

"We're not going there anymore."

This didn't make any sense at all. A US Marshal had us right in the middle of his sights and would surely pull the trigger very soon. Everyone knows you go to Mexico when that happens.

"Why?"

"Why what?"

"Why not Mexico anymore?"

"Because we're going to Alaska now."

This didn't make any sense either. Alaska is still in the goddamn United States, where a US Marshal can arrest you easy as fishing, but you still have to cross two international borders to get there.

"Let's go to Mexico instead. We're close to Mexico."

"It's too hot down here," Billy said. "I hate it."

"That's not it."

"Look at this shit. There's no water. Do you want to live in a desert?"

"Mexico has coasts. It has the ocean."

"Look, kid. We're going to Alaska."

"If you don't tell me why," I said. "I'm gonna stay right here with this creepy dog."

"No way. It freaks you out too."

I sat right down by the dead dog and pet its bony, dead face. The short fur was still soft, even with mummified skin below it. I looked up at Billy and grinned. "How about that?" I said.

"You're a lightweight. I'll just throw you over my shoulder."

"I'll piss myself. It'll run down all over you."

"Jesus Christ, kid."

"Tell me why."

Billy breathed in and squinted across the great hot plain. "We just tried Mexico, kid. It was a bloodletting."

I looked at my hands. The creases still held black flecks of blood. The blood of a man I killed with a knife so I could paint the wall with the blood of another. Two dead men turning rancid in the borderland heat. Men I killed for Billy. No more Mexico. I got up.

"Okay," I said.

Billy smiled. "And there's another reason."

"What's that?"

"Because I'm the big brother," he said, and punched me in the arm, "and I say Alaska."

• • •

We walked until the sun slanted low. Then Billy crossed the ditch and a barbed-wire fence and led the way through ankle-high grass to the only stand of trees in a hundred miles at least. He found some fallen limbs—all dead and dried white. Oak turned to bones and horns. With it he sparked a fire that burned slow and quiet and threw clean light. The wind picked up and brought cold with it. I edged in close to the fire. Billy kept some distance.

He took his shirt off and laid it out on the ground. The dirt was hard and dry, and grass stood the shirt up in small peaks. He knelt down and smoothed it with his palms. Then he took his .45 in both hands, dropped the clip with a press of his thumb, and levered the bullet from the chamber. It landed like a cut fingertip on the shirt. Three quick movements had the gun in pieces. The slide and frame, one in each hand. The barrel and mainspring slid out neatly. He could have done it in his sleep by then but moved slow and exact over the parts.

He took a corner of the shirtsleeve and cleaned the barrel and the inside of the slide. The shirt came away black, the barrel shiny. The glint of it held my gaze across the fire. He laid it down on the T-shirt and reached for the clip.

"You alright, little brother?" he said, unloading bullets into a little pile. He counted the rounds silently. Four left.

"I'm okay, Billy."

It was cold out there with the sun gone down. A relief at first after so many days of heat, but my fingers ached with it. They stiffened, and I held them out toward the fire.

"You got a look in your eye," he said. "I know that look."

"We lost all the money."

"I don't care about that. You know what I'm asking."

In that light, my scars were suddenly red as blood, like the tears were wide-open again. I pulled my hands from the fire, but it was no trick of the light. Blood still stained the creases, deep in my skin. It stuck there like ink. I kept forgetting.

"There's a line, isn't there?" I asked. "Between what's bad and what's real bad."

His hands worked the gun back together. There were many small bits to get right, and he did not respond. When the last steel pin clicked smoothly into place, he laid the gun aside and leaned back on his elbow. His face was all shadow but for the eyes.

"This line," he said. "Who drew it? Who stands guard?"

"I don't know."

"You think it's God, like that preacher said?"

"Maybe."

"We've been over this." He ran his hand through his hair and leaned-in over the fire. "Look," he said. "I've made mistakes, little brother. All these things we've done. I asked too much of you. It was cruel. I know it. You deserve better than me. But we're past that now. If there is a God—there's not, by the way, but if there is—if he drew some line, we've crossed it."

The light washed him in flickers of red and orange, turned his eyes to embers.

"But you listen here, kid. This is your foundation. You lay this down and build on it. The thing you did was justified. A man brings violence to your family, you find a gun and you blow his head off. That's a truth older than God."

"Okay."

"Do you believe me, little brother?"

"I believe you, Billy."

Then he grinned and balled up his T-shirt. "There you go," he said. "We got it sorted."

He stretched out on the ground with the shirt as a pillow and his long arms behind his head. "Sleep now," he said, and in a minute, he was out like a light.

I watched him breathing slow, comfortable in his skin in the cold blackness of things. Something was different about my brother. He seemed younger than before . . . like that sixteen-year-old version who found us a trailer house and a job and laughed through everything. He wasn't so worn down anymore. Not so long ago, he had a great big bag of cash and a Firebird. There on the Plains all he owned was a pistol and four bullets. Yet Billy smiled in his sleep. Warm on a night that chattered my teeth and made my hands into claws.

It didn't make any sense at first, but I kept my eyes on him, and it came to me. He was lighter. That's what it was. All that weight from Radium—the robberies, his abandoned child, and poor Maggie-Grace—gone. When exactly it had slipped from his shoulders, I wasn't sure. Maybe it was the moment he saw death coming and reached out for it, or when he rose up from the concrete floor, roaring through a mist of blood.

It don't really matter. Point is, he was unburdened. He looked clean, way deep down, like a sinner fresh from baptism. The way he might have looked that day on the river if he hadn't turned the whole thing into a joke. Maybe it *was* a sort of baptism that lightened his load, just not the regular kind. Billy, after all, was not a regular man. He was capable of things other people weren't. Maybe his sins were different, too. They needed more than a dunking. More than water.

• • •

In the morning we kicked the ashes of our fire to dust and went back to the road. We only had to walk about a hundred yards. Billy barely got a cigarette lit before a dumpy, old RV coasted past and stopped on the shoulder. It was the first vehicle I'd seen since the cashed-out Taurus. Billy never even stuck out his thumb.

We jogged up, and a pretty, plump woman leaned out the passenger window.

"You fellows need a ride?" she said. And then, "Oh! Hello again."

It was Anna, the pregnant missionary's wife. Here she was again, freckles and all.

"Well, I'll be damned," Billy said.

"Actually," she replied, "I think you'll be saved."

23.

We piled into the RV and let our eyes adjust. What a dump. My memory did not do it justice. The mold smell was even worse than before. But we weren't complaining. If someone hadn't picked us up, we would have died of thirst in maybe four hours. That is not an exaggeration.

Billy leaned in between the two front seats.

"Thanks again," he said.

John turned around and looked Billy up and down.

"You seem different," John said.

For one microsecond, Billy froze. You see, the situation had to be handled correctly. Billy hadn't come off well in previous meetings. He'd subtly mocked John's direct line to God, talked his disciple back out of the faith, then slipped away with no explanation—and that was just the first time we hung out. During our second run-in, Billy bounced his pecs at John's pretty wife. John must have seen it. Everybody did. That was fine when we thought we'd never see them again. But they kept showing up! We couldn't seem to get away.

The microsecond passed, and Billy's face adjusted like a new skin. He smiled in an honest, respectful sort of way. A way that said, "Don't worry, I'm a basically happy, all-around okay dude. I would never try and sleep with your pretty, knocked-up wife." Then he opened his mouth, and spoke in a tone so simple and true, for a moment I thought I was sitting beside a stranger.

"I needed to make a change," Billy said. "I don't know that I ever gave you my name. Will Conner."

Billy's mind worked just that fast. A tiny pause, invisible to anyone who was not his brother, then he was someone else entirely. Will Conner. That's a good name. Honorable and clean sounding. Will Conner is a guy you trust . . . but also a pretty good outlaw name, when you think about it.

"Good to meet you, Will," John said, and reached one hand around to shake my brother's.

"And what's your name?" Anna asked me. She turned around in her seat wearing a big smile like she honest-to-goodness wanted to know. I was already a little fazed-out, and I guess the question caught me off guard.

"Bernie," I said. Shit. I spend all this time convincing people I'm not challenged, and then I go and call myself Bernie. What a moron.

• • •

We rode with the missionaries all morning. At noon John pulled into a rest stop and jogged off to a tiny cinder-block bathroom. He was gone a long time. Longer than a dump should reasonably take. Anna wasn't concerned. She cut thick hunks of brown bread and hummed a little song to herself, and perhaps to the baby she carried.

As she worked, a little Honda Civic pulled in at great speed and parked right by the bathroom. The driver leapt out and pounded on the door. He tried the handle, and then he waddled around gripping his crotch with his hand. I could hear him cursing.

"How long has he been in here?" the guy shouted.

Anna ignored him. She just got out some hard cheese and sliced it real thin. She hummed and arranged cheese wafers on the bread. After a while, the guy slammed back into his Civic and squealed his tires. A half hour later, John came out of the bathroom wiping sweat from his face with a wad of toilet paper.

"You made cheese sandwiches!" he said. "I love a cheese sandwich."

Anna kissed him on the cheek. We all ate some sandwiches, and no one talked about John's bathroom issue. No one talked at all actually. The bread was so hard and salty and dry it was all I could do to get it down. People just can't make enough spit for bread like that. Every bite required large amounts of water. I went through five or six glasses just to keep from choking. Billy killed at least half a gallon. By the time we were done, we both had to piss like racehorses. We didn't use the rest-stop bathroom though, just walked around behind it and went in the grass. Who the hell knows what the missionary had done in there?

Whatever it was, it made John real tired. He tried to read his Bible while Anna washed the dishes but didn't make it far. Less than half the book of Job, which he said was very short to begin with.

He rubbed his weary eyes with his palms. The lines of his face slanted down over his bones. He was an old man suddenly—a change so swift I worried for his health.

"Do either of you drive stick?" he asked.

• • •

We rolled on into the afternoon, with Billy in the driver's seat and me in the back next to the preacher. One fairly long dunk in the river and a couple hours of conversation was enough for John to trust us completely. He just tossed Billy the keys and sprawled out on the RV bed, and that was that. As we pulled back onto the highway, John looked up from the bed. His eyes were glassy and wide.

"Hey," he said. "What did you say your name was?"

For a moment, I considered changing the alias. Something manly, like Brock or Jesse. Better not to risk it.

"Bernie," I said. His eyes narrowed.

"If you say so," he said, and rolled over.

Damn that guy could sleep, even better than Billy. John was way on down in the REM cycles in less than five minutes. He rolled eerily close to me and stacked his hands under the left side of his face like children do in greeting cards and nowhere else. His limbs twitched, and I could see the eyeballs tracking back and forth under thin lids. This was some real sleep, man, the kind doctors recommend.

I watched John breathe in shallow puffs as his wife gave us a long and emotionally complete history of his religious chops.

"He was only thirteen when he heard the call," she said. "Imagine that! Thirteen. His folks thought he was nuts."

Billy nodded and drove. "Wow," he said.

• • •

Late that afternoon, Billy touched the brakes in a speed-trap town somewhere in North Texas. Maybe New Mexico. Hard to tell. Plates and silverware slid around in Rubbermaid bins, and John sat bolt up-right like a dead person brought to life.

"Here," he said. "Stop here."

Billy pulled over, and John leaped right out before the RV even stopped. We watched him sprint across the road, nearly trip over the curb, and make for a distant line of hills. The hills were dry and brown and looked like the end of the world.

"What's wrong with him?" Billy said.

"He's had another word."

Billy pulled the RV across two lanes of traffic and followed the jogging missionary down a side road. Anna clapped her hands and her face turned bright pink.

"You're about to see something you won't forget," she said.

"We're already in that ballpark, Anna."

Turns out John wasn't running for the hills. There was a little Presbyterian church back there with a dozen cars in the parking lot. John went right through the doors of this place with no hesitation at all.

Billy parked and followed him in. I followed Billy, and Anna waddled behind as best she could. By the time we got in, John was already up on stage with his hands clamping the podium and three church deacons trying to drag him off. They held him by the shoulders, and one guy had his belt. The belt was already on its very last notch and the deacon wasn't pulling too hard because I think even he was worried John might snap in half.

"I've come to you as fire to the chaff," John shouted. The deacons lifted John's feet clear off the ground, but he never let go of the podium. I guess they must have bolted that thing down. Billy stared like the circus was in town. And it sort of was, you know. This was just a little Presbyterian church having a little Wednesday-night church service. About twenty-five people in the pews. They had low expectations, I'd say, but here came John, bringing the fire.

"You've been sitting so long you've forgotten how to stand," John said. "It's like you're already dead."

A collective gasp rippled back through the pews. John kept talking. The deacons loosened their grip a little. His feet settled back down to the ground. Anna beamed.

Would you believe me if I told you John brought that tiny crowd around like a broke colt? Would you believe he did it in five minutes? Well, that's all it took. Five minutes and he had them shouting amen. They shouted and prayed and wept, and the very same deacons who once gripped John by the shoulders rushed out after tubs of water for impromptu baptisms. People who had gone to this church fifty years and were pretty damn sure they were Christians had John dunk them again for good measure.

Billy blinked many times. Anna watched like John was Christ himself, returned in a campervan to give her a baby. She held her belly with tender hands as he preached.

John had mojo and that's a fact. So much mojo, as it turned out, that re-saving a small Presbyterian congregation did not satisfy. On the way out, John asked the pastor what the most unholy place in town was, and the guy said the Tasty Beaver with almost no hesitation. This place was a dive bar and occasional strip club a few blocks from the church. John marched right down there and jumped up on the bar.

Right off he started praying over the four or five lowlifes getting their slant on that Wednesday evening. He pointed right at one guy in the corner and told him God forgave him for leaving his family in Tucson, but liquor wasn't going to help anything. That guy started crying and threw his whiskey across the room. In twenty minutes, all the poor drunks in that place, even the bartender, followed John out to the parking lot and got down on their knees and prayed. John said a blessing and told them they were changed and not to go back to their shitty, old lives.

He didn't say "shitty." I added that because he used a lot of religious sounding words I don't know.

With the Tasty Beaver emptied of Wednesday drunks, John slumped down on a barstool and shut his eyes. Anna came up behind him and rubbed his shoulders.

"Isn't God amazing?" she said, and sent Billy and me off to get the RV.

• • •

That night, we ate some more dark bread sandwiches with the missionaries. John could barely chew, he was so tired.

"These things take a lot out of him," Anna said. "Miracles don't come free."

She tore off small pieces of crust, and John tucked them one by one into his cheek to dissolve. He looked like a collection of sticks and string.

When Billy was done with the food, he stepped down from the RV. He nodded to John, sprawled out on the bed, and to Anna, up to her elbows in a pail of dishwater. He said thanks for the food, and we were off now. But John caught up to us halfway across the parking lot. He actually roused himself, jogged thirty feet on clattering bones, and grabbed Billy's meaty arm in his own desiccated hand. What he had to say meant that much to him. You bet we listened.

"God has brought you across my path three times now," he said. "Do you not think he has a purpose?"

"Hadn't considered it, Preacher."

"I think he wants you to ride with me," John said. "He wants you to bear witness to the revival he is bringing."

"If that's his plan, with all due respect to the man upstairs, he don't know me very well."

John smiled and nodded. His teeth were way too big for his head. He looked like he'd been dead for about eight days, out in the desert sun drying out. I bet he weighed ninety pounds. He gripped my brother's arm, more to stay upright than to keep us tethered.

"I should tell you that God has delivered some clarity on my destination," he said. "I had a dream last night. I saw mountains, and craggy, small trees, and in the dream, I was very cold. God wants me to go north, to Colorado. Maybe further. Canada or Alaska—it's not yet clear. I say this in case the knowledge changes things for you."

Billy scratched the stubble on the side of his jaw. He squinted and made a bad face. The knowledge did change things. We were headed north. Free rides are hard to find. It was too good an opportunity to pass up.

"Plus I need a driver," John said. "Anna doesn't drive stick."

So we stayed. Billy and I leaned back in the captain's chairs to sleep in our clothes. They said goodnight, and we said goodnight back. These missionaries were a strange sort. Maybe they were crazy . . . I'm not sure. They were too kind, I know that, and must not have looked all too close at the men they picked from the side of the highway. If they had, maybe the blood still held in the creases of my hands would have put them off. Maybe the .45 riding under Billy's shirt, or the look in his eyes—that hellfire left over from cheating death—maybe they would have tossed us out. Maybe they should have.

24.

We traveled with the missionaries for a couple weeks, and John never did manage a proper shit. Something was really badly off with his colon. It reminded me of little Clive, back in Radium, and the deer turd that rolled out of his pant leg that one time. Except deer turds dropped from Clive without permission. It took every ounce of John's meager strength to pass the stones his guts produced. There are things you can take for a problem like that, but John refused medical attention and basic over-the-counter laxatives.

He suffered bravely. The intestinal traffic jam never shortened a sermon or dulled the spiritual fervor. He could get just about anybody to pray the sinner's prayer. Drunks and stiff churchgoers, and a stripper he pulled right off the stage one night with a wave of his hand and a few choice scriptures. For a while, I wondered if the constipation actually gave him power. If it might have some unpredictable and positive side effect—like people with brain tumors who can suddenly speak Latin. John's mojo was astonishing. John himself was not. There had to be an explanation.

So one morning, in the back of the RV, I just asked him outright. "What's up with your stubborn shits?" or something to that effect. He just smiled and leaned back against the brown carpet wall.

"Ah, yes," he said. "The thorn in my flesh."

John huddled under a quilt, sipped hot water, and held forth on God's loving punishment. God, he said, was like a dad from the Great

Depression. He loved his many children. He showed it by watching them all the time and spanking their bare asses with a belt when they misbehaved. God did a lot of spanking, because the vast majority of his children were headed straight for hell. Not just bad people, but kindhearted Lutherans and agnostics too, and every single Catholic.

Anyone who thought they were doing "okay" was no friend of God. Being just "okay" was the worst possible thing, John said. John wasn't "okay." He couldn't take a dump, for God's sake. He felt bad all the time. That's when he was happiest, and that was the right way to be.

He said the pain in his guts was very likely punishment for something he'd done wrong. He wasn't sure what, but said he'd figure it out someday and be better for it.

"God sees all," John said. "He's keeping me on the straight and narrow."

He told a Bible story to really nail down his point. It was about some guy in the Bible who fell off a mule and went blind, and then un-blind, and then had to travel around preaching and getting tossed in prison. Apparently, this guy had a thorn in his flesh that was always causing him grief.

"I got a thorn in my heel once," I said. "I pulled the little bugger out with some pliers."

John shook his head under a little hood he made from the quilt.

"It wasn't an actual thorn, Bernie. The Bible speaks in parables."

"Two weeks later I stepped on a nail in the same exact spot. Pulled that dude out too. You gotta do it fast or you get tetanus. Then you gotta get a big shot. The shot hurts worse than the nail."

"You're missing the point, Bernie. I think you're doing it on purpose."

The thorn was metaphorical, he said. It was proof of God's watchful eye. Without punishment, how would this Bible guy ever know when he'd gone astray? Constipation was John's thorn. He thanked

God for it. This kind of sermonizing was real common during our time with the missionaries.

The travel was slow on account of all the tiny revivals God wanted John to do. Less than a hundred miles a day usually. Once we only made it ten. It made me crazy. There was all this down time, and John had so many ideas he wanted me to understand. He didn't try so hard with Billy for some reason. Billy got to hang out with Anna, who was fun. I had to sit with John and learn. Maybe I put off a receptive vibe. I don't know. I shouldn't complain. They were so nice. But goodness' sake! It was exhausting.

• • •

Billy took the first available opportunity to score cigarettes and whiskey. Slipped away during one of John's revival services and hit up a liquor store. That night, after the missionaries were asleep, we crept from the RV. We sat on the hood of an abandoned Geo Metro and got truly blasted.

"Been too long," Billy said. He had a cigarette between his two fingers and the neck of the whiskey bottle wrapped in his palm below. The words came out in smoke, and he chased them with liquor.

"Jesus fucking Christ," he said. "I haven't sworn in a hundred years."

"Fuck," I said. "I never fully appreciated that word till now."

"It's a great word."

"Maybe the best. It means so many things. Pass that whiskey. You're gonna fucking drink it all."

He passed it. I took a good pull and then a draw on the cigarette. The liquor fumes and smoke mixed in my lungs and made me feel as light as a feather.

"We should just go," I said. "Right now. We'll nick a car, turn up the radio, and swear like sailors all the way to Alaska. Please, Billy. Let's go."

Billy took back his whiskey. He drank in silence. However much we wanted to bolt, we both knew we were gonna stay. There were a bunch of great reasons. Billy didn't have to explain. The missionaries were excellent cover.

See, every person you run into has a bank of faces in their mind. They've got their neighbor in there, college roommates, and the features of men in wanted photos—guys like Billy and me. Make eye contact and they run a mental background check. It's fine if you only talk to one or two folks at a gas station from time to time. They probably won't recognize your face. But see enough people and eventually somebody will see you back. It's hard to stay invisible for long, especially when there's a determined US Marshal right on your heels. But not if you're driving a missionary from church to church. You hold the door for his pregnant wife, you smile at the parishioners, and man, they just smile back. You are judged godly and clean in their eyes. That's how you evade the law for weeks and across a thousand miles of open country. That's how we did it, anyway.

We smoked and drank a while and I tried not to think about how John would look at me in the morning. He'd see my bloodshot eyes and know my secrets. He'd know I was going to hell. The judgement would be silent, but heavy.

Billy pulled a little pamphlet from his back pocket and flipped through the pages.

"Get a load of this," he said, licking his fingertips to grip the paper. He had a spot he wanted to start . . . read it before, I guess.

"Just be good to people and be kind and you'll make it to heaven just fine," Billy read. "There's no such thing as sin."

He held up the pamphlet so I could see. A newsprint illustration showed two young guys in a car. The guy behind the wheel looked like a real moron. His friend had a smug grin and some very inclusive spiritual ideas.

"God is love," Billy read. "Why would he send his creations to hell?"

Then he cleared his throat and made his voice sound like Beaver Cleaver.

"Gee, mister," he read. "I guess I won't pray to let Jesus into my heart after all. I was right on the edge after what that preacher said, but I guess he was wrong. I guess I'm doing okay."

That's when I knew the pamphlet was about to go really dark. It was terrible to be "okay."

"BAM!" Billy shouted. "A train comes out of nowhere and T-bones the shit out of these guys."

He held up the pamphlet again so I could see the cartoon carnage. It was gruesome and very detailed. It made my balls shrink up into my stomach. Billy laughed and tucked the thing away under his arm while he lit a new cigarette off his old one. He chuckled and smoked, and I figured he was done.

"Where did you get that thing?" I said.

"These churches have them all over," Billy said. "They've got more pamphlets than Bibles."

He shifted his cigarette to the corner of his mouth and found his place again in the pamphlet.

"Oh, no!" he read in his Beaver Cleaver voice. "We're in hell now. Fuuuuuuuuck!" That last part wasn't in there. Billy added it. I checked over his shoulder, and then I couldn't look away. The dumb guy and the smug one stood on a little stone island in a lake of cartoon fire. The dumb guy looked scared shitless.

"You were wrong about all that hippie shit," Billy said, still ad-libbing as Beaver. He flipped to the last page. I read the final lines before he could adjust his voice.

"No," the smug guy said. "YOU were wrong!" And he took off his face like a rubber mask. His whole face! Underneath was a grinning devil head. He was the devil the whole time! I thought I was gonna barf.

"Aw, shit," I said, but Billy was laughing. He laughed so hard he almost fell off the hood of the Geo Metro.

"Straight to hell," he said. He could barely choke out the words.

Everything was funny to Billy after a little whiskey. Death was funny to him. Hell was funny. Not to me. I just wanted to forget about that grinning devil head and the lake of fire. That's all I'd been trying to do since we took up with the missionaries.

For fifteen years I trotted through life, pretty much unaware of the possibility of eternal damnation. It was great. When things got real bad, I could just close my eyes and imagine stepping into traffic. Here comes a big old bus and BAM. It always put a smile on my face. The end sounded like rest to me. Now there was no rest to be had. John stole that away from me. Now if I stepped into traffic, I'd have to go right to hell after. There was no other option. John said even the Catholics were going to hell on account of the infant baptisms. If Catholics were going, what about me? I'm a killer. A thief. It took great concentration not to fall into depression. Now there was this cartoon, so I knew just what hell would look like when I got there. Shit.

Billy calmed himself and looked around for his cigarette. He'd dropped it in all the hilarity. When he couldn't find it, he lit a new one. He leaned back and breathed out a torrent of smoke.

"I read a whole gang of these things in the can," he said. "There's one about a sergeant in Vietnam who makes fun of a super religious private for being, I don't know, no fun at all. Then the sergeant gets blown up. Straight to hell."

He took a drag and went on.

"In another one, a rich guy dies after spending all his money on sports cars and parties. Hell. One has this ninth-grader blowing his coach. They both get AIDS and die." Billy pointed his cigarette at me. "And guess what?"

"Hell?"

"No, actually. The poor little shit repents and goes to heaven. Still dead though."

"And the coach?"

"Straight to hell."

I forced myself to laugh, but it was too high pitched. Billy heard the fear. He clapped his arm across my shoulders.

"Kid, you know all this is bullshit, right?"

"What?"

"All this stuff about hell."

"So it's not real."

"I don't know. Maybe, but not for us."

"That don't make sense, Billy."

"Look over there," he said, pointing his cigarette across the parking lot at the dark RV. "Say those two missionaries go on a bender. They really cut loose—snort a load of coke and have a devil's threesome with the town bisexual. Then they kick off somehow. T-boned by a freight train or something. They might end up in hell. It's possible. Because look, they're still missionaries. They've read all these stupid pamphlets. They believe in hell. They gave it power. But you and me, kid, we don't believe in anything. For us, there is no hell."

"Okay."

"Say it."

"Say what?"

"You know."

"There is no hell for us, because we do not believe."

And here's the thing, it sounded right to me. I said it, and it became true. Before that I was pretty worried. I did a lot of bad things. I knew I'd do more. Hell seemed built for me, but Billy understood how things were. He had clearer eyes than me. He wasn't so easily convinced. I was lucky to have him to keep me right.

"Good," Billy said, and handed me the bottle. I took a sip, but he caught the bottom and raised it up. A huge slug poured down my throat. I pulled back coughing, and booze ran down the front of my shirt. Billy laughed hard and punched me in the shoulder. He waited till I got my breath, then he pinched up a flap of skin at the base of his jaw.

"How scared would you be right now if I tore off my whole face and I had a devil head on under here?"

I laughed then like Billy had before. I laughed until I thought I might pass out. That grinning devil head was so funny! So childish. How had it ever frightened me?

We smoked and laughed till late that night. Stars shone clear through slashes of heavy cloud. It grew cold. We drank more whiskey to keep warm. When it was gone, we went back to the RV. I eased open the door and slid up in the reclining passenger seat. My hands moved slow with drink. Clumsy. I made the door close soft, then pulled till the latch clicked. Billy did the same, peering around in his seat to check on the missionaries.

"They're still asleep," he hissed. "We're in the clear."

I turned in my seat and looked. Their bodies made two spoons around the child Anna carried. I watched them breathing, low and soft in the small RV bed. What a safe place they made for their child. And just a few feet away lay two wanted men. Killers and thieves, drunk, and reeking of smoke. The kid didn't know. It was better that way. I put my head in my hands. My face buzzed with alcohol.

√ 25.

We coasted into Colorado Springs on a Saturday night. About an hour of daylight left. John directed Billy to an empty parking lot. We settled in near the back. Anna had got it in her head that John needed a haircut. I guess he did look a little wild. She set up a folding chair right there on the tar and broke out a buzzer and some scissors and gave him a trim. She hummed as she did it. Billy propped himself up in the doorway of the RV and smoked a cigarette while he watched.

"You worry too much," John said. "No one would have minded my hair."

"Damn right," Billy said. "Made you look like a prophet. Now you're gonna look like a youth pastor."

Anna waved a tiny pair of scissors at Billy.

"Language," she said, but smiled too broad to mean it.

The missionaries were really happy. Everything was a good-natured little argument, like newlyweds before the honeymoon. Something big was happening and it wasn't hard to figure out. Across the parking lot was the largest church I'd ever seen. The building had more in common with a sports arena than the white steeples of the Midwest—all angles of roofline and windows. It was the sort of place where thousands of well-off people go to sing songs and feel like they're doing "okay." I figured John planned to hijack the morning service and attempt the largest gorilla revival in history. That takes some balls right there. Almost as many balls as it takes to walk into a liquor store with a loaded gun. Arguably more. I was impressed.

Anna wanted John's hair to look just right for the big day, and when that was done, she decided mine should look less shitty too.

"Get down here," she said, dusting off the folding chair. I was up on the RV roof. I'd started spending a lot of time up there. There was a ladder built right into the back of the RV, and John was usually too weak to climb it. Billy had talked me out of hell, but John was always trying to talk me back in. I had to keep my distance.

The roof wasn't safe that evening. Anna pointed up at me with her scissors.

"I won't have you looking homeless tomorrow," she said. "It's a big day."

I feared those sharp little blades and didn't move. "I am homeless," I said.

"Don't make me send your brother after you."

"Just say the word," Billy said, and lit another cigarette. Usually she would have gotten after him for all the smoke, but just then it was my hair that bothered her. I get it. My hair was long in some places and burned short in other places. I slid down the ladder and eased back into the folding chair. She pinned a towel around my neck and fired up the buzzer. I shied like a spooked horse when it touched my neck skin.

"Hold still," Anna said.

She gripped the top of my head with one hand and took off all the hair from my neck up over my ears. She did the buzzing fast, then dipped a comb in warm water and dragged it across my skull. It stopped in tangles and my head snapped back into her chest.

"Ow."

"Your hair's a rat's nest," she said. "Have you ever combed it?"

I expect this was a joke, but honestly no. I never combed it. I never really cut it, either. It just sort of broke off at about four inches. Bad follicles. Faulty like the rest of me. Once I looked at a strand really close under a magnifying glass and there were little knuckles in it every little distance. The hairs broke off at the knuckles.

"I leave it alone most of the time."

She tried a different angle and this time she really got her back into it. Tangles ripped out with a sound like tearing cloth. My neck cords strained to keep my head on my shoulders. Then something gave way with a pop. I figured it was a big chunk of my head skin. I imagined it dangling from her comb. Scalped by a missionary! But it was the comb itself that gave way. The handle broke right off.

She tried a beefier comb and broke that too. Two combs down, Anna got out a tube of oily hair product and rubbed it into my head with her fingers. This part didn't feel bad at all. Her hands were so warm and gentle. All the knotted tendons in my neck and shoulders relaxed. Little muscles in my face loosened up for the first time in maybe years. I wondered what sort of stupid ape face I'd been making this whole time without knowing it. Anna's hands felt so good I didn't even worry about it. I didn't worry about going to hell, or how the haircut would look, or the fact that I had a partial hard-on. I just closed my eyes and smiled. Who knew having a woman rub your head could feel so good?

I was just about asleep when she reached another comb from her little hair cutting kit. She whispered kind things and moved slow, like a veterinarian approaching a sedated cow.

"You're going to look great," she said. And then, "Oh fiddlesticks!"

She'd broken her last comb in my stupid, knuckly hair. That grease didn't do jack shit. A big chunk of the busted comb hung from the tangles. She had to buzz off a patch to get it out. Then she just buzzed the whole thing, right down to the skin. She did it real fast while I was still all dopey and relaxed from the massage. She said it was better that way.

When it was all gone, Anna squatted down behind me and held a mirror out in front of us. She made a big happy face.

"Meet the new you!" she said.

There's a reason Billy never took me to a barber. It was a horror show. My head was even bigger somehow without the hair. How is that possible? The shape was worse, too. The ears poked out in differ- ent directions and that flat spot was super obvious. Anyone walking past, even a hundred yards away, would notice. They'd point and say, "Look over there. That kid has a flat spot on his big old melon head."

And the scars—they were worse than I remembered. Big, fat, white things crawling up from the base of my skull, right over the top and down the other side like the stitching on a baseball. Windshields do bad things when you go through them. They open you right up. They leave proof.

Anna held her happy grin, but her eyes traced my scars in the mirror. I could feel her questions. That kind of damage requires an explanation. There was a car accident—that's what I told people. It was long ago. I'm better than I used to be. Billy helps me so I don't get lost.

But she did not ask, and I did not answer. She unpinned the towel and brushed the last severed hairs from my head.

"Well, darling," she said. "You look great."

"Really?"

"You bet."

I glanced around to see what Billy thought, but he wouldn't meet my eyes.

"Looking great, buddy," he said, and gave me a big thumbs up.

• • •

When the sun went down, the missionaries broke out a board game they said was really good. They explained all the rules, but I just couldn't grasp it. It involved dice and cards and pretending to be made-up old-West characters. Anna was the town hooker, John was a gunfighter, and Billy was the sheriff. The sheriff! Billy! It was a bullshit game. They kept having to remind me it was my turn to roll, or discard, or whatever.

"You're the gold-miner," Anna said. "Use your gold-miner voice."

I didn't have a gold-miner voice, and I didn't feel like inventing some embarrassing shit right then.

All I could think about was my naked head. Every time I looked around, I could feel their eyes darting away—like they'd been staring a second before. I get it. It's hard not to notice a giant Frankenstein head, especially in such a confined space. But they all just refused to acknowledge the situation. It was like walking around with shit on my face. I knew about the shit. Everyone else knew about the shit. And I knew they knew. There's no moving on until someone brings it up. It stressed me out so bad, I started to worry that my naked fucked-up head was spinning around without my permission. I had to reach up and touch it all the time to make sure it was pointing the right direction. Sometimes it was. Sometimes it wasn't.

Finally, I just slipped out the side door and climbed back up on the RV roof. They could get by without their gold-miner.

I lay on my back and looked up at the sky. It was so dense with clouds not one star showed through, seemed like there was nothing out there at all. Just us. Down here. The stubble on my head rose in goose pimples with the cold. Below me, Billy made the missionaries shriek with laughter. He had a good sheriff voice. It was like Dirty Harry.

"Make my day, punk," he said.

• • •

When Anna's laughter quieted and the windows dimmed, I heard Billy's boots on the tar outside the RV. The sharp rasp of his pocket lighter told me he was smoking. A draft of tobacco rose a second behind. It's a good smell. I breathed it in. Then I heard John's voice, low and thoughtful as he always talked. I had to listen hard to pick out the words.

"You should quit that," John said. People were always droning on at Billy about the evils of smoking. I smiled at John's effort. It would do nothing.

"God has great things in mind for you," John said. "Too bad if you die of cancer before getting it done."

Billy chuckled. "If he has plans, the cigarettes won't matter."

"What's that?"

"A little thing like cancer, seems like he could clear that right up."

Billy had dropped his solemn Will Conner act. Not all at once. He let it erode over time so no one would notice. By Colorado he was himself again in all but name. He grinned and smoked and turned things into jokes. "Who needs chemo when you've got the Holy Ghost?" he said.

"Sometimes God heals, that's true," John replied. "But sometimes, he kills his darlings."

Billy took in a long breath. By now my ears were tuned so hot the crackle of burning tobacco came clear as church bells.

"Good night, John," Billy said.

The RV door scraped shut, and we were alone. Billy dropped his cigarette and crushed it with his boot heel. I could hear the sole working back and forth on the tar. He cleared his throat.

"Hey, kid," he said. I considered pretending I was asleep, but that never worked with Billy.

"Yeah?"

"If you're wondering, your head looks really messed up still."

"It's terrible, isn't it?"

"Terrible. But I don't know, it kind of fits you. You're a bad motherfucker, kid. People wouldn't guess that. Now you look the part."

"Thanks, Billy."

"Any time, little brother."

26.

John did plan to speak at the megachurch, just not in the way I expected. He actually called ahead and set things up, like a normal human being with a calendar and working phone. You see, it wasn't a dream from the Lord that brought us all north to Colorado. It was an honest-to-goodness scheduled event. The megachurch knew John was coming. For the first and only time, his name was in the program. No hijacking required. That Sunday morning, he walked into church with his new haircut and his best clothes on and no uncertainty at all. And then, God wound up and punted him in the nuts. Right directly in the middle of his nuts . . . metaphorically speaking.

John made his way through acres of filling pews and found Pastor Kenneth Munsey at the foot of the stage. He held out his hand to shake.

"We made it," John said. "By the grace of God, we are here at last."

"Oh," Munsey said. "That's good."

Pastor Munsey had a good polish to him. His skin was tan and wrinkle-free, his teeth white as fluorescent lights. He wore one of those microphones that hooks behind the ear so he could move around while he talked.

"This means so much to me and Anna," John said.

"Excellent," Munsey said. "What's your name again?"

• • •

Here is what happened. I got it all out of John in an unguarded moment later on, but it makes more narrative sense to tell it here. Months before, as John considered his cross-country revival crusade, he'd called Munsey on a whim. He was on the fence at the time—torn between providing for the coming baby and following that profound religious calling he'd first heard at the age of thirteen.

Crusades are expensive with wives and children attached. Munsey's church was renowned for financing the crap out of missionaries.

As luck would have it, Munsey was attempting to book "missionary day" when John called. One set of missionaries, the Stalwarts, had just backed out. They were somewhere in a Chinese prison. No telling when they'd get back. The Stalwarts were compelling speakers, and good looking, too. What a loss! Munsey was feeling pretty down about it when John called. It seemed like a sign. I'm spitballing here, of course. I didn't talk to Munsey. But I do know he booked John right away—even spent a few minutes expounding on the generosity of his thousands of parishioners.

That was it. John bought the only RV he could afford and set off, knowing that on a certain Sunday, in Colorado, God and Pastor Munsey would provide.

In the intervening months, Anna got bigger and the RV rattled louder and the Stalwarts got out of prison. As near as I can tell, Munsey just plain forgot about John.

"The Stalwarts were just delivered from a Chinese prison," he said. "So . . ."

John's bony shoulders sank further and further away from his head. It looked like his arms were about to drop off and crawl away in shame. Finally, he just turned and walked away. He took Anna's hand and led her slowly back toward their dumpy RV. Chinese prison trumps a long road trip every time. No way around it.

Then Billy put his arm across Munsey's shoulders and spoke softly to him. I can't imagine what he said, but that man's skin turned ashen from the top of his shiny forehead to the tips of his fingers. He blinked many times, and then he nodded.

"Hey, John," Billy called out. "John the Baptist. You're on in twenty."

• • •

I'd like to tell you our slight missionary preached a glorious sermon. That many were saved or re-saved that day on the battlefield of the Lord. That people fell on their knees for the power of his words. Let the little man have his day. But I will not lie.

John stepped up on stage and his voice broke. Timid is the word. He spoke a little while on something having to do with loving one's brother, but I couldn't bring myself to listen. The whole thing took on a pleading nasal air. Imagine erectile dysfunction on a public stage. No one listened.

Five minutes in, a six-foot-tall pillar of muscle in a nicely wrinkled suit strolled up on stage and made like John was introducing him.

"Thanks for warming up the place, buddy," he grinned, slapping John on his round back. Then he turned to the church with a solemn face. His words were quiet, but they carried well.

"I'm Geoff Stalwart," he said, "and Jesus has delivered me from prison."

The place went nuts. Two or three thousand people cheering their heads off. The sound of it vibrated my lungs. It was infectious. Even I clapped. Geoff calmed them with a wave of his hand. Then he launched into the saga of how he and his wife, Ashley, whom he mentioned only once, were arrested for spreading the word of the Lord.

"The cell was just a hole in the ground," he said. "The guards spit on me as they passed, and I prayed for them."

We sat up front with Anna and John. I kept waiting for him to regain his mojo and rush back up on stage—preach some hellfire and brimstone—really tear the place a new one. Instead, Anna held his hand in her lap like he was dying of cancer. He looked at the floor while Geoff told his story.

Geoff was really nailing it. I don't think anyone in that whole crowd looked at their phone one time. He talked about how he converted a prison guard, and how that guard was gang-raped by all the other guards for his new beliefs. I mean, it *was* a hell of story, but there was something off about Geoff. I don't know. He was different than John. Better looking, for sure, but that wasn't it. Something about the way he talked. Or maybe the way his face moved while he talked. I could feel him leading me where he wanted me to go. That's common enough in good talkers. They take you places. But I got the sense Geoff was bringing me somewhere I wouldn't like.

This thought was just coming into my mind when Geoff paced by on the stage above us. His gaze swept along. His face was strong and sad and victorious all at once. But a darkness flashed in his eyes when they landed on me. He paused for a moment. So short I bet nobody else noticed, but we stared at each other. The muscles around his black eyes quivered, and I swear he showed me his teeth.

Then he moved along, and I sat in my chair with my heart thumping in my chest. Geoff returned to the middle of the stage. He put the microphone carefully back in the stand and moved in close to it so he could speak softly and still be heard. The lights made him glow.

"The guard was so brave," Geoff said. "Jesus made him brave." He paused. He let tears fill his eyes. I could hear women crying in the seats behind me. A whole crowd with a lump it its throat. "We need to go back," Geoff said, "or that guard's sacrifice means nothing. We need to go back, and we need your help."

Offering buckets came out in stacks. Ushers ran around almost frantic. The Stalwarts needed that money right now! And wow, did people give. Guys ripped bills in half trying to empty their wallets. There was no mention of John and his road trip.

I told you that nobody noticed the moment between Geoff and me, but there's a chance Billy saw it, because I could feel him getting angry. You know. There's a vibe. Plus, he was working his hands open and closed. Then he was gone, and I had to jog to catch up. He dodged out a side door and walked fast through a network of halls and stairways.

"Wait up," I said. But he didn't wait. He didn't ever turn around. Finally, he stopped at a glass office door. The door said "Secretary-Treasurer" on it. He turned to me with a smile.

"Just wait," he said. "This is gonna feel so good."

In no time at all, a forty-something dude in loafers and a gray sweater rounded the hall corner holding a garbage bag full of money. I shit you not. This guy used a garbage bag to carry all the offerings. He stopped in front of Billy, leaning against the office door.

"Hello," he said.

"Hello," Billy replied, and punched the sweater guy right in the throat. The guy stood off balance, trying to get air back into his lungs. He looked confused and offended. Then Billy cracked him in the face with a spinning elbow and dropped him like a dead person. The guy was out so cold his body made a funny hollow sound hitting the carpet.

"What the hell, Billy?"

"I can't go splitting my knuckles," he said. "The missionaries would notice."

We dragged the sweater guy into a janitor's closet and left him wrapped in duct tape with a mop bucket over his head. Then we locked ourselves in the unisex family bathroom and opened the trash bag.

"That Stalwart guy is a dick," Billy said. "We're doing God's work here."

"I thought you said there was no God."

"Figure of speech."

He flipped up the toilet seat and sorted the money from the checks like a stack of mail. Bills went into our pockets or down our shirt, and the checks got flushed. Unless you're some kind of white-collar criminal, they're not a whole lot of good.

"This breaks my heart," Billy said, holding up a check made out for $10,000. "Goddamn you . . ." Billy squinted, "Filbert Gunderson. Why didn't you carry more cash?"

Our jeans bulged with money as we left the church. We timed it just right. John and Anna were already retreating across the parking lot.

"Get us out of here," Anna said.

• • •

Billy started the RV and took us out onto the highway. The engine sounded bad. It had never sounded all that great, but there are only so many miles in a dirt-cheap RV, and this one was near its end. John put his head in his hands. Anna looked out the window at the big tile-roofed houses of Colorado Springs. I could hear the breath catch in her throat. She was trying not to cry. Goddamn, it was uncomfortable.

After a while, Billy couldn't take it anymore. He eased a big stack of bills from his pocket, quiet as he could. He smoothed it out with one hand and slid the whole thing into a cup holder. He left it there for a minute or so, then rediscovered it with a flourish.

"What's this?" he said. "This wasn't here before."

John's slight fingers took a long time shuffling through the cash. He counted it once, then again. His voice came out as a whisper.

"Five thousand dollars," he said, "at least."

Anna laughed aloud and wrapped her arms around John. There were some tears on her part, but they were happy ones. When she let him go, John looked at Billy's face in the rearview mirror.

"How did this happen?" he said.

Anna laughed again and wiped her wet cheeks. "It was God, of course," she said.

Billy grinned. "Yes sir," he said. "God."

27.

John was always tired after working his small miracles. That's how you know a preacher believes the words he says. It costs him more than it costs you. And it cost John a lot. Every time he spoke to a crowd, he came away smaller. Every person took a slice of him. But then he'd eat and sleep and maybe, if he was lucky, pass a small turd. Eventually he'd rebuild himself. If his miracles cost a slice here and there, his failure to work magic on the stage of that enormous church was a crippling blow.

He held the money a long time without speaking. He weighed it in his hands and flipped through the bills. Then he made Billy stop the RV so he could throw up on the side of the road. I still remember the look of his bony spine arching like a cat as he hacked up several days' worth of Anna's brown bread.

I had to help him back to his bed after. No one said where to go, so Billy drove north on Colorado freeway. When he finally asked, John said, "Mountains. Take me up a mountain." That's all he said—all anyone said—for quite some time.

Billy turned west into the Rockies. We stopped for groceries in a little tourist town, where Billy loaded the cart with salmon and beef cuts, anything Anna pointed to and many things she did not. He paid for it all, and we drove again.

The roads began to change. Tar narrowed and coiled in switch-backs. The shoulder dropped away so suddenly you could almost reach out and touch the sharp crowns of trees. Beyond them the earth rose and fell in crags and peaks. It's hard to grasp that jagged horizon if you've spent your life on the flatlands. It looks carved on purpose. There's a symmetry in the sharp edges.

Forests shrank to bonsai trees, centuries-old pines the size of toddlers and wizened as elves. Then the trees stopped altogether, and alpine tundra rose out in desolate humps. The shoulders of ancient slumbering creatures. It was there we camped. I don't believe it was an actual campsite. There was no power or pump-out facilities. Seems like that sort of land would be protected and super illegal to drive on. But John roused himself from under a quilt and pointed out the window. "There," he said.

Billy nursed the RV off road and out across the tundra. He parked in a stony hollow.

We stepped out for a cigarette while Anna set to work on supper. I was pretty excited. She had all kinds of tasty stuff to work with. But I could hear her and John talking, and the news wasn't good.

"No meat tonight," John said. "I couldn't hardly manage it."

"Yes, darling."

Billy's face sank. He stubbed out his cigarette and stepped back into the RV. John was holed-up in the back corner of the bed. He tilted his gaunt face toward the cloudy back window. He looked like a skull balanced on a pile of quilts. Anna cut meager slices of brown bread and layered them with bitter green leaves and small crumbs of cheese. She got out a stick of butter. John winced at the sight of it.

"No butter for me," he said. Anna whispered apologies and put it away.

"Salmon is good for the stomach," Billy said. "What you need is salmon and some mashed potatoes."

"I couldn't manage."

Billy looked at the brown sandwiches and shook his head. He reached into his front pocket and came out with a chocolate bar. He opened it and broke off a little piece.

"Have some chocolate," he said.

He reached out toward John with the candy in his palm, like he was tempting wildlife. John stared at him from way back in his sunken eye sockets.

"I don't like sweets," he said.

"Chocolate is medicine."

"Sugar is a temptation of the flesh."

Billy shrugged. "Okay then," he said, and ate the chocolate himself.

"It's been a long time since I had any chocolate," Anna said. She said it real quiet, like she hoped John wouldn't hear, three feet away.

"I don't know if you'd like this kind," Billy said.

"It would be a mistake," she whispered. "Of course, you're right."

"Don't abstain on my account."

John really said it that way: abstain. I think that's the only time I ever heard the word used in regular conversation. Anna looked at Billy with pleading eyes. He broke off a piece of chocolate and passed it to her, then another piece and handed it to me. These were really small pieces of chocolate. The bar was divided up into about a dozen sections, and Billy was breaking those sections in half. It wasn't like him to skimp. The missionaries were rubbing off.

We chewed the tiny pieces of chocolate, and then we ate the sandwiches.

Or course they did not satisfy. Brown bread and leaves are no kind of meal. When we were done, Billy and I walked some distance from the RV and smoked more cigarettes. They usually have a hunger-blunting effect, very useful when traveling with missionaries. Out on the tundra, those cigarettes did nothing. My guts shifted with their emptiness. They growled so loud Billy looked at me sideways.

"I can't help it," I said.

Billy crushed out his third cigarette. He shook his head and fished the chocolate bar back out of his pocket. Only a square and a half was missing, still pretty much a whole bar. He broke it in half and handed me the small end. I ate right away. I didn't even break off sections, just bit the corner and chewed. It tasted a little strange, but I didn't care. I ate the whole thing and licked my fingertips and then I looked at Billy. He still had most of his half left, sucking on each little piece real slow and careful.

"Wow," he said. "You just dove right in."

"What do you mean?"

"Don't get me wrong. I respect it."

"What did I just eat?"

"About thirty-five doses of medical Marijuana."

"Well, shit, Billy."

But he grinned wide, and I couldn't be mad. "Strap in, kid," he said.

A gust of wind rippled the blue-green tundra grasses. With it came the smell of hot butter. Something was frying in butter! Fish maybe, or beef. It didn't really matter which. We both turned sharp and looked back at the RV. It rocked with activity. Pots and pans clattered, and steam rolled out the open door.

"Holy shit," Billy said. "It worked."

We were almost running when we got to the RV. Butter has a strong hold on the human brain as it is, and the weed probably helped. Anna was hard at work when we piled through the door. She peeled potatoes into a big pot of water. Her face was flushed with the heat of it.

"Finish these," she said. "Fast, or the fish will get done miles ahead."

Billy and I took up paring knives and set to. It was hard going. My hands were slow. That's not out of the ordinary, but Billy's hands were slow too. He dropped a whole potato in the water and laughed as he tried to spear it back out with the point of his knife.

John huddled in the corner and pulled the blankets up over his head. Without his deep-set eyes glaring out, we just sort of forgot he was there. Anna smiled and sweat as she cooked, smacking at Billy and me when we tried to sample things before they were done. She put big gobs of butter in the potatoes and on the cooking salmon. Plenty of salt. When it was done, she pulled the pans off the stove, and we ate right from them with spoons and plastic forks.

It's hard to explain how that meal was for me. It was like filling empty places, near as I can tell it. Not just an empty stomach, but little gaps in my limbs between the nerves and the bones and skin. As I ate, I could feel the buttery potatoes moving around to the places I'd worn thin—to my bony elbows and knees, to my skinny ass. I could feel the surplus. An end to months of famine. The tight cords of my neck relaxed, and my head seemed to float off my shoulders. My skin felt good inside my clothes, like the skin of my loins, all over my body. Marijuana, I thought, was an excellent thing to have. It improved food, and sex too probably if I could ever line up both experiences at once. Good times!

We ate all the food, and then Anna broke big chunks of bread to clean the pans. She took a bite and started to laugh.

"This tastes like sawdust," she said. "Has it always tasted like this?"

"It has," Billy replied.

"I'm so sorry."

As the sun went down, Anna sat between us in the RV doorway. She swung her plump legs back and forth as the sky turned red. Warm colors reflected off Anna's eyes and the sheen of her skin. Her hand glided slowly over her taught belly.

"Feel this," she said, and moved Billy's hand.

"Goodness," Billy said. "It's kicking."

"John wants a boy," she said. "But I think it's a girl."

My brother's big hand rested soft on Anna's belly. Knuckles made thick and hard from work and violence. Fingers of leather stained with cigarette tar. Below them a new life was growing. "It's good to have a daughter," he said.

The food made heat in my body. It had been comfortable at first, like a campfire. But as I watched Billy and Anna, both looking down at her squirming belly, the heat began to rise. It traveled up my throat so I could hardly breathe, then spilled down my face in tears. I wiped them away with the back of my hand, confused by their presence and by the aching in my chest.

"It's okay, Bernie," Anna said. She patted me on the back, but when I looked up, I did not see the gentle kindness that was in her voice. The mouth was right—the nose, the flushed cheeks. But the eyes were wrong somehow. I stared back. Her eyes were on upside down! I rubbed my hands over my wet face and looked again. The small lid was on top and the big one blinked from the bottom up like a jungle lizard. Billy's, too. They both looked at me with their lizard eyes.

"You okay, kid?" Billy said.

"I have to go," I replied, and jogged out over the tundra.

• • •

I walked a long way in that last red light and walked still when the light sank to blue. And when there was no light left at all, I tipped my head back and gazed up at the universe itself. Stars whirled in their paths from horizon to horizon and turned the earth between to silver and shadow. Peaks grew up around me like the surface of the moon.

How long do thirty-five doses of edible marijuana last? Perhaps, I thought, Anna's eyes would be right-side-up by now. But I didn't want to risk it. It's a bad thing to see, and besides, I couldn't remember how to get back to the RV. Instead, I wandered farther.

My head spun and spun as I walked—stars and black peaks and silver earth below. It didn't feel like a defect out there with so much to see in all directions. Who wouldn't spin their head around in such a place?

I covered some large distance that way. Then great stones rose up before me. Spires and round boulders. The ground became steep and rugged underfoot. I slid several times, sliced my hands on sharp stones, left bloody handprints on the boulders I climbed. I don't know why I continued. There were easier places to walk. Paths that took no toll in blood.

The rise ended in a narrow ridge like the spine of a pack animal. I picked my way out along it. Loose stone clattered down steep slopes on either side. I carried on, and soon the ground widened into a garden of sorts. Thick trees grew harsh and branchless in that high place. Vines coiled about them, etching the trunks with shadow. I reached out and touched one of these trees, but it was just stone under my fingertips, carved by the wind and rain. The place was quiet. I walked slowly there, on my toes. I was careful to move nothing. It would have felt wrong to do otherwise.

Out on the very edge of the furthest rock a man sat cross-legged. His body was as harsh and windswept as the garden of stone around him. His ribs and neck bones showed through his shirt. He did not move with my approach. Did not wince when my feet turned a stone.

"Who is it?" the man said, when I was near.

"Just me," I replied. The man on the rock was John. I hadn't seen him slip out, though he must have quite some time before to climb so high in his diminished state.

"Come sit beside me," he said, and patted the lip of stone. His seat ended in hundreds of feet of vertical drop. It may as well have been the actual edge of the earth. The place where explorers turn back, where the map is shaded and monsters rule.

"I'll stay back here, thanks."

"Suit yourself."

For a while we were silent. He bowed his head into his hands, so he looked like the stones around him. I began to doubt his presence. Then he spoke again.

"Think for a moment on what has happened in this place," he said. "The men who came here from the valleys . . . the sacrifices they made to their gods when fire itself was new."

The stone where John sat was black with ash and ancient blood.

"They knew nothing of the one true God," he said, "but maybe they felt something of his presence. If the almighty speaks anywhere, he speaks in the mountains."

John rubbed his scalp with his fingertips so hard I worried for his skull.

"In this place, God spoke to the heathens," John said. "But he will not speak to me."

I didn't know what to say to him, could not trust the thoughts in my head. Words born of drugs sound stupid when said aloud. I watched his bony spine lift and fall with his breath and said nothing.

"Things were clear to me once. I could see a man's sin in the lines of his face and the set of his shoulders. And when I baptized his soul into heaven, I saw those sins washed away in the current. They are like ashes in the water. Mortal sins look like crow feathers. I became this way when I was young."

Something caught in his throat as he breathed. He coughed hard, his chest collapsing in as he did.

"I called your brother down into the water because I could see the things he did," John choked the words out in a rasp. "I wanted to take the weight from him. But when I put him under, nothing washed away. Why is that?"

"I don't know."

"Maybe someone carries the weight for him," John said, "or God does not hold his wrongs against him."

"He is a good man."

"He is no such thing," John replied, "but good's got nothing to do with it."

He coughed again, harder this time. He could not seem to get his breath. "Do you have any water?" he whispered.

I could have used some water myself. My mouth was dry as Anna's dark bread. Now that he said it, I was almost crazy for a drink.

"I have no water."

He nodded, and I could see his throat working, trying to swallow spit from his dry mouth. When he had calmed himself, he got to his feet and stood at the edge of the stone.

"Let me tell you a story," he said. He turned to me, full-on this time so I could see his whole face in the starlight. His skin was drawn; his lips shrunk back from long teeth. His eyes were glassy and dark. They too were on upside down, but the preacher looked right that way.

"There's a shepherd in the hills," he said. "He owns a hundred sheep. Do you know what a shepherd is, Bernie?"

"Yes."

"One day, a single sheep leaves the herd on his own. Lights out for the territory. Gone."

As John spoke, his narrow body swayed perilously out over the cliff's edge. His heels were just a few inches from the drop.

"What do you think that shepherd does?" John didn't pause long enough for an answer. "He goes after that one sheep, is what he does. Leaves ninety-nine to bring just one back into the fold."

John's feet edged back toward the cliff a little with every word. "And when he finds that one sheep," John said, "he carries it home on his shoulders and tells his friends. Bernie, you have to stop spinning your head around like that. I can't concentrate when you do it."

"Sorry."

"Honestly, I've tried not to mention it, but jeez."

"I'll work on it."

"Okay. So this shepherd gets home and says, 'Rejoice with me, friends. I've found my lost sheep.' Do you know who told that story?"

"I don't know. You should come away from the edge, John."

"Jesus told it," John said, stepping a few feet toward me. "God is the shepherd. Men are the sheep. Most people take that story to mean God loves everyone and wants them all in his flock."

"Do you think different?"

"On nights like this," he said, "I think God loves that one sheep and doesn't give a damn about the ninety-nine."

He turned back to the ledge. This time his toes hung right over. He spoke words into the void.

"Am I that one sheep?" he said. "Pursued by God. Protected. Tell me, Bernie. If I leap, will God catch me?"

"Please don't."

"I've washed sinners clean. I've cast out demons through faith. He rewards me with silence."

"Let's go back. We'll have a long drink of water."

"You think I'll fall?"

"Jesus Christ, John."

"Don't blaspheme."

"Sorry."

John leaned out over the edge. I thought he'd go, but he tilted back at the last moment.

"Do not put the Lord your God to the test," he said, stepping away from the ledge. "Jesus said that, too."

John reached out his hand.

"Help me down from here," he said. "God is busy tonight."

He put his arm around my shoulder—not out of love, but exhaustion. I carried half his weight down that slope. He wasn't much more than bone, and the path was not so hard as I remembered. Soon we reached the rolling tundra, and he let go of my shoulder, slumping back on the dry earth to rest. He breathed fast in the thin air.

"Thank you, Bernie," he said between gasps. "My wife says God sent you and your brother to us. Maybe she's right."

"I don't think so."

"She calls you a wild boy. A motherless child. She wraps her hands around my unborn baby when she speaks of you."

"I'm not a kid anymore."

"True enough. No one who has done the things you've done can be called a child. You have done things. Have you not?"

His eyes were on right side up again. The chocolate was wearing off. I nodded.

"When I saw you on the banks of that river, you looked different. If I saw then what I see now, I would have called you down into the water beside your brother."

John sat up and tried to stand. I reached out to help him, but my hand was black. Covered in blood. We both looked . . . then John caught my stained hand, and I pulled him to his feet.

John was rested and did not need my shoulder. It was a long walk. John told me many things. He talked about his work and the megachurch and all that weighed on him. It was very compelling, but I couldn't stop thinking about that shepherd story. Something was missing. A question appeared in my mind. I needed an answer like I needed water.

"What happens if the sheep doesn't get found?" I asked. "If he doesn't want to get found."

John smiled and looked down at the ground. "It's a short parable, Bernie. Like three verses. There's not a lot of detail."

"Take a guess, Preacher."

"Eventually a wolf will get him."

"And then?"

"What do you mean?"

"What does the shepherd do, when the lost sheep is dead?"

"I expect he finds the wolf, and snares it, and crushes its head with a stone."

We walked a while longer. Then a light grew behind the sparse hill we climbed. I thought perhaps the sun was rising, but it was the wrong horizon. As we crested the rise, I saw the RV down below. The whole thing was lit up by the headlights of another vehicle—a black Dodge Charger parked out on the tundra. Anna stood in the gleam. Her pajamas were lit up white, and her arms were wrapped around her belly. A man stood before her in the headlights. He was tall and wore a black leather jacket. I could hear their voices, though not full words at that distance. Anna pointed in our direction, and the man turned to look. He could not have seen us out in the darkness, but I saw him clear enough.

John squinted. "Who is that guy?" he said, but I never answered him. We never spoke again.

28

I came down the hill at a sprint. Rocks turned under my feet. Too loud of course, though I don't know if the marshal heard. I didn't care. Billy could sleep so hard. I imagined him with his head tipped back in the captain's chair, out like a light right up until the marshal snapped on the cuffs. I had to wake him. It was time to run.

Then Billy's hand reached out from the shadow of a boulder and caught me by the arm. My feet rose off the ground with the force of it, and he swung me around behind him. Then he gripped me by both shoulders and looked into my eyes like he could see my brain in there.

"How high are you right now?" he said.

"Your eyes are on right-side-up. I think it's wearing off."

"And I'm right in thinking there's a US Marshal questioning our missionaries?"

A beam of white light swept across the stony ground. We dropped to our bellies. For a moment we lay in the boulder's black wake. The air itself glowed around us. I did not breathe. When the light passed, Billy rolled over onto his back. I crept out a little from behind the stone and peeked back at the RV. I couldn't make out the Charger or the marshal. Maybe he moved on, I thought, or maybe it was some other cop all along, just telling the missionaries to move their dumpy RV off the delicate alpine tundra. Marijuana can cause paranoia. Maybe this whole thing was just a bad side effect like the lizard eyes.

"I don't . . ." I said, then the spotlight blinked back on, unmoving this time and dead in my face. My eyes burned. The world turned white. Shouts rang in my ears. In the midst of it, I felt Billy's hand clamp down around my wrist. His words were calm and clear.

"Time to run, kid," he said, and we ran.

The ground slid and clattered under my feet. I sank to my shins in loose stones, sprinted blindly. Billy dragged me along by the wrist. I saw nothing for a long time. When my vision returned, it came slowly. Closer objects appeared first. Billy running. That's what I remember. He clutched the .45 in his right hand and my wrist in his left. He moved as a beast moves when pursued—like he was made for it from the beginning. He leaped over stones with a clean sort of efficiency and pulled me behind with brute force.

When my eyes cleared, Billy sensed the change in my stride and loosened his grip. We ran together then. Both our lungs sucking thin air. We ran and slid and clambered down sharp stone ledges. My limbs shook, and still we ran.

There's so little time in these situations, you see. The marshal would call in the local meatheads again. He probably did that already. They'd arrive with choppers this time, and dogs and many men. They'd draw a big circle on their maps and scour every inch of the land inside. There is no hiding from these people. There is only running. You have to get farther than the meatheads think you can. You have to get outside their circle before it's even drawn.

The air thickened with every step. More oxygen. More strength in my legs. Soon we ran among short mountain trees, then taller ones, then the earth below our feet grew soft with moss. Billy's form came to me like a flip-book character between the trunks. He bounded and was gone so fast I thought he'd broken something. Instead, I found him up to his knees in a cold mountain stream, laughing and cupping palmfuls of water up into his mouth. I waded in beside him and we drank. When our guts were full as bowling balls we staggered out and ran on cold feet. We ran, and we did not stop.

Sometimes I think our ancestors take pity on us, let us access again that animal nerve, that state that lets horses run themselves to founder. Break the body to save the life.

In the first light of day, I heard the helicopter. It came from far off but grew louder. We were jogging by then—our throats like bullet wounds sucking wind. The sound drove us on. We stumbled over stones and logs. We covered miles, till the blisters between my toes tore and made my shoes wet with blood—till Billy's breath came in coughing jags. Finally, when we could run no farther, Billy hunkered down below the roots of a great pine tipped over in a storm. He gathered branches and long spears of dry grass. We covered ourselves and slept.

There were a few times the beating of helicopter blades reached my ears, but they never came too close. I never heard dogs or the shouts of a search party. And when the sun sank again and Billy crawled out into the open, there were no sounds at all. We ran too far for the law to follow.

• • •

Clouds rolled in thick and dense that night, and there was almost no light from the stars. We picked our way over uneven ground on limbs shaking from hunger and cold. I stayed close to Billy, strained my eyes to see him in the dark, strained my ears to track the crunch of his steps. We did not talk much, but I asked questions sometimes just to hear his voice and to know what little I saw and heard was not just in my mind. Billy answered with one or two words at a time.

"How much butter do you think Anna put in those potatoes?"

"A lot."

"Do you think they'll make it to Alaska in that shitty old RV?"

"Probably not." He was right, by the way. To my knowledge those missionaries never made it farther north than Colorado.

"What did John say to you when you were baptized?"

"What?"

"He whispered in your ear when he pulled you from the water. What did he say?"

"He said God chooses some people. Malarkey."

There was one question I did not ask. "Where are we?" I already knew the answer. Nowhere. We weren't exactly navigating when we made our run. Even if we had been, the mountains are no kind of forgiving. There are few roads and fewer homes in the backcountry. Hikers die in the Rockies every year. They get lost and eaten by bears and their jackets show up as tattered rags years later—and those people generally have some sort of equipment. Tents and maps and dehydrated food and those special pills you can put in a bottle of swamp water to purify it.

Billy had a .45 and four bullets and some money in his pocket. That's all. We'd slipped the marshal, but at what cost? My feet bled into my shoes. My pants fell away in shreds from the knees down. Billy wasn't much better. I could hear a hitch in his stride. He'd turned an ankle or worse.

How long can a man walk with nothing to carry him? How long can he wander, lost in the mountains, before he's lost for good?

Somewhere in the small hours of the morning, Billy stopped to breathe and lean against a tree. The bark crackled like dry scales as he slid down to the earth.

"How're you doing, kid?"

"I'm okay."

"Me too." But he didn't get up. He coughed into his arm, spit into the pine needles and dry grass. I put my hands under my arms and tried to calm the chatter of my teeth. Billy would worry if he heard it, like I worried at the shallow rattle of his lungs. The run burned everything. It used us up, left us cold and empty. We hunched in the darkness. It seemed stupid to walk with no direction.

Then came a rustling sound out in the trees. Sticks breaking and the clatter of wood on wood. It was not far off. Billy staggered to his feet and sparked a flame from his pocket lighter. His hand curled around the .45, but he thought better of it. Search parties might hear a shot. Instead, he felt around in the underbrush, came up with a baseball-sized stone.

"Stay behind me," he said. His shadow lurched in the flickering light. One hand before him carrying a tiny flame, the other clutching a stone. A caveman.

Fear beat blood back into my hands and feet. Deadened nerves awoke in pain. I imagined grizzlies . . . wolves . . . search parties. The clatter grew loud and crisp, and still Billy crept nearer. I wanted to turn and run. Run till my heart stopped.

Then Billy straightened up. His shoulders relaxed, and he waved me in. The caveman stone fell to the earth.

This was no grizzly rooting for grubs in the wilderness. No bloodhound followed close by deputies and a US Marshal. Billy's lighter reflected in the wild eyes of a mule deer. Its wide antlers tangled in a low-hanging pine bow. It strained and wrenched and blew steam from its nostrils but could not break loose. Billy set the lighter in the crook of a tree and ran his hands down the animal's flank. The sleek hide twitched below his fingers.

"Be still, my friend," he said.

He gripped the antlers in one hand, and in his other, he took the branch and broke it.

"Don't gore me now," he said, and let the deer go. It ran away into darkness. Billy laughed and closed his lighter.

We walked on. In less than a quarter mile, our feet crunched the gravel of a road. That road passed an empty cabin with hot running water for showers and thick wool coats to wear after. In the driveway was an old Buick. It had a full tank and keys under the visor. Do you believe that? It sounds too good to be true, but things had a way of lining up for Billy when he was in need.

29.

We drove north fast. As fast as we could in the old car. An end run. You see, the marshal was close. Not that he hadn't been close before. He had me in his car that one time. That's about as close as you can get, but we were unpredictable then, always bolting in different directions. This time he knew where we were headed. The dead coyotes on the southern border likely caught his eye, and for a while maybe he thought we'd escaped into Mexico. Perhaps he even wasted a few weeks searching the villages of that dusty country, but he was done with that now. He pieced together our northern route. It's no great mystery where that road leads. The Canadian border.

The way I figured it, we had two options. We could hunker down stateside and hope to outlast his curiosity, or we could make one last sprint for the border. The way Billy figured, we had just one option. He got his foot down hard and made that old Buick roar.

He took surface roads and stopped only for gas and cigarettes. He drummed his fingers on the wheel and spoke little. The law was closing in. Billy knew it. I knew it. No point in bringing it up.

We crossed into Wyoming in the midmorning. It was only then I noticed something was wrong with our radio. It came on with the car and picked up a single AM station. It could not be shut off or shifted to other frequencies. The volume too, was stuck in place, so low I could barely make it out. At first I thought it was all static, but words began filtering in as we drove. Regular benign ones at first, then more specific phrases. "Goddamn Muslims," was the first line to really leap from the white noise. By noon we were getting full sentences . . . conservatives discussing the evils of gun control and of the Middle East. The signal was quiet enough to ignore for a while, but every mile made it stronger.

By the time we rolled into Buffalo, we knew the hosts' names and voting records and roughly where their bomb shelters were buried. Billy rubbed his face with his hand and said he needed a drink real bad. We parked on the street and found a bar.

Buffalo is like an old-West cowboy town. They've still got a bunch of the original buildings. The locals probably don't give a shit, but at certain times of the year tourists swarm the place. This was not one of those times. The bar Billy chose was totally empty.

It was one of the old-school-y places, with actual swinging saloon doors. Animal heads and portraits of outlaws lined the walls. The guy behind the counter wore a vest and boots and a big cowboy hat. He even had a good cowboy-looking hitch in his step when he moved around back there.

"Hello, boys," he said, and poured two shots of whiskey before we even sat down. It was barely 3 p.m. He didn't even ask. Billy knocked his back and eased down on a stool.

"Another," he said. The man poured. Now, my brother did not look like a guy hoping for conversation. If he did once, it was when he was young. But we'd been on the run a long time and his face was as hard as the long-dead outlaws glaring down from their sepia-tone portraits. The bartender did not grasp this.

"Welcome to Buffalo," he said. "I'm Flat Foot Chuck. The drink's free if you can guess the origins of my name."

Billy closed his eyes and let out his breath.

"I do not know," he said.

It turned out Flat Foot Chuck wasn't an old cowboy at all, but a former Suzuki salesman from Ohio. He acquired the place two months back with a $300,000 settlement against the driver of a pickup truck kind enough to back over his foot in the parking lot of an Applebee's.

"Right over the thick, bony part," he said. "It was like a flipper for a while. They took bits of skin from all over my body for repairs. It looks quilted now. Grain goes every which way."

He offered to show us his quilted flipper, and then just kept rattling on without circling back.

"So people started calling you Flat Foot?" Billy said.

"I guess I sort of chose it myself—like a nom de plume."

"So, you got the name because you made it up."

"I guess."

"Well, that's a shit story, Chuck. Now what kind of food do you have here?"

"We got some chili on special, but I wouldn't recommend it. It can be volatile. That guy over there ordered a bowl, and he's still in the bathroom. I hate to think what he's doing to my plumbing. They didn't plan for this a hundred years ago. People took delicate shits in those days."

Billy turned his head down the bar. Five stools away was a bowl of chili, a folded newspaper, and a heavy leather jacket draped over the counter.

"Aw, shit," Billy said.

"Speak of the devil," Chuck replied, gripping his stomach. "I think nature's calling me too. Watch the bar a minute, will you?"

Chuck limped off at full speed, his old-style cowboy pants creased between clenched cheeks. He pushed through the door marked "Gentlemen." I turned to go, but Billy did not. He reached over the bar and took down a bottle of expensive whiskey. He filled our glasses and knocked his back.

"Billy?" I said.

He filled his glass again, then pulled the .45 from the back of his pants and laid it down on the counter beside the bottle.

"We have to go," I said. He sipped off the top of his glass and squinted at the bathroom door.

"Do we?"

"Yeah, I think we do."

He finished his glass and set it down.

"How about this, little brother," he said, tucking a cigarette into the corner of his mouth. "If Flipper gets back first, we pay the tab and run." He sucked flame into the tobacco. "But if it's the marshal who walks through that door, I put my last four bullets through his chest. We still run, but it's more leisurely."

"I don't know, Billy."

He pushed my whiskey glass toward me. "Do we have a deal?" he said. I took it and drank.

"Okay," I replied.

Billy picked up the .45 and levered a round into the chamber—a familiar sound I'm sure, for the walls of that saloon. Come to think of it, there were few places better suited for a standoff with the law.

The cigarette burned down to the filter, and Billy left it cooling between his lips. He watched the bathroom door and I watched him. A toilet flushed, muffled by the old walls. Billy's hand tightened on the gun. Then the door swung open, and the gimp cowboy tilted in, laughing.

"Oh, man," he said. "I'm clean as a whistle now."

Billy tucked the gun down his waistband and slapped a fifty on the bar.

"For the whiskey," he said, "and the old man's chili."

• • •

We were out on the street without another word, driving north in a cloud of dust and engine smoke. Billy took a ramp to the freeway and really opened the tap. The car labored up the wide rolling hills outside Buffalo and nearly shook itself to pieces on the slopes.

Billy kept his foot down and said nothing for fifty miles. Profanity broke his silence.

"Damn it to hell," he said. To my eyes, we were alone on that stretch of freeway, but Billy pointed in the rearview mirror.

"Watch," he said, and I watched. As we crested the next hill a black car came up the back side of the last. It was visible for a moment, then gone again as we descended. Billy's eyes stayed on the mirror as we climbed another rise. For a blink at the top, there it was again, far behind. This time I could make it out. A Dodge Charger.

"Damn it," Billy said again.

There were no towns for a great distance on that road. No place to turn. We drove and let the Charger close the gap. Billy wrung his hands on the wheel. He looked in the mirrors. With each hill we caught a glimpse. In each valley we lost it.

The radio developed a new condition about this time. Static shrieked on the downhill runs. And when we climbed, fearful right-wingers called into question the mental health of certain presidential candidates. The station grew louder and louder every mile. The bursts of rage and white noise were deafening.

Somewhere south of the Montana border, Billy smashed the butt of his .45 into the radio dial a bunch of times. Then there was silence, and our situation didn't seem so bad anymore.

Billy took the first exit into Billings at such speed we left black tire streaks on the off-ramp. We lost ourselves in the turns of residential streets. Then Billy hot-wired an old pickup and drove north again. He looked in the rearview. Nothing. He turned on the radio to some thumping, good classic rock. He lit a cigarette and grinned.

"I'm the man," he said. "The marshal can go fuck himself."

The ground opened up and the roads became straight. Distance melted away. We shared a bag of peanuts somebody left in the glove box. Then, a hundred miles north of Billings, we passed a gas station with a black Dodge Charger parked out front. From the highway it looked empty, but I kept my eyes on it in the rearview. When we were good and far away it pulled out behind us.

"Billy," I said, but he saw it, too.

"I should have shot that son of a bitch," he said.

The marshal hung some ways back and didn't seem to be gain-ing. I figured he was waiting for the right moment to force us off the road, or call in some meatheads with barricades and spike strips. Very serious stuff, I know, but the highway rolled on and no spike strips appeared. No barricades or squad cars. Signs popped up—Canadian border eighty miles, sixty miles. Fifty. As the sun sank in the west, a giddy sort of mood descended on us. You can only be on high alert so long.

Billy rolled his window down. The cool air kept us awake. He watched the Charger in the rearview for long stretches at a time.

"Remember that show Carl liked, about Africa?" he said.

"The one with lions or the one where the tribesmen put pointy sticks through their peckers?"

Billy laughed aloud.

"I forgot about the pointy sticks. I'm talking about the bush peo-ple who could chase down antelope on foot."

"Those little dudes just ran and ran for days. Finally, the poor an-telope fell over dead. Its eyes were so big and scared."

"That's the one. I think this guy watched the same show," Billy said, pointing his thumb back at the marshal. I turned around in my seat and looked. The angular headlights barely moved. They did not close the distance or fall back. They just sat there.

"I think we need to take a minute here and acknowledge the balls on this guy," Billy said. "He tracked us a thousand miles in the last two days alone. That's some serious bushman-level endurance right there. Not even explosive diarrhea slowed him down."

"I guess so."

"Plus, he's really old."

"Late fifties."

"That's old, kid."

"Yeah."

"Hold on," Billy said. "We haven't stopped in hours. Imagine his fifty-year-old sphincter right now." He made a fist with his hand. "The will power!"

I laughed so hard I thought I'd pass out.

Another sign grew out of the darkness. Canadian border, ten miles. We quit laughing. Billy scratched his head and glanced in the rearview. We knew what was happening—both realized it at once. The marshal didn't have to call in the locals. There are barricades and spike strips built in on the northern border. Agents guard that line with firearms. He wasn't chasing us to exhaustion. He was just chasing us off a cliff. I think Great Plains tribes used to do that with buffalo. The marshal watched a different documentary, that's all.

I waited for Billy to come up with some sort of a plan. He pretty much always had a plan, and pretty often it was a good one. But soon it was just five miles to the border, and still he said nothing. Four miles. I began to wonder if he was just going to hit the gas at those big steel gates and hope for the best.

Then Billy slid his seat back as far as it would go.

"Get behind the wheel," he said. Suddenly everything moved fast.

He crawled over into the passenger seat, and shouldered out of the wool coat he'd lifted from the cabin—told me to put it on. He pushed a stocking cap down over my weird buzzed head. He pointed at a narrow gravel road and told me to turn. In a minute, the Charger's low beams lit our mirrors again. We rolled on a few miles. Billy tucked the .45 down the back of his pants. He tightened his belt around it and cracked his knuckles. He took deep breaths.

"See this curve up here," he said. "Where the road dips?"

"Yeah."

"I need you to hit the brakes at the very bottom. Hard. Then stomp right back down on the gas."

"What are you going to do, Billy?"

"Never mind," he said. "He's going to pull you over. If he doesn't, drive one mile and stop. One mile and not a yard farther. I'm not as fast as I once was."

"What?"

"Brake hard," he said.

I did. The wheels skid on the gravel as we dropped down the hill. The lights behind us blinked out for just a few moments. Billy popped his door open. The wind tore at his hair and clothes.

"One mile," he said, and jumped. Just like that. Billy never told me the plan. He could have explained it. I'd have felt a lot better about things. No. He just jumped out of the car. But what the hell . . . I did what he said. I floored it. Acceleration slammed his door a second before the marshal's lights came into view.

I squinted at the odometer. One mile. It's not as far as you'd think. I kept waiting for the marshal to race up and pull me over, and he kept not doing it. I drove slower and slower as the mile rolled by. Finally, I just had to stop. The marshal drifted up real slow and parked behind me. Then he turned on his flashers. The weirdest traffic stop in history.

The whole cab flashed red and blue. I closed my eyes and tried to think. Billy never told me his plan, but I had an inkling. There was an old bandana in Billy's coat pocket. It was crunchy with snot from the previous owner, but I pulled it open and tied it around my neck. Then I lit a cigarette. I took a long drag, pulled the bandana up over my nose and mouth and let the smoke filter through the cloth like I was breathing fire.

The Charger's door slammed. I could hear the marshal's boot heels on the gravel. No more time. I thumped my fist three times across my chest, then stepped out of the truck. I spread my shoulders as broad as I could. I slid one hand around my back to where the gun would be if Billy didn't have it. I tried to make myself taller and to focus my eyes in the flashing lights.

"Thanks for the chili, Mr. Quinn," the marshal said. "That was some powerful stuff."

He was a silhouette edged in blue, then red, then blue. He looked big in the leather jacket. His posture told me he had his gun level.

"Maybe I'll buy you a bowl on our way back to Minnesota. It's only fair. Now take out that gun real slow."

I really hadn't thought this far ahead. I left my hand where it was.

"Not that slow."

I didn't move. Didn't speak.

"You don't have it, do you?"

I let both hands fall down at my sides.

"Aw, shit," he said. And with that, Billy appeared out of the night at a dead run. He brought his pistol down on the back of the marshal's head with the full force of his sprinting bulk. The marshal was on the ground so fast I didn't even see him fall. He twitched and groaned. Billy whooped—danced a little jig in the flashing lights.

"Look out," I said.

The marshal had found his gun and was attempting to point it at Billy, or me, or maybe the North Star. Hard to tell. We ducked for cover, and he fired off a bunch of rounds in random directions. A concussion usually makes aiming difficult. Billy waited for a break in the shooting, took a little run up, and soccer-kicked the gun from the marshal's slow hands. It arched off into the ditch. Then Billy kicked the old marshal in the ribs a few more times.

"Take that, you son of a bitch," he said. "And that."

The marshal held his guts. Billy leaned against the car and panted.

The old man made crawling motions with his legs, but didn't go anywhere. It looked like he was on a really slow treadmill. We watched him for a while as Billy got his breath.

"Good thinking with the bandana, kid," Billy said. "And you look good in that coat. Better than I do."

I'd forgotten about the bandana. I tugged it down and smiled.

"You're still fast."

Billy laughed and wiped sweat from his forehead with the back of his hand.

"Did a 4:30 mile in high school," he said. "What was that just now. Six?"

"You didn't have to jump out of a car first in high school."

"True enough!" Billy laughed and nudged the marshal with the toe of his boot. "Did you hear that asshole? I still got it."

The old man made a gurgling sound in his throat.

"You think he called for backup?"

Billy coughed and spit. "Let's ask," he said.

He rolled the marshal over and sat down on his chest. He back-handed him across the face.

"Hey!" he said. "Did you call in the locals?"

The marshal blinked and struggled, but Billy drew the .45 and put the barrel straight down on his concussed head.

"Always call for backup," the marshal said. His words were all slurred and fucked-up.

"Bullshit. They'd be here already. You're all alone, old man."

The marshal sighed and nodded. He didn't have much fight left in him.

"I've called the meatheads too many times, and you keep getting away," he said. "They don't listen anymore. My boss won't listen. My ex-wife won't listen. Nobody cares what I think."

"And you're still chasing us."

"Technically, I'm on vacation."

Billy laughed aloud. He climbed off the marshal and dragged him upright against the side of the truck. He put a cigarette in the old man's mouth and lit it. Then he yanked the leather jacket off the marshal one arm at a time and shouldered into it himself.

"Well, don't I feel special," Billy said. "Kid, this guy wants to vacation with us."

"Wow," I said. "That's real special."

"We should have a spa day together. We could get a couple's massage."

"You don't have to be mean about it," the marshal said. He puffed on the cigarette and touched the side of his head with his fingertips. He winced, but spoke clearer. "Jesus," he said. "You punch like a freight train."

"I used the pistol. It's heavier than my fist."

"That explains it. Why do my ribs hurt?"

"Kicked you a few times. You tried to shoot me."

"I don't remember any of that. Goddamn it. You gave me brain damage. I'm going to be one of those old people who can't tie his own shoes."

We let him finish his cigarette, then Billy and I hauled the marshal back over to his car and propped him behind the wheel. He turned off the flashers and rubbed his face with his hands.

"What's your play here, kids?"

Billy got in the back and put his .45 through the steel grate so the barrel rested against the base of the marshal's neck.

"You're going to drive north, old man," he said. "And if you make one move I don't like, I'm going to squeeze this trigger. Hell, if you hit a big enough pothole I might pull on accident, but that's a risk we're both gonna have to take."

The marshal nodded. He didn't look so good. His skin was pale.

"Kid, ride shotgun. And grab the wheel if he passes out."

"Or if your brother blows my head off."

• • •

The marshal turned his car around and took us back to the highway. He went north. It seemed longer than it really was. Long and dark and silent. I couldn't see Billy's face in the back seat, just the barrel of his gun.

The marshal cleared his throat and glanced over at me. "Cost me $300 to replace the back window," he said. "How's your hand?"

"Stop talking."

"A swing like that would shatter every bone in my wrist. Jim, I don't see a cast."

"Shut up."

"Maybe you've got the same problem your brother's got," he said. "You know, up here." He tapped his forehead.

"Shut the fuck up," I said. "And don't offer me any more of your stupid deals."

"There are no deals left for you. Not since Laredo."

Then Billy's voice came from the back seat. "It's time," he said.

Before us the road siphoned off through great steel gates with concrete buildings on either side. It was the only structure for miles, and brightly lit. I tugged the bandana from around my neck and jammed it into my pocket. Billy pulled his gun back through the grate. The three of us squinted in the bright flood lights.

The marshal slowed and stopped beside a small window. Behind thick plexiglass a man in uniform rubbed his bald head and put down a magazine.

"Roll down your window," he said through a crackling loudspeaker.

"Think very carefully," Billy said. "You want us caught. I know it. My brother told me how it is with you. But would you die to make it so? Decide now, old man."

The marshal sat for a moment. I watched his face but read nothing on it. He rolled down the window.

"Hello, sir," he said.

"Passports," the speaker crackled. Instead the marshal held his badge out against the plexiglass window so the little bald man inside could see every detail.

"US Marshal," he said. "Returning two fugitives to your wonderful country."

"You've got one riding shotgun."

"He gets carsick. He already barfed like three times back there."

The man nodded and waved us through. That's all. We pulled back out on the northbound highway. No one followed. My heart rate settled.

Canada. It was my first time in that country. You'd think I'd have been there at some point, living all my life in northern Minnesota, but we didn't travel much before the outlawing. I squinted out the window at the desolate land. I'd expected some shift in the landscape. Something exotic to mark the new territory. It looked the same. A disappointment.

"What now?" the marshal said.

"Drive until I tell you to stop," Billy replied.

• • •

Billy gave the order outside a small town maybe fifteen miles north of the border. He forced the marshal out of the car and down the ditch to a picnic area on the side of the road. It was empty and cold that night. The grass crunched with frost. The marshal walked slow and without fear. Lazy even.

"Keep moving," Billy said.

"Let an old man rest."

Billy shoved the gun in his back, then suddenly the old man moved with unnatural speed. He stepped aside and caught the pistol in his hands. He ripped it loose. But before he could raise it, Billy sent his fist into the marshal's already damaged head. The gun clattered to the ground. The marshal covered his face with his hands.

"Goddamn," he said. "You're giving me Alzheimer's."

"You won't leave us alone," Billy said. "Shit. What am I supposed to do?"

"You could turn yourself in."

"Go to hell."

The marshal straightened up. He looked much older than he probably was. His hair was thin enough for the scalp to reflect silver in the moonlight. Deep lines crossed his face. He spit blood onto the frosted grass.

"I have just one question," Billy said.

"You want to know why," the marshal replied. His eyes were bright all of a sudden. "Why you, and not one of the hundreds of fugitives I could be chasing? Well, Billy Quinn, you bother me. Consequences don't stick to you. You steal and fuck and smoke like a chimney, and look at you. You look like a goddamn male model. You are an abomination, and if fate will not punish you, I will."

"That's not the question."

"Well shit, you could have stopped me before the big speech."

"Seemed like you were on a roll. Did you write all that down first?"

"You don't have to mock it."

"No, really. The 'abomination' thing sounded super cool."

"Enough. What's your question?"

"My jacket. Why did you take it?"

The old man laughed.

"To scare the hell out of you," he said. "That's what I told myself, but I guess I should be honest, considering my situation. I always wanted a leather jacket like that, but I never had the stones to buy one. Didn't know if I could pull it off."

Billy nodded and thought. Then he picked up his gun from the grass and pointed it at the marshal.

"Get on your knees," he said. The marshal sank down. I could hear his joints pop. He was so old. Billy circled around behind him and put the .45 to his head. "Well," he said. "Should I kill you?"

"That's up to you, Billy."

"Will you come after me if I don't?"

"You know I will."

Billy held the gun to the old man's skull. He held it there a long time. Then he backed off and paced around awhile.

"Fuck," he said. "Just say you'll let us go. Lie to me if you have to."

"It's not in my nature."

The marshal was surprisingly calm. Billy grit his teeth. He slammed the gun into his chest and yelled. His knuckles turned white around the grips. He forced the barrel into the marshal's temple. He held it there long enough it left a red mark when he pulled it away.

"Fuck," Billy said again, and wiped his sweaty face on his sleeve. He paced. He rifled through his pockets looking for cigarettes, but found none.

"Give me the gun, Billy." The words were so quiet I didn't realize I'd said them until he turned to me.

"Let me do it," I said. "I can. You know I can."

Billy thought. He looked at the gun in his hand. Then he snapped the safety on and tucked it back down his pants.

"No, kid," he said. "No more of that."

The leather jacket looked all wrong on him suddenly. Way too big. The shoulders hung loose and collapsed, like a kid playing dress-up in his dad's clothes. Like I would look if I tried to wear it. He took it off and draped it around the marshal.

"It's a cold night," Billy said. "And anyway, I want to see you coming."

SHITHOLE ALASKA

30.

Not too far north of the border the water rose in my ears and I took my leave a while. A long while, it seemed. The road comes back in flickers. Billy shaking hands with a bearded farmer, a stack of American twenties for a red 1970s Chevy pickup. A Canadian waitress on Billy's lap with one bra strap flipped down over her shoulder and the morning sun lighting the peach fuzz on her smooth arms. A fourth of something dark emptied in a low-ceilinged motel. I blinked between and finally opened my eyes in a grainy half-lit place called Winner.

There was a sign. Sign said, "Winner, Population . . ." and the rest was blasted away with bullet holes. If you've been in rural southern states you think you know what I'm talking about—a big crater-y dent. Missing paint. You're thinking shotgun blast. Rednecks get drunk and drive around with pump-action Winchesters. This was different. Near as I could tell the sign was carved up by .30-06 rounds. Heavy-caliber rifle, one bullet at a time. Half the sign was chewed off. That's persistence.

Billy leaned over the wheel, straining his eyes in the dim headlights.

"Winner . . ." he said, and just trailed off.

The town was in the depressed middle of Alaska. An hour or two north of Fairbanks. No oil. No fishing boats. No curbs or sidewalks. Probably no zoning commission. The houses were built low and far apart. Stacks of firewood and piles of trash filled the empty space. Snow on trash and trash on snow. Shoveled paths to the firewood.

Billy pulled over. He got out and walked into the headlights, snapping a pack of cigarettes into his palm. It was full-on winter. Hadn't been when the water filled my ears back in Canada. I wondered how long ago.

Billy pointed off to the east. The sky was starting to turn colors like a bruise.

"See over there?" he said. "Sun won't break that horizon till almost noon. Won't stay up past four."

He coughed smoke and steam. I hunched in my coat. The Chevy rumbled.

"Let's hole-up awhile," he said.

I'm still not sure of Billy's reasoning on this one. Hell—I'm not sure how he crossed the Alaskan border. There are ways, I suppose, but it probably would have been a really good idea to stay in Canada. Billy's grinning mug got a lot less airtime in that country, and the marshal didn't have jurisdiction. Barring that, we could have pushed through to the coast. Jobs live on the edges of Alaska. But there we were in Winner. I got out of the truck, and Billy passed me his cigarette. I smoked it.

"Winner it is," I said.

I already mentioned the trash, but it really bears talking about. I had to wonder if there were garbagemen in Winner, or even a dump where industrious truck owners could take their own shit. My guess was no.

Billy drove around real slow, just looking at all the shit. He pointed out the most egregious examples. One house had little black patches all over the snow, where the owner had burned each individual bag of trash. Another homeowner just lined up beater cars in his front yard and filled them with trash. There was a Care Bear pressed up against one window, pinned with trash.

Billy wedged his knee against the wheel and pointed his lit cigarette past me.

This place had a big old pile of trash bags layered with snow. On top of the pile was a huge Ford truck. The thing had big tires and red shock absorbers, like the monster trucks you see on TV. It had those smokestacks that go up the back of the cab instead of out the rear end.

The truck was parked at a steep angle, cresting the trash hill. It was taller than the house behind it.

A lot of people have strange priorities in rural areas. Great trucks and terrible houses. It's confusing to people from suburbs. Vehicles depreciate, says the corporate middle manager. Houses do not. Yes indeed, but the wilderness draws a special sort, people just a generation or two removed from nomadic roots. They don't care about a house, or some shit in the yard. But a truck . . . trucks are the new horses. Nomads take great pride in their horses.

Anyway, Billy wasn't pointing at the truck, or even the trash hill. He was pointing to a scribbled cardboard sign out front: "Room for Rent."

"We have a winner," Billy said, then chuckled at his own joke.

• • •

We were greeted at the door by a grinning mullet also smoking a cigarette. The burning tobacco lit hefty features with each puff. This guy was strapping. We're talking knife-fight-a-bear strapping. Think Daniel Boone . . . if Boone wore acid-washed Wranglers and drove a monster truck.

"Afternoon," he said around the cigarette. It was some time in the morning but we didn't correct him.

"The sign says you've got a room," Billy said.

"Come in. Have a beer." The mullet turned and sloped back into the house. He had a primal way about him. Small, round eyes. Pale and sharp. He moved slow, loose-limbed, but not from laziness. If I had to guess, he was just saving his great strength for a specific task in the near future. Some swift, violent action. He scratched his lower back and thumped down in a frayed La-Z-Boy.

"Rest your bones," he said, nodding at an old tweed couch.

The place was littered with full ashtrays. Stuffed animal heads lined the walls. He even had a neon Budweiser sign propped in one corner, but it wasn't working. It was an average, grimy bachelor pad, but if you looked real close, there was evidence of a woman. Very little indoor trash for one thing, and somebody hung curtains. Golden brown cakes of fry bread cooled on the kitchen table. They leached rings of grease into layers of newspaper. Yes. There was definitely a woman around.

"Few souls visit Winner this time of year," said the mullet. "Fewer still come looking for a place to lay their head more than twenty-four hours."

Billy kicked his legs out on an old wood crate the mullet used as a coffee table, matching the mullet's level of relaxed. "Seems like a nice enough place," he said. Near his feet, a Barbie doll lay tangled up in stiff clothing. A child, too, was in this house.

"It's a shithole," the mullet said. "And it's dark all the time. These are truths you will come to shortly, if you have not already."

Then he shot forward and snapped his palms down on the crate so hard Billy's heels bounced and the Barbie leapt like a living thing. "Goddamn, woman!" he shouted. "We have guests. Bring out some beers."

The mullet leaned back in his chair and listened. No movement. He got up and sauntered off to the kitchen, shaking his head. "She sleeps through the dark months," he said. "Useless."

I didn't want a beer. What I wanted was some of that fry bread. It smelled great, even with all the cigarette smoke. I thought of asking, but I didn't do it. The mullet returned, juggling three cans of Budweiser as he walked. His big hands were faster than you'd think. I bet he could have kept five or six cans up at once, like a circus clown. He tossed two beers in our direction and caught the third behind his back.

Billy snapped his can out of the air without even looking, but mine rolled on the floor and I had to run for it. The mullet cracked a beer and Billy cracked his. I opened mine to a geyser of suds. It went everywhere, but the mullet just laughed and told me not to worry about the mess.

Billy took a long drink off the top.

"Damn," he said. "It has been too long."

"Always has," the mullet replied. Billy took another long drink and leaned back, getting into the correct mindset for macho talk. They exchanged some discussion on the stuffed elk heads lining the walls and one massive grizzly mount with a deeply sad look on its face.

"I shot this brute right in the vitals man, but damn if he didn't make me track him up half the mountain."

The mullet dove right into a long hunting narrative, eventually ending with the skin and head of the mournful grizzly submerged in a bathtub of borax and alcohol. He was somewhere in the middle of this story when a small girl appeared in a doorway behind him. She was about three feet tall with dark hair and a smooth face. Her eyes glowed in the dim house, and her feet made no sound on the floor. She glared at Billy and me.

"It's harder than you think to tan a bear skin," the mullet said. "A lot of the hair falls out and clogs the shit out of your drain."

Billy nodded and stubbed out his cigarette. As the mullet talked, Billy reached around in his pocket and came out with a match. The old kind with the tip you can strike anywhere. He held it down low, at the girl's eye level, and flicked it lit with his thumbnail. One hand . . . no easy thing. The girl shrank away into the darkened house till only her eyes were visible. Two floating pinpoints of light, like a fox in the woods.

The mullet talked. Billy listened and nodded and worked the match up between thumb and forefinger as it burned. At the last moment, when all that remained was curled ash and a tiny stub of wood, Billy flipped it around and closed it in his fist. The girl's eyes started at the quick motion. He clenched his fist till the knuckles turned white, then opened it real slow. Inside was a fresh new match and not even a smudge of ash. The girl could not resist. She drifted over on her toes. Careful, but curious. She drifted slower and slower the closer she got . . . like a snare trap might close any second. Finally, her tiny hand darted out and took the match from my brother's palm. She flashed a grin of baby teeth and ran off.

"You have a beautiful daughter," Billy said.

"That's not mine. Jesus, do I look like an Indian?"

"What now?"

"Oh, shit. You're not supposed to say that anymore. They've got a word they like better." He snapped his fingers and made a face. "Nope. Any attempt would be an embarrassment. Indian. You know what I mean."

"And you're a white guy."

"White as fuck. I just let her mother live here—we've got an arrangement, if you see what I'm getting at."

"I see."

"I highly recommend getting a similar arrangement," he said. "Gets you through this endless darkness."

"I'll keep that in mind."

As he spoke, the little girl rode back into view in the arms of a larger version of herself. A teenager, if I had to guess, with the same smooth, observing face and drifting feet. For a moment I thought she was an older sister, but the way she held the little one . . . she was a mother, just north of childhood herself.

"Hey Laina, what's that word you use for your people now?"

"Athabascan," she said, real quiet.

"Holy shit," the mullet replied. "It changes all the time."

"Not since the ice age," she said, and winked so quick I'm still not sure if I imagined it—if I saw what I wanted on her pretty, impassive face. She hefted the small girl to her hip and drifted off to the kitchen.

"Look for a skinny one though," he said. "Most of them aren't like Laina here. Whales, man. Just a warning."

Billy looked straight across at him in a way most people can't do. Most people want to fill silence, and they'll say stupid, meaningless shit to do it. Billy was good at silence.

"Do you want to see the room?" the mullet said. "It's small for two, but you could make it work if you like each other."

"We're not that close," Billy said, and left his beer half drunk on the coffee table. As we walked out, Laina looked up from the kitchen sink, her arms up to the elbows in suds.

"Go see the widow Krone," she said. "Edith Krone. She takes people in sometimes."

"Thanks," Billy said. "I owe you one."

"And have some bannock for the road," she said. "I guess you'd call it fry bread, where you're from. The elders call it bannock, and I call it frog bellies, but it doesn't matter. Take some."

Billy didn't, but I sure did, and it was good.

• • •

The widow Krone lived on the ragged edge of town. Her house seemed too big for the survivalist moonscape of Winner. Behind it were trees, and beyond those a whole lot of cold acres and grizzlies and slumbering trolls probably all the way up to salt water.

There was no "For Rent" sign out front of this place, just a sagging porch covered in snow.

Billy knocked, and straightened his hair. He brushed the cigarette ash from the front of his coat. Then he snatched the stocking cap from my head and ruffled up the half inch of matted stubble. He stepped back and looked.

"Nope," he said. "Bad idea." He pushed the stocking cap back on just as far as it would go without covering my eyes.

"Don't take that off," he said.

"What if she asks? Old people have a thing about wearing hats inside."

"Well, then you've got to take it off, but only if she asks. Like explicitly asks."

Locks thudded open one by one. Hinges creaked, and the face of old Edith Krone appeared in a narrow gap. Startling is the word. Her face was startling. Edith had one cataract eye, which looked like a white marble, and one good eye, which looked like a black marble. At least I think that was her good eye. You can never be sure.

"Hello, ma'am," Billy said. "I'm Eric. This is my brother Forrest. We're . . ."

"Mormons?" she said. "If you're Mormons there's no point in you being here. My mind's made up."

"We're not Mormons."

"Jehovah's Witnesses?"

"No. Do you get a lot of them up here?"

"What do you want from me?"

"Just a room," Billy said.

Edith glared with what was probably her good eye. "You smell like smoke," she said. "If you smoke we need not continue this conversation."

"No ma'am—we just came from a place down the street."

"Lester's?"

"The man I talked to had a mullet and a lot of stuffed animals. I didn't catch the name."

"That's Lester. What was your opinion of him?"

Billy scratched the side of his face. "I hate to judge a man I don't know," he said.

"Your first impression."

"He and I won't be friends."

Edith smiled wide and swung the door all the way open.

"Come in," she said.

We rented the widow's attic for $150 a week, along with another $50 for dinner each night. She shook Billy's hand and then mine, and I

felt the strength in her knuckly old fingers. It takes a strong woman to
live alone so long in a dark, empty place like Winner. A strong woman
with strong morals and a very strong grip—both on reality and on the
hands of strangers.

Her knees were not so strong as her grip. She insisted on showing
us our new living situation in person, but navigating the stairs was
a whole big process. Her joints made as much noise as the creaking
boards underfoot. Billy and I just followed and tried not to rush her.
Halfway up she stopped to breathe and to talk.

"Does he still have that Indian girl living with him?"

"Who?"

"Lester. Does he have a girl with him?"

"Laina," Billy said. "She sent us over here."

Edith nodded and started back up the stairs.

"And the little one, how did she look?"

"Smart and quick on her feet."

"And well fed?"

"I think so. Hard to tell."

Edith made the last step and hunched over to rest. The smell of
old things was strong up there. The widow's main floor was tidy as
an Amish home. Her attic, on the other hand, looked like an antique
shop. A really badly managed one. An out-of-business antique shop is
what it looked like. One entire end was a jumble of old furniture, old
dust, and a lot of other old shit. Just from one angle I could make out
a buffalo hide, the front end of a motorcycle, and a very lifelike cat
carved out of a red stone. All of it lumped up together in shapes that
could have been absolutely anything when the lights clicked off.

"This looks real nice," Billy said.

Edith managed to straighten up.

"You can stop sucking up," she said. "My late husband, Earl, was
a great man, but he sure collected a lot of useless trash. The crafty old

Jew waited to die till I was too weak and old to drag his crap to the dump. The beds are over there."

She pointed to a tall mound of things that appeared to be supported by bunk beds. Then she turned and started down the creaking steps, just as slow as she had climbed them.

"Did you say how Laina looked?" she said, about three stairs down.

"She looked okay, I guess," Billy replied.

"What about this one?" she said, pointing at me. "Do you speak? How did you gauge her situation?"

"Her face don't give much away, Miss Krone, but I guess maybe she's not so happy over there."

Edith shook her old white head and started down the stairs alone. "I tell her to bring her daughter here, and live with me. I have a room saved for the both of them, but an old lady doesn't have what she needs."

And with that she crept back to the level floor of her own domain—a place where her knees worked and the doilies were tidy and clean.

"She has other rooms," Billy said, looking at dead Earl's pile of crap. "We should have asked. Shit."

Out among the pile, that red stone cat caught his attention. He went over to it and felt the curve of its back with his hand. "Oh no," he said. Its whole head was a lid . . . the body a stone urn. "There are ashes in here."

31.

Winner was a terrible little shit town. Lester the bear killer warned us about that, but it didn't really sink in till the next day, when Billy and I went job hunting. That's what you do when you hunker down in a little shit town. You get a little shit job.

I'd guess a few hundred people lived in Winner, though I'll never know for sure because the population signs on both ends of town were shot full of bullet holes. I'll never know the speed limit either, or any of the road names, because all those signs were shot up, too. Billy drove slow and looked out the windows at all the shot-up signs. We kept expecting to find the nice part of town, a main drag lined with businesses and intact signage. But there wasn't a nice area, because Winner was a terrible little shit town.

The longer it took to find Winner's economic hub, the fewer words Billy spoke. We passed a log cabin with a single unsheltered gas pump out front and cigarettes advertised in the windows. Yellow housepaint made the words "Don's Food N Fuel" right on the logs. The logs were all ripped up with bullet holes, but you could still read it.

Billy drove past, and a hundred yards later the town just petered out. No more buildings. Just trees. Slowly, a truth became apparent— one Edith could have shared in about five words but didn't for some reason. Winner had no economic hub. The jobs were in Fairbanks, miles to the south. Fairbanks had a military base and a university. The villages around it had grocery stores and gift shops, ski rentals and guide services. Winner had nothing of the kind. It was just a bit too far for the tourism dollars to travel.

Billy rubbed his face with his hands.

"Alright," he said, and turned the truck around.

He parked at Don's Food N Fuel and got out, left the engine running. I stayed in the truck until he came around my side and opened the door.

"Edith told me to stay out here," I said.

"If I have to come to grips with the depths to which I've fallen," he said, "so do you."

• • •

You should probably know a couple things, on background. On our first morning with the widow Krone, Billy let it slip that we'd be looking for work. She asked if he was planning to wear what he had on, and Billy said yeah, he was. Then she made him wear some of her dead husband's clothes. Earl wore a lot of polyester leisure suits. The one Edith picked out was orange.

I was supposed to stay in the truck because dead Earl's clothes didn't fit me, and because Edith thought my head might scare people. But she wasn't along, so Billy and I went in together. I didn't really mind. He had to wear a stupid orange suit, and I had to wear my stupid head. We were finally equal.

• • •

Don's smelled of cigarettes and deer tallow. Card tables and folding chairs lined one wall. Pallets of groceries and beer took up the rest. Flour, Campbell's soup, and Budweiser. All the basics. Behind the counter, a wiry, middle-aged Alaska Native read a paperback. He glanced up when we came through the door, then returned to his book. Billy took a little walk around the place. He looked at everything. He read the prices. It took less than one minute. Then he went back up to the counter and took a deep breath.

"Are you looking for help, Don?" Billy said.

Don shrugged. "You looking to be help?"

Billy squinted. He rubbed his face with his hand. "Screw it," he said. "Just give me a carton of smokes and whatever the kid wants."

Don set his paperback face down to keep his page. On the cover was the silhouette of a big-breasted woman in a window, fixing her hair. I could see her nipples and everything. They drew the eye. "Sinner's League," scrolled across the top in big neon letters. I wondered what sort of book deserved a cover like that. Sex on every page probably. The only books I ever got in school were fat hardcovers about history or hastily published pamphlets about the bad effects of bullying. I ignored both, but silhouette nipples would have got my attention.

"It's a mystery," Don said.

"What?"

"That cover is deceiving," he said. "The sex is occasional at best."

"Okay."

"Not that I give a shit what you think of my reading material. Now what do you want?"

I grabbed a handful of beef jerky sticks from a barrel on the counter and handed them over.

"Good choice," Don said. "And hey, dude. Nice suit."

Billy gave him the finger and Don gave it right back. They both smiled.

• • •

Back in our parked truck, Billy revved the engine to get some heat going. I peeled the jerky and he peeled cellophane from the cigarettes. He smoked. I ate. We did not talk for a while. When his cigarette was just ash and settling smoke, he lit another off the smoldering filter and passed it to me.

"Trade?" he said. I took the cigarette, gave him a jerky stick, and again we did not speak awhile. When he was done, Billy balled up the jerky wrapper and cleared his throat.

"This town is a shithole," he said.

"Lester told us that."

"Yes, he did."

"We could leave."

I passed the cigarette back to Billy. He returned it to the corner of his mouth and pulled smoke into his lungs, then blew it out his nostrils in two narrow streams. Far from us, over the trees, a sliver of sun broke the horizon. Those cold first rays lit Billy's smoke and closed our eyes with brightness.

"A shithole is a good place to hide, kid," Billy said. "Most are hesitant to come looking."

I nodded and squinted into the rising noon sun. "I was hoping it wouldn't come to this."

"Me too, kid," he said. "Me too, but at least I've got these fine-ass dancing pants."

• • •

There's one more thing you need to know here. Winner had an annual dance called the Things Were Better Then Senior Swing. Years back, some well-meaning community-minded individual organized the event primarily to get old white people like Edith out of the house. See, Winner was about half Alaska Native and half white. There were plenty of native kids running around, but no jobs meant no new white people. So Winner's aging white population was left alone in low-ceilinged homes to spoon up oatmeal through the long dark winters. Bleak as hell, I'm telling you.

Anyway, the Things Were Better Then Senior Swing was sort of a big deal in Winner. Edith told Billy to come by if we happened to strike out on the job hunt. She said Winner's two or three biggest employers would be there. They'd be happy to hire such an upright and well-dressed individual as my brother.

So, we killed a bunch of time smoking cigarettes and eating beef jerky, and then we went over to the Winner Lutheran church, bingo hall, and community center to schmooze some old people. Most towns would have three separate buildings – one for each organization. Winner had just this one steel pole barn with plastic sheeting stapled over the windows and three different signs on posts out front.

There was a big old hole in the sheet metal right by the door. A ragged strip of pink fiberglass insulation fluttered from it, like a hand reaching out, waving at us. We both stood in the parking lot, watching the insulation move in the wind.

"That's the saddest thing I've ever seen," Billy said. "Wait . . . Nope. I was thinking about John's RV. But no. This place is sadder."

"I don't want to go in there, Billy."

"Listen, can you hear the polka?"

"Aw man. I don't like polka."

"There comes a point in every man's life when a terrible thing is required of him. Sometimes, kid, that involves polka."

We followed the music to a basement room full of old people. It played over a modified guitar amp and tape deck system. Oldsters shuffled slowly under a ceiling of fluorescent lights. Out in the middle of the dance floor, Edith stepped with the spryest of the old guys. He was short and narrow in the waist. He looked hopeful about his prospects, but when Edith saw Billy, she left her partner gawking mid-song and caught us on the stairs.

"Don turned you down?" she said, a smile creasing her old face.

"It wasn't a good fit."

"So, you just gave up and smoked cigarettes the rest of the day."

"I cannot tell a lie."

Edith scowled and grabbed Billy by the elbow. "I have someone you should meet," she said, and dragged him away. On a flat surface, that woman was quick. Too quick for me to follow, and in a moment I was adrift in a crowd of crusty dancing Alaskans.

In all fairness, they probably weren't actually that old. Sixties maybe? But Winner was hard on people. They shuffled around in little circles. Men held women in fingers thick as bratwurst—faces red with cold ruptured capillaries and alcoholism. The women stood straighter, as if braced for disappointment. They shuffled in close on me, eyeing me from under hooded lids. Closer and closer, till every way I turned was a stiff elbow or steely gaze.

My heart thumped in my ears and my hands cramped into damp-palm fists. The tendons rose in cables and valleys. The knuckles turned white. I looked for Billy, but all I saw was a lot of suspicious old people. I closed my eyes and tried to settle my breathing. I told myself old people are nothing to be feared. But it was no use. They are formidable in large numbers.

Then a hand touched my shoulder, and I opened my eyes. It was Laina—the fry-bread girl. Her daughter trailed at her heels.

"You're lost," she said.

"I am."

"Well, I guess I found you. You can come with me if you want."

She drifted off across the dance floor to some folding chairs in a quiet corner. The child ate from a baggie of Cheerios, and Laina ran her fingers through the little one's hair.

"Why are you here?" she asked.

"My brother brought me."

"And you lost him."

"Yeah."

"Lester drags me to these things. He hates the music, but hanging out with old people makes him feel strong. He likes feeling strong."

"You lost him too?"

"He's probably burning one in the parking lot."

The child finished her Cheerios and dug in Laina's purse without permission. She found a granola bar and bit the wrapper like a clever raccoon. She sat down on the floor and ate. Laina watched her. When it was clear the child didn't plan on swallowing the wrapper, she turned her gaze on me.

"I hate this place," she said. Her voice didn't seem right, too happy for the words themselves.

"You should leave it then."

"My people are no good at leaving," she said. "Sometimes one tries, but they always come back and soon we forget they left at all."

Laina was a pretty girl. She had sleek hair and good cheekbones. I'm not sure how old. Seventeen at the time, maybe a year give or take. When she smiled it was something, but her eyes were like black holes. They were the saddest eyes I ever saw. Goddamn. They were sadder than Winner's Lutheran church and pole barn bingo palace. I wanted to say something to make whatever bad thing she carried a little lighter, but I didn't know where to start. Her sadness was this great big confusing thing. Maybe it was Lester making her sad. He was an asshole. It made sense she'd be sad living with him. Maybe a family member just kicked off. Maybe the child had leukemia and only Laina knew about it. I'm no good at reading these situations.

"I'm afraid of old people," I said. "I didn't know until today."

She laughed and I laughed, and that did sort of improve things. A happy groove replaced the weird old polka music. Beach Boys, I think. The oldsters kicked up their heels—lost a decade or two in the rhythm. Edith's abandoned partner danced past alone, pulling a fairly good moonwalk.

"Young people!" he said. "Dance! Dance before the song of life passes you by."

He snapped his old fingers down at his sides with the beat of the music. He moved his old hips. He stole an old lady from another old man and they danced like crazy.

Then Laina and I were out on the dance floor. She swayed. I reached out for her, and found my hands capable. We whirled and stepped, and the happy child darted around our awkward feet. Why not, after all? It was just a lot of old people. Not such a scary thing.

Laina swept up the child and put the little thing on my shoulders. Small legs hung on either side of my neck, and tiny warm fingers laced across my forehead.

"I'm not so good with little children," I said, but Laina just laughed and kept dancing. Her eyes weren't so sad anymore, and a little slip of her long black hair was caught up in the corner of her mouth. I remember that.

How quick a day can turn around. One minute you're in a shithole town surrounded by creepy old people. The next, there's a little girl on your shoulders. She's laughing—way too happy to have leukemia—and her mother's holding your hands in hers. A hell of a thing for a guy like me.

We danced through a few songs, and Laina didn't get bored with me. I was starting to wonder what would happen when a slow number came on. Something romantic. Maybe she'd let me put my arms around her. Then Billy caught my eye from the corner of the room. He grinned wide and beckoned me over. I looked at Laina. She was happy right then. She didn't see Billy. Her hair was still in the corner of her mouth.

"Hey," I said.

"Hey yourself."

"I think I have to go."

Her eyes were sad again in no time at all. It was like flipping a light switch. She took the child from my shoulders and turned away.

"My brother," I said, but she was already walking. I should have just ignored Billy. Maybe she would have slow danced with me. But ignoring Billy is not in my nature. Besides, he had a dangerous sort of look to him—the look he got before something exciting happened. I didn't want to miss it.

Billy punched me in the arm.

"Want to see something cool?" he said.

"Yeah." Of course I did. I always wanted to see cool stuff. Billy couldn't keep the smile off his face. He took off his leisure suit jacket as we jogged up the back stairs.

"Hold that for me," he said. "I don't want to get blood on it."

"Blood?"

Billy pushed through the back door and out onto a gravel parking lot, layered with ice. "Not mine," he said. "Come on kid. Have some faith."

Drifts of fresh powder slithered over the earth, alive in the wind, yellow with the outdoor lights. Hunched in a heavy Carhartt was a strapping big guy—and hell, it was Lester the bear killer. Small towns, right? When he saw Billy, he dropped his cigarette and turned around like he knew what was up. Even I didn't know what was up, but somehow Lester read it all over Billy. Right away he shrugged out of his coat and let it fall behind him.

"Lester," Billy said. "Boss man caught you skimming."

"I know."

"He sent me out here to fire you. Nothing personal."

"He's a coward and you're a fool." Lester rolled his sleeves up over his meaty forearms. I still wasn't exactly sure on the details, but one thing was clear. My brother was about to fight. No wonder he was grinning. I was grinning, too. It had been a long time since the great Bare Knuckle Billy Quinn had a proper match.

"We can handle this peacefully," Billy said, but he didn't mean it. Lester ignored him and pointed his big old hand at me.

"Stay over there, kid," he said. "When this is over, I promise I won't kill you with my hands." He flexed his fists and watched the tendons ripple in his own forearms. "Strangling a retard just wouldn't feel right. You are retarded, aren't you?"

I felt the blood thump up into my face, but I just laughed. I knew Billy would make him pay.

"Come here, Lester," Billy said.

And Lester did. He ran at Billy so hard his feet cut through layered ice and raised jets of gravel. Billy's heels left the ground as Lester's sprinting bear hug met his sternum. It reminded me of an illustration I once saw in a Tarzan comic book, in which Tarzan gets the living shit kicked out of him by a rabid and personally slighted alpha male silverback. Billy wore a dead man's leisure suit instead of the leopard print thong, but other than that, the similarities were striking.

The two of them came to earth in a pile and slid six feet over ice, stopped hard against the bumper of a Chevy Suburban. Lester rose up. He dropped his great fists down on Billy's face. Right and left and right again. Enough to brain damage an average man. But he wasn't fighting an average man. He was fighting my brother. Lester's fist rose again and dropped. This time, Billy's left hand reached up and caught it. Just stopped it dead, like Lester punched a wall and it was closer than expected.

Lester looked confused for about half a second as Billy's right fist sliced up through the air. The force turned his whole head sideways and sent him sprawling. They both staggered to their feet. Lester kept shaking his head back and forth, trying to make his eyeballs point in the right direction. Billy grinned fangs of blood. He spit black onto the snow. Lester came at him. He swung twice. Big windmills. Billy stepped between and punched Lester right in the middle of his nose, just hard enough to wobble him. Then, while Lester tilted, Billy punched him twice more in the same exact spot.

Lester fell like a dead person. He was out colder than anyone I ever saw. My brother still had it! I cheered and clapped. What a day! I became very riled up. It's not my finest hour, but I sort of kicked Lester a little bit while he was down.

"Screw you, Lester," I said. "I'm not retarded. Not all the way." Billy let me do it, because Lester was a tool, and because I wasn't very good at kicking. My boots just bounced off his tree stump of a body. I couldn't get purchase on the ice. I missed a shot at his temple and fell on my butt.

"You're an asshole, Lester," I said. "I don't feel bad at all."

Billy helped me up and patted me on the back.

"Are you okay, little brother?"

"Yeah. I just fell down is all."

"Looked like you were working through a thing."

"He shouldn't say retard. Everybody knows that. And I think he makes that Laina girl sad."

I was cooled off and already a little embarrassed about kicking a guy while he was down. I wished Billy would stop asking questions.

"Do you want to know why I had to shut his lights off just now?" Billy said. "It's not just because he's an asshole."

I nodded.

• • •

Here's what happened. Lester worked for a lumberjack named Bud, and he was skimming the books. Bud knew it, and Lester knew he knew, but Lester was a big guy and Bud was old and afraid to fire him. The widow Krone also knew about this because Winner is a very small town and people know things there. She didn't like Lester, and when Billy showed up on her doorstep with his broad shoulders and strong jaw, I guess she saw an opportunity.

So, as I danced with a beautiful woman for the first time in my life, Edith introduced my brother to the old tree cutter, and they all made a deal. The fact that Lester was out cold meant Billy and I were lumberjacks now.

• • •

Back in Edith's kitchen, we celebrated with whiskey. Edith's long-dead husband kept a bottle for special occasions, and Edith said this was one of those. She poured it over ice. Billy drank his in a single gulp, then put the ice on a quickly darkening black eye.

"I'll assume Lester looks worse," she said.

"He does."

"Anything broken?"

"It's just a shiner."

"I meant Lester. Did you break his ribs?"

Billy stepped back. "Miss Krone," he said. "You have a vindictive streak."

"Come now, Eric, don't claim to be a peaceful man."

She went to an old record player in the corner and dropped some vinyl. Sinatra, I think. "The Way You Look Tonight." She caught Billy by the elbow.

"We never got the pleasure," she said.

They spun slow in her tidy living room. I sipped the booze—topped up the glass when Edith wasn't looking. A great day indeed, and it started off so bad. You just never know when things will turn around on you.

Sinatra was just gearing up for his big chorus when a knock came at the door. Edith peeled away. She did a twirl across the room . . . in such a great mood, she swung the door all the way open without even checking through the peephole.

It was Laina, with her child in her arms, and blood running down her face.

32.

There were no tears and no words from Laina. Edith put the child in Billy's arms and sat Laina down on the couch. One of Laina's eyes was swollen shut, the lip below all busted and bleeding. The open eye was glazed. It focused on nothing at all. Laina looked worse than Billy by ten miles—worse than we left Lester.

"Go get a bag of frozen peas," Edith said. "And Forrest, wrap it in a towel first."

I did as she said, but after that I wasn't much help. Billy set the child in a chair and padded across the floor in his stocking feet. He knelt down into Laina's blank stare and spoke.

"Tell me just one thing," he said. "Does Lester know where you are?" She didn't nod, or move, or anything. Her child curled up in the chair where Billy left her. The little one wore footie pajamas. The pajamas had little buffalos and horses printed on them. This situation was beyond me. The air was too warm . . . too thick. I grabbed my coat and slipped out the door.

• • •

The stars were clear that night, the snow glowing blue. It was cold out there. Too cold to sit still, but I sat anyway. I sat on the deck and waited for something to happen. What exactly, I did not know. All I knew was I couldn't go inside. I pulled my stocking cap down over my ears. My breath made frost on the rolled edge.

In a few minutes, the door opened behind me and Billy's weight cracked the frozen deck boards. He came down the steps and sat to my right, an unlit cigarette between his lips.

"Lester did this," he said. "She won't say it, but you know it and I know it."

He lit the cigarette and breathed. "I screwed this one up worse than usual," he said. "A beating like that changes a man. He wakes up angry. I didn't even think."

Billy passed me the cigarette. I slipped my hand from the mitten and took it, put it to my cold lips and took a drag. The smoke was warm.

"He'll come for her," Billy said.

"What do we do?"

"We wait," he said. "And we put things right."

We sat for a while like that. Billy didn't have a coat on, but he seemed fine. He lit another cigarette and smoked it down. When it burned low he flicked it out onto the ice.

"You alright, kid?"

"We can't keep doing this, Billy," I said. "Laina's face . . . did you see it? Everything we touch goes to shit."

"I know."

"I can't go in there. I can't look."

"It's okay, kid. We'll do better. I promise."

He reached around behind his back and drew out the .45. For a minute, he held it in his hands. Then he gripped it by the barrel and passed it to me.

"As long as you're out here," he said, "take the first shift for me."

I took it from him, and tucked it down by my ribs under the coat. My skin shrank from the cold steel—hairs prickling below layers of wool.

"I'll be back in an hour or two," he said.

Time passed with the moving of stars and with the slow march of cold through my limbs. I'm not sure how long. I made fists inside my mittens for warmth. The fingers were stiff with the cold and the old scars. I used to wonder if they'd ever fully heal, but I quit that when I was young.

Violence follows me like vultures follow the dying. We were well acquainted, violence and I, long before Billy burned that elevator and made us outlaws. I've seen my brother thrashed bloody. I've seen him thrash others, and I've asked the same of my own two hands. I know how things look after. Purple and broken. Wounds leave scars. They don't go away, and that's just how it is. Live through enough and the scars build up. Nerves go numb. It's not so bad when you think about it.

But somehow, I could not look at Laina's face. Maybe some things always slice deep.

• • •

I heard the truck before I saw it. The engine roared. A tuned-up beast. Headlights turned down Edith's driveway. They rode high on a lift kit. I stood, bit the right mitten and pulled my hand free. I let the mitten fall to the ice. The headlights rolled closer till I stood squinting in their halogen glare. He left the engine running. Tart black exhaust rose in clouds. The lights bounced with his great bulk leaving the cab.

"Hello, retard," Lester said. I couldn't see his face just then, or any part of him past the lights, but I knew the voice. I reached into my coat. The .45 was warm with my body heat. I drew it out.

"Oh no," he said. "The special kid has a gun." He laughed and walked into the glow of his headlights. The fringes of his mullet became a halo.

"Go to hell, Lester. I should kill you."

Lester raised his hands.

"Fine, fine," he said. "Hear me out. You can have my job. I don't give a fuck about lumberjacking. I'm past it. No hard feelings. But you can't take a man's woman like this. There aren't nearly enough of them in this shit town."

"I didn't take her. She left you."

"We had a misunderstanding is all."

"I'm pretty clear on the situation, Lester. You couldn't beat my brother, so you beat someone else. I might be a little retarded, but you're a coward."

"Okay, kid, you've said your piece. Now send her out or I'm coming in."

He looked relaxed. His bulk slumped with ease, and his voice held no edge of guilt or rage. In the bright headlights I could see his knuckles. They were just barely pink after doing all that damage to Laina's face. I'd been cold before. Numb and tired. I wasn't anymore.

"Try," I said, "and you'll be dead before you reach these stairs."

He leaned back and laughed.

"You think you have the stones?" he said. "Alright, retard, take a shot."

Bad guys in stories are always saying things like that. Have you ever noticed? They figure the good guy doesn't have it in him, and they're always right. The good guy can't seem to pull the trigger. Stories are this way because a good man isn't supposed to have killing in him. But I'm no kind of good man, and killing is in me. I raised the .45 at Lester and fired. I didn't hesitate—just pulled the trigger and felt the gun snap into my naked hand.

Lester jumped back.

"What the fuck?" he said. He wasn't dead. Not even shot, actually. I missed him clean, sent the bullet through one headlight of his big old truck. It crackled in the cold night air. The world looked different with the brightness turned down by half. Lester was no longer a giant backlit silhouette. He was just a man. I could see his scared, bruised face and did not fire again.

"What's wrong with you?" Lester said as he hopped back up in his tall truck. He slammed the door and floored it back out Edith's driveway. The transmission squealed in reverse. I held the gun straight out in front of me until the engine faded away. It smoked in my hand. My ears rang in the quiet.

When I turned, Billy stood in Edith's doorway.

"Come inside," he said.

Edith was still up when I got in. She held Laina's child on her hip. The child was slow and quiet with sleep and did not cry. Her mother was gone from the couch.

"What did you do?" Edith said.

"He shot out Lester's headlight," Billy replied. He grinned and helped me with my coat, took the .45 and tucked it away in the band of his pants. "Like a boss," he said.

"You have more of your brother in you than I thought," Edith said. "Though you could have got him in the leg. Made him hurt."

"He didn't have to," Billy said. "I bet Lester shit himself."

"There's no need to use that kind of language."

After a while Edith took the little one back to bed. When we were alone, Billy got dead Earl's bottle of whiskey and filled two glasses.

"Sit down," he said, and I sat. He slid one glass across the kitchen table to me.

"Drink," he said, and I drank. It burned in a pleasant way.

"He won't be back," Billy said. "Not tonight."

I nodded and took a longer drink. I gripped the glass in my gun hand. The nerves in it hummed under the flesh.

"I should have been out there," he said.

"It wasn't your shift."

"Kid, it's always my shift."

He refilled my glass and I drank again. I could feel it now. My eyes watered and the glass clinked against my teeth.

"You did a good thing, little brother," Billy said. "Now it's time to sleep."

"Head up," I said. "I need to sit a minute."

So he went, and I sat a while longer. I laid my hands out next to each other on the table and looked at them. The gun hand still felt different than the other. It vibrated up to the elbow but when I looked, it lay still and calm and symmetrical.

It was a near thing. A few inches to the right and the evening would have gone very differently. How does one get rid of a body? We had access to a woodchipper. I saw that in a movie one time. It seemed to work pretty well. Edith would have been fine with it. I didn't know about Laina though. Women are a mystery.

And there was this other question . . . how does one justify the killing of another? Billy told me once, if a man comes after your family you get a gun and you blow his head off. He said this truth was older than God and I tried to believe him. But I was ready to kill Lester for taking a swing at his woman. This woman was lovely and kind to me, but she was not my blood. Billy's code did not allow a killing for her sake, yet I fired without pause.

Maybe that's why I missed. Maybe the hand failed me because it obeyed a greater truth.

This line of reasoning lit my sluggish thoughts. If my hand knew right from wrong, then it was right to kill those men on the Mexican border. It was justified—to do it for Billy. The weight of my wrongs slipped a bit from my shoulders. I refilled my whiskey glass.

All those times my hands cramped and refused their tasks . . . those other times they moved swift and strong to do terrible things . . . it made sense in my drunkenness. Evil was in me, but only a certain kind. Only what helped Billy. For him, all was justified. My hands would allow nothing else.

I sipped and smiled a big numb smile. And hey, jerking off must not be wrong either. A few thousand sins erased from the ledger right there. Good times! I finished the glass and considered another, but I was already drunk. My vision was slow. My skin was warm. I lay my heavy skull down on the table. The world spun and warped with the motion. I laughed at the funny shapes.

Maybe I'd crossed no lines after all. I could stop worrying, after so long. I closed my eyes. My muscles relaxed. Then, right at the point of sleep, when there's no coming back, a crack opened in this joyful new logic.

Maybe I tried to kill an unarmed man and missed. Maybe it was just that simple.

33.

I woke with my face stuck to the kitchen table. Edith was up early, frying bacon and slamming the hell out of every single one of her pots and pans. The clatter hurt my head. So did peeling my face off the varnish. She cracked a cup of coffee down in front of me. BAM! She had no mercy in her.

"You should wash," she said. "Bud will be here in a few minutes."

"Thanks," I said.

I'd forgotten about the new job. Too much violence going on. It seemed all wrong to go to work after everything that had happened. But I guess we already paid the cost, and it was far too expensive to back out now. I drank the coffee and splashed water on my face and met Billy on his way down the stairs. He was shouldering into a flannel shirt.

"Morning, champ," he said.

Billy was in a great mood. He rolled up his sleeves and powered through most of the bacon and enough coffee that Edith had to make more. Then Laina's daughter drifted out from a back room and he lifted her up into his lap. He fed her the leftover bacon. He poured a bit of coffee into a saucer to cool so she could get a taste. He ruffled her hair.

"Miss Krone," he said, "will you be alright here? One of us can stay."

Edith went over to the broom closet and pulled out a great long bolt action rifle.

"We'll be fine," she said.

Then Bud honked his horn outside and it was time to do some lumberjacking. "Work like God's watching," Edith said, and we went out to meet the headlights.

• • •

There was something wrong with Bud. It was dark in the cherry picker, and we were in back, so I couldn't really nail it down at first. His hand moved funny . . . that was part of it. The left was fine, but the right one acted more like a tentacle. It sort of wrapped around the gear knob. And there was something off with his voice too.

"Make room," he said. "Gordon is not small."

At least, that's what I think he said. Bud sounded like he was talking through marbles. Like he had four or five good-sized shooters in his mouth all the time. Billy and I scooted to the far edge of the back seat and pretended like we were sure that's what he told us to do. He didn't correct us, so I guess it was.

He nodded and made a smacking noise with his mouth as he drove. Then he told us a story. Near as I could gather, it centered around a great big white pine he took down many years ago and a former employee named Vernon. I understood more as he talked. The marble mouth thing wasn't so bad once I got used to it.

"Vern was good with the chain saw," Bud said. "But he was not observant."

Apparently, this Vern guy didn't notice Bud was standing right under the heavy old branch he was cutting. Bud noticed, but couldn't move fast enough.

"I tell him, no! Stop!" Bud said. "But he just keeps cutting, the dumb fuck. Branch comes down and hits me right in the noggin. Peels back half my face like an orange rind."

Bud turned all the way around in the front seat and pushed the loose skin of his face back with one hand. His teeth and the whites of his eyes glowed under folds and thick seams of scar tissue. His hand, now that I got a good long look, had just one finger. The middle one—grown thick and strong with constant use.

"So I'm holding my face on with my damn hand just like this." Bud continued. "Then it's hospital time."

There was one thing I didn't know when Billy pitched our new job. Bud Larson wasn't an ordinary lumberjack. He and his little crew took down trees in dangerous situations. Leaners mostly. If a tree was threatening to fall on something important, like a roof or a power line, Bud could take care of it. The thing is, you can't just chop down a tree like that. You have to start at the top and cut it up into little pieces, right down to the stump. Mistakes have dire physical consequences. Those consequences caught up with Bud. Rather, they caught up with certain parts of Bud. Each decade of his thirty-year career claimed substantial pieces of his extremities. Fingers. Toes. The mobility of his face.

I squinted at Billy, tried to send my thoughts into his head without words. "No to this job," I thought. "Hell no. Lester can keep it. Let's leave this shithole with our limbs still attached to our bodies."

Billy just laughed. "They stitched you right up," he said.

Bud shook the loose skin of his face back into alignment. "Doc did a pretty good job," he said. "Wish I had him when I lost the fingers. Probably could have saved them. But I guess he'd have to find them first."

Billy caught my eye and grinned. He raised his middle finger real slow.

The cherry picker shuddered and stopped in front of a small cabin made of unskinned pine logs. Curls of smoke came from a tin chimney. As we watched, a small door opened and the shoulders of a huge man forced their way out. Here was Gordon. He stood slow and stiff. When he reached his full height, his head cleared the peak of his tiny cabin by six inches at least.

"He is one tall Indian," Bud said.

Gordon raised his arms above his head and let them down slowly. Bud tapped his finger on the steering wheel.

"One tall Indian," Bud said again.

Gordon climbed up in the cab without a good morning or a hello or anything. He just slid the passenger seat all the way back so it hit the back seats, and Billy had to scoot over into the middle. Even then, Gordon had to fold his legs up against the dashboard. Out on the road he turned in his seat and silently shook both of our hands. Nearly a minute later I heard him mumble some words. "Good hands," he said.

"Gordon here is a poet," Bud said. "Or a stoner."

Gordon nodded in the passenger seat. His head bumped the ceiling.

• • •

The work was just outside of Fairbanks. That city is ringed with vacation homes and high-class hunting cabins. Bankers and executives bring money from the Lower 48. They want to own wilderness. Instead they build pretty log cabins on good roads that lead to the Fairbanks airport. They decorate with animal hides, killed and preserved by other men. And when a tree threatens to crush the whole thing, they call Bud Larson. Bud brings chain saws and muscle down from the true wilderness.

It was a long drive, passed in silence. Finally, Bud turned down the client's driveway and parked. Billy and Gordon and I set to work unloading the equipment while Bud tilted his weird old body toward the house. We hauled a diesel generator out into the snow, and Gordon ripped it to life. We set up nine industrial-grade lights. In their white blaze, we saw our job for the day . . . an enormous pine grown beyond its strength. The whole thing leaned hard over a crisp new log home. Snow-laden branches scraped the roof. Limbs creaked with the pressure. Bud stood at a distance with the client. He explained the protocol like the guy was going to help, which he wasn't.

Gordon blinked up at the tree. "I'm sorry old girl," he said. "It's not your fault some rich white people built their house beneath your branches. Not your fault they find you inconvenient now."

He didn't say it loud, but Gordon was a big guy, with big lungs. The words carried. The client went inside and Bud returned shaking his head.

"He heard you," Bud said. "He's not happy. No tip for us."

Gordon nodded, and we all set to work. Chain saws roared and Gordon rode up in the cherry picker. Billy chopped up the limbs as they fell, and I tossed sap-reeking branches through the woodchipper. All of us rushed to stay warm. All except Bud. Bud watched.

Hours later, the sun crested the horizon. Gordon let his chain saw idle, then shut it off. He raised his big arms and stretched the long muscles of his back. Billy took off the fur bomber hat Edith had given him from her husband's closet.

"Lunch," Bud said.

Billy shut off the generator and the lights dimmed, crackling as they cooled. For the first time in hours, there was silence. Bud poured steaming coffee from his thermos and passed around mugs.

"Look at that," Bud said, motioning to the dismembered pine. "That poor old girl grew for two hundred years. In ten more there won't even be a stump."

"Grass will grow from my rib cage," Gordon said. He scooped lard from a tin can with a piece of bread. He seemed pleased with the flavor and totally at peace with mortality.

"Shut up, Gordon," Bud said.

Billy and I sipped coffee and ate the roast beef sandwiches Edith made for us. Snot ran from my cold nose. Some of it got on the sandwich but I didn't care. The sandwich was still good. When we were done, Billy sidled over to Bud.

"Hey," he said. "I don't have to fill out any tax forms do I? Like a W-4 or something?"

"Not unless you feel the need to waste your time. I gotta piss."

Bud walked away, swinging his legs like he was carrying a fishbowl between his knees. Gordon stayed. He wiped the grease away from his mouth with the back of his hand.

"What'd you do?" he said.

"Many things," Billy replied. "Narrow it down for me."

"There are just three types of people who worry about the tax man's paperwork."

"Yeah?"

"Misers, libertarians, and criminals."

"You're not wrong."

"We've not known each other long, but you do not seem like the type to get wound up by little deals. So what did you do?"

Billy looked at Gordon a long time. Sized him up. He was hard to read. His face looked like something carved into the side of a mountain. Billy grinned, and decided to take a chance.

"Robbed about twenty-five liquor stores," Billy said.

Gordon leaned back and laughed a big booming laugh. "And yet you are here," he said. "Breaking your body for a few dollars. Breaking Lester's body, too, for the privilege."

"That's about the size of it."

"Ill-gotten cash is very slippery. Hard to hold onto."

"Sounds like you've got experience."

Gordon laughed again and sipped his coffee. "Me and a friend knocked over three banks in Montana in the mid-90s. We were like wild creatures then. Young men. We were tired of living poor on the Blackfoot reservation. Angry. Taking the white man's money felt good. Felt like payment for our grandfather's lands. But the money spent fast. Burned through a quarter million in less than a year. Then I'm wanted, and broke too."

"Damn."

"Ah well. Nothing I couldn't fix with a long road trip and some new papers. You picked a good hideout by the way. You can relax here. Nobody ever comes to Winner."

A few minutes later we were back at work. In another hour, the sun vanished, and many hours after that the great old tree lay in neat piles of firewood and mounds of chipped mulch. Bud handed out envelopes of cash.

"That's a man's work," he said.

• • •

Laina's little child was still in her buffalo pajamas when we got back. Or maybe she was in them again. Either way, her mother wasn't around and Edith looked tired as hell. The little girl ran to Billy before he even got his boots off. He caught her up and raised her over his head.

"Waaaaaaaa!" he said. She shrieked and laughed. When he set her down, she ran and hid behind a chair. Billy pulled his big fur cap down real low. He got down on all fours and ran after her like a bear. He made bear sounds too. Convincing ones. He grunted and sprinted around on his hands—grinned through what was left of his black eye. It wasn't even black anymore. Just a fading shade of yellow, healing well less than twenty-four hours after the crushing blows.

Billy told me once he had a deal worked out with his body. He told me he had it licked. Muscle and bone would do as he said, and he said heal. Bullshit, you're thinking. Maybe. But there was yet a little fire in him after so many breathless miles on the road. A light in his eye. A glimmer of something other people don't have. The small child could see it. She feared it . . . and was drawn to it. And when he made bear noises, she felt every emotion available to a developing brain. The whole palette at once. She wanted him to catch her. She fled for her life.

34.

Things were simple for a while. Every morning we climbed into Bud's cherry picker. Every day we worked till my hands ached and my ears rang with the sound of chain saws. Cash piled up under Billy's mattress. He paid the widow Krone in folded twenties, and at night she made us huge pans of hotdish. We ate like kings. We laughed aloud.

It wasn't long till Laina came out of hiding. Bud dropped us off, and she was in the kitchen making frog bellies. They smelled just great. I think she used lard instead of vegetable oil. Oh man!

She kept her distance at first. Kept her back turned, looked down when people spoke to her. When the fry bread was done, she took some and slipped away. The next day was better, and the one after that. Soon she was sitting with us at the kitchen table, eating and smiling at jokes. She didn't talk much, but I guess she never really had.

Then one evening, she put her hand on my shoulder as she cleared the table. Her fingers grazed the skin of my neck. Lightly and for just a moment, but it raised goose pimples all over my body. I wanted to jump up and run around and maybe dive into a really cold lake. Electric!

Billy saw her touch me. He caught my eye and winked.

After the food, we had to go down into the crawl space and perform surgery on some plumbing. The kitchen sink was stopped up with bacon grease like a bad artery. The blockage was so deep, Edith's twenty-foot drain snake was useless. We had to drag ourselves down a narrow dirt tunnel under Edith's kitchen and cut through the clogged PVC pipe with a hacksaw. Our breath made steam in the cold. Billy worked the saw and I held a stockpot underneath to catch the bad water that sloshed out with each stroke.

"Careful, kid," Billy said. "A little more to the left."

The goopy stuff spattered down on Billy's shirt. "The other left. Shit. This smells like death."

I adjusted the stockpot. The bad water came faster the longer he worked. It was rank.

"Save some room in that pot," Billy said. "I might have to barf."

I should say, the plumbing repair wasn't Edith's idea. It was Billy's. This home-maintenance stuff was our regular pastime now. Ever since moving in with Edith, Billy was going through a serious DIY phase. He'd come home after a day of lumberjacking and just start fixing things for no reason. He went to Don's and bought about three dozen 60-watt light bulbs—lit every dim corner of the house. Whole rooms nobody had visited without a flashlight since Earl dropped dead. He got steel wool and cans of spray foam, also at Don's, and filled up all the mouse holes he could find. He hummed while he worked. Happy songs. He was way on in.

He even went under the house and jacked up a few of the saggier beams. That's how he knew where the drain pipe was.

"Hey," I said. "How long are we gonna be here, do you think?"

"I can only do this so fast, kid. The angles are all wrong."

"No—here in Alaska, with Edith."

Billy cracked a smile. "You mean with Laina," he said. "A girl brushes your shoulder one time and now you've got it bad."

"It felt weird. Her hand on me."

Billy stopped sawing long enough to punch me in the arm. "She's pretty," he said. "And she's got a kid. You got a *ready-made family* right there!"

This was also a thing . . . *ready-made family*. Edith liked the way Billy and Laina looked together. She liked the way he carried around her child on his shoulders. Basic mathematics required them to fall in love and get married and have a whole lot of great-looking babies together. Edith told Billy that Laina was, you guessed it, a *ready-made family*. She told him to quit smoking soon, and settle down. She took steps to force the issue. She brought out these really big puzzles and suggested Billy and Laina work on them together. Farm tractors and puppies and stuff. Thousands of pieces. That's a lot of puzzle—and a lot of pressure too. Thus, the DIY projects. They created distance.

"Do you think she likes me?" I said.

"Probably. You shot at Lester. That raises your stock, I expect."

"I did do that."

"Although," Billy said. "Remember that woman back home?"

He didn't have to go into detail. I knew just what he was talking about. There was this lady back in Radium who had to call the cops because her husband was chasing her with a cast-iron fry pan. The cops got there and did their jobs and pretty soon the asshole was chained up in the back of a squad car. Then the woman changed her mind and jumped on the arresting officer. She just about clawed that cop's eyes out. His buddies had to pry her off. It made the newspaper.

"A woman goes through something like that," Billy said. "Her reactions become unpredictable."

"You think she wants to claw my eyes out?"

"Just biding her time, waiting for an opening? Probably not. Sixty-forty. Forget I said anything."

Billy kept sawing. He was nearly through, and the pipe was flexing and pinching the blade.

"You never said. How long are we gonna be here?"

Just as I asked, Billy's saw sliced through the last thread of PVC. Brown water and congealed grease shot out like somebody having the runs. I was distracted and the whole stream missed my stockpot. It was my one job.

"Mother!" Billy shouted, but Edith was standing on the floor above, and the little kid too, so he couldn't finish the thought.

Filth rained down on both of us for a solid thirty seconds. When it was done, Billy lay in the rotting grease and laughed. He laughed so hard he started coughing. I laughed, too. He leaned back and wiped tears from his eyes. Lying in a cold dirt crawl space, covered in rotting shit; it was the happiest I'd seen him in a long while.

This sounds crazy of course, but listen. When we were done reaming out the clogged pipe, gluing it back together with an eighty-seven-cent PVC coupler, we knew we'd go upstairs and wash ourselves clean. We'd drink cocoa before bed. I could hear Edith stirring it on the stove, clear through the kitchen floor. We'd have that good cocoa, and Billy would hold the child on his lap. I'd sneak glances at Laina's healing face—try to read what little I could.

I'm telling you, for us it was green pastures. Lumberjacking all day. Tinkering at night. It was medicine. It was life as life was intended to be. There was even a pretty girl and a child, which are the cornerstones of any paradise, however meager. In Alaska I realized what I wanted, and it was mine already. For a time, anyway.

"So how long will we stay?"

"Not forever," Billy said. "Take it in while you've got it, kid. Use it all the way up. It's the only way this works."

"Okay, Billy."

"Now hold the pipe steady so I can scrape out all this crap."

• • •

We did go upstairs, and we did have that good cocoa. And then we went to bed for some good sleep. Billy was out immediately, but it always took me longer to doze off. Downstairs I could hear footsteps on the creaking floorboards—the only thing that gave away Laina's drifting gait. She did this a lot, after everyone was in bed. Paced around for hours. I thought she'd stop when she came out of hiding, but the pacing continued.

I thought about getting up, going to find her, but I never did. Didn't know what to say I guess. Didn't know what she thought of me. Maybe Billy was right. She might love Lester still, in spite of the beating. Maybe because of it. Women are confusing to me. It's because I don't have any sisters.

So I stayed in my bed that night. I did not go looking for her. And finally, she came looking for me.

I was a few hours into sleep by this point, in the middle of a nightmare. You know the one. Billy's trapped in a burning car. His face is covered in blood. I saw it so often it wasn't even scary anymore. Except this time, he looked up and started talking to me. "You have to do it, kid," he said. "Promise me." I had the .45 in my hands. I was bloody to the elbow. The gun was bloody too, and smoke rose from its barrel.

I sat right up out of the dream and smacked my forehead on the ceiling. BAM! When I fell back, Laina was there, watching it all happen. Her face hovered just above the edge of the mattress. Her skin was smooth and her eyes were wide and dark, like an empty mask. That scared me worse than the dream. I sat back up and hit my head on the exact same patch of ceiling.

"It's just me," she whispered.

"Yep. I see that now." I propped myself up on my elbow and rubbed my face. "You shouldn't ghost up on a guy like that."

"I didn't want to wake you. It's bad to wake someone in the middle of a dream."

Wind screamed through the eaves of Edith's old house. The windows shook like a bunch of kids were throwing gravel. A storm was sweeping through. A bad one. Laina's voice was nearly lost in the sound of it. She stepped up a few rungs on the bunk ladder so her face was even with mine.

"Tell me about the dream," she said.

"Just a rerun," I said. "I know how it ends. What's on your mind?"

"Lester," she said. "I keep thinking. I've tried, but I can't stop." She left a pause, but I didn't know how to fill it, so she had to go on alone. "Edith says you shot his truck on purpose . . . says you only meant to scare him."

"That's right."

"My room faces the driveway. I watched you out my window. I was watching before he arrived." She leaned in very close to me. So close I could smell Edith's shampoo in her hair and see the last fading marks of Lester's fists. "You were small and cold and folded in on yourself, and then you weren't anymore. Forrest, you didn't draw like a man aiming at headlights."

Her face was different than before. With everyone else asleep in bed, her quiet sadness had fallen away. What remained was an edge not immediately obvious in the scant Alaskan daylight. I wriggled back in my bunk till I hit the wall. I thought of that poor, unpredictable, battered woman back home and the cop whose eyes she tried to claw out. My eyes were about the only thing on my body in reliable working order. I couldn't afford to lose them.

"I don't know what to tell you, Laina. I already said how it was."

She reached out and grabbed a fistful of my T-shirt. "Here's what I think, Forrest," she said. "Either you're some kind of a white knight, or you're a killer."

I stared back into her eyes. They were dark and wet. I said nothing.

"Heroes don't come to Winner this time of year," she said. Her hand tightened on my shirt. Her arm quivered. She was about to go for my eyes. I could feel it coming.

"If I'm a killer, then I'm no good at it," I said. I made my voice sound light—like it was a big joke. "I couldn't hit the broadside of a barn. I'd be the worst assassin that's ever walked the earth."

"That don't matter, Forrest. It's the intent I'm after. Everything else can be learned."

I couldn't think of what to say next. I was so confused. There was just no way of knowing what she wanted to hear . . . or what she'd do when I told her. She was right on the edge of something, and she had a really solid grip on my shirt. Sixty-forty, Billy had said. High stakes, I'm telling you.

"So," she said. "Did you mean to do it?"

"To do what again?"

"Jesus, Forrest, you are kind of slow, aren't you?"

"A little."

"Did you mean to kill him?"

If I knew what she wanted, I'd have said exactly that. Lied through my teeth if I had to. It's not some big moral issue for me. But I didn't know, and the truth is just easier to remember.

"I missed, Laina," I said. "If I hadn't, he'd be through the wood-chipper already."

She dragged me forward by the front of my shirt. I clamped my eyes shut. Grit my teeth. Then her lips landed hard on the corner of my mouth. She pressed in, and pulled me to her at the same time. She was so swift and active, it took me a second to realize what was going on and start kissing back. I couldn't keep up—couldn't breathe. She got my tongue between her teeth and I tasted blood.

When she let me go, the world was spinning. Well, no. My head was spinning, as usual, but Laina didn't even seem to notice. She put her hand right in the middle of my chest. Her nails pricked through the crumpled shirt.

"His heart's right here, Forrest," she said. "Next time, don't miss."

She dropped to the floor and drifted away down the stairs. When she was gone, Billy sat up in his bunk. He scratched the stubble on the side of his face.

"That was some crazy shit, man," he said. "She was this close to taking your eyes out."

"Jesus Christ."

"That cop back home had to quit the force and get one of those special dogs to lead him around places. You could have been like that guy!"

"Aw man. Why didn't you step in?"

"Thought about it, but it seemed like she might kiss you instead. I had to play the odds. Made the right call."

"What if you got it wrong?"

"I'm pretty fast, kid. I'd have stopped her before she got both your eyes. Worst case scenario, you lose some depth perception. Tell me you wouldn't roll those dice."

"Damn it, Billy."

"Come on, you're fine. You are fine, right?"

"She bit me a little."

• • •

Billy was asleep again in about two minutes. He had a good laugh about Laina's aggressive brand of kissing, told me to be careful if she ever offered to kiss a certain other part of my body, and went right back to sleep. Just like that. I couldn't do it though. No sleep for me.

After an hour of sweating into the sheets, I gave up. I fumbled downstairs in my stocking feet and made coffee. I thought maybe Laina would be there and I could get some clarification on things. She wasn't. Everyone was asleep but me. Me and the storm outside. It was really tearing shit up out there. I could hear trees falling. The floorboards of Edith's old house shifted under my feet. I sipped coffee and put my hand on the picture window. It shuddered with the force of the weather.

I got the sense there was a beast on the other side of the glass—something too big and strong for a physical body and too angry to be still. A huge, ancient creature, raging and throwing itself at the mountains and the pines and at the shelters of men. There's a reason northern peoples put their faith in violent gods.

I was in a very weird mood. Probably it had something to do with the kissing. I really liked the quiet, sad Laina, who made fry bread and cared for her daughter. Anyone would love that girl. But that wasn't who kissed the hell out of me and told me to shoot Lester in the middle of his bear-killing chest. She looked the same, but it was a whole different Laina. The wild night-owl edition . . . very confusing. I wouldn't have believed my own memory, except my tongue was still bleeding.

Really though, if I'm honest, it wasn't the kiss that kept me up. It was the dream. "You have to do it, kid," Billy had told me. "Promise me." Billy visited my dreams many times. He came bloody and burned and silent. Always silent. He didn't have to speak because we understood each other—me and that bloody version of Billy who lived in my head. There was an arrangement. He kept me steady. Fed me. Led me through this world. And I did what he needed me to do. I was strong when I had to be. I ruined my hands for him, when it was required. I picked up a gun for his sake . . . killed men so he could live. I would do it again, but goddamn it took a lot out of me. What else was there for me to do? Was it worse? It must be, since he had to ask. I couldn't get my mind off it. It made me sick. It took my sleep away.

35

I drank coffee till the storm blew itself out. A few hours later, Billy came downstairs with an unlit cigarette in his mouth, reaching around his pockets for a lighter. He headed for the front door, but it didn't open. He checked the bolt and tried again. Nothing. Finally, he tucked his cigarette in his front shirt pocket, and stretched his neck cords. Warmed up his shoulders. Then he grabbed the doorknob in both hands, braced his foot up on the frame, and heaved. I mean, he really threw his whole body into it. Then all of a sudden it crashed open. Billy fell back on his ass and chunks of ice slid all the way into the kitchen.

"Holy shit," Billy said.

Two inches of clear ice covered the whole outside world. The wind stripped the sky of clouds before calling it quits and the earth glowed with starlight trapped in ice. Billy peeled a chunk of it off the door and flung it low, like a skipping rock. It raised a shrill whine across thirty feet of driveway. Then he peeled off another chunk of ice and lobbed it high into the trees. Every branch it touched snapped off and fell. Broke like gunshots—crashed down like grenades. Billy scratched his head.

"We're going to be busy," he said.

• • •

Except we weren't. We cleaned up the ice chunks from Edith's floor. Then Billy poured and drank three or four cups of coffee. We packed lunch kits, waited for Bud's headlights, but none came. By 6:30 Billy was pacing and flexing his hands. By 7:00 he had a dangerous sort of look in his eye.

"Maybe he's putting chains on his tires," I said. Billy didn't respond. Instead he grabbed his coat and stepped into boots on his way out the door.

"Get your stuff," he shouted back. I put on clothes till my body turned into a great soft potato. I found him hunched over the Chevy windshield with a rubber mallet in one hand and an ice scraper in the other. Ice chips flew. He smiled while he worked. When he was done, he got in and unstuck the tires with the gas pedal, then pumped the brakes across twenty yards of skating rink. He laughed smoke and steam.

"Get in," he said.

The road crackled under our tires and shone bright in our headlights. Glassy limbs lay thick over everything. On the road and parked cars and on the desolate homes of Winner. It was frightful and beautiful and Billy smiled with the sight of it.

He took the roads at ten miles an hour and even that was too fast. The truck turned sideways at any hint of gas or brake. It jolted over fallen branches. Ahead, a raven stood bolt upright on a mailbox, frozen solid and smooth as glass. It lit up with the headlights. Billy passed his cigarette to his driving hand and punched me in the arm.

"And you wanted to stay in," he said.

"I never said that."

"I could see it on your face."

We found Gordon standing still and silent in his huge canvas jacket. The hood wasn't quite huge enough. It made a tent of his shoulders. Behind him, his small cabin door hung in pieces on icy hinges. Splinters clung to the shoulders of his tented jacket. He said nothing of the storm or his ruined door. He just climbed in the truck and nodded.

He showed us down a long forest road to Bud's place. The cherry picker was out front, parked by a collection of rust- and ice-covered machinery. Between the machinery and the house lay Bud. Dead.

"Holy shit," I said.

Bud lay spread-eagled on his back six feet from his front porch. His warped old arms were flung out at his sides, as a man does when he loses his balance. His eyes looked in two different directions. Frost covered his face. Billy leaned down and felt for a pulse.

"Dead," he said. And then he looked up at us. "Say some words, Gordon."

"Bud is dead," Gordon said.

"Better words. You're the poet."

Gordon blinked in his tented hood and said nothing.

"Get his feet," Billy said.

Billy and Gordon dragged Bud's stiff body up onto the porch and propped him in a chair. Then we all went inside to get warm. Gordon tossed some birch in the woodstove and rubbed the head of a fat black lab.

"Your life will take unexpected turns now," he said to the dog.

With Bud rapidly cooling outside, we had two options. We could make a phone call and let the local government auction off the cherry picker and the log home and whatever other crap Bud owned. He had no children, you understand. Or as Billy put it, we could let old Bud sit a few more hours on the porch he so loved and use his equipment for one last payday. We all thought this second option was a good and respectful plan.

"The people of Winner need us," Billy said. "Bud would have wanted this."

We scraped a small mountain of ice from the cherry picker and rolled into Winner like a liberating army. Billy hoisted me up on top of the cab to shout out our services. People ran into the street waving their hands.

Bud found most of his work on the fringes of Fairbanks, where outside money was plentiful—that's true. The people of Winner could handle a few trees. But this wasn't a few. Wind and ice brought down pines on just about every roof in town. Limbs crushed cars and sparked in tangled power lines. People were desperate. They paid in cash.

We worked like animals for a long time. The sun rose and briefly made the whole world too bright to look at. Then it sank, and we kept working. We halted for sandwiches and cups of steaming Campbell's supplied by grinning children. Once in the darkness, I had to smack my hands into the side of the truck, just to get them moving. The old scars . . . they don't always respond so well to the cold.

We cleared whole blocks—left chain-sawed rounds in massive wood piles. For many hours, I thought of nothing—not the pain in my muscles or the money we made or the crazy look on Bud's dead face when we found him. Thinking does no good at such times.

When we could work no more, Billy parked the cherry picker back in Bud's yard. He divvied out fat wads of cash. That's how things are in Alaska. You work till your body breaks. Then you keep going. You keep going because you know, at the end of it all, there's a big stack of bills. You're a king and a slave at the same time.

We let Gordon off at his cabin with its ruined door. Billy leaned out after him.

"Call dispatch," he said. "Tell them about Bud."

• • •

There was fry bread on the counter when we got home, soup warming on the stove, and a note from Edith that said she was way too old to be waiting up for house guests. Billy drank the soup straight from a mug and chewed the fry bread on his way to bed. I couldn't get the soup down so fast. It was real hot, and Edith didn't like us bringing her dishes to our room. Finally, I just abandoned a half mug and headed for the stairs. I was so tired I thought I might throw up. That's when you know sleep is going to feel really good . . . when you think you might barf first.

It made me happy to know I'd be sleeping soon. And probably for a long time. Bud was dead, which was no good for him, but it did mean we'd get to sleep in. I figured I could reasonably expect fourteen solid hours. How lucky was I?

I was halfway up the stairs when I heard her whisper.

"Hey, Forrest," she said.

I turned around. Laina stood at the foot of the stairs in a flannel sleep shirt. The shirt was big and loose and she looked very sexy in it. It hung down just low enough I thought maybe she wasn't wearing anything else under it. Night owl Laina. God she was enticing.

"Hey," she said again. I glanced back up the stairs. I could see my bed. That looked great, too. The sheets would be cold at first. They'd get warm just about the time I drifted off. Dang that's a good feeling. Maybe the best feeling in the world.

Laina reached out her hand. "Come here," she said. Of course I went . . . just to talk for a few minutes, then I'd go to bed and have all that good sleep.

But she didn't want to talk. She just slipped her hand in mine and led me down the hall to her room. It was much better than the attic. There were drapes on the windows and nice rugs on the floor. The child slept in a pile of blankets at the foot of a small woodstove. The stove cast orange light on the little one's face. Laina closed the door behind us. Before I could say a word, she pushed me down on her bed and climbed up on top of me. It was shocking. I might have cried out except I was very tired, and tiredness makes me amenable.

Right away she pinned my head down with her face. I couldn't see a thing through her long hair, and I couldn't breathe because her mouth was covering all the airways. I tried to keep up with her tongue—tried to participate. I felt blindly for her waist, and she slapped my hands away.

This was not at all how I imagined things might be with Laina. It wasn't like any of my fantasies. There was no tenderness. I wasn't sure if I liked it . . . but you don't just stop a girl once she's started. You roll with it. Plus, she was very strong. Small but solid. It would have taken a lot of energy to throw her off.

When I was down to my last gasps of air, she pulled back just long enough to strip the sleep shirt off over her head. Not a stitch on underneath. It didn't seem real. I was too tired to understand. Then her lips were on me again. She went after my clothes without looking. The buttons flew off my shirt. The belt from my pants. Her skin was hot on mine—like standing too near a bonfire.

I didn't know what to do with my hands. It was weird just lying there. I wanted to hold on to something . . . to steady myself. I grabbed her thighs and I guess maybe that was a mistake. A quiver went through her and she pulled away. She caught both my wrists in one hand and pinned them down above my head. Then she slapped me real hard across the face.

My ears rang and my cheek smarted. Laina froze, wide-eyed. She looked at me, then turned to her daughter real slow. The little kid was still fast asleep.

"Are you okay?" Laina whispered.

I smiled. "It's fine," I said. "I don't mind."

So she slapped me again, and it really was fine. It was more than fine. Adrenalin poured into my blood—turned the pain to heat and energy. It was like she reached down into my brain and threw some ancient switch. Then we started in earnest.

Maybe it wasn't like my stupid fantasies, all those pretty JCPenney models. So what? It was a lot nicer than what happened with Candice. Miles nicer. In fact, things seemed to be going rather well. The occasional slap to the face did wonders for my abilities. Laina was pleased. Silent. I mean, her kid was asleep on the floor five feet away . . . but still pleased.

When it was done, we lay sweating on top of the covers. She rolled up on an elbow and glanced down at her daughter. The little girl was peaceful in the warm light of the woodstove. Laina sank back with a sigh.

"She can sleep through anything," Laina whispered.

I looked Laina all the way up and down. Really took her all in. It's rare to see a woman like that. Relaxed in her nakedness. I could see the proof of her motherhood. Her breasts were low and full, and she had stretch marks around her middle. That didn't bother me none. My head was way more fucked up, and I didn't create an entire living person getting it that way. All I did was go through a windshield at sixty miles an hour. Besides, it kind of fit Laina. She seemed gentle all of a sudden, now that it was over.

I reached out and touched her hip. She glared back, but didn't hit me this time. I slid my hand up toward her waist. I liked that place where the hip narrows. It was like a warm, sunny hillside.

"Don't go exploring," she whispered.

I smiled at her, and she smiled back. She blinked heavy eyelids—stroked my throbbing face with her fingertips. Some tenderness after all.

"I'm tired," she said. "You should go."

"Now?"

"Soon."

Not much tenderness. Maybe it was enough.

"Shouldn't we, maybe, talk?"

"About what?"

"I don't know."

She touched my lips. "You may ask one question," she said, "if you promise to go away right after."

"Any question?"

"Sure."

This was a tough one. I had a lot of questions. I wondered how she knew her daughter would sleep through all the sex. That seems like a high-stakes bet. I wondered if she could maybe fix my shirt at some point. And I wondered if she planned to hit me every time we did this. Not that I minded—just nice to know, moving forward. But she'd only answer one, so I narrowed it down.

"My brother's right upstairs," I said. "He's taller than me, and good looking, and he doesn't spin his head around. He's just plain better in all the ways. So why me?"

Laina ran her fingers through my ratty short hair. "Oh, Forrest," she said. "Your brother's not nearly broken enough for my tastes."

She leaned in and kissed me softly on the forehead. "There are some things a normal person can't do. Bloody things, Forrest. But sometimes, those things need to be done."

"I guess so."

"I might ask you to do something for me one day," she said, and kissed me again on the forehead. "Your brother is handsome and strong, but I don't know what he's capable of. You, Forrest, you'll do what I ask. You are capable, because you're missing all the right pieces."

Then she kissed me on the lips.

"Now go away so I can sleep."

• • •

I poured a cup of coffee and paced around Edith's house. My whole body felt different. Charged. I flexed my hands and then I did some push-ups on the hardwood floor. That always helped Billy clear his head. It didn't help me though. I remembered my bed like a long-dead friend. Laina stole my sleep. I mourned the loss. Then I got my winter clothes on and went outside.

Edith had a pile of pine rounds out back. They were very old and well-seasoned. I went to the garage and found an axe. It was far too big for an old lady to swing. Too big for me, if I'm being honest. The single blade was the size of a dinner plate and pitted all over except for the bright sharp edge. I took it out back and swung at those rounds as hard as I could. The wood flew apart. It was a good feeling. The brief shudder, then release, as pieces fell in two.

I chopped wood until my hands quit working. Then I went in and ran cool water over them. When the fingers moved, I chopped some more. It calmed me. The flash of steel and splitting pine. I swung and swung. My thoughts became ordered. Time moved quickly.

Soon there was movement in the house. Lights came on and coffee brewed. A new day. New things to do and think about. Billy told Edith about old Bud Larson. I watched them both make somber shapes with their faces, but I was disconnected from it. Time was still fast for me.

They talked about his work ethic and upstanding character. Then Gordon drove up in the cherry picker with some strange news. Bud left a will stuck right to his fridge with a magnet. Gordon got it all. The house, the dog, the machinery. There was some paperwork to be done, but the local government was being very understanding. We could keep the business going while all the official crap got ironed out. We still had jobs! Edith made pancakes to celebrate. Gordon ate three dozen all by himself. Billy slapped me on the back and grinned. Good times for all. Though not for Bud, who was still dead.

36.

"How depressing is this gonna be?" Billy said. He drove the Chevy with one hand and shoveled spoonsful of Tater Tot hotdish into his mouth with the other. Right from the pan. The pan was on his lap, and the tinfoil Edith used to cover it was balled up in the ditch a mile back. "I have a strong feeling this is gonna be real depressing," he said.

Gordon was hosting a small memorial gathering for Old Man Larson. A man should not be forgotten, Gordon said, even if he has not one single family member left on this earth. According to Gordon, everyone dies three times. The first death is when the heart stops. The second is when the body is laid to rest, and the third is when the name is no longer spoken. The third death is the most painful, Gordon said. Getting together and telling a few stories, he said, would ease the old man's suffering. So, basically, we had to go. Plus, Billy was nearly done fixing Edith's house and didn't feel like a night of puzzles.

Edith was pissed-off she wasn't invited but sent a hotdish along anyway. It was in her nature to send hotdish, and it was in Billy's nature to eat the hotdish on the drive over.

"Goddamn," he said through Tater Tots. "That woman can cook."

He handed me the serving spoon and I took a bite. It tasted like cardboard. A lot of things were starting to taste like cardboard recently. Pot roast. Pancakes. Even bacon. I had a theory that Edith was losing her mind and adding the wrong sort of spices to things. Everyone else was pretending so she wouldn't feel bad about herself. That theory got less and less viable every day. Edith wasn't even around to see Billy chowing through her wretched hotdish.

There was a very small chance the cardboard nature of recent meals could have been caused by changes in my sleep patterns. Loss of sleep patterns, actually. I hadn't slept a wink in four nights. I wondered if that could be having some effect. No. Couldn't be that. I felt great. Life had never been better. Four nights running, Laina took me to her room, and four nights running my dick performed like a plank of solid oak. I was a rockstar! Not really. She did all the movement stuff. I was more like sturdy infrastructure. Point is, I was a non-disappointment. So what if I couldn't sleep after? So what if I spent seven or eight hours chopping wood every night while everyone else rested, and food wasn't good anymore, and my clothes were getting too big? I was fine. I was better than fine.

Billy parked a quarter mile from Bud's place. He didn't want to be blocked in if the gathering became too sad. Then we came around a corner in the driveway and saw Bud's old place all lit up and shaking with loud music. The windows rattled to the base line. We could hear people laughing inside. For a second, we thought we'd misjudged Gordon's little get together. It wouldn't be sad at all. But it was. It really was.

We knocked on Bud's door and a woman I did not recognize let us in. She was very thin and her eyes were glassy. She carried a bottle of Absolut Vodka.

"Hello you," she said to Billy. She talked loud to make herself heard over the music, but I suspect she'd have talked loud anyway. "Do you want a drink?" she said, holding out the bottle. We slipped past her and immediately regretted it. A few dozen people crowded Bud's living room. A few women danced. Men lounged on couches with their legs spread wide apart. Everybody looked like they were running real hot. They ran so hot they didn't seem to have any gums left . . . smiles as long as horse teeth. They smelled like chemical smoke. Like if you burned cleaning products.

"We shouldn't be here," I said.

Billy couldn't hear me. "Where's Gordon?" he said.

We found Gordon sitting on the floor in a quieter corner, with his back to the wall. Bud's dog lay beside him, with his head in Gordon's lap, and Gordon's big hand resting on top of it.

"Welcome," Gordon said. "Make yourselves comfortable."

All the couches were taken so we squatted down on our haunches. Billy lit a cigarette and passed it to Gordon, then tapped out another for himself. Gordon took a long slow drag. Burned half the thing in one go. His words came out so low and rumbly it sounded like he was talking from the back of a cave. "The situation got away from me," Gordon said. "The people I invited, invited other people."

Billy nodded. "It happens," he said.

"Then they put all manner of substances into their veins and now if I kick them out, they'll get into car accidents and be killed."

"Seems like their problem."

Gordon shook his head. He was very low. "No one is talking about Bud," he said. "Bud has been forgotten already. His third death has come and gone. His light blinked out and this place we live in is darker for it."

Billy nodded. I tried to reach back for a good Bud story. I figured it would prop Gordon up a little. But I knew him such a short time. I had very little to say about the man.

A couple came down the log stairs from Bud's old loft. Their hair was all messed up. People clapped. Gordon let out a sigh that sounded like a gust of wind. "I will not sleep there tonight," he said. He finished the cigarette, stubbed it out and went back to petting the dog. The dog was old and her face skin was very loose. Gordon's fingers pulled up huge wrinkles of the stuff. Suddenly I remembered a great Bud story—the thing about Vern chain sawing a branch right down on Bud's head and tearing half his face off like an orange rind. I brought up this story to Gordon but it didn't seem to help. He shook his head.

"Vern was not a good lumberjack. He was not good to Bud. And now he's had sex with a woman in Bud's bed, and I will have to burn the sheets and maybe the bed, too."

"That was Vern?" Billy said. He turned around to get a look.

"Vern was not good to Bud," Gordon said again. He looked at the floor. He pet the dog. People laughed and danced in the living room. There were so many bad chemicals in the air, I was starting to get a real sick feeling in my guts. Like something bad was about to happen, or was already in the process of happening someplace else, and my guts knew about it before the rest of me. Or maybe I just needed to barf. Anyway. I wanted badly to leave, but Gordon was in the middle of a thought.

"Vern is a good metaphor for Bud's time on earth," he said. "Everything went wrong for Bud. Bad luck all the time. No wife. No sons. Life dropped trees on Bud's head. Tore his face off. Took his fingers. Took his youth. Then fucked a woman in his bed during the time of remembrance. Bud's life was one big Vern, from beginning to end. And after the end, too."

Gordon's eyes became like two round stones. He said more sad things, then trailed off and sat quietly. We watched his face for a long time. Billy got to his feet. We'd been squatting so long his knees popped.

"Well, Gordon," he said. "See you tomorrow."

We headed for the door. What a relief. I had such a bad, sick feeling in my guts. There'd be cocoa at Edith's place. Cocoa was the only thing that still tasted good.

But we didn't quite make it out. Billy was just a couple steps away—reaching out for the knob—when that heavy wooden door exploded into splinters and dust. He fell to his back, covered his face with his arms. The night roared with sounds I did not at first understand. Concussive blasts. Gunfire.

I dropped down behind the couch and took a quick little peep around it. Billy was moving still. Crawling away from the door, rubbing chunks of wood from his eyes. Bullets flew. Everybody took cover except the woman with the vodka bottle, who just stood there screaming. The screaming made it hard to maintain my calm. I took another look around the couch. Billy had his hands over his face. I didn't know what to do. It was all so sudden. Being in a gunfight is one thing when you're the one who started it. There's a certain logic. But as an innocent bystander—dang. It's all just fear and confusion. I don't like to admit it, but I got so scared I couldn't seem to move.

Finally, the shooting stopped and a group of men slammed through the door. Even half deaf from the gunfire, I could hear their heavy boots on the floor. One of them shouted.

"Gordon, get out here. We need to talk."

I recognized his voice. It was Lester, the bear killer. Shit. I peeked around the couch in time to see Lester haul off and kick Billy in the ribs.

"I'll deal with you later," he said. "Gordon! Get the fuck out here."

Lester wore a big black coat. He carried a semiautomatic rifle, and so did two of his guys. The third had a pump-action shotgun. I wanted to throw up. Whatever he wanted with Gordon, he was gonna shoot Billy and me right after. Of course he was. Billy beat him up and took his job and I was banging his girl. He'd probably have his guys torture us first.

"Jesus Christ, Gordon," Lester shouted. "You know what I've come for, just go ahead and bring it out."

Finally, Gordon emerged from a back room. He carried two big paper bags in one hand, and something else in his other, but it was sort of tucked away behind his back so I couldn't see what it was.

"I told you my decision about this money," Gordon said. "My mind's made up."

"Think this through, buddy," Lester said. "There are a lot of people here. People you'd rather not see shot to death."

Gordon thought for a long time. So long I started to wonder if he was gonna say go for it, you know. Shoot a few people, see if I care. But he didn't say that. He tossed the bags over to Lester. Lester motioned to one of his guys, and that dude picked up the bags. He opened them and nodded to Lester. Lester grinned.

"Don't feel bad, Gordon," he said. "You're not getting robbed.

You're just settling Bud's accounts. Don't I deserve severance pay? Plus a little extra for pain and suffering."

"Bud did not like you."

"And I didn't like him. The old fuck didn't appreciate my skill set."

Gordon shook his head. He thought a long time before each thing he said. It made the conversation stretch on forever. "I knew about your stealing. And I knew about your other activities. This skill set you speak of," he said. "It was ugly to me, but I did not want to get tangled up in the white man's problems." As he spoke, Gordon loosened his hand and an axe slid slowly down through his fingers. The head of it was even bigger than the one at Edith's house. The handle was long and slender, and when the blade hung nearly to the floor Gordon tightened his grip. He looked down at the axe, and then he looked at Lester. "I see now I should have taken action."

Lester laughed a nervous laugh. "You know what they say about hindsight," he said.

"You will die soon," Gordon said. At this, Lester's guys all raised their guns to their shoulders. Then, around the room, I heard other men racking bullets into their pistols. Three of Gordon's uninvited guests were armed as well. At least that many. Rural areas, man. I'm telling you, everybody's armed to the eyeballs all the time. Everybody except Billy, who left his gun at Edith's place. I looked around the couch again to see if he had some plan of action—something he could communicate to me with his eyes—but Billy wasn't there. The floor was empty where he'd been.

"That's not the hindsight thing," Lester said. "You got your sayings all messed up, Gordon."

"Your throat will be opened and your life will pour out into your hands. You will watch it go. You will mourn your own passing before it happens."

"Come on, buddy. Think this through." But Gordon must have thought it through already, because he lifted the axe above his head and ran straight at Lester. Lester raised his gun and fired. All I heard was a pop and a long whine, and the top of Gordon's left ear evaporated in a bloody mist. And then, all at once, the whole scene just blinked out. Blackness. I'd have thought I was dead, but gunfire lit the place in flashes, like a lightning storm. Just images. Gordon with the axe before him, mid-swing. Lester diving away. Couch stuffing floating down like snow. I made myself as small as I could. I was so afraid. Where was Billy? And why did he have to leave his gun at home? And why did everybody I know feel the need to take drugs and do violence on each other?

In the midst of it, Billy's hand caught my shoulder. I rolled over and saw his face. It was white in the muzzle flash. A bit nicked up, but calm.

"Where were you?" I hissed.

"Looking for a damn pistol," he said. "Found the fuse box instead." Then he pointed four or five yards to a busted-out window. "See there? When I tell you, I need you to go through it."

I nodded.

"Now," Billy said, and I rose like a sprinter. My feet barely touched the ground. In that brief moment I did catch a glimpse of Lester and Gordon—both somehow alive still. Lester was scampering on all fours with Gordon in hot pursuit, chopping at the floor behind him with the axe. Blood streamed down from Gordon's missing ear. His eyes were like round stones again. Then I was at the window and leaping through it.

I ran till I hit the tree line, sank down behind an old pine and watched the house. I waited for Billy, but he did not come. Shots cracked in the cold night air. "Goddamn," someone shouted. I didn't know the voice. A man left the front door at a run, tripped, and fell on his face, then got up and limped away. It was not Billy. The shots slowed, just enough bullets to keep everyone pinned down. And still Billy did not burst out into the night.

I breathed and tried to let my heart settle. I felt really weird. I was always wound up after close calls, but this was different. My body felt disconnected from my head. My guts were water. I wondered if it had to do with the not sleeping thing. No. It wasn't that. I'd been in a gunfight. Of course I felt strange. It was probably PTSD. I pounded my forehead with my hand till my thoughts leveled out. I was okay. Billy would be okay. He had a sense for these things.

I scanned the woods around me. A few yards off another man sat with his back to a tree. Another fleeing partygoer, no doubt. He sat very still.

"Hey," I said and waved.

The man didn't wave back. I thought maybe he'd been wounded. Maybe he was bleeding out. I crawled over to help, but it wasn't anyone from the party. It was the man I shot down in Laredo. His brains stained stucco walls four thousand miles to the south, yet here he was in Alaska, with a bowl carved in the top of his head. His eyes were like red grapes. I fell back on my ass and opened my mouth, but no scream came out. This dead man had followed me. He blinked his red eyes.

I threw up on the ice. A stream of tar and blood. I tried again and failed to scream. Then strong hands gripped my shoulders and pulled me upright. It was Billy.

"Breathe, little brother," he said. My eyes focused on his face. So calm and steady. Wind returned to my lungs. Shots popped from the house, but they seemed far away now. I looked down. My barf was just a lot of Tater Tots and burger. The dead man was nobody I killed. It was old Bud Larson, frozen these many days. His head was totally intact.

37

Of course I did not sleep that night. I didn't even try. When Laina was done with me, I went right out to the woodpile. I took the axe in my hands and swung. This was my life now, I thought. A new defect to deal with. Unpredictable hand problems, missing things, and now there'd be hallucinations. I saw a dead Mexican in the Alaskan wilderness. The men I killed were coming back for visits. I was crazy now. Shit. I swung the axe.

Everything was falling apart. Everything except the sex. Laina and I were really figuring each other out. Getting the angles right. Soon even that would be over. Billy said it was time to leave. The firefight at Bud's old place would bring swarms of cops. The marshal too, probably, and soon. We'd be gone already, except Billy wanted forged papers this time. He wanted to do it right. Head for Argentina, or one of the non-extradition countries where it's always warm. Sun and mixed drinks, he said. No Laina. I swung the axe.

How did things get so heavy all of a sudden? The stuff I did for Billy. The robbery and murder and whatever he needed next. I could live with it. But now there was Laina to think about. When we were gone, Lester would come for her. That, I could not live with. I don't know if she loved me then, or if she took me to her bed because I was broken and stupid enough to kill if she asked. Either way, I knew I would kill for her, if she asked. For her and her little daughter, and for Billy. Where would it end? . . . this list of people asking me to do terrible things. Or not asking, just knowing I would. It was too much for my defective head. Reality was breaking down. I swung the axe. I swung and swung till my lungs burned and my hands felt nothing at all.

"Hello there, kid."

I looked up mid-swing. There was a great huge pit bull not six feet away. His skin and hair were black. Blood ran from three bullet holes in his flanks. The blood was black, too. He grinned long white teeth. Grin is the correct word. He didn't have a dog look on his face.

I made a bad scream—embarrassingly high pitched—and my hands let go of the axe at the very top of my swing. It sailed away into the night. The dog watched it go and laughed.

"Tightly wound tonight, are we?" he said.

"Aw shit."

The dog paced. He put his head really low to the ground and moved his spine like a snake. The muscles in his back rippled and bulged.

"You don't look so good," he said.

"You look better than you should," I replied. "My brother shot you for mangling my hand. You're dead. I'm seeing dead things now."

The dog grinned. "Hallucinations," he said, shaking his big head. "That's no good at all."

"No shit. Did you come all this way to tell me that?"

"Nope."

"Why the hell are you here, then?"

He eased down onto the ice in a pile of muscle and bone. He let out a long dog yawn so I could see every one of his pointy teeth. My bit hand tingled and ached just looking at them. "You really don't know?" he said.

"I don't."

"You will."

I went and found the axe and split some more wood. I figured the dog might go away. You know, like an itch goes away when you don't scratch. I chopped a good long time, and then I glanced up to see if the dog was still there. He was. He lounged on the ice, chewing and smacking his lips. He looked relaxed.

"Hey," he said. I looked away fast.

I swung the axe. I swung and swung and swung. I chopped the wood into kindling. Smaller and smaller pieces. Soon it'd be tooth-picks. All the while, that dead dog smacked his lips. Louder, and with increasing joy.

"I bet you're wondering what I'm eating," he said. I sunk the axe and looked up. His upper lip was full of something, like a dip of chewing tobacco.

"Not really."

"It's good," he said. "I'll share."

"No thanks."

The dog padded over with his head almost scraping the ground, and his two tiny eyes looking straight up. He came right to me and spit a chunk of something at my feet. It was an ear. Gordon's shot ear, only it was the whole thing instead of just the top.

"You can barely taste the gunpowder," he said, and then he laughed. It sounded like barking. I threw up on the ground. Except there was nothing in my stomach, so I just heaved.

When I was done, the dog had trotted off somewhere. He'd taken the ear with him. I went back inside . . . back to my room. I took off my clothes and climbed into bed—waited for Billy to wake—waited to begin again.

38.

We found Gordon in a hospital room in Fairbanks. He'd called Edith's house phone in the early morning, from a burner cell. Told us to come. Told us he needed our help. Beyond that, he didn't say much. He was more talkative in person.

"I see you are unharmed," he said. "I worried."

He was sitting up and smiling with bandages wrapped around his head. His limbs sprawled out in the tiny hospital bed. One of his arms was bandaged, too, and one of his legs. His feet were bare and sticking out from the bottom of the blanket, because there wasn't a blanket in the whole facility big enough to cover all of Gordon at once.

"We bolted," Billy said. "I'm not proud of it."

"It's okay. You have your brother to worry about. If the boy was killed, I would have been sad. No. Don't worry about me. I am heavily medicated, and the doctors say I will make a full recovery, except for my ear, which is a lost cause."

Billy took a seat in the corner. "How long did the fighting go, after we left?"

"Long time."

"Who's dead?"

"Nobody. Axe murder is harder than you think. Lester is fast, like a squirrel. Have you ever tried to chop up a squirrel?"

"Nope."

"Impossible if they don't stay still."

"What about all the shooting?"

"Hard to hit anything in the dark," Gordon said. He nodded and scratched the bandages over his ruined ear. "It was real dark," he said, "and of course, no one was still. Hard to hit anything with an axe or a gun, unless it's still and the lights are on."

"Looks like they hit you a couple times."

"I paused a moment to get my breath. That was my downfall." Gordon folded his hands in his lap and looked at them. He seemed like he was going to continue, but we waited a long time and he did not. Finally, Billy spoke up.

"You said you needed help?"

Gordon nodded. "Well," he said. "There is something you should know." Gordon fessed up about the whole thing. He never found a will stuck to Bud's fridge. Never called the local government to handle the paperwork. No. He just dragged old dead Bud out into the woods and moved into his house. He cared for Bud's dog, and kept his stove burning, and found stacks and stacks of cash in a shoebox in his basement. Bud didn't trust banks, which was wise, Gordon said. "Banks get robbed," he said. "This should be common knowledge."

Anyway, it would have worked out great for Gordon, except Lester came by one day looking for an investor. Lester had a lot of side hustles. Car repair and welfare fraud and also a meth-cooking operation out in the wilderness. He used a bush plane to bring the crystal to a group of buyers in Anchorage, then returned with cash and raw materials. After his run-in with Billy, Lester turned cooking into his main hustle. He hired some local muscle and expanded his deal with the guys in Anchorage.

"But that big storm broke his plane," Gordon said. "He needed a new one, and he wanted Bud's money to pay for it. I told him Bud wouldn't want to finance his murderous trade. I told him his products caused disproportionate harm to my people. And then I told him to go fuck himself, which was probably a bit much."

Billy hadn't hardly taken a breath since Gordon began. When he was done, Billy blinked many times.

"You just dragged Bud out in the woods and left him there."

"It's what he wanted."

"You're joking."

"He told me, 'when I pass, take me out in the woods and put my back against a tree. Let the wolves come for me. Let the bears and the birds and all manner of creature enjoy my flesh, as I have enjoyed theirs.'"

"He said that?"

"Not word for word. The general idea."

"You can't just leave a body in the woods, Gordon."

"It is not mine to ignore the wishes of the dead."

Billy rubbed his forehead. He reached for a cigarette, then realized he was inside and put it back. "What do you want me to do about all this?"

"Bud's house is full of police officers now. I told them I was burglarized while house sitting. I told them Bud's out of town. If they find his body there will be many questions that I cannot answer, given my history with the law."

Billy breathed in deep through his teeth and looked up at the ceiling.

"Why the fuck did you leave him in the woods? We have a professional-grade woodchipper."

"I don't understand why the wolves didn't partake."

"The why don't matter. You need me to move him, don't you?"

Gordon nodded. Billy got up and paced around the tiny hospital room. He flexed his hands. He wanted to smoke so bad. He sank down on the edge of Gordon's bed.

"I will do this for you," he said, "Because I like you, and because you're shot and I feel bad about bolting on you yesterday, but I need something from you, too. You said you got a new name when you came here. New papers. They must be good since you're not in jail. My brother and I need the same treatment."

Gordon nodded again. They shook hands. Then Gordon extended his broad hand to me, and I shook it. His fingers wrapped all the way up around my wrist.

"He was frozen already," I said. "That's how come the wolves didn't eat him. Would have been like chewing rocks."

"Yes," he said. "You are a smart boy. I'm glad you weren't killed in the shooting."

39

Billy parked on the road, and we followed our boot prints from the night before. We used a flashlight until we got close, and then Billy shut it off and we stood in the woods waiting for our eyes to adjust. I could hear Billy breathing. I moved my shoulders around in my coat for warmth. In a minute we continued, and soon we could make out bright lights through the trees.

We dropped down on all fours and crawled the last hundred yards to the corpse of old Bud Larson. He was right where we left him, though I still wonder how the cops missed him. Their floodlights made the woods as bright as day.

"Hello again," Billy said. Then for some reason, we both just kept crawling in toward the house. Toward those big lights and bustle of investigators. Curiosity, I guess. It's deeply ingrained. We crawled right to the edge of the woods and peered in.

Bud's house was a crime scene. Red tape crossed all the doors and windows. A couple squad cars were parked in the driveway, a big black van. A handful of guys in uniform milled around under floodlights. They carried guns and beer bottles and blood-soaked towels out to the van. Everything was in plastic bags. All the guys wore latex gloves.

As we watched, another car arrived. A black Dodge Charger. The door slammed. Billy got up on his elbows and squinted. I squinted too. Probably we both needed glasses.

"What in the actual hell?" Billy said.

A tall, thin man strolled up to Bud's old place, stepping over crime scene tape and pulling on rubber gloves. He wore a black leather jacket, along with a big scarf, on account of the leather jacket not having any insulation to speak of. He shook hands with the investigators. Glasses or not, we both knew that man.

"It's been less than twenty-four hours," Billy said. "Incredible."

My heartbeat rang in my ears. My mouth tasted like pennies, and I had to flex my hands to keep them from cramping.

"We didn't even do this one," Billy said. "Gordon lost his ear totally independent of our criminal endeavors."

I said nothing because I knew it would come out as a whimper or a shout. Billy was almost laughing. He sounded crazy.

"If you look at it a certain way," he said. "I did drive Lester deeper into the meth business, which did eventually lead to Gordon getting his ear blown off. But goddamn that's a lot to deduce. That marshal is even better than I thought."

He busted a piece of ice off the ground and chewed it. Then he turned and crawled back into the woods. When we got to Bud, Billy stood up and brushed himself off.

"Well," he said. "Grab his feet."

I couldn't believe it. The marshal was on us again. It was time to run. Time to steal a car and drive like hell. We needed to do something about Laina, but that was in the future. Maybe we could wire her some money from Argentina. Right now it was time to run. But I couldn't say that, because I knew I'd scream it. The marshal would hear and shoot us both dead right where we stood. So I just grabbed Bud's feet and Billy got his shoulders and we staggered off into the darkness.

Bud was frozen at a right angle. His old butt kept dragging on the ground. Halfway out of the woods, my forearms burned. Sweat poured down my face and palms. I lost my grip. Bud landed on his rear end and tilted slowly upright – like he was just sitting there. His frozen eyes stared at Billy and me, and we stared back. Billy got out a cigarette and lit it, then he offered one to Bud.

"No?" he said. "Good for you, Bud, these things will kill you."

"What the hell, Billy?"

"Too dark?"

It was too much to handle. I groaned and slammed my fists into the icy snow. "Why are we doing this?" I said. "We have to run."

Billy smoked his cigarette. He was silent a long time.

"True enough," he said. "But not yet."

"What do you mean not yet?"

"We go right now and we'll never stop. Understand?"

I wanted to shout. I wanted to leave my brother in the woods with dead old Bud and run. But I didn't do it.

"He doesn't know we're here," Billy said. "Not for sure. Hold tight, little brother. We'll get those new names. Just give me a day or two. We'll do this right."

I put my hands over my face . . . breathed in and out real slow.

"Okay?"

"Okay."

Billy stretched and flexed his hands and got a good hold on Bud's shoulders. This time he rolled Bud over so he faced down. I got his feet and we lifted. His big old rear end poked straight up. Billy grinned at me.

"The things we do for people."

• • •

We took Bud up the side of a mountain on switchback gravel roads. Trees leaned out from rock and snow, and the earth fell away sharp at the edge of the road. When it got too narrow, we stopped and pulled Bud out onto the ice. He made a dull thump hitting the ground. Billy dragged him over to the edge of the road and crouched down low. He got his hands under the side of Bud's ass and hove up and forward like he was flipping a tire.

Bud rolled and bounced. His head and feet broke through the film of ice and sent streams of snow up into the air. I bet he was tumbling at forty miles an hour by the time we lost sight of him.

"Damn," Billy said.

We went back to the cherry picker and sat on the running boards. We looked out over the land. A few lights pricked the darkness. The homes of Winner. Not many and not very bright. Somewhere down there, a skinny old US Marshal puzzled over bullet holes and torn couch cushions. He looked for traces of Billy and me, but he would find none. Billy was right. I could see it now that I was calm. There's no way he tracked us to Winner. We were so careful. Probably he just set up shop in a bigger town—Fairbanks or Anchorage—and drove out to investigate the more significant gun crimes. One day he'd find us, but not today or tomorrow. We had a little time. Better to wait for our new names. I wondered who I'd be.

Above us streaks of green light appeared in the night sky. They flexed and danced like living things. At first I thought these lights were in my mind alone, another product of insomnia. Then Billy leaned back and I saw the green reflection in his eyes, too.

"Pretty," he said. The northern lights. Postcards don't do them justice. We sat a long time with our heads craned back and our mouths open.

"I wonder if the missionaries had that kid yet," Billy said.

"She was big as a house last we saw."

"Do you think she got her little girl?"

"A daughter is good to have."

Billy rubbed his neck and blinked. He got out a cigarette but didn't light it. He held it between his fingers.

"We need to do something about Laina," he said.

"I know."

"Lester will come after her."

"I'll just kill him this time," I said. "She told me to do it, so it's okay."

Billy decided against the cigarette. He put it in his pocket. "We'll be gone, kid, remember?"

"We'll stay till he comes back, and then I'll kill him."

"I thought you were in a big old hurry."

The lights above coiled and writhed. In my mind they took on the form of a great snake eating its own tail. Teeth scraped along smooth scales. Glassy eyes peered down at Billy and me, and Bud below. The Vikings had stories about a great serpent like that. It outgrew the oceans, swallowed its own tail. I met the snake's glare without fear. It was captivating. I hardly caught Billy's words when he spoke again.

"Be careful with her, little brother," he said. "She's awful young."

"I'm young too."

"Men like us," Billy said. "The things we touch don't come away clean . . . understand?"

I blinked and the snake was gone, just green light again. "I understand."

"Maybe we just buy her a pair of plane tickets," he said. "That would work."

"Yeah, that's better."

• • •

Billy tried to get me to sleep with some Nyquil. He found an old bottle and made me drink about half of it, and then some whiskey. He watched me get into bed and close my eyes, and when my breath came slow he went to bed himself. But I wasn't sleeping—just lying really still. When he slept, I climbed back into my clothes and slipped away. I didn't go to Laina's room either. It seemed all wrong now, after what Billy said. I went straight out to the woodpile.

The dead dog was already there, just lying on the ice and waiting for me.

"Hey, kid," he said.

"Hey." I was almost glad to see him. Night gets long when you are the only one awake. It is not good to be alone. I set up a log and swung the axe. The dog sat by and watched, silent except for the occasional yawn. Maybe this thing was manageable, I thought. Chopping wood is sort of fun. And one hallucination isn't so bad, is it? It was like having a pet dog. Never mind the bullet holes, this one could talk. A lot of people would love to have a dog like that.

"So you got rid of Bud?" the dog said.

"Yeah, we did."

"How'd you do it?"

"Tossed him down a big hill. He rolled and bounced till I couldn't see him anymore."

The dog made a big dog grin and licked his many sharp teeth. His tongue went up to his eyes.

"Did you happen to save any bits for me?"

"Bits?"

"I don't know. Like a hand, or a foot. Anything that sticks out and might be easy to snap off."

"Of course I didn't snap off any bits. What's wrong with you? First you ruin my hand, and now you want Bud's. Shit."

"Sorry, kid. It's in my nature."

I went back to chopping. Stacking and chopping. The pile of split wood was getting pretty big. Much larger than the pile of rounds. There wasn't much left to do. One, maybe two more nights of work. I wondered what I'd do when it ran out. I'd be gone. That's what.

The dog edged a little closer. He looked concerned.

"Forget about Bud and his delicious-looking bits," he said. "How are you doing? You look pretty tired."

Even a dead imaginary dog is still a dog, still a good friend to have. His eyes were big and watery all of a sudden.

"I am tired. I haven't slept for a long time. And now the marshal is closing in and I might have to kill Lester and the whole thing is really stressful."

"Soon you will find rest. I'm sure of it."

I bent down and pet his muscly face. "You're a good dog," I said. "I forgive you for biting my hand. Do you have a name I can call you by?"

"I am known by many names, in many different regions of the world."

"Is one of your names Kevin?"

"No."

"Damn."

"You will know me one day, but not tonight." He reached out his long tongue and licked the palms of my hands. Between my fingers. He was a good dog.

"Kid," he said. "Have you taken anything for the insomnia? There are pills."

"Billy gave me Nyquil. It's not working."

The dog shook his big head. "That's no good at all," he said. "Have any bits fallen off yet?"

"What is your deal with bits falling off?"

"Like a fingernail, or some hair?"

"No. Goddamn. Don't talk like that."

"That's good. When bits start falling off, that's when you've got real trouble."

40.

Billy and I got our portraits taken at the Fairbanks Walgreens and sent the files off to Gordon's passport guy. Then Billy took me to a diner and ordered burgers and milkshakes. I knew something was up when he asked for the milkshakes. Burgers were a staple of our diet, but Billy only ever bought milkshakes when he knew I was having a bad time. Like when I'd catch hell at school, or when he'd done something that was about to make my life harder than it already was.

"So Gordon called," Billy said. "He sounds better. That's good."

"Yeah."

"He says these passports are something else. His guy has access to government microchips, or some shit. You can board international flights with these things."

"That's gonna be really nice."

"The passport guy is in high demand, on account of the micro-chips. But Gordon says he got us to the front of the line. It wasn't cheap, but they'll be done tomorrow night. We'll all meet at Gordon's old place. Two days, kid, and we're out of here."

"That's great, Billy."

We both nodded and looked at the table. I waited for the bad news.

"How's that milkshake? Pretty good, right?"

It wasn't. I'd barely touched the shake. I knew I'd just have to throw it up later. I even snuck my burger under the table for the dog to eat, which was disturbing on about five different levels. One level was the sound his teeth made. Another was the fact that the dead imaginary pit bull I saw every night had followed me into my daytime activities.

"Real good," I said.

Billy met my eyes, then looked away. "Your burger is on the seat next to you."

I glanced down. The dog was sitting there with his tongue out, panting. "Sure enough."

"The Nyquil didn't work, did it?"

"Not really."

"Damn."

Billy sipped at his milkshake. "Listen, kid. Some things are hard to get over. I know it."

I nodded and tried to resist my urge to pet the dog. That would be real weird. Petting a burger, or perhaps the air above a burger. I wasn't sure how it would look to other people.

"You've carried a lot," Billy said. "I just need you to carry it a little further."

He laid out the state of our finances. How much the papers would cost. The travel. Life in some new place. I'm sure it wasn't complicated, but I couldn't focus. The dog was growling. The bloody black hairs on his back bristled and spit ran down from his bared teeth. He barked. I followed his eyes out the windows to a tall, thin man on the sidewalk. The man wore a black leather jacket. A scarf coiled around his neck. Here was that US Marshal again on the streets of Fairbanks. My hands made fists right there on the table. The dog barked and barked and barked.

"Are you still with me, little brother?" Billy said. I blinked. The marshal was gone. Maybe he was another hallucination. Maybe not. It didn't matter. In two days, we'd be gone.

"Excuse me," I said. I went to the bathroom and threw up a tiny amount of milkshake. It was acid now. Nothing left in me. I drank some water from the faucet and spit. Something clattered like a stone in the sink. I picked it up and squinted. It was a tooth. I looked at it a long time. A molar I think. It seemed bigger than a tooth should reasonably be. Like a cow's tooth. The tooth of a creature who eats grass.

I leaned in close to the mirror and opened my mouth. My remaining teeth were long as fingers. The gums were gray. Beyond them blackness. It was like a hole in the ground. A vision of death. No wonder dentists are always killing themselves. A career spent staring into the void. No amount of golf can make that okay.

How many days since I slept? Six? I couldn't remember.

How many days can a guy live without? Well, things were starting to fall off, so not a hell of a lot longer. I put the tooth in my pocket and washed my face, found Billy eating an extra order of fries at our booth.

"We don't have enough money for these papers, do we?" I said.

"No. We do not."

"And we have to be outlaws again. That's why you got me a milkshake."

"We don't have a lot of time, kid."

"Fuck it," I said. "Let's burn a path."

The dog leaned back his head and howled, and the howl turned to laughter.

41

Billy had a place picked out. A liquor store a few miles outside Fairbanks. We drove past it pretty often on our tree-cutting trips. It was always busy. Booze is a stable commodity, even in hard economic times. Just this one place, Billy said, would close our funding gap. Then we were done.

We waited till it closed and did our work. Billy parked a few hundred yards down the road and tossed me one of Edith's white flour-sack towels. It had a teapot with a happy cartoon face embroidered in one corner. The teapot winked at me and pointed a Mickey Mouse hand in my direction. "Good luck, buddy," rolled across the towel in neat rows of thread, stitched by an invisible hand.

"I agree, kid," the dog said from the bed of the truck. "I'm sure this won't go south."

Damn hallucinations. I closed my eyes. Concentrated. One more job.

"Do you have a good feeling about this, Billy?"

"Always have a good feeling," he replied, pulling his flour sack up over his face.

He grabbed an extra-large sledgehammer from the bed of the Chevy and weighed it in his hands as we walked. Billy had a stabilizing effect on me. Everything was going to be fine.

We walked around back and found a door. Billy didn't even check to see if it was locked. He just swung the hammer as hard as he could. The knob came right out of the door and clattered on the floor behind. He swung again, just below the empty knob hole. The dead bolt tore loose and the door tilted open.

Billy dropped the hammer like a home run slugger. Even through the towel I could tell he was grinning. We raced in. I went for the till. He burst through office doors, hunting the lock box. In the darkness,

I could hear things tipping over. Bottles smashing. Boxes torn apart. I got the register open, but it was empty except for the pennies. I left them and met Billy in the vodka aisle.

"Nothing," he said.

Then there were sirens. Not approaching sirens. Present sirens. Unlike Winner, Fairbanks had no shortage of cops.

Billy moved fast. So fast his feet skid back on the waxed lino-leum and the wind he drew behind him moved bottles of liquor as he passed. We'd left the back door open a few inches and flashing lights came through the gap. He went right at it. Right at the flashing lights, and I followed at a sprint.

The door swung open. For the space of one heartbeat I saw an of-ficer raising his pistol. Billy's hand reached out. The shot was nothing but a clean whistle. A tuft of Billy's hair and blood rose into the air. His head snapped back. Then his momentum carried the two of them down in a pile. In another heartbeat, I was over them and running out into the flashing red and blue.

It took some distance to stop. To realize what I'd seen, and turn. When I did, two officers were dragging Billy out onto the ice. They had him by the arms. Blood streamed down his face. His head hung loose, like a dead deer, and bounced when they let him drop. I waited for him to rise. They thought he was knocked out cold, or dead, but he wasn't. This was Bare Knuckle Billy they were dealing with. Any sec-ond he'd jump up grinning and give the cops a thrashing. Any second.

Billy lay still. One officer nudged him with his boot and shook his head. The other picked up a radio. He said a few words, then let out a gasp as my shoulder met his sternum. He looked confused as he fell. I was confused too. I didn't really decide to rush him, but I did. I didn't decide to smash his face in either, but I did that too. I swung till my knuckles bled. Then his partner got an arm around my neck and dragged me back. My heels slid on the ice. My vision narrowed.

I clawed and writhed—tried to get a breath. There was so much pressure in my head I thought my face would explode. Things were going dark. So little time.

I worked my hand up between his elbow and my throat. I pried with everything I had, made just enough room to fit my chin in the crook of his arm. Then I bit him right through his coat. He screamed and let me loose. He ran backwards, fumbling with his holster. He pulled his gun, but I just took it from him and beat him with it.

When it was done, I stood among three limp bodies in the flickering lights. Red. Blue. Red. Sirens came back into my ears. More of them coming. It was time to go. I knelt over Billy. There was so much blood I couldn't make sense of things. I pulled the flour-sack towel from around my face and wiped the blood from his. Then I felt around for the wound. There was a big old groove in his scalp, but the skull underneath seemed solid enough.

I gripped Billy by the shoulders and sat him up. The sirens were getting closer. So little time.

"Wake up," I said. "You're okay."

I shook him hard.

"Please wake up."

His head rolled to the side. It was a few hundred yards to the truck. More cops on their way. I pulled him over my shoulder and stood. Our shadow looked like a great monstrous creature. Top-heavy. A troll teetering on chicken legs. I gasped under his weight. My knees creaked, but I walked. I had to. I heaved him into the bed of the truck, dug the keys from his pocket, and drove.

• • •

"Hot damn," Billy said. "That's going to be an awesome scar."

Back in our attic room, Billy leaned down and looked at his wound in the mirror. He'd been awake when I pulled into Edith's driveway. Sitting up, and pretty much okay. He took a shower, rubbed Neosporin in the bullet groove, and drank some whiskey. Now he grinned and touched his own skull with his fingertips.

"I should probably get stitches," he said. "I bet most people would get something like this sewn up."

As I watched, a single drop of blood made its way out onto his forehead. Billy didn't notice. "Aw screw it," he said. "I'll be fine."

The drop ran down right between his eyes and hung off his nose. Then a whole river flowed down behind it. His head was a bloody canyon. Brains puckered and shrank in the dry winter air. He turned around and looked at me with purple eyes.

"Unless you want to give it a shot," he said. "I think Edith has a sewing kit downstairs." He laughed as blood ran from his chin.

I blinked and his head was whole again. No blood or exposed brain. The wound was already healing. It would be closed in three days.

"I hope the hair comes in white," he said, "Just this little streak. That would look really cool."

"Yeah. Real cool."

"Hey," he said. "What happened? I was out like a light."

"I did what was required," I said.

42.

The dog paced. He seemed excited. Restless. His head hovered low to the ground and his eyes looked straight up, bright as two polished silver dollars.

"I saw you, kid," he said. "I saw that big old tooth you lost."

I was back outside with the firewood. All that good seasoned pine was split and stacked by the door so Edith wouldn't have to walk far when we were gone. Only a handful of huge rounds remained, and they were from a different tree. I'm not sure what kind, but the wood was old and dark and laced with knots. Really twisty stuff, nearly impossible to split.

"You put it in your pocket instead of just throwing it away. That's weird, right? Just keeping a tooth like that."

The axe hit a knot and bounced off—nearly flew out of my hands. "You ate Gordon's ear," I said. "So shut the hell up."

He laughed and paced. He circled in close, just outside my kicking range.

"What do you think is going to fall off next?" he said. "Let's take bets."

"Nothing's going to fall off. We're going to bust out of this shithole and I'll be able to sleep again."

I swung the axe. The big round ate two inches of blade and refused to split. I strained to get it out. Wouldn't budge.

"My money's on a finger," the dog said. "Or your pinky toe."

"What the hell? Bad dog. Go away."

I heaved. The handle flexed to its limit, then dragged the blade free so quick I fell back on my rear end. He laughed his barking laugh.

"Once the fingers go, it's just a matter of time." he said.

"Till what?"

"You know, kid," he said. "I bet you don't even make it through these shitty old logs." He eased back on his haunches and licked his whole face with his long, wet tongue. "I'm going to eat your guts first."

I leaped up and went after him with the axe. He dodged away, laughing, wagging his little nub tail. At the edge of the woods, he paused. He sniffed the air and grinned. "Better ease up on the crazy," he said, and vanished.

A light snapped on in the house. Edith's back door slid open a crack, and Laina drifted out. She wore a thick blanket around her shoulders and a big fur cap on her head. She sat down on one of the unsplit rounds, crossed her legs, and tucked the blanket around them.

"Hey," she said.

"Hey back."

She watched me work awhile. Bad timing for an audience. The blade kept bouncing off the gnarled old wood, or sticking so hard I could barely get it out. After about a hundred swings, a single tiny chunk split loose. Laina clapped.

"Mr. Krone laid this wood away," she said, "before he passed."

"He's upstairs in an urn shaped like a cat. Sometimes I think it's moving but it's not."

"You know, he died right here, holding that axe—trying to split that very piece of wood."

I dropped the axe and backed away from it. "Aw man," I said.

"Dropped dead," she said. "Heart attack."

Maybe the dog was right. These logs already killed one guy. It was a matter of time. My fingers would turn black, then fall off. Then my heart would explode like old Mr. Krone. And the worst part . . . Laina was laughing. She laughed like the dog. Bark bark bark.

"Your face right now," she said. "Oh my God. Priceless."

I dropped to my knees and threw up. I heaved blackness onto the ice. Laina quit laughing. Her hand touched my shoulder.

"Oh, Forrest," she said. "I was just joking around. He had cancer.

He died in the hospital like every other old person. It took him years and years."

I wiped my mouth and spit. "You scared me."

"It was kind of funny, though. I'm sorry you threw up."

"Don't feel bad. I throw up all the time now."

She helped me up and stood back. She looked at me longer than was comfortable.

"You're not totally okay, are you?" she said.

"A floozy in Nebraska asked the same question," I replied, "The answer is still no."

"I'm not totally okay, either," she said.

I reached for the axe, but Laina stopped my hands. She said that's not what I needed. She had something better. She went inside and I stayed where I was, just hoping she wasn't talking about a sex thing. I didn't have the energy. I was also kind of worried my dick would fall off before my fingers.

Pretty soon she came out with a rifle and a box of shells. She led me away from Edith's place on foot. Alleys and ditches by moonlight. She loaded the rifle while she walked. I had this thought that Laina might be leading me out into the wilderness in order to blow my head off. I had a follow-up thought that maybe she was really just another hallucination and it was me with the rifle, and I was going to blow my own head off. I had complex feelings about this. It might be nice to just end things. I decided to roll with it.

"I hate it here," she said. "I told you that."

"I remember."

"It's a terrible town. Full of sad people who can't get the hell away."

"Winner can't be much worse than my home town. Radium. Very sad little place."

Laina laughed aloud. "Are you serious?" she said.

"Yeah. Why not?"

"Okay, big shot. Tell me about the saddest person you know in Radium, or wherever you said you were from."

I had so much material to work with. So many depressing people. I had Deer Turd Clive. I had my own parents for goodness' sake. But one story just blew the rest of them away. I rubbed my hands together. Laina didn't even know what she was in for.

"I used to know this guy. We called him Unlucky Luke," I said. "Big strong guy. Always talked about going into the military. Wanted to serve his country, you know. True patriot. He joins up right out of high school. Marines. All in."

"If your buddy Luke dies a hero in the Middle East, that's not the type of sad I'm talking about."

"Halfway to Basic, the transport stops for the night. Little barracks in, I don't know Iowa or something. Drill sergeant gets everybody up in the middle of the night and makes them sprint laps around the compound. And Luke, he's just so excited to be there he can't contain himself. He's way out in front. Then he trips on a root. It's dark, so nobody sees him. Every single guy runs right over him. Fifty, sixty big farm boys. They ship Luke home with a busted hip and a lot of back problems no one can figure out."

Laina nodded her head. She looked unimpressed. I'd been so confident in Luke's sad-sack story. His youth, his eager patriotism, literally trampled into the dirt. It was like a metaphor for all of Radium—everyone who lived there. Laina didn't understand. I threw out more details.

"He didn't even make it to boot camp, so technically he's not a soldier. No disability payments. Nothing."

Laina scuffed her feet on the ground.

"So now he's all stove-up, shoveling grain at the elevator for minimum wage." I was almost shouting. "Except he's not anymore. Because my brother burned that elevator to ashes. Luke's probably homeless now." Aw, man. I hadn't even thought about feeling bad for burning Unlucky Luke's one place of gainful employment. I hadn't thought of him at all for years. After the boot camp-thing, he just sort of faded away.

Laina nodded again. "Are you done?" she asked.

"Luke made one big mistake," I said. "He tried to be out in front. People from Radium . . . they have to stay in the middle. They have to be mediocre, or the world crushes them."

"Nice," Laina said. "Poetic."

"Now I'm done."

"Okay. I'm about to make Luke seem like the luckiest dude in the world. You're going to think he won the lottery, just by being born in Radium instead of Winner. Are you ready?"

"Give it your best shot."

"I had a cousin once who was all set to leave. Headed to South Dakota to live with his old man. Then his grandma—my grandma—faked a letter from the dad, saying he changed his mind and my cousin couldn't live with him anymore. My grandma couldn't stand to be without him, you see. Two weeks later, my cousin walks out on the lake ice with an axe and chops a hole. Then he gets in the hole and drowns himself."

"Aw, man."

"It was the middle of winter, Forrest. The ice was three feet thick. I bet it took him all night. Just chopping and chopping."

"Aw, man. I think I'm gonna barf again."

"This place gets to people."

You win."

We kept walking. We were a long way from Edith's place. If Laina was going to blow my head off, I figured now would be the time.

"Did you ever wonder how I've managed to cope this long, Forrest? How I've kept from taking an axe out onto the lake like my cousin, or stabbing Lester to death in his sleep, or drowning my daughter in a bathtub?"

"Jeez, Laina. Do you really think about that stuff?"

"Were you listening to the thing about my cousin?"

"Fair enough."

"Do you want to know how I got through?"

"Yeah."

"This is how," she said, and put the rifle to her shoulder. She fired four times real fast. Levered in shells like a trained killer. When she was done, one of Winner's ruined road signs had four new holes.

She held the gun out to me. I took it and fired. It kicked like a mule. Deafened me—made my body hum. Spent cartridges landed on the ice and melted out of sight. We passed the gun back and forth till the road sign dropped from its post. Then Laina propped it up in a snowbank and we kept firing. When the box of shells ran empty she hefted the gun over her shoulder, and we turned toward home. My ears sang like church bells, but I could think clearly for the first time in days.

"Does everyone up here shoot signs, or is just you?"

"We all have our own special ways of blowing off steam. Booze, or cigarettes. Or beating women."

"Okay."

"I've been blowing off steam with you these last few days, and that's been working great. Thank you for that, by the way."

"No problem."

"I wish it worked for you. It's okay that it doesn't. Maybe shooting road signs will work."

We walked the rest of the way in silence. I liked walking with her like that. It felt like sharing something. I wondered if people would still drown themselves in frozen lakes if they had someone to walk with at night.

Laina stopped on Edith's front porch. "You were talking to somebody when I came outside," she said. "Who was it?"

"There's a dog who visits me. He bit my hand and my brother shot him to death, but he still comes around. I wanted to call him Kevin, but he says that's not his name."

"Fuck," she said.

"I know."

"You're crazier than me, Forrest."

"That's not really my name, you know. My name's Jim."

She helped me off with my jacket and hung it up. Then she led me over to the couch, pulled me down after her. She put my head on her lap and ran her hands through my hair. Her fingertips found the old scars and followed the length of them.

"I'm glad your name is Jim," she said. "Forrest sounds like a challenged person. Forrest Gump. We've all seen the movie."

"I'm not challenged. People always think I am, but I'm not. I promise."

"I believe you, Jimmy. Now go to sleep."

43.

I woke with my head in Laina's lap. The warmth of her legs against my skull felt good. I enjoyed the softness of her living body. Air came clean into my lungs, and the blood no longer ran as acid through my veins. I was alive again, and with a pretty girl, too.

"You stayed," I said. She looked down at me and smiled.

"You're heavy."

She had the TV on. A newscaster chattered too fast for my sleepy brain. I sat up and rubbed my eyes. Everything was brighter. Clearer. I raised my arms over my head. The shoulders popped, then moved easily.

"You twitched like crazy all night."

"Sorry."

"It was endearing. Like watching a dog sleep."

I smiled and thought of coffee. Coffee would be good, and some of that fry bread. I wondered if Laina could be convinced to make some on short notice. Food would taste good again, now that I'd slept. The first meal should be something special.

But the newscaster was getting clearer all the time. He reported an attempted robbery at a liquor store near Fairbanks. My robbery. Two police officers were in the hospital, he said. Serious, but not critical condition. One suspect was wounded, the other described by investigators as "dangerous."

He talked over B-roll shots of the liquor store. Crime scene tape crossed the door. Sheets covered a bloody patch on the ground. A few cops milled around. Then a tall, thin man appeared right in the foreground. He wore that great leather jacket and grinned at the camera. He waved.

"Officials say the investigation is still . . ."

The sound faded under Laina's hand on the remote.

"You did this," she said. "Didn't you? You and your brother."

It was up. I could tell from her face. Laina wasn't fishing for a confession. She knew. Really knew. No point in talking around it.

"Yeah," I said. "How did you know?"

"Look at your hands."

They were black and blue and scabbed-over at the knuckles.

I couldn't meet her eyes. I looked at the floor, waited for her to do something. She'd hit me in the head with a lamp, or one of Edith's heavy vases. Then she'd grab her daughter and get as far from me as she could. Call the cops, probably. She knew what I was now. She should run.

"You're going away soon, aren't you?" Laina said. Her voice was steadier than I expected.

"We need papers first," I said, "and money to get them."

"Looks like you botched this one," she said, nodding to the TV. True enough. I hadn't thought of it that way in my sleepless state, but now it sunk in. We still had to come up with the rest of our passport fund, and we had just a little over twelve hours to do it.

"Shit," I said, and slumped back down on the couch next to Laina.

"I might be able to help you," she said, "but you have to promise me something."

• • •

Laina knew a few things she hadn't said before. Things about Lester and his business. Of course, we knew about his meth-cooking operation thanks to Gordon. We knew he lost a plane. But actually living with the man made Laina privy to certain details. She knew where he cooked. She knew he kept some money there.

"So you're not going to call the cops?"

"Not if you make me a promise."

"What is it that you want?"

"Lester will know I told you," she said. "If you're careful it might take him a few days to line things up, but he will. You need to promise me, if you do this, you'll leave this place in a hurry."

"I believe that's the plan already."

"And one more thing," she said. "You have to take me and my daughter with you."

"Edith won't be happy."

"I don't care. Promise me."

• • •

The trail was just two tire ruts in ice, snaking away from the plowed road. Easy to miss if you're not looking for it. Billy revved the engine, kept the truck working for a long way. He parked when the tires spun. We walked from there. It was a long trail, winding through rock and trees, always up. Up and up with no light but the stars. My legs burned by the time we reached Lester's cabin. It was squat and old, perched on the shore of a mountain lake.

When they first met, Lester took Laina to the old cabin and flew her around in his bush plane. It was summer then and the plane had floats. They took off and landed from the water like magic. Laina smiled when she spoke of it, in spite of herself. It was the only place for miles to land a plane. This, according to Laina, was where the meth was cooked.

We came out of the darkness slow and quiet. The cabin windows glowed yellow, but there was no movement inside. We slipped passed Lester's huge truck and up the cabin steps. Billy eased the door open— went in gun first. He cleared the rooms, then waved me in. There was nobody home, so we just set about the place.

Every surface was covered in glass beakers and tubes and all kinds of science-type stuff. Sheets of plastic hung from the ceiling. All of it was dirty and singed brown. We dug through drawers, closets, every little place. Then Billy flipped a ratty old mattress. Under it was a manila envelope of cash. He tore it open and rifled through the bills.

"Well shit," he said. "There's twelve bucks in here."

He slumped down on the flipped mattress. One hand clutched the gun, and the other opened and closed in white-knuckle fists. It was important not to talk at times like this, when Billy was up against it. He was unpredictable. I stood real still, and just watched him think.

Something wasn't right about the cabin. The lights were all on, and there was a fire in the woodstove. Lester's truck was outside, but there was no one around. Billy scratched the side of his head with the .45. He got up and went out on the front porch. He squinted into the darkness.

Down on the frozen lake was a speck of light. It looked like a single lit match. Billy tucked the gun down the back of his pants and set off. I had to jog to catch up. We cut into the woods, felt our way to a dark clutch of trees at the shoreline. Billy stopped there and held up his hand for me to do the same. Some distance out on the frozen lake, a bonfire flickered. Billy watched. The flame lit two small reflections in his eyes.

A group of men gathered close around the fire.

"Three," Billy whispered.

We crouched, watching the black figures lit by flame. Billy thought.

"Too cold for a party," he whispered. "They're waiting for something."

He popped all his knuckles and thought some more. Then he grinned wide.

"The plane," he said. Billy was right. The bush plane Lester bought with Gordon's stolen inheritance was missing, and so was Lester. Billy leaned back against a tree. He slid his hands under his jacket to keep warm. We hunkered down . . . ready for a long wait.

I thought about how it would be. Any minute the plane would drift down from a dark sky, full of toxic chemicals and cash. We still had a few hours before Gordon's passport man arrived with our new lives. Plenty of time for one last score. I closed my eyes and imagined the warm southbound cab of our truck. Billy behind the wheel. Laina in the middle with her child on her lap. The child would sleep while Laina made cooing sounds and moved the hair from her face. I imagined the sun rising sooner, and setting later.

But the plane did not come, and soon my fingers and toes ached with cold. Frost grew on Billy's whiskers. I envied the fire out on the lake, and I began to worry. Maybe those guys really were just hanging out around a bonfire for fun. They were Alaskans, after all.

The improbability of an airplane load of money arriving within driving distance on the very night we needed it most began to sink in. Things often lined up for Billy when he was in need, but honestly, what are the odds?

I used to do this thing when I was a kid. Billy would take me deer hunting. I was too young to shoot, but we'd sit together in one stand. I'd get so cold out there. Hour after hour in silence, till the thought of a deer became impossible. When it was too much, I'd make these silent deals. Billy told me there was no God, but there *was* something, wasn't there? A great power governing the movements of deer and men. When I was a small boy, and quiet for long stretches of time, I sometimes felt a presence. A kind, if distracted sort of presence. I made my deals with this unnamed thing. "Send Billy a deer," I'd whisper into the woods, "and I'll quit stealing cigarettes. I'll stop masturbating all the time." Of course, the deer rarely showed up. When they did, I forgot my promises with Billy's rifle blast.

I quit that sort of thinking long ago. You can't bargain with fate. But on that cold Alaska shoreline, my brain slipped back into old habits. The plane would not come. I knew it deep down. No plane. No money. No traveling papers. The marshal would find us. Maybe in a day, or a week, but he'd find us.

"Let the plane come," I whispered, but what could I offer fate? Or the universe or God or whatever. I'd done all the bad things already—couldn't take them back.

Thick ice coated Billy's whiskers. Below them, his skin was drawn. The lines around his eyes sank deep. I hadn't noticed. Until that morning, I was busy with my own rotting body. He looked tired, like a man who has smoked a hundred thousand cigarettes in a row. Billy had one more great effort still in him, and nothing more. I guess even the hottest fires burn low eventually. So little time now.

I thought again of Laina holding her child in our dim truck cab . . . Billy drumming his fingers on the steering wheel, smiling when the child sneezed in her sleep. A beautiful thing, but it wasn't meant for me. I am not a whole person. I'm two-thirds of one at best. Laina knew it just looking at me. Maybe she could use my brokenness in a temporary sort of way, but eventually it would poison her.

Billy didn't feel for Laina the way I did. But maybe he would one day, if I wasn't around. Maybe she'd bring him peace. Maybe that child would call him father.

"Send the plane," my lips formed the words without sound. "Give this new life to Billy. You can take it from me if you let him have it."

• • •

The plane sounded at first like a lawn mower, a long way off. Billy raised his head and listened. Out on the lake, the men stood back from their fire. Their murmuring voices rose with excitement. Two lights appeared over trees down the shore. Red and green. The roar of wind and engine climbed.

Billy pulled his hand from his jacket . . . and the gun with it. He reached down around his neck and pulled Edith's dish towel up over his nose. I did the same, and the two of us blew steam through cloth.

The plane landed on a pair of skis far down the lake and coasted into the light of the fire. The engine gasped. The prop slowed in halting circles. The door swung open, and a duffel bag flopped out on the ice. A man jumped down behind it. Even at a great distance I could make out Lester's bulk. He opened the bag and lifted out a handful of bills. His men cheered and clapped and raised bottles of beer. I started out onto the ice but Billy's arm stopped me. He held the gun like a finger to his lips. "Hold," he whispered.

The men lifted a panel from the side of the plane and dragged barrels and boxes into piles. They talked as they worked. They were loud, distracted. Billy leaned in close to me.

"Listen, kid," he said, "if this goes south, I want you to run. Grab that woman and her daughter and drive, or find the missionaries if you feel like doing penance. Just don't turn around."

I looked at his face. It was half covered and his voice carried nothing with it.

"If this goes south," I said. "I will turn the ice red."

Billy let out a hushed laugh and stood.

"Stay behind me," he said, and he ran.

I kept pace for the first stretch, both our feet light enough not to break the crust of ice left by the storm. When we drew near, Billy's gait changed. He pulled away from me like I was walking. In a moment he sprinted well out in front, a wild shape making no sound. He closed the distance with animal speed. At the fringes of their firelight, he rose in a leap. His gun hand coiled back, then snapped out as he returned to earth. The .45 struck Lester in the back of the head. Billy landed on his toes. Lester fell in a pile.

When I got there, Billy had his gun leveled at the three men still standing. The fire lit their faces. Lined, angry faces. Faces changed by greed and harsh chemicals. I recognized them from the shoot-out at Bud's house.

Lester lay motionless on his stomach. He never saw who came at him.

"You know how this works," Billy said. None of them moved.

"Someone toss the kid that bag of cash or I'll start shooting." The men looked at each other and did nothing.

"We will find you," one of them said.

"How about I start with you," Billy replied, adjusting his aim.

The talkative one grabbed the duffel by the strap and tossed it. I caught it in the gut and nearly fell backward. It was heavy. At least fifty grand depending on the denominations.

"Okay kid," Billy said, his gun still leveled. "Head out."

I put the strap over my shoulder and backed slowly from the firelight. The cookers twitched like leashed dogs.

"Run," Billy said, so I ran.

The duffel slammed against my legs as I went. Cash jostled around inside. Halfway to shore I glanced over my shoulder. Billy was still out there—his gun raised.

At the shore I dropped the duffel and snatched it back up with my other arm. My shoulder burned with the weight and my lungs with the cold air. I climbed the hill with pain in my side and turned again. Billy was gone from the firelight. So were Lester's three men. I ran harder, past the cabin and Lester's parked truck and down the narrow trail. Billy caught me at a dead sprint. He took the duffel as he passed. We flew through the trees on glare ice. It wasn't so far as I remembered. I hit the side of the Chevy so hard I knocked the wind from my burning lungs.

Billy tossed the duffel in the bed and we leapt into the cab gasping for air. He turned the key and we were gone.

• • •

You'd think we'd be laughing. Punching each other in the arm and congratulating ourselves on the big win. I guess we did a little of that. So much money in one go. But we didn't have a lot of time just then. The dashboard clock said five to midnight. That's about when Gordon said his passport guy would arrive, and we were still a good half hour out. Billy kept the truck in low gear and revved its old engine to the red line. He took us down the mountain at sickening speeds. He drifted around corners, ran two of Winner's three stop signs.

There was also this. Lester would wake, and he'd know. He never saw our faces, but he'd know. And he'd go right for Edith's house. It was hard to think about much else.

Billy skidded to a stop outside Gordon's old cabin. Gordon sat out front in a lawn chair shoved down into the snow. The hood of his jacket tented up over his head and his face looked like something carved into a mountain. He waved his un-shot arm.

"Are we late?" Billy said.

"Don't know," Gordon replied. "If you are, so is Mr. Passport. Wait with me."

So we did. We sat with our butts in the snow, me to Gordon's right and Billy to his left.

"How are you feeling?" Billy said.

"Old," Gordon replied.

I believe that was as true a thing as Gordon ever said. His body barely moved, even when breathing. He'd always looked like a person made of rocks and stones, but now he looked as immobile as rocks too.

"I see you fixed your door," Billy said.

Gordon nodded. "Had to use big nails," he said. "Like the kind they used on Jesus. Only nails I had."

I looked around and sure enough, the door was spiked together with nails as big around as my pinky finger. That whole cabin was in bad shape. It looked even smaller than before. Small and cold and rotting. The bark was peeling off the logs in gray strips, like an animal shedding fur. I don't even think he had a fire going inside.

"Is there anything we can do for you, before we go?" Billy said.

Gordon shook his head. "Just sit until the man comes," he said. "I feel that I will be alone for a long time, and it is good to have friends here."

Time passed slow. I thought of Lester, waking angry on the ice. Arming himself. Coming for us. But there was nothing we could do. So we waited and said very little, and finally an SUV coasted up and stopped on the road. Gordon nodded to Billy. Billy unzipped the duffel and took out a stack of cash. He went out to meet the car alone. As Billy came, the window rolled down, but the cab lights were off, so I never saw the man inside.

Gordon's big hand slid down from the lawn chair arm rest and patted our duffel bag.

"My friend," he said. "Be careful of this money. You think it is a good thing. It is salvation to you. But it brought Bud no joy and me only pain. Pain for Lester, too, I suspect, though he had it coming."

"Lester spent the money you're talking about. This is new money."

"Same money," he said. "Careful."

"Okay, Gordon," I said.

Then the SUV drove away and Billy came back with a manilla envelope.

"Okay," he said.

"Okay," Gordon replied. And so we left him there, and never saw him again.

44.

Edith's front window glowed with warm light. No sign of Lester. We had the money, the traveling papers, and still a little time. Such long odds, but we made it. Billy grabbed me by the shoulder and we just smiled at each other across the cab. Didn't even say anything. We didn't have to. Everything felt good. Everything felt blessed. The sound of the truck dropping down into park . . . the rumble of the idling engine. It was all beautiful. I wondered if Laina made some of that good fry bread for the road, if Edith made coffee. I bet they did. Today was a good day.

We jogged up the steps. Pushed through the door. Laina's few bags were stacked just inside. Laughter filled the room. Edith puttered in the kitchen. Laina held a full coffee pot in her hands. And sure enough, fry bread leached rings of lard into layers of paper towel. I wanted to leap and dance. I wanted to kiss Laina on the mouth and raise her child above my head. For just a second I forgot the violence and blood I carried with me, and the deal I made with fate for Billy's freedom. Of course I forgot. Wouldn't you?

But something was wrong.

Laina's face was stone. There was no excitement in it. No smile. She wasn't laughing and Edith wasn't either. Then I saw it. Beside the cooling fry bread, a heavy leather jacket was draped over the edge of the table. Beyond it sat a man too tall for the chair he occupied. His legs sprawled out under the table. A US Marshal in Edith's house, bouncing Laina's child on his lap. Laughing aloud, and waiting for us. Things always get fucked up right at the end, do they not?

"Get in here, Eric," Edith said from the kitchen. "You didn't tell me your friend was coming."

The marshal turned his head real slow. Laughter flushed the sharp lines of his face. He raised his cup in Billy's direction like he was making a toast.

"Hello, friend," he said.

Persistent bastard! Heat rose in my chest, and my hands clenched to fists. I guess Billy and I should have run just then. The truck was still warm. We could have made it to the highway, probably even lost that old marshal just long enough to leave the country. I didn't even think of that. I wanted to rush him, to tear the little girl from his grip and put my thumbs through his eye sockets. He wore a pistol on his belt, but could he draw before I reached him? He'd have to set down his coffee first, if he was right handed. I was willing to chance it, but Billy caught my arm, steadied himself while he slipped off his boots.

"You cut it pretty close," Billy said. "I didn't think we'd get to see you again."

"I made pretty good time, considering." He hugged the child close with one arm and patted her soft belly. "Mrs. Krone, your renter gives terrible directions."

"I'm sure he did his best," Edith said. "Should I brew another pot?"

"Yes ma'am," the marshal replied, and bit into a lump of fry bread.

Billy shrugged out of his coat and took a seat at the table, easy as you like. Laina put a mug in front of him and filled it. He took a long drink—looked right at the marshal the whole time. The marshal ran his fingers through the child's hair and stared back.

"Easy to get lost up here," he said. "Some men never turn up."

Billy set the mug down and wiped his mouth with the back of his hand. "True enough."

Silence spread. I stood at the door, sweating in my winter clothes. My heart pounded. Limbs twitched and locked, torn between fight and flight. Billy finished his cup, and Laina filled it again without a word.

"Tell us something about Eric," Edith said. "He's lived here for months and never told me a thing."

"Well. Let's see." The marshal put on a cartoon scowl and rubbed his chin. "He's got a way with women."

"Oh, I know that already."

"You don't know the half of it. In fact, dang, how old is this girl?" He pinched the little one's cheek with his thumb and forefinger. "How old?"

"Three," Laina said.

"Dang. I'm no good with ages. I thought maybe Eric here sired a little person already, but the dates don't add up, do they?"

Edith laughed hard from the kitchen. She laughed so hard she dropped a cup and it exploded on the floor.

"Look what you made me do," she said. "You old rascal."

The marshal smiled his long teeth. He tore off a piece of fry bread and fed it to the girl like a dog. She took it, but only bit the places his fingers hadn't touched.

"I didn't see your car," Billy said. "Did you walk?"

"Parked down the road a piece. I wanted to surprise you."

"A wonderful surprise," Edith said, shuffling over to the broom closet, "even if you did make me break a mug. I never get company up here."

Something was off with her—too quick to smile. I couldn't put my finger on it exactly, and in a moment, I didn't have to. She reached into the broom closet, but instead of a broom she came out with the old bolt-action rifle.

The marshal had his back turned. He ate and drank while Edith's gnarled old hands brought the gun level. The child saw the barrel hovering six feet from the marshal's brain stem and leaped to the floor. She ran to Laina and hugged her leg. We all watched Edith press the stock into her bony old shoulder—all but the marshal. It was almost more than I could do not to cover my ears.

"Have some more coffee, old friend," the marshal said. "We have a long drive ahead of us."

Billy shook his head real slow. "I need a cigarette," he said, glancing up at Edith. "It's real dangerous to smoke inside. Especially with a little girl right here. Let's take a walk, you and I."

Edith nodded and eased the rifle back into her closet.

"Just the two of us?" the marshal said.

"My brother quit. Edith straightened him right out. But it's too late for me. My lungs are black."

The marshal didn't move, but the smile dropped from his face. He thought for a while. "Okay," he said.

They rose at the same time. Chair legs squealed on the smooth wood floor. The marshal shouldered into the leather jacket. "I'm glad you quit, kid," he said as he passed.

Cold air rushed in with the opened door. It prickled my sweaty skin. I hadn't moved an inch since I came in . . . didn't realize till just then. Billy tapped out a cigarette and put it in his mouth. Then he took my shoulder again while he stepped into his boots. I could see the .45 under his shirt as he bent over to tie them.

"Remember what I told you," he said. "Take that woman and her daughter. Drive."

He spoke so calm it sounded like he was talking about the weather.

"If things go badly."

"Yeah," he said, with a weary smile. "If I miss."

"You should let me do it. I have before. It doesn't hurt me so bad."

"No, kid. It's my shift."

He closed the door behind him. I went to the window and looked out. The marshal was just a black shape against the icy driveway. Billy sparked his cigarette as he walked out. The ember lit his face. He breathed smoke, then reached for his gun.

I waited for the crack, but it did not come. It would not. Billy held the gun out to the marshal, but it was the wrong way round. The barrel was in his hand, not the grip. And his fingers were open. He spoke words I could not hear.

This is not how it ends. We run. That's what we do. We run into the woods and keep running. Maybe Billy was tired, but I could carry him. Surrender is no kind of finish. I went out the front door at a sprint and down the steps. My hands were strong. I'd snap the marshal's neck. It wouldn't be hard. The bones would sound like knuckles popping.

Then the world went white. I saw nothing at first, but felt the cold night air shake with an angry roar. A big engine, running hot. I turned an ankle in my blindness and fell, squinted up from my knees.

The blaze split in two bright headlights. Lester's truck.

Billy raised his hand to shield his face. I could see each one of the fingers. I could see the wild fringes of his hair, lit like fire, and the easy way he held his body. Then I saw his shoulder snap back and a haze of red fill the bright light around him.

It was after this I heard the shots. Dozens of them coming fast atop each other. Many guns at once, probably. I ran into the light and sound and flying lead. I found Billy on his back. I knelt over him. His shirt squeezed with blood in my clenched fists.

"Get up," I said. "We have to run now."

He blinked and focused his eyes on my face. I gripped his greasy shirt and lifted him a few inches from the ice. Heat filled the air between us. Heat from the blood that burbled up under my balled fists and the tears that fell from my face to his.

"What do I do?" I said. Bullets creased the ice around us. He opened his mouth, but no words came out.

"Tell me," I said. "Anything."

He pressed the .45 into my side. I took it, and he grinned bloody teeth.

I crawled from my brother, low across the ice to our truck. The marshal huddled behind the front wheel. Bullets screeched overhead and cut holes in the Chevy. Shattered the windows.

"What the hell, Jim?" he said. "Who are these guys?"

"Meth cookers."

"Aw shit," he said, and pointed his gun around the front of the Chevy. He fired blind. A volley returned. Lead rattled through the old truck frame.

"You ripped off some meth cookers, didn't you?"

"Yeah."

"Goddamn it. Your brother is still fucking me from the other side."

"Maybe he's not dead."

The marshal made himself as small as he could. He popped the clip from his gun, squinted, and slid the clip back in.

"He's dead, kid. Now cover me. When I get to the house, I'll cover you."

He looked up from his gun. "Ready?" he said. I nodded, and he nodded. "Sorry about your brother."

I stood and leveled Billy's gun just above Lester's headlights. The marshal rose in a sprint. The gun leapt in my hands. Three shots. That's all I could squeeze off, and I doubt they hit anything. The marshal made it as many steps before he fell. His gun slid across the ice. Bloody holes opened up in the leather jacket. Then something caught deep in my chest and robbed my limbs of their strength. I fell back. The .45 clattered beside me. The volley of gunfire ceased, and for a time all I saw were the stars above.

• • •

Footsteps cracked the ice to the right and left. Three or four men. Heavy boots. They spoke loud, deafened by their guns. One of them laughed. A few shots rang out at close range. Finishing shots, but they did not finish me.

Lester's big voice silenced the rest. "Why did you do it, Laina?" he said. "I didn't even hit you that hard. We can work this out, can't we?" He was answered with a rifle blast.

"Go fuck yourself, Edith. You never liked me."

Another blast, and the boot heels left at a run. I could hear the duffel bag of cash jostle and scrape against their legs. Truck doors slammed and the engine roared away.

My strength returned in the minutes that followed. I tried to roll over—to stand—but I could not. I waited and breathed and tried again, and then again, and finally my arms pushed me upright. I staggered. Crawled when I had to.

Billy was where I left him. I put my hand on his chest and felt no rhythm. I looked into his eyes, and saw no fire there. They were just regular eyes now, looking at nothing. I wept, and closed his eyes with the palm of my hand.

Slowly, I became aware of Laina. She had drifted out of the house, wrapped in a blanket and her own long hair. She waited and watched. What that poor girl saw that night . . . nobody should have to see that. Billy lay on the ground below me, his blood running into freezing pools. The marshal was a torn dark form, yards away. The man she trusted to bring her safe from Winner had blood up to his elbows and a gun in his hand.

I had Billy's gun. Don't even remember picking it up again. It was just there. My fingers wrapped around it like tree roots grow around stones. She saw all of this. All I lost and the little that remained, and she did not look away. I stood.

"You're shot," she said—these first words were nearly lost to the ringing in my ears. I blinked at her, and she said it again. "You're shot."

I looked down. Blood spread across the left side of my chest, and my shoulder sagged badly. The socket was down in my armpit. My knuckles hung low, like an ape arm. I could not lift it. When I tried, the ends of bones made sharp tents of my skin.

I tucked the gun down the back of my jeans and put my right hand over the bullet hole.

"Come inside," she said. "I'll call an ambulance."

"I can't do that, Laina."

"Your arm looks really bad, and you're bleeding a lot. Come inside."

"My brother is dead."

Laina wrapped the blanket tighter around her shoulders. "You're going after Lester, aren't you?"

I nodded.

"I don't want you to kill him," she said. She shivered through the blanket. I could see her small fists pulling through the thick wool. "I changed my mind. You told me you'd take me from here. I want that, instead."

"I cannot give you the things I promised. I'm sorry. But I can make it so he never comes for you. I can do that."

"Maybe I can patch you up," she said. "We can drive south like you said we would."

"The police will come. When they get here, tell them my brother is the outlaw Billy Quinn. That other man is a US Marshal. I never knew his name."

Laina nodded.

"And tell them where I've gone. Tell them everything. It will go easier on you that way."

I climbed into the old Chevy. Broken glass crunched in the seat cushion. I swung my left hand up onto the wheel, but the keys were out of reach. I had to leave my right hand over the bullet hole in order to not bleed to death.

"Can you get this for me?" I said.

She leaned in through the door and turned the key. The engine coughed and sputtered, then came to life. Those old trucks are tough. You can shoot right through them and they still run. Then I pushed in the clutch and Laina shifted it into first for me.

"Go slow or you'll burn out the transmission," she said. "And if you live, meet me in Fairbanks."

I nodded and drove. In the rearview mirror I saw her alone among the dead. Behind her Edith stood in her open door, a rifle in her hands and the child at her feet. I thought then that I would not see any of them again as long I lived, which would not be long at all. It was okay. Laina would be fine. When I was done, she'd be fine.

• • •

I drove out into the darkness with the gun wedged against my back, my right hand pinned down hard over my chest and my bloody left propped up on the wheel. It was just strong enough to steer, though every turn and bump twisted the jagged bones. Wind screamed through the windowless cab and through the many gaping bullet holes. Out past the houses and the trash of Winner I drove . . . miles . . . until my face was frozen by the wind and the dim Chevy headlamps lit the path to Lester's cabin. I floored it up the icy ruts. My head slammed back and forth in the cab and out the missing driver's window, but I kept it going. I passed the place Billy had parked not so long ago. I forced the truck on.

The trail to Lester's cabin was long, and I worried about the placement of my bullet wound. It was very close to the heart. People in movies die from bullet holes in that region. Except Bruce Willis. He got shot there once and then shot himself again through the same hole in order to kill a guy standing behind him. Bruce didn't die from that, but I was not him, and I didn't want to bleed out on the hike. I pressed down hard on the hole, kept the truck climbing over rocks and ice until I smelled burning clutch and rubber.

Then I got out and walked. My heart pumped steady. I could feel the blood swirling in my palm with each beat. It's a strange thing to feel the current of your own rushing blood. It was warm and thick and glued my palm to my chest. The hole was not in a good place.

I saw lights through the trees—the yellow glow of cabin windows. The men were loud inside. They talked over each other with excitement. The smell of bear steaks and smoke came thick from the place. There were cheers. Somebody laughed. I leaned against Lester's parked truck to rest, waited for the rage to fill me. That heat and strength I had sometimes. But it did not come. All I had was an understanding of facts. I needed my right hand to do this last thing – the same hand damming up the hole in my chest. Without it, I figured I'd have only a few minutes of real strength. It had to be done quickly. I took a deep breath and peeled it away. Heat slid down my chest as I pushed through the cabin door. I drew the gun in my blood-slick right hand.

The first shot went through a man's cheekbone. All was silent then but for the ringing in my ears. Men dove for shotguns and rifles. I leveled the gun and tried to remember how Billy used it when he was alive. He breathed steady. He pulled the trigger slow and let the shots surprise his hand. One man reached a shotgun, and I sent two bullets through his chest before he could lever in a shell. Another raised a heavy assault rifle, but the clip had been emptied in my brother's body. The hammer fell on an empty chamber. I let the man understand before I shot him dead.

I stood breathing the tart powder smoke, and let the ringing leave my ears. Three dead men sprawled at my feet. They lay in broken glass and shell casings and pools of blood. Lester was not among them.

Then a gust of wind cooled the wetness leaking from my chest. The kitchen window was open. Old curtains blew in. A dangerous man, but Lester was also a runner. A coward.

I pushed back out the door and scanned the woods. Nothing moved but trees in the wind. Then I saw him far off. A black shape out on the frozen lake. He was running—making for his bush plane. I followed. Out there on the flats, a layer of ice still glazed the snow. It caught the moonlight, bright as a cold sort of day. It carried my weight so my feet were quick atop the deep snow. I ran hard. Faster and faster till I felt something break loose in my bullet wound—some membrane not yet breached. The blood spattered my face. My own blood. There was too much of it, but still I ran and brought the dark shape of Lester closer.

His bulk sank through the crusted ice, deep in the snow beneath. He struggled and slowed, but Lester was a strong man and plowed ahead. Clouds of white powder rose in the moonlight as I closed the distance. He neared the plane, still too far ahead for a clean shot. He reached it . . . stepped up on the landing ski and fiddled with the door. I couldn't make a shot at that range. Not with a handgun. I kept running. The wood propeller jolted to life. It turned once then stopped, then spun to a blur.

I dropped to one knee and steadied my breath. I put the sight on his hulking form through the fuselage windows. He revved the engine and the skis crept forward an inch, then a foot. He was a long way off and I didn't have a good record when it came to Lester. My hands failed me once before when I held him in my sights. That was before he killed my brother.

I pulled the slack from the trigger, slow and steady as the breath in my lungs. The gun started back and the night rang.

I waited. I thought I'd missed. Then Lester tilted out the door of his plane and flopped down on his face. The engine shuddered and stopped. For a moment all was still. I rose and staggered forward on unsteady legs. I touched my chest. There was too much blood. I tucked the gun into my pants and pressed my palm down over the bullet hole. I wanted to lay down and rest, but I needed to see Lester. I needed to see his face. I forced my legs on and found him on his back under the wing of his plane. One of his big hands clamped around his throat and blood ran through his fingers.

"Who's there?" he said. His head tilted away from me.

"Hello again, Lester."

"You? I shot you."

"I got back up."

I walked around him and knelt down so he could see me. His eyes were wide and crazy—all white around the edges. Blood splattered his jaw and his breath rasped with effort.

"Your brother stayed dead though," he said.

"He did."

"Good. He deserved what he got."

The words sounded stupid to me. False. How did Lester not see what I saw? It was clear if you looked closely. If you paid any attention. But Lester did not understand. He would not. He didn't have time.

"My brother was a good man," I said.

Lester blinked his scared eyes. "I've been killed by a retard," he said. "Shit." He let his hand go from his throat and laughed aloud, blood gurgling out into the snow. He died laughing.

45.

One night in the mountains of Colorado, John the missionary told me about a shepherd with one lost sheep. He said that shepherd left his whole flock to find just one, that he loved the lost sheep more than the rest. And if that sheep was killed, he'd snare the beast that did it and crush its head with a stone. John told me to figure out which I was. The loved sheep, or one of the many left behind. I am neither of those things. I knew it right then, looking down on Lester's still, cold face. I'm not of much value, you see. A boy of scraps. A killer and a thief. Some people are meant for big things. People like Billy. I'm not. I'm just a blunt instrument. I'm the stone the shepherd raises to crush the evil beast. The one he gets bloody and tosses away because it won't ever wash clean.

There's a place for people like me. John talked of it often, but I didn't want to think about it just then. I rose from the ice and looked out across the lake. The sky was turning colors. You forget what time it is in Alaska's deep winter. Morning. Still dark purple, but days would get longer soon. I could feel it.

I could also feel my bloody shirt turning to ice and the fingers of my crippled arm going numb. It was time to go. Where, I was not sure. Laina said she'd meet me in Fairbanks. It was as good a place as any. Maybe I could make it.

It was a long way to the truck. Longer than I remembered. My legs went weak halfway off the lake. I broke three times through the crusted ice. I wallowed in the snow. Crawled. Got my legs under me. The fourth time I could not. I lay breathing—looking back across the lake at the spot where Lester died.

Down below the changing sky, a pair of eyes caught my view. Canine eyes. A wolf, I thought, very far off. It would eat Lester. They start with the guts, you know, the wolves. By the end, they're cracking bones in their teeth. I imagined Lester reduced to a bloody spot in the snow. Gone come springtime. Disappeared from this earth. The idea made me smile.

But the eyes drew nearer, and a form clarified around them. It was not a wolf hungering after Lester's soft organ meat, but a wide-headed pit bull coming my way. He trotted right up to the edge of my snow wallow, panting through bright, bloody teeth.

"Hey, kid," he said. "You don't look so good."

"I've been shot."

"Sure enough. Are you gonna die here?"

"I don't think so. Laina's waiting in Fairbanks. I'm just taking a little rest."

"You don't want to go to Fairbanks."

"I think I do."

"If you say so, friend."

I crawled out onto the ice and got up. I couldn't use my right hand, because it was clamped down over the bullet hole. My left was no help either. It swung loose and low down at my knees. The dog watched it with hungry eyes.

"Don't even think about it," I said.

He padded along beside me. I made it off the lake and up the slope to Lester's cabin. The money was there in its duffel bag. I ducked under the shoulder strap and found the strength to lift. The dog shook his head.

"Silly boy," he said. "That's no good at all where you're going."

"Maybe Laina can use it. She has a kid. Everyone says kids are expensive."

"The kid will be fine without you," he said. "They both will."

Things were getting really weird. I wasn't surprised to see the dead pit bull, and that seemed like a pretty bad sign in itself. Something was badly wrong with me, but I didn't dwell on it. I had to get to the truck. And I did. I swung the duffel up into the bed. Then I had to scream, because the bones were slicing around like knives in my chest. I leaned against the Chevy and looked at the dog. His face was solemn, but his little nub tail wagged like crazy.

"If you want a ride," I said, "go ahead and hop up in the bed. I don't mind."

He didn't move. He watched me struggle with the door handle. My left hand just barely worked if I sort of swung it back and forth. I got the door open and fell back on the bench seat. I got my legs inside the cab and pushed upright. I was feeling really strange now. Like my head was floating a foot above my shoulders.

"Are you sure you're good to drive?" the dog said. Suddenly he was sitting upright in the passenger seat, looking super concerned. I saw his point. It takes two good arms to drive stick. My crippled one was getting more crippled all the time, and the other was occupied. I peeled my right hand off the bullet hole as quick as I could—used it to start the truck, lift my left hand onto the wheel, and shift into reverse, then slapped it back over the wound.

"How about that?" I said.

"Good one, kid. I bet you only lost about half a cup of blood right there."

I got the truck turned around and limped it down the trail. My hand was slow on the wheel. My eyes wandered and blurred, but I reached the plowed roads. Then I screwed up and forgot to turn, went right across two lanes and into the ditch. The engine sputtered and died, and refused to start.

"Hard luck, kid," the dog said.

I went out to see the damage, but it was no good. My legs went weak, and I had to sit down on the ground. I rested my head against the side of the truck. The dog nuzzled his big head into my lap. His eyes pointed straight up like one of those bottom-feeding catfish. My right hand slipped off the bullet wound and pet the dog's bloody black hide. He was a good animal. I was lucky to have him around, even if he was a hallucination.

"Kid," he said. "You're not going to make it to Fairbanks."

I scratched the top of his head with my fingertips, like dogs like you to do. He wagged his little nub tail. It felt good to make him happy.

"Good dog," I said. "I wish you would tell me your name."

"You know me, boy. Your brother spoke of my work. He told you what I do in war, and when the plagues come. Maybe you put it out of your mind. But now. Here. You must remember."

I looked at him. His fur prickled with dried blood. His tongue lapped up around his nose and his teeth and his drawn lips. He was right. I did know what he was, and not just from the creepy stuff Billy told me. I felt the truth of him deep down in that part of my guts that still knows the old things. The stories our ancestors told, when houses still had dirt floors and it wasn't just children who feared the dark.

"Are you the death dog?" I said.

He showed me his long teeth.

"But I'm not going to die."

His eyes became huge and watery all of a sudden. "Oh, my boy," he said. "Don't you see? You're out of blood."

I looked down. Nothing more flowed from my chest. It was all gone.

"You've lived long enough, kid," he said. "Killed enough. You can be done if you want. You can come with me right now."

"Where are you going? Is it heaven?"

He rubbed the side of his head against me. His skin twitched.

"Come on, kid," he said. "You know it's not heaven."

"I know."

I'd killed people. Five, by my count. Or six. I couldn't remember. Maybe it was right—to do it for Billy, and Laina, and that little girl. Right, but not free.

"It's hell then?"

"It's not so bad down there," he said. "Well, that's not true at all, but I'll go with you. You will not be alone."

His long tongue lapped the blood from my shirt and from between my fingers. It felt funny. Ticklish. I giggled. What a good dog. He was making a ton of sense. It wasn't so bad. Hell was a fair price for the things I did. I was glad to pay. You can get used to anything if you know it's justified. It's the wrongfully convicted that piss themselves in the electric chair. The guilty ones just close their eyes.

"Okay, my friend, I'll go."

The dog picked up my crippled left hand in his teeth. It didn't hurt at first. He was careful not to squeeze too hard right away. A very good and careful dog. I closed my eyes.

"You've done everything that's been asked of you," he said. I was a little curious how he was talking with my hand in his mouth, but not curious enough to look. "Now it's over."

I felt his teeth tighten down . . . grind against the bones of my hand. The pain was warm. It was good. Laina would be fine without me. Maybe she'd leave Winner on her own, raise her daughter where the nights are short and oranges grow from trees. They'd be okay in that sunny place, and I'd be okay in hell. There was nothing left for me. It was time to go. What a relief.

"You'll see your brother again," the dog said. "He's waiting for you."

I know he meant it as a comfort, but it was exactly the wrong thing to say. I opened my eyes and looked down. "Hey," I said. "Billy's not in hell. Death works different for him. It's like falling a long way into cold water. He's stronger than me. He'll swim for the surface—find a place for himself. And if there's nothing to find, he'll make a place. He is very strong. He will do it."

The dog let go of my hand. "Really?" he said.

"Why not?"

"Okay, well, you can't just design your own afterlife. That's the first thing."

"Maybe *you* can't. Billy's special. Even John said so."

"God has his favorites from time to time—that's true—but that doesn't change the rules. There's heaven and hell and that's it. Jeez. Special only goes so far."

"Well, he's in heaven then."

The dog tilted back his muscly head and laughed. "You think God's favorites make it up-stairs?" He could barely handle himself. He sneezed a bunch of snot all over my shirt, and then he licked his chops. "Kid, the old man's pets are all out of their minds. Tortured. Violent. It's the narrative tension he finds compelling. What will they do when everything is taken? When there's a loaded pistol in their hands? Will they see the light—repent?—or will they go out in a hail of gunfire? Usually it's the gunfire, followed by eternal fire. But which show would you rather watch?"

I hung my head. I felt so weak and sick and cold all of a sudden. I may have cried a little. "I had hoped God would be kind, if he turned out to be real," I said. "Seems like he would be, with sunrises looking like they do, and women all being so pretty. But if he's mean I guess there's not much I can do."

"It's a hard truth," he said. "If it's any consolation, you're handling this really well." He shook his head in a serious way, like he was really sad for me. Like he cared. But I looked into his face, and something was not right. Maybe his tone was off, or the way he held his eyes.

"You are a brave, strong boy," the dog said. And right then I saw it. His mouth quivered in just the hint of a smile. The same smile kids back home used to get when they were playing a joke on me and thought I couldn't tell. The smile of a liar, when suckers buy in.

"Maybe it is as you have told me," I said. "I would go with you. I am willing. But I do not think I believe you."

Suddenly his eyes were bright as fire. He bared his teeth and they glowed in his head.

"It doesn't matter," he barked, and snapped my crippled hand back up in his teeth. I couldn't pull it free. There was so little strength left in my arms. But my legs still had some juice. I snaked them up around his throat and laced the ankles together.

"Hey," he growled. "What are you doing?"

"I'm sorry, but I think you're trying to trick me. It's easy, because Billy isn't here, but I can't let you do it."

"Wait a second, kid." But I didn't wait. I squeezed my legs together with everything I had left. The dog gurgled and thrashed and I kept squeezing.

"I don't believe in your hell," I shouted. Spit and blood frothed out between his lips and my hand. It ran down into his eyes. "I don't know about God. Maybe. I wish I had more time to decide, but you're lying about hell. Yes. I'm sure of it now. And you have no power if I don't believe."

The dog's body began to slow. Vertebrae moved in his neck. His legs twitched. His face was wet with spit and half crushed by my legs. I lay back on the ice.

"My brother will find me," I whispered. "We will make a new place. I will not disappear."

I felt very cold then. My body shook for a little while and then stopped. A sound like a roaring current rose up in my ears, taking me away somewhere for the last time. Death is just a long drop into cold water. Deep water. Black water. That is what Billy told me, and that is how it would be for us. He told me to swim. Demanded it. Promised he'd be there, if only I didn't lose myself in the blackness. It seemed like a lot of effort just then, but I decided to try. Maybe he'd need me over there, in the land he built for us. I closed my eyes. My ears roared louder and louder, and then there was silence. Swim, I thought. Swim! I will not disappear.

Then a pair of strong hands gripped my wrists. I've never been clamped like that in all my life. Hands of iron. They jerked me around by my arms. My shoulders popping. My broken bones grinding against themselves. I laughed aloud. Billy had me. I recognized his power. His joy and his terrible strength. He had kept himself, just as he said. Found me in the dark empty and dragged me to the light. We would be together in the new place. He promised me, and it would be so.

But when my eyelids parted, I did not see my brother's face. Instead, I saw my own feet sliding over the earth . . . the heels scraping thin white lines in the ice. Between them walked Laina's child. She held Billy's gun in both her small hands. For a moment I was sad. I so wanted to see Billy again. But then the little girl noticed me looking and grinned. What a smile she had. Gap toothed and pure in that surprising way only small children can manage. It was the prettiest thing in all the world. Worth sticking around for, I thought. And I smiled back. Moving my face was a great effort though. The darkness came back down on me, and I was in and out for quite some time.

46.

When I came 'round, Laina was there to greet me.

"Hello," she said.

I lay in bed in a place I did not recognize. Stiff hotel blankets covered me. Laina sat beside me.

"Hello," I replied.

"I need you conscious today. Mister . . .," and she raised a small blue booklet in her hand, "Mr. Grant Liddle. The border patrol doesn't let corpses through."

It was my passport. She held it up so I could see. My face looked back at me with a stupid, gumless grin. Below it was my new name. A good one, I thought.

I sat up and felt the pain return to my shoulder. Laina put her hand on my chest to stop me. Her fingers touched the base of my neck.

"Take it slow," she said. "You've been shot, don't you remember?"

White bandages bulged under a clean shirt.

"I forget many things."

"You slept three days here in Delta Junction," she said. "Canada's a day's drive. We couldn't stay in Fairbanks."

"I guess not."

"I found you in the ditch," she said. "You were nearly dead. For a long time, it seemed you might go that way." As she spoke, the child crept out from the bathroom with a mouthful of toothpaste. She took her hand off the brush and waved. I raised my hand the little I could and rippled the fingers at her.

"You bled so much on Edith's back seat, she gave us the whole car."

"She is a good woman."

"She wasn't happy about it. Now you should get dressed and eat something."

So that's what I did. Laina helped me into a stiff new pair of jeans. The child dragged my blood-spattered boots over to the bed. Laina put them on my feet one at a time and tied them. Bending double was more than I could manage just then, but I healed quickly. The skin closed up in a hard, white scar. Torn tendons and shattered bone reached out to each other. Rebuilt. The structure never did get quite right. One arm hangs a few inches lower than the other. It's been years now, and my shirts still don't fit, but it's no big thing. The pain is gone and both hands work mostly fine. And when they do cramp up, Laina rubs lotion into the knotted places. She rubs my tight neck cords. She kisses me. That's better than I could have hoped. Don't you agree?

• • •

There's one night years ago that slips into my mind now from time to time. Billy's up on the roof of our trailer house with a fistful of Roman candles and his pocket lighter. He's a silhouette at first—an empty place where there are no stars. Then the sparks fly.

I see his face, lit blue and red and green. Streams of fire rise from his outstretched arm. I see that, and I see the pretty face of Maggie-Grace, long before she realized how things were and had to separate herself from us. Long before Billy took his rage and a bottle of grain alcohol to the Radium elevator. The night I remember was beautiful still. Maggie's carrying the first ember of Billy's child. She's smiling up at him, and he's looking down. He winks. That's what I see now when I close my eyes.

It should have been Billy driving south with an honest woman in the passenger seat, her sleeping child curled up between. Should have been his wounds she stitched closed and his blood she bathed away. And when the sun rose close and hot, far from Alaska, it should have been my brother's broad shoulders carrying a laughing child and his hands laced in a woman's gentle touch. His clean, strong hands. Not mine, scarred and forever stained red.

But sometimes things don't turn out like they should.

End reading

ACKNOWLEDGMENTS

Over the years I've had the fantastic luck to learn from and work with a long list of brilliant and largely under-appreciated creative types. I will list some here in no particular order.

Bruce Eastman
Kelly de la Rocha
Lin Enger
Ed Munger
Kate Smith
Jen Ehrlich
Dan Gunderson
Meg Martin

And finally, I'd like to thank the resilient people of Minnesota—especially those who live on the northern plains. They welcomed this long-haired English major into the fold more than a decade ago, and inspired, in large part, the wild young men of this book.

ABOUT THE AUTHOR

John Enger is a writer, woodworker, and former journalist. By the end of his ten-year news career, John's award-winning work reached one million listeners each week on Minnesota Public Radio and countless more through the dozens of platforms that picked up his stories. His byline appeared in USA Today, U.S. News & World Report, and on regular contract work for National Public Radio.

Now he splits his time between building custom furniture and writing fiction. John lives with his wife, Emily, and their two children in the woods of northern Minnesota.

See more of John's writing at johnenger.info. Find his woodwork at engergrove.com

ABOUT THE PRESS

North Dakota State University Press (NDSU Press) exists to stimulate and coordinate interdisciplinary regional scholarship. These regions include the Red River Valley, the state of North Dakota, the plains of North America (comprising both the Great Plains of the United States and the prairies of Canada), and comparable regions of other continents. We publish peer reviewed regional scholarship shaped by national and international events and comparative studies.

Neither topic nor discipline limits the scope of NDSU Press publications. We consider manuscripts in any field of learning. We define our scope, however, by a regional focus in accord with the press's mission. Generally, works published by NDSU Press address regional life directly, as the subject of study. Such works contribute to scholarly knowledge of region (that is, discovery of new knowledge) or to public consciousness of region (that is, dissemination of information or interpretation of regional experience). Where regions abroad are treated, either for comparison or because of ties to those North American regions of primary concern to the press, the linkages are made plain. For nearly three-quarters of a century, NDSU Press has published substantial trade books, but the line of publications is not limited to that genre. We also publish textbooks (at any level), reference books, anthologies, reprints, papers, proceedings, and monographs. The press also considers works of poetry or fiction, provided they are established regional classics or they promise to assume landmark or reference status for the region. We select biographical or autobiographical works carefully for their prospective contribution to regional knowledge and culture. All publications, in whatever genre, are of such quality and substance as to embellish the imprint of NDSU Press.

Our name changed to North Dakota State University Press in January 2016. Prior to that, and since 1950, we published as the North Dakota Institute for Regional Studies Press. We continue to operate under the umbrella of the North Dakota Institute for Regional Studies, located at North Dakota State University.